# Contaminated Games:

---

## Anybody Can Get Caught Up
### Vol. 1

# Contaminated Games:

---

## Anybody Can Get Caught Up
## Vol. 1

### By

### Minnesota Baps

Asta Publications, LLC
www.astapublications.com

Copyright © 2010 by Minnesota Baps

Library of Congress Cataloging-in-Publication Data
Baps, Minnesota, Contaminated Games: Anybody Can Get Caught Up Vol. 1
p. cm
Includes index.

ISBN13: 978-1-934947-44-9
LCCN: 2010928063

1. Urban Fiction 2. African American Fiction 3. Fiction I. Title

Printed in the United States of America.

# ACKNOWLEDGEMENTS

Deep within my soul there are a lot of people and things that I would like to show my deepest appreciation to and commend them all for making me into a humble individual:

To the most high God (Allah), for bringing me into existence

My sanctuary: Camden, New Jersey, my backyard: Centerville projects

My mother (Olynthia) your priceless, my father (Kenny T. Mahan - R.I.P ), my sister Ashley, Marshall (O.G.), my grandparents - Cora, Delores, Mr. Kenny, my Aunts: Carolyn, Linda, Arlene, Gloria, Maxine, Betty Ann, Yvette, Tracey, Kim, Keisha, Cheryl, Vicky, my Uncles: Sadler, Howard, Willie, Lance, Marvin, Dandy, Wayne, Herman, Butch, Doc, Moses

Ms. Boo, Sadiqa, Ab, Nana, Radee, Anwar, Safiyah, Duron, Hakim, Nadiyah, Elgin, Ebony, Fatman, Missy, Lil Timmy, Lamar Janell, Donell, Meechy, Kye, Onya, Nicky, Booper, Cole, LaCreia, Sadie, lil' Lance, Miles, Imani, Takeya, Spring, Taylor, Kera, Diggy, Toure, Twig, Myesha, Sylvia, Shaun, Dana, Boo, Tonya, Danique, Danny, Cease, Lavell, Keyonnie M., Ronnesia, Aniyah, Donny, Auntie Gwyn, Deanna, Angel, Derrick, Rasool, Leesha, Taneya, Kuwan, Wakeelah, Ernie, Critter, Dajaun (Wag), Pud, Lisa, Krissy, Dotsy, Muttis, Bernadette, Big Mama, Lil Heemie, Kwamiere, Destiny, Sylvia (Net), Manda, Tammi, Boop, Tina Mar, Yara, Vigi, Veronica, Nicky, Leslie, Missy J., Setta, Gwynail, Vonda Cook, Gee-Gee, Aneesah, Waheed, Empress, Ms. Darlene, Aunt Virgina, Ms. Buttons, Ms. Tye, Ms. Myra, Sweet Pee, Ms. Kat, Ms. Lynette, Mr. Charles, Cousin Keith, Sissy, Hengie, Uncle Stevie, Uncle Sonny, Uncle Balloue, Aisha, Woodie, Tiombe, Taniesha, Aunt laura, Neen, Sheena, Rochelle, Shay, Mommy Ree, Mommy Butler, Mommy

Black, Fofo, Kelli, Latisha, I-Savior, Keya Judge, Mary, Mome, Tasha, Corey C., Keisha C., Khalia, Tiffany J., Reek, Summer (Dog), Shonie, Caneeka, Jada, Tia, Aunt Ronnie, Burger, Shaneeka, Goosey, Nicky, Pooh, Fu, Shannon, Lil Shake

Sonny, E (Lefty), K.Y., Dice, Shabar, Tim, Brian, Shock, Shamar, Sutan, Reg, Boon, Uncle Buck, Lil' Sai, Mighty, Stacks, B.O., Lashay, Tyson, Dave (Duke), Doughboy, Vito, G-Rap, J.D., Yusef Marlin, Uncle Gumu, Dollah, Screw, Shoes, Malik, Spliz, Bino, Fonzy, Dev, Gee, Mark Butler (Biz), Biz, T.L., John Doe, Dave Doe, P-owe, Curt, Justin (Jkp), Porta Rich, Mikey High, Heem, Reem, Butchie, Dave T., Big Jerry, Mally, Dad da, Boo Bop, Mo Betta, Two Shots, Ruck, Bam, Uncle Bam, Big Marheem, Saheem, Shoobie

Assuanta Howard, ASTA Publications, Terry, Shawn Roche, and the Spanky's tattoo shop, The Progressive Democrat club, My Elite street team, To everyone I've ever meant and got to know and understand on a personal level One Love

To all I've lost: Grand Mom Sadler, E.B., the Twins, Marheem, Relly, Tanon, Turron, Uncle Zeek, J-Mar, Kaz, Big Meek, Rash, Fess, Lil Hengie, Radio, Ajia Blaze, Cousin Scotty, Pete, Scott, Nuke (Esco), Kalee, Tee-Tee, P-Hall, Butta, Capone, Coco, Ivy, Damon, Brian C., Nick Perry, Meatball, Troy, Baby K, Chip, Susan "Susie" Williams, L.B., Daddy, Jennie, Big Nate, Johnny Abdul

*"Only through knowledge intelligently organized with direction a self leader master's detail connected to position."*

# CONTENTS

# Chapter. I

The winter of 1980, a legendary ending to a year which many would vision as ordinary just like the boring one that preceded America's society in '79. Prior to everyone bare witnessing to the riveting hit television show "Dallas" circulating through heavy rotation on the American air waves. Boxing young, poster boy Sugar Ray Leonard defeated Roberto "No Mas" Duran for the welterweight championship of the world. Stevie Wonder released his Grammy speculated album "Hotter than July," no pun intended but July was far from the disco inferno album. And, Jesse St. James was beyond a playboy bunny at Hef's mansion of exoticism, she truly was the peak of her career.

I (Kyle Marcus Moore) was twelve years old at the time of all these extraordinary events were taking place. A courageous adolescent at heart, still in the stages of a growing child into a young man; very frail physically and wet behind the ears. That was the perception that the OG's had of me at the time in the neighborhood. Ironically, I was extremely strong minded, vigilant to my surroundings but hid behind my potentials as much as the moistness behind my ears made my eyes water.

I was the only child to an on going mother (Olivia Moore), who gave birth to my month old baby sister Aniyah; she became the better half of me and my new inspiration to the meaning of life. Prior to Aniyah coming into this mysterious world of opportunity, I was my entire family's spoiled brat of a baby boy. Sulking or whining wasn't even apart of my quiet attitude like it had been for my other cousins and relatives who pursued materials that were never needed; only wanted but, seen it and their hands had to have it.

My Uncles Muscles (Lamont H. Williams) overindulged in giving out gifts, priceless material, and money when it came to all of

1

his nieces and nephews. Especially when it came to me, I wouldn't consider his generosity as being a favorite but, he always use to tell me that I was a mere reflection of him when he was my age; whatever that meant?

Besides my Uncle Muscles there was someone else that I admired as a passionate athlete, the great Reggie Jackson. As an overwhelmed baseball fanatic I thought Reggie was the best professional player to swing a bat in the major leagues. Only certain games caught my eye during baseball season but, Reggie and the Yanks were scheduled to play on regular television; I was always a heedless statue stationed in front of the TV until the ninth inning finalized. Named after this popular café in my neighborhood, I played for Sophia's Sunketts, a little league team that won the championship every year that I was apart of it since 1976.

Growing up as the only man child in the entire household I grew to be a shy roach amongst wild insects for peers in my environment. I was always apart of the in crowd but my naiveté made me feel that I wasn't; due to growing up I presumed. There was no older brother to turn to for that tough love or sister to lean on for advice and guide me through. My mother was very candid when it came to the well being of my livelihood and survival to the cold outdoors. "You're the key," She would emphasize. "And life is the round box that we live in with all the answers."

Olivia basically was telling me to open my own doors, experience life's air and, never stop questioning throughout my quest of success; in lamest terms she wanted me to understand that shit stunk. For starters, I wanted to open my psychological quest with, "Why the hell was my father a phantom in my life." But, I feared losing my teeth more than the rational answer that would never rise to the surface to fathom it all.

Camden City, two-hundred years after it was founded by a British settler and named after Earl De' Camden and, here I was able to be born and raided in a place that was named after a single man; that's a hell of an honorary stigma to have left behind for people to glorify. Since the day of studying the history of my home hometown and the information that was shared on Big Earl, I had visions of making

2

the same accomplishments; having a town named after me called "Moore town."

Approximately nine square miles in depth, the Garden State's environment was the sister to the city of brotherly love "Philadelphia." Philly was a five minute travel timer across the Ben Franklin Bridge or either the Walt Whitman depending on where you were coming from. Every city had its signature nickname which had been a reflection of its' lucrative, economical services or industrial plantations. Well, Camden was branded the "Sugar City," not because it had a productive sugar cane agriculture but, how smooth things functioned in the atmosphere due to the citizens being so kind hearted and trustworthy. The city's gaudy nickname was truly unimpressionable and ironic to what I was use to observing in the urban area and battlegrounds. Even though I was young I was far from incompetent and I knew life and the people within it weren't perfect.

I resided at 2141 South 7th Street, Centerville Projects was home of the brave for me. I happened to live in the Chelton Terrace Townhouse section of the projects though; the main entrance before you entered into the jungle. My mother, Aniyah, my sister's pop and I all lived together in a three bedroom row home. Donald was pretty cool but he was rarely home due to working two shifts as a security guard at a bank downtown on Broadway. My mother was a registered nurse at the Dayton Manor nursing home for elderly people; she just like Donald was rarely home either.

Now my father, Kyle Tommy Moore Sr., was a living mammal roaming the city streets like a lost pet without a home. He and I never had a sturdy father-son relationship, so his whereabouts really was none of my concern. He was simply a human in my eyes, not a man, just Kyle for that matter; I never referred to him as my pop, dad or father. He was just another mendacious, dead beat nigga whom disowned his child for the wealth and glory of the contaminated streets. When I use to question my mother about Kyle Sr. or his whereabouts, Olivia would nicks me off in haste and become discursive, going from one topic to the next. And, I don't even think she knew what she was talking about half the time. She just tried to refrain from hearing or speaking Kyle's name as much as she possibly could.

Out of a full year of school, I went about three-fourths of the time, mainly because I took advantage of my entire home alone. I use to have the house all to myself from the morning to the mid-evening. There were many days that I became a live wire and on other days I was truly an indolent soul to make it through my classed. School was the life though, from expanding my mind from taught knowledge, having free time with my crew an, getting to flirt with damn near every pretty girl in class. What more could a young man of my stature ask for? I truly had no other options and, being kicked out of the house at twelve wasn't something I could grow with.

I use to walk to and from school with my little cousin Wadeelah, known to my family as "Lady Weight Down," because she was extremely boney and frail. Wadeelah was my Aunt Gracey's oldest daughter; she had one brother Mobart and a younger sister, Malika. They all were like my mother's adopted waifs because they always stayed with us; more than often I stayed with them too. Gracey was my mother's youngest sister out of five other girls and three boys including my infamous Uncle Muscles.

Wadeelah and I were two peas in a pot, our family called the two of us Vanilla & Chocolate, she was light skinned and bright like the sun and I was dark as midnight; we both have been going to the same schools since kindergarten.

Reminiscing back, I could recall getting my as whooped on Halloween in kindergarten because I misplaced the costume that I was suppose to share with Wadeelah; I went to the morning session and she came in the afternoon. My Uncle Sammy - my grandmother's younger brother - beat me first for losing the costume and then I got it even worse after my mom came in from work. Until this very day I hate Halloween with a passion, not because it frightens people but I always have nightmares about the ass whipping and the lost of the shared costume.

My second year in junior high school, Wadeelah and I attended Morgan Village Middle School after graduating from Henry L. Bonsall. The entire school was split into levels and homerooms from the honor students to the incompetent students; the six grade new

4

boots had the entire first floor. Ms. Carter and Ms. Harris had the top two homerooms, 7109 & 7133; Wadeelah was in Ms. Carter's class she was a very virtuous and intelligent girl when it came down to academics. I was in homeroom 7114, Ms. Martin's class; this short brown skinned lady with a patch of tiny mole under her right eye. I was leveled average class, not because of my comprehension level but due to my lack of effort into my school work. My capabilities were just used to get by in school, not to become valedictorian of the entire school. I was a getting by kind of guy, don't fail, pass by the skin of my teeth and be happy with that.

On report card day, my grades were exactly like the homeroom I sat in everyday, Average! More C's than B's but in my mother's eyes they still were failing grades, Olivia would reiterate the same statements over and over again every time I received a report card. "You can do better," meaning those B's and C's could be Straight A's. Those same statements went in one ear and out the other because I wasn't beat to hear that shit. For a willing seventh grader I though I was doing damn well, well up until I met this chocolate girl like the Whispers' song name DaVita Mills.

DaVita was in Wadeelah's class and it was through Wa-Wa that I had learned that DaVita had the biggest crush on me but, I never foreseen her likes in me; until two week prior to Christmas break.

One monotonous morning in social studies class I had got a hall pass to use the restroom which happened to be directly across the hall. But, my hard head ass pursued to roam the halls after I came from the bathroom. The long boring lecture had me nodding off at my desk and that's the only reason I asked for the pass in the first place; I couldn't afford any detention though. I started to sit in the bathroom until the bell rang but Ms. Martin wasn't going for that, she wasn't always on high alert but she was far from stupid.

Bypassing one of the school bulletin boards on my way back to class which had a big sign on it that read "CHRISTMAS KISSES," and under it was these green papers stapled to the board. They were Christmas - O- Gram sheets that were made out for students in the school who had a crush on the opposite sex. After skimming through about half of the board I ran across one that caught my undivided attention. A crush - gram to me that read:

*To: Kyle Moore,*
*From: DaVita Mills*

*I watch you at my locker every morning before I go into home-*
*room; it's something about you that makes me warm inside. I don't*
*know if it's your eyes, your skin tone. Or the blue and orange base-*
*ball jacket that you wear. I want to be your girlfriend and I don't*
*take no for and answer because when I see something I like, I GET*
*IT! HUGS & KISSES.*

*DaVita*

I just used the bathroom seconds ago and I almost pissed in my
pants right there in the hallway after reading the brief crush notes. I
was only twelve for Christ sake, GIRLFRIEND? She had to be fucking kidding the kid I thought, I couldn't even walk and chew bubble
gum at the same time and she was talking some boyfriend/girlfriend
foolishness. Not for nothing, after I read the brief note I was a tad-bit
mushy on the inside but, in the same sense I had an STD syndrome
(Scared to Death). Even though I didn't know DaVita personally,
through observation of her character gave off a vibration filled with
aggression; I was a shy little guy.

Prior to Christmas break, for an entire two weeks I would come
to school late just so I wouldn't run into DaVita. Wa-Wa would call
me everyday after school just to tell me what DaVita said in class.
I got so frustrated with the annoying news that I told my mother to
tell Wadeelah that I was on punishment and couldn't receive calls
for three months.

$ $ $ $ $

It wasn't until the New Year that I gained enough courage to approach DaVita and converse. Young, fresh to death and
dipped in my new Christmas gear when we came off break there
was no stopping my confidence. I was at my locker in search of

some old homework that needed to be turned in when DaVita walked up and made it her duty to come over and talk to me.

"A Kyle," she said, in an endearing tone."Why do you always run away from me when we see each other around school? What am I ugly or something?"

I felt my Adams apple slide down my esophagus and hit my testicles as she stood an inch away from me as I hesitated to answer.

"Um... Nah, you're not ugly I just... I just-." Now I was stuttering and becoming very tongue tide like I had a speech impediment. "I just was waiting for the right time." She smirked knowing I just said one of the dumbest lines in the flow game.

"The times been right your watch has just been a little slow."

"Oooool." A couple other ear hustling students gestured by the lockers, listening in on our conversation; denoting that I had gotten played.

"Look here's my number, feel free to call anytime but if you choose not too it'll be you're lost," she said as she turned to walk in the classroom.

What put the icing on the cake was when she turned and walked away, the tight, blue Jordache Jeans she wore smothered her rear end like plastic wrap on a cold cut sandwich. DaVita's physical structure was an optical illusion; a girl her age at thirteen couldn't possibly have an ass that big; she stood only 5 feet even. But, prior to losing focus from her thunderous backyard while heading to my next class, I glimpsed at the number that she wrote in the palm of my hand in black ink (541-1229).

Throughout the next couple of months preceding my thirteenth birthday in March, DaVita and I had each other's undivided attention. My routines changed drastically - for the better of course - because I was no longer walking home with Wadeelah or my boys after school; DaVita replaced them. I used my allowance to purchase her snacks at lunch and goodies after school, my money helped sometimes but DaVita managed to keep a bank roll full of cash in a black leather pocketbook that she wore across her cleavage. I was looked at like a sucker in a lot of my peer's eyes but who cared, DaVita loved my attention and I was one step away from getting my ears dried. More so, I was two steps ahead of my boys who were trying to walk in my size eights.

My phone privileges were constantly being taken away from me because DaVita and I talked to the wee-hours of the morning; I had to be off the phone by eleven p.m. With the careless attitude that I possessed Olivia couldn't stop us from communicating so she could have kept the phone and the jack that was inside the wall too.

Lucky thirteen, it was my birthday and it arrived ordinarily as if turning another age wasn't meaningful to me. It was just another day in my eyes of the same shit that was happened yesterday and another day that was closer to my unpredicted death bed. My mother told me specifically before I went to bed to come straight home from school because she had reservations at this elegant restaurant and she didn't want to be late. I wondered all night of why she made a big deal about taking me out when we could have had a home cooked meal and some ice-cream and cake at home. But, knowing my mother and how she maneuvered there was a trick up her sleeve somewhere.

The next morning before I headed out of the door the phone rang, it was DaVita.

"Hello," I answered. She had asked me not to go to school and if it wasn't a hassle for me to stop over to her place before I went to school. At first I was skeptic about going to her home as I began to ask myself unfamiliar questions about why she wanted me to come by so early. She wasn't about to get me into any trouble on the most special day that only came around once a year; knowing there were lots of presents to be consumed at the end of the day.

DaVita emphasized that everything was cool and I needed not to worry but, that was prior to my mind being boggled and forcing myself into an early grave. She was home alone and her mother wasn't coming in to late and she had a birthday gift that she wanted to give to me directly.

I practically ran from my house to the beginning of her street corner on Patton Street in the Fairview section of the city. The Fairview area was partially like a suburb milieu in the city but it was blacked owned property but was divided into two sections; a quarter of a mile in distance sat White Fairview and the name spoke for itself.

After regaining my breath by leaning on this elderly lady's fence so DaVita wouldn't notice that my breathing routine had changed over to that of Carl Lewis. I rang her doorbell twice as I awaited her presence from the brown and white patio. She answered the door wearing a knee length, purple nightgown and a matching pair of slippers which looked like a pair of socks from a far due to her having tiny feet.

"Make yourself comfortable," she said, as she headed up the stairs.

I took my coat of and laid it across my lap as I took a seat on the tan plush carpet; which happened to run wall to wall. There was too many expensive valuables floating around the house for me, I wasn't trying to touch nothing because I damn sure didn't have the money to replace any of it. DaVita trotted back down the stairs slowly as she observed me stretched out across the carpet with my head propped back on the white, fluffed sofa having the hard, clear plastic; the type of plastic you set fire to and it never melted.

"Why are you sitting on the floor silly?" she asked, in a light giggle.

"You have too much luxurious stuff for me not to be."

"Boy this cheap stuff isn't luxurious it just happens to look good." She grabbed my coat and my hand and directed me to her bedroom. I stood by the entrance of her room's door looking confused as hell, still not trying to get as comfortable as she wanted me to become because I was nervous as a muthafucka.

The last thing I remembered was the bedroom door slamming behind us and me getting into her full size bed with about thirty other comfortable stuffed animals. The entire experience felt weird, I just knew I was in fantasy land once my eyes were shut and I curled up like an indolent cat.

DaVita's cool hands slid up under my white V-neck T-shirt smoothly, awakening me at once. I remained motionless from DaVita's chill as I gazed at her in weary eyes and rolled over to return the favor. I was extremely tired and I pushed her hands away a few times so I could roll back over into hibernation. Every since Aniyah was born I hadn't been getting much rest like I normally would when I was the only child. Every time I sat my ass down it was either, "Kyle get a pamper… Get a bottle… Wash the bibs… Throw this in the trash… Do this, Do that." I felt like a fucking maid, I wanted severely to zip my mother mouth shut and put a padlock on them.

With persistence DaVita continued to caress my arms and shoulders with her lava like hands and, at that point my garden snake began to rise from the mist of the wilderness.

"Happy Birthday," she whispered, softly into my ear, unbuckling my pants in unison. I looked up and there she was - all of her thirteen year old body - straddled over me unclad; having a twenty year old physique, I just knew I was still dreaming.

Not being able to utter a word, DaVita stripped me down to my multicolored tube socks and then guided me into her tunneled sauna. That was the best feeling that had ever come over me since my conception back in '68. While mounted over me, I couldn't help but to squeeze her hand size melons and for every bounce she gave I held on tighter and tighter.

"Um Kyle, you feel so good," she moaned seductively. "Ah! I love this moment of pleasure, please don't stop. She kept on.

Subconsciously, I said to myself, 'She's been watching too many of her parents nasty tapes.' But, she continued on saying just about anything to keep my sex drive invigorating and me inside of her. Not for nothing, her obscene vernacular was quite intriguing and from the way it rolled of her tongue it drove me to stand firm inside her warm house longer than I expect to.

We traded places and I was on top in full control even though she had to guide me to the right gold hole at times. My mission was to have her speaking in tongues after I got done but she was too highly advanced. When I finally got into the rhythm that I needed to be in, it felt like I'd mastered my stroke decades ago. DaVita's tiny munchkin feet locked a good grip around the nap of my neck as my chest rested on her leg tendons to continue penetrating her like a flexible basketball team. The sensation thrilled her minded with passion as she continued to suck on my neck and carve lines down my backside with her nails.

After I reached my ten second heart attack for a climax I lied beside DaVita, dripped in sweat and extremely breathless. We cuddled for about an hour or so after talking about how her first experience of sex had been no comparison to what we indulged in. Ironically, it had been my first and only experience and of course it was great and truthfully I didn't care if didn't get any better. In the spare of the moment though, I truly loved what DaVita had to offer. Another hour passed us by like wind on a cold winter day and it was time for me to head on home so I could prepare myself for the birthday dinner that my mother scheduled for me.

When I woke up from my reposeful sleep, DaVita who still happened to be naked was mounted over me for a second time with a stainless steel .38 revolver pointing me directly in between my eyes. Instantaneously, I felt my heart beat slowly drop to a beat every minute as I began to take short breaths; wondering what I had done to tick the malicious deer off.

"If I was to kill you do you think it would be for the love of you or the hate of something else?" she asked, holding the gun firmly.

"Why would you want to kill someone you love and don't even hate?" I asked, out of mere fear knowing a trigger had a mind of its own.

"I just want to see if you fear love or hate life."

"I don't even know what love really is but I know how to love and how can hate something that doesn't hate me?" I asked, lying at the same time so she could disarm herself with the gun.

After dropping the unloaded gun which happened to be her fathers, I put forth as much effort to make my way out of her home before she had time to reevaluate the situation and change her mind. I was scared shitless while searching for my clothes that she hid from me. She convinced me though to stay a little while longer after making me things clear that everything was some sort of prank. And, the bitch had the nerve to partake in another round of coital intercourse.

Vacuous mind me, I seeped through her warm peaches from behind, not because I desired the feeling but because I felt death surfacing the room. While she rested on all fours, her soft succulent ass shook like billowing waves like the ocean on my inner thighs as I watch in motion.

"Aaaahhh, continue to go on after you cum, keep it in Kay," she muttered, sensually biting on one of the teddy bears which garnished her bed.

I felt like stopping, she must have been crazy to think Olivia's oldest boy was focused on shooting tadpoles inside of her young, psychotic ass.

"Hold up, hold up" I said, pushing away from her. "How many other niggas have you been with and did this same process too?" Being very concerned to see if I was the first one, I had to inquire about it.

"Three! Two before you and you make the third person."

"At thirteen!" I was so confused, I wanted to scream out, 'you fuckin' little whore,' but I kept my composure. She had been with three guys including myself before she was even eighteen. While I sat on her bed in deep thought, I calculated how many boys she would have slept with by the time she was twenty-one. My perception of a good girl gone bad at a tender age was what I envisioned as the number twenty-four lingered into my brain; including me and the two other guys. Subconsciously, I didn't mean to compare but she was worse than my Grandmother Ann who had ten children and eight different baby's daddies.

"You might as well become a call girl or something," I suggested, putting on the rest of my clothes that she finally gave back to me.

She sucked he teeth and replied, "You'll be worse than me before you graduate high school, I know girls my age that are worse than me in fact I know a few that you know all too well."

"Yeah like who? I asked, trying to guess myself as she stood in front of me putting a pair of clean panties on and a T-shirt.

"That's for me to know and for you to try your entire life to figure out," She retorted, walking me to the door; she tried to kiss me but I resisted.

"Come here," she said, gripping my face, forcing a kiss on to my lips as I headed out of the front door; I wasn't trying to look back at the aggressive nightmare.

A blue, four door Lincoln town car was pulling into the driveway as I made my way onto the side walk. The man driving the Lincoln who I assumed was DaVita's father, flashed a pistol out of the window and asked me, "Did you just leave from inside of the brown and white house with the brown screen door?" I had no heart beat this time after seeing some steel for the second time.

To save both our asses I responded, "No sir I did not I come out of the house next door to your home." and, then I took off running fast as I could down the street.

$$ \$ \$ \$ \$ \$ $$

My birthday ended pretty smooth, I had dinner at this Italian restaurant name the "PUB," with my mother and my cousin Wadeelah, the set up artist. The entire place was packed; it had to be at least two-hundred people in the place. Mainly Italians with their retinue in attendance, mirroring a Mafia gathering had been the stark view of the night. One of the Pub's chiefs pushed over a two laired cake to our table which had about a thousand candles decorating both lairs. Pandemonium and cheer filled the entire restaurant as everyone stood to their feet singing happy birthday to me. For a split moment I felt like a phenomenal actor receiving an Oscar Award, when it was time for me to blow out the candles I wished to live a long, enduring life and one day to have a few children. But, the weirdest thing happened when I went to blow over them, they remained lit. I blew a second time and the same thing occurred, that's when everyone yelled out "Make another wish." I closed my eyes took a deep breath and did exactly that, only this time I wished to be successful in all my endeavors and making a huge name for myself. In one immense breath I blew every candle out and smiled as everyone clapped and continue to cheer for me.

The imaginary genie couldn't go in his bag of wishes and make that wish come true, I thought to myself. The ratio of that happening was like 1: 1,000,000,000, I was very indolent when it came to putting in that extra effort to do anything progressive or beneficial. Plus I was born with a skunk on my back, I lacked walking a straight line and played around with everything I put my mind too. There were only three things I had in the world and I wouldn't cross them for nobody like Al Pacino in Scarface.They were my word, my balls and my heart, why my heart? Because that was what got me through life and kept me optimistic so I could better myself each and everyday.

The year of 1980 came and went like the rising sun on the east in the morning and set on the west at night. I had remained friends with DaVita, to bad things didn't go as I expected them to go but, she transferred to another school before the school year terminated in June; due to a fight she had with some girls that she stabbed for trying to take her jewelry. We encourage each other to stay on track and promised to meet up in the future later. But before the next school year came around in September, DaVita was a disappearing act and so was I...

# Chapter. 2

A few years later around mid '83, Kangols, Adidas sweat suits and sneakers with the thick shoe strings was the sure thing. Afros and bellbottoms were quickly fading away, and Olivia still kept me looking young and fresh to death. I cut my fro and began wearing my hair low, dark faded with thick side burns. I grew approximately seven more inches throughout the previous years, standing a firm 6'1" and weighing an even buck-eighty.

I had found a little gig at this hot pizza turnover shop out in East Camden, owned by this Jamaican man named Teddy. Who the fuck knew that a brother from Jamaica, straight off the Caribbean boat could make hot pizza turnovers? I thought only Italians knew how to do that shit.

My boy Dontae had put in a good word for me to land the job, somehow Ted knew Dontae's pop and it was sort o f a favor for a favor kind of proposal. Which in fact, didn't bother me none I was just trying to make a little paper. Since Donald had left our home after being put out by Olivia for getting caught in her bed with some whore he met at a local bar one lonely night. It was a must and only right that I contribute and help mom out the best way that I could, financially. Even though my funds were mediocre the extra bread came in handy, in more ways than one.

I began feeling like Aniyah's guardian after putting in so much time with her when my mom obtained a third shift job at the super-market; which paid close to Donald's yearly salary. I walked her to the Martin Luther Day Care Center each morning before I went to school and my mother picked her up after she got off work. But, during the evening it was just Aniyah and I doing the potty training thing and teaching her how to sound out her name and master the alphabet.

My grades were above average, making the honor roll two straight marking periods in a row; with effortless studies. I never imagined the day that I would be persistent with school work, it wasn't that I was excited to learn, truth be told I was trying to impress my teachers. Majority of my classes was taught by woman of all nationalities, being in their late twenties early forties; none of them married. You wouldn't believe at fifteen I was fishing in a pool of great white sharks, trying to catch one when I was nothing more than wasted bait, waiting to be baited.

There was this one female staff member whom happened to be my 4th period English teacher, whose gorgeousness stood out amongst her colleagues. Her name was Ms. Janice Thornton; she was every man with a dick - dream wife. Standing approximately 6'1" inches tall in high heel shoes, light skinned, having light spotted freckles which ran horizontally across the bridge of her nose. She was stacked like dirty laundry; her ass was so huge that she couldn't even wear a pair of regular denim jeans to work without her thighs splitting the inseam of them. Her fingernails matched every outfit that she had ever displayed, if her attire was blue, so was her neatly, manicured nails; if she wore pink, her nails were the same color, and she was a walking coordination from head-to-toe.

I always lounged in the back of the room in my other seven period classes, just in case I wanted to fall asleep or joke on people. Ironically, I sat in front of Ms. Thornton's class just so I could watch and observe her demeanor.

Ms. Thornton had this long, unique, brownish-tan braid that hung over her right eye, clipped to a beret. And, no matter how many various hairstyles she wore, the long braid always distinguished her facial area. It was like the braid was a mere aphrodisiac, it drove me fucking crazy. But, insignificantly most of all, when Ms. Tee missed a day at work, I missed a day of class; class was less important without her in the classroom, to me.

After class, some days she use to give me all kinds of goodies, snacks, and fruit once the bell rang and I was late for the next period; I felt like her black stallion. "Now don't let anyone no that I gave you this," She used to say. I love my job, catch my drift." Given me a flirtatious wink of the eye, having a loss for words, I anxiously wanted to say in return, I fucking love you, catch that, ya' dig?" But I feared that her respect level for me would wane.

$$\$ \$ \$ \$ \$$$

I drifted into a mere reverie about Ms. Tee, one day I stared at her for a long time in class. She was standing at the blackboard seductively in some Pink, leather pumps, totally unclad; tits and ass everywhere. My skin was burning through my pants because I was so erect and my thighs were numb from the ultimate fantasy. Just before the mental orgasm, my daydream had been shot by her sensual voice, asking me to take a few documents to the main office for her; what a fucking coincidence? It was like she was reading through the obscenities the entire time and timed my every thought. I declined in the opportunity and lied with my head down for the remainder of the period.

One day, I came across some lucrative information pertaining to Ms. Tee's personal life from this comical - jokester named Syrus; one of the school's security guards. He also was a friend of my family, well he use to roll tough with my uncles and exchanged war stories with my junky of a sperm donor. Ms. Thornton's husband was a big time stock broker and he gave her practically anything she desired, long as she remained loyal to him and their family. Syrus felt that he was looking out for my best interest and my worst just in case Ms. Tee tried to pull a fast one and try to get me into any trouble, I guess I could blackmail her. But, Syrus stayed true by revealing his past observations of how I was firmly the teacher's pet in a great way; he said, he wouldn't put it pass her if she passed me for the year just for general purposes.

$$\$ \$ \$ \$ \$$$

For future references, he also put a priceless bug in my ear that would help me score with the breath taking, crafty, English dame of seventeen years. Her long, bereted braid that she wore with a bulk of confidence, was her birthmark. She loved all different kinds of berets and beads to give her birthmark some extreme center of attention. Her birthmark was a thing of beauty, sort of a sex symbol and definitely the key to a man's heart.

"How do you know all of this remote information?" I asked Syrus, curiously, thinking he's been where I tried getting at. "You were fucking the star or what?"

"Nah youngin' she already did her homework on this fat cat, with nothing but the dog in me. She knows a nigga tricks more than magic, dig it?" He replied gleefully, giving me some skin. "Understand this, I know a source who knows sources that know sorcerers. You'd be surprised what kind of information you can find out when you keep your ears to, and in the streets." Leaving me with some heat seeking wisdom, and endless jewels to find a spot on my brain to burn Syrus walked away from me like he and I were never conversing.

$ $ $ $ $

A few weeks had came to past and I hadn't appeared in Ms. Thornton's class the in fact, I had skipped out on school the entire time; sixteen days wasn't so bad, being as though I had not missed a day at school in a long time. Whimsically, instead of me chasing the dream that I couldn't seem to catch, I thought that I would use a psychological tactic of my own to try and bait Ms. Thornton in the way I seen fit. On evenings that my mother was at work Ms. Thornton would call my home to try and get some kind of insight as to why I haven't been appearing in her class when I was suppose to. Pretending to be my own father, I would intercept the call, to hear Ms. Tee's concerns about my well being and how important it was to show up on time for English; I began to fill that I had her right where I wanted her.

Making up one of the poor excuses of the year I was hoping I could keep Ms. Tee aloof but, worrying about me somehow that her interest would grow stronger. Over the phone one night, I told her that my grandmother - dad's mother - had past away and I would be out of town for a few weeks bereaving her death with distant relatives. Without thought she understood totally and told me that she would stay in touch as much as possible and would help out as much as she could if needed.

I was hanging out with my crew at Luby's pool hall on Kaighns Avenue, and at different friends' houses the entire time I had cut Ms. Tee's class. Ahmad and E.B. -short for Ibraheem - two of my childhood cronies use to be adamant in there repetitive statements to me when they felt that I was fucking up, by saying " That I was real stupid for skipping out on Ms Tee's class and, that I was losing a huge amount of cool points with her." Clairvoyantly, Ahmad an E.B. seen something that I was too blind to color, they knew and, she knew that it was more than infatuation. But, what they didn't know was that she wasn't trying to lose everything that she came to gain; whatever that was?

In the closing days of May, I decided to take one more day off from school before returning to the closing chapters of the school year. But, I made it my duty to go and see Ms. Tee no soon as school had been dismissed and she left for the entire afternoon. Eighty-degrees under partly cloudy skies, the calm breeze from the wind made it seem like the sun wasn't in control this particular afternoon; it was a beautiful day. And, I was dipped in the finest dapper that I could purchase, a Sergio Techini shirt - turquoise an white - a pair of navy blue Adidas sweat pants and some white on white sell top Adidas sneakers to bring out my outfit even more; Ted's hot pizza turnover money was definitely paying off for me.

Ms. Thornton was approaching her pearl - white four doors Cadillac Deville around 3:30 p.m. when I arrived, just to meet her in time in the half vacant parking lot. Tapping her on the shoulder from behind, Ms. Tee damn near went into immediate shock because she assume I was some kind of purse snatcher, while putting her belongings in the trunk of her car.

"Mr. Moore," she said in a frantic manner."Your approach shouldn't be as silent the next time, I thought you gave up on me and school by now from all the days you've missed. You know my seventh period class hasn't been the same without you there."

"Oh really?" I planned on returning a lot sooner but you know how it is when there's death in the family with close relatives from a distance?"

"Yeah, sure I do, everything is truly understandable, so I hope that I will be seeing you in class on Monday?" She asked, igniting the car engine.

"Sure will," I replied firmly. "But before we part ways may I ask a favor of you?"

"Sure, how may I help you?"

"I spent my last few bucks through my travels up here and I'm in need of a ride to my next destination."

"No need to explain, will do, get on the passenger side." I loved Ms. Tee's professionalism and morality as a woman, she was extremely cordial and it was a hard thing to shake at my age; my mother was exactly the same way. But, everything was going according to plan, the flow was streaming smoothly and all I had to do was stay calm. Slouched back on the red leather interior, to keep from looking in her direction, I leaned my arm upon the arm rest and lied my face inside my palm and stared out of the passenger side window the entire time; avoiding any eye contact. Through peripheral vision, I saw her curious looks in my direction while watching traffic.

She was kidnapping me I assumed, from the opposite direction she was traveling in to get to my house; I only lived about a quarter mile from school. "If you don't mind me asking, where are you taking me?" I asked nervously. "I live back in the other direction." I said pointing over my shoulder.

"Oh I'm so sorry honey I was trying to get to the bank before it closed but, if you're in a hurry I'll get you home and just go to the bank in the morning," She responded, tapping my thigh gently. A quick chill shot up and down my spine faster than the speed of sound and my feet locked on me like cramps simultaneously.

"I'm in no hurry Ms. Tee, the extra stop is alright with me. It's a free day today," I said through a lying tongue, knowing that I had to be to work at 4 o'clock; Ted was going to scold me verbally for this one.

We pulled into the bank's parking lot on Broadway and Federal Street, where Donald worked for a living. "Out of all banks in the city, she had to come to this one,' I thought to myself, slouching down in my seat even more just in case I spotted Donald's ass. Ten minutes... Twenty minutes went by and there still was no sign of Ms. Thornton's ass, she was still inside doing God knows what? Aggravation filled my brain gradually as I waited patiently, the leather seats had heated up like volcano juice from the sun reverberating off of the car windows; truly in an uncomfortable situation. She could have at least turned the air-conditioner on before she got out the muthafucka. While observing the bank like I was on a stake-out, I managed to get the two boxes of berets out of my right pocket and station them on top of the astray, beneath the radio.

Another ten minutes disappeared and it wasn't until then that it was Friday-payday-the bank was probably extremely consumed and she was fucking up my money. Donald came outside the bank to spark a cigarette, leaning on side of the bank's wall he went into full motions of retrieving his pack and lighting his cigarette. At an instant I wanted to hop out of the car, run up on him and began to give him some crucial boxing lessons. For doing the most incompetent shit a cheating man could ever do to a woman. When you're fucking another woman you don't shit where you sleep and fuck her in your comfort zone where your family lives. I haven't even ventured into the despising affairs that social life had to offer and I truly understood that golden rule. I wanted to slap the shit out of him in his Mr. Clean, bald ass head.

Syrus walked out of the bank a few seconds behind Donald did, right then I assumed that the bank has some sort of board of education reform to prevent any check defaults. Donald and Syrus shared a few laughs and then they shook hands before Syrus jumped into this gray Chevy pick-up truck and burned rubber down Broadway. Finally, Ms. Tee came walking her fine ass out to the entrance of the bank, where Donald stood still blowing cigarette smoke. Donald then pulled Ms. Tee's arm with force and whispered something into her ear, giggling, she gave him a flirtatious shove to the shoulder. They conversed for a few seconds more and before she got back into the car I figured the scrambled, mental puzzle which Syrus gave me insight too two weeks prior. The source was the bank, the sources were Donald in singular form and, Ms.Thornton was the sorcerer. Your ears aren't the only things that formulate things in the streets; your vision gives everything a perfect view. Ironically, I wasn't the type to believe half of what I seen and none of what I heard, anyway. I was to tender to do that, what I heard or seen I ran with until someone showed me other wise. And, in my eyes Ms. Thornton was fucking my sister's father.

"Who's the guy over there in the security uniform with the bald-head?" I asked unhesitant, wanting to see how sincere she really was.

"Who, Donald? A friend, why are you inquiring anyway?" she asked, in a nonchalant manner. "He's such a gentleman, with the prettiest little girl, she's too adorable." I hated Donald with every bone in my body from that moment on and, somehow someway I had to avenge my mother's agony with Ms. Thornton in mind.

"You can take me to Buster's Pizza place on Marlton Pike if you don't mind," I forcibly requested.

"You got a change of plans to day huh? Okay, no problem," she answered, turning on the gadgets to the radio and the air-conditioner. Ms. Tee observed the two boxes of berets lying on top of the ashtray like she put them there herself; they really took her by surprise.

"These have the prettiest colors in them, are they yours?" she asked, in an astonished voice. "Where'd they come from?" Ms. Tee had more questions then a kid in a candy store.

"Nah... Not at all... There not mines," I answered, vacuously. Knowing she had knew where they came from. "They were for my baby sister, I had placed them there because they were giving my pant's pocket a hard time, but since you're so amazed by them you keep them."

"No not at all, I can't accept something that you've already brought for someone else. She must be a doll baby because berets bring out your inner beauty."

"It's not a problem Ms.Tee, seriously, if you want them you can have them. I'll get here a few packs some other time. Besides I know you have a thing for them anyhow." I needed an enticing reaction from that statement.

"Oh you do, how so? 'Cause you notice them in my hair as often and much?" she answered my own questions for me with a seductive blush, touching my face fervently with a simultaneous glide. "Kay-Kay you are so generous," She whispered softly. "I wish I was fourteen again because--"

"Red light!" I yelled instantaneously, watching the road the entire time; traffic was moving at a much swifter pace than usual. Hitting the breaks with a bricked foot, we managed to jerk forward and brace ourselves from a painful crash of the dashboard and steering wheel.

"Are you alright?" I asked, aiding her shock.

"Yes, I'm fine, a little scary but I'm fine. It was a heart stopping moment for a second. How 'bout yourself?" With a firm grip, she grabbed my hand for comforting purposes. While the light was still stop sign red, Ms. Tee leaned over in my direction and kissed me right near the corner of my lip; half cheek, half lip. In an instant I became hypnotized, I was truly immobilized, unable to believe what my face just felt. As bad as I wanted to taste her cherry red lipstick, it dried up in haste, giving me a master piece to walk around with for the day.

"Remember what we've discussed in the past, what goes on hear stays here, everything isn't for everybody. Understand that I have a lot to lose and nothing to gain if things got into the wrong ears." I just sat there in a daze, nodding my head, agreeing to her every word as I remained mum, never saying a word.

I was approximately a half an hour late when she dropped me off in front of the Rotti Shop around 4:30p.m. But, who cared? In my eyes Ms. Tee was a full time occupation; it takes toiling labor to cater to glamour, charm, class, and wealth. And, I wouldn't hesitate to earn every drop of sweat for her. The looks on a few of my cronies' faces, when Ms. Tee pulled along side the curb in the pearl-white caddy, had been filled with profound enthusiasm; Ms. Tee's glow even got there dicks hard.

"You know those young men right there?" she asked, while eyeing them as they stood on out front of the shop. "Their some eye catchers as well, I see why you all hang together? I never knew fines could come in packs." She smiled passionately, handing me a piece of paper. "Feel free to call me anytime you'd like too, I don't see no harm in checking up on your whereabouts throughout the course of the summer. I don't see why I can't arrange a few days for you to come and stay at my place and meet my family."

I'm like 'Spend a few days with you and your family?' DAMN! I really got more than I bargained for. As I watched Ms. Tee's caddy smoothly sailed down Marlton Avenue, I was imagining how the trip would turnout while walking over to my homeboys. Breakfast in bed, massages, a few shopping sprees, and SEX, SEX, and more SEX…

"KYLE!" Wayne called, shattering my fantasy. Snapping back into reality instantaneously.

"Yeah?" I said, dumb founded.

"Give me ten cat daddy and some extra skin on the back hand side. 'Cause man she's a priceless fox," Wayne added, combing his wavy hair backwards. "That's your squeeze slim?"

"Nah man, she's my English teacher. She was just giving me a ride home from school, that's all."

"Nigga, school was dismissed almost an hour and a half ago," Ahmad said, taking a few tokes from the slow-burning joint that was being passed around in rotation. "Who you trying to fool? FOOL!" Everyone burst in laughter.

"Aye ol'blood, I told you its' nothing of the sort."

"Yeah we bet, she probably told your young ass not to say anything," Rasaan, the crew comedian, said biting in to a slice of pizza, holding the joint with the opposite hand. "I can dig that though, silence is golden and it gets you the gold when needed."

Ahmad, Rasaan, and Wayne were my three older brothers from another mother that I never had biologically; Dontae and Kyron were too. There were no special exceptions between the five of them, I treated them with the utmost respect and love and, the feelings were mutual but theirs came with a little more discipline.

"You just keep practicing your swing to be the next homerun king with that bat," Rasaan continued, giving me motivation. "I'm trying to see you become the next Reggie Jackson, you under dig?"

"I can dig it, I always go hard at the mound," I responded, with a gaggle of lies on my tongue, I didn't know the last time I swung a bat?

Even though I was three years behind them, I felt like their senior because I was sort of their boy next door and they knew that my love was truly genuine. Everybody knew them as the three main stars on Camden High's basketball team, they were the coolest dudes walking the streets; sort of like the Cooley High gang in its' prime. But, there Achilles heel was there absences from school often as much, they felt that they earned the grades by a shot at the ball, not by the ball of there pen. I couldn't say that about Ahmad though, he was a scholar-athlete, very studious person, plus his father Champ Mack was a strict over-seer and would kick his ass if he failed at anything. Other than that though they were either in two places, at the Stanley park playground or right out front of the Rotti shop, where they were hanging when I pulled up, flirting with every P.Y.T.(Pretty Young Thing) that they could spot in the atmosphere. But, they were my boys, my extended family and there wrongs were mines, we never judged each other. The only thing I would ever judge is the unconditional love if ever it waned.

# Chapter. 3

It was another never ending story of the summer going into my eleventh grade year, everybody was preparing themselves for another crucial school year and what was to be expected; but I never made it. I had finally stop lying to myself about being a corporate success story and dropped out of high school, it wasn't because everyone expected so much for me, I wasn't fit out to handle that conservative task anymore. In fact, that day Ms. Thornton had given me that ride to my job, where Rasaan, Wayne, and Ahmad were hanging out, jiving; about two-months prior. That was the last time I came close to Woodrow Wilson's gated property. Ms. Tee's number definitely came in handy during the fall; I had no excuses as to why I never used it the first time she gave it to me; I guess I was intimidated and my balls were the size of sun-flower seeds.

On another note, every since my mother had kicked Donald's ass to the sidewalk a ways back, she had been doing extremely well for herself. He would come around from time to time and try and see Aniyah but my mother was adamant in her decisions of denying him visitation rights. After about a month or so of persistence, Donald stop coming around, in fact he just vanished from the mysterious milieu without a trace. But, that didn't stop Olivia's growth and goals; she was on a mere paper chase. She had two supervising positions at both day/night jobs (Dayton Manor nursing home, Woolworths); she was grossing more income than she could bear.

She and my sister moved across town, down in the fifth ward into a five bedroom home; leaving me our old townhouse. As long as I kept a job she was willing to pay all of the utilities and mortgage. The mystical nature and liberalness which my mother shared with me was very bewildering, I probably was the only seventeen year old kid in the 'hood whom lived and managed like a grown man. But that was my mother for me though, always wanting to be distant and aloof. It was very strange but I didn't care it kept her off my back.

I wasn't doing to bad myself, I got a dollar raise at my job and Dontae and I got promotions to better positions; he was one of the cashiers and I drove the delivery trucks for the company. Ted was the boss, but his first lady - Jane - called all the shots and ran the take out joint with profession and progression. Their two daughters' (Rose-Angel and Dena) done all of the other pacing labors in the shop. None the less, I was an instant attraction to the six foot, modeled body Rose-Angel. I could remember my first day on the job of how she fraternized with me the entire day like we hung out everyday. Since my third day on the job, she's been giving me sex- quickies -on her lunch breaks, on the days she had to work. And, even though she was my only second piece of trim, she was an acrobat on the dick, Man! There was something different every time we had an impulsive encounter.

Rose was the eldest daughter of three, Ted and Jane also had a son, she was a senior in high school and her parents spoiled her. But, not how this chubby, black, jive ass clown named Poohshaun catered to her every want. Word on the wire was that he was so knee deep in the underworld that if you bypassed him you could catch a freeze off of his knee cap. Ted praised this cock sucker like he was the Pope or some divine god whom made all things possible. One day Poohshaun came to pick up Rose and Ted was all over him like he was a stalking groupie. I was far from being mad at the cat, maybe a little envious of his life style but, I was fucking his dame; why should I be mad?

Slyly, there was some thing dishonest going on between Ted and P. S., I just couldn't pin-point what it was. P. S. would come in empty handed but would leave out with a duffle bag strapped to his shoulder, every time he came and went. From my clear observations through aloofness, everyone else was playing on deaf ears and didn't seem to know anything; inquiring wasn't even the answer.

On Dontae's day off one day, I was asked by Rose to fill in at

Dontae's position and help stock the freezer in the basement. I assumed that she wanted a quickie, because that was sort of the norm for us on inventory days; we used the staff's second bathroom in the basement frequently. But, for some odd reason on this particular day, Rose's demeanor towards me was a bit off and irate. She didn't care to explain her bottled-up issues and I didn't care to ask. We ran out of room in the holding freezer while stocking all the frozen goods but, there was this other door - adjacent to the freezer - which I assumed was another freezer that had been rarely used. But, to Rose's knowledge I was wrong and she berated me for even going close to the shallow door. Expressing to me that 'I should make it my last time going anywhere near that door.' Oh! Believe me, that was the last time I stepped close to the lousy door and it was Rose's last time getting anywhere as close to me as she use too. Rose's demands didn't stop the curiosity of what could be so sacred behind that door from running through my fragile mind; I was eager to find out the mystery through patients.

$ $ $ $

By early October I had a new roommate, one of my closest homeboy's (Kyron Owens) had been staying with me after his mother found a .380 handgun and a sneaker box full of money that he consumed from hustling people out of on the courts at the play ground; Arlene thought otherwise and just knew her son was into some type of criminal activity. But, in my eyes if criminality activated the fascinating game of basketball, then Kyron was the most renowned criminal that ever played on the paint. His source of income was menial corporately, but it was superb in the sport of basketball; hoop hustling was the only way he knew how to manage.

Every night (mostly), down at the Stanley Park playground, guys from all parts of the city would meet up to show off there extraordinary talent that didn't get many of them to the collegiate level of stardom. Wayne and Rasaan ruled Stanley's street courts, along with Ahmad, Dontae, and Kyron; they were truly the fantastic five. They played jokers who had there talent and skill, if not better and punished them like amateurs who knew nothing. Stanley Park was a local Rucker park special, only without the referees and top scouts there to make the game even more interesting; only a lot of liquor dwellers, locals, hustlers, bookies, and pure talent.

City superstars such as, Billy Thompson, Kevin Walls, Milt Wagner, Donny Bunch, and Itchy Smith, who were all - if not - College and high school All-Americans, came through to play full-court, rough house ball for respect and there love for the game. Games were so intense, the jokers whom betted against the bookies upped the ante anywhere from a $1,000 to $5,000 dollars a game. That's how much confidence was directed towards the talent on the court and, in 1983, that was a lot of money to throw up for grabs at a playground game.

$ $ $ $ $

Ms. Thornton finally found time to mingle with me at her summer home up near the Jersey shore; where she was spending her entire summer vacation. One of her relatives at the house had given me the number where she could be reached at her summer home; the number was only given to me out of the finagling sense of urgency for educational purposes.

Within forty-eight hours of me receiving the phone number, Ms. Tee had returned my call and was overwhelmed by my persistence because she had assumed that I forgot about her offer of staying with her for a few says over the summer. The same night she drove down to my pad and picked me up without the thought of hesitating. But, in our short conversation of brevity, she told me that she had been going through some rough times, on an emotional rollercoaster and, she just needed a piece-of-mind and comfort. I really pondered on what type of comfort would she possibly get out of a sixteen year old kid, after giving her the okay?

Kyron knew the rules and regulations that were instilled at the fort, and he was willing to maintain those responsibilities until I returned in a few days. Olivia's foot was concrete and she didn't have a problem with kicking his ass out on the street. Due to Ted going out of town with his family on a business trip, Dontae and I had two week off from the shop - with pay - to roam freely until Ted returned.

The entire ride to the shore was an emotional down pore for the luxurious fox, which had been a little over an hours' worth of Cathartic expressions; truly a learning experience for me too. Jackie had been going through an elongated love crisis which seemed far from monumental. Her husband, whose name she didn't disclose - the stockbroker - was having a ongoing affair with some one close and dear to her; a twenty year ongoing affair that went into effect after they eloped. Jackie admitted that she was twenty-two when she got married in 1963. Back then, Kyle's sperm was too premature to be trying to create me. She confessed that the bitch her husband was committing adultery with was her childhood best friend, the godmother to her two daughters (Janaya and Jasmine), and knew about every furtive secret and dark skeleton that was ever acted upon.

Her appearance showed that the crucial, love conflict was causing her stress and pain, far from looking like her usual self. She had her hair tide in a Louis-Vutton scarf, heavy bags garnished under her eyes, and there was butts of marijuana joints filled in the debris of ashes in the car's ashtray. I concluded her vigorous pain to have come from being dick strung, a manipulated profound love that couldn't be escaped, or the money had her and she didn't have it.

The woman that her so-called husband was having an affair with had been her biological, youngest sister True; her own contaminated blood. That statement fucked my immature, sixteen year old mind up because I was always told that blood was thicker than water; I guess some needed water to survive.

"She didn't do that to you?" I asked, knowing it happened, but I was very perplexed.

"Yeah that stinking bitch did, she's been fucking my husband in my face for the past twenty years. After all I've sacrifice for her," She implied, banging her fist on the steering wheel.

That point of the conversation frightened me, I thought she had convinced me to come to her summer home so she could kill me; I don't know why, that's what I thought though. She then went on of explaining to me how her first and last night coitus with Donald went in to play. Mentioning, that it wasn't supposed to have happened the way that it turned out - for the worst - but she was inebriated and Donald was enticing to her wrong eye at the time and she acted upon her infatuation for him. In her twenty years of marriage she said that was the first time she had ever slept around on her husband. But, it wouldn't of never of happened if she didn't find the explicit photographs of him and True in his office desk drawer.

Between the long ride up to the shore and Ms. Tee's depressed love story, I didn't know what exhausted me more. But, once I was in the comforts of her summer home, I made my way to her bedroom. My mind was in dream land in a maximum of ten seconds from the feel of the marshmallow comforter, covering the water bed. I could have sworn that I had a bad case of Déjà vu when I awoken around midnight. I had been taken advantage of, stripped down to my tube socks and no sheets to cover my nervous anatomy.

Ms. Tee was partially naked, wearing nothing but laced panties with a garter that latched on to some white, silky stockings. Having a phenomenal shape and build, like that of Vanessa Del Rio; I mean oatmeal thick. My eyes felt like they were gazed in a mirage, I'd never seen someone so sexually divine before. My abdominal area was covered with streaks of a powdery substance and, before I could even touch it or find out what the fuck the Arm & Hammer baking soda was doing down there, Janice began snorting the shit between her nostrils like a vacuum cleaner; licking the residue remains off with her sultry tongue.

My mind became vacuous after she fiercely pushed me back down on the bed and started to blow me like gusting winds. Janice's volcano mouth engulfed my dick and balls like a snake on a rat's ass, making my toes curl from the amazing sensation. She asked me to talk dirty to her in the heat of my explosion, I did exactly that, and it aroused her to the point of snorting some more cane. Only to have given her an adrenaline rush to fuck me like a professional porn-star.

Mounted over me like a lady cop making a resisting arrest, Janice guided me inside of her pulsating pussy walls and went for an invigorating bull ride. Her cat was extremely moist, had my chocolate éclair looking like a pair of leather pants. With her head in a backward relaxed position, she began talking to me as her pace and gyration process slowed gradually.

"I lied when I told you that I had everything to lose and nothing to gain. I been lost everything, I just was in denial of holding on to everything that was once dear to me. I gained and I lost all in one stark breath and, if I could turn back the hands of time I would want my life to be much different. Being the freak of nature through my spirits' guide and enjoying life… Better than being some miss-goodie-two shoes and a miserable whore."

Truly disinterested at that point of another heart aching moment and the vision of profuse tears, my mind didn't want to continue. Janice's soul was still filled with relentless agony and I felt like I was the cause of her troubles.

"It took for me to be around a care-free sixteen year old, that's full of life and energy to understand that real eyes realize real lies and, to believe in myself," she continued, showering me with multiple facial kisses.

"Facing your troubles aligns with facing yourself day in and day out, if you run from them then you'll always run from yourself. Life, beauty and, everything that you live for comes from the soul… Heart felt," I replied consoling her gently.

The succinct advice I'd given Janice came from my grandmother Ann a firm believer in Karma, her favorite book in the bible was Proverbs (Exhortations to seek wisdom), the book of wise sayings.

The night skies were clear and serene and the sound of the shore's water filled the air like rain showers as I gazed out onto the deck from the bed. Janice rested beside me with her head lying on my chest while my stomach absorbed her tears. Lying in deep thought, thinking how fortunate I was to be a sixteen year old young man, who stepped in the shoes of his father at an early age but, yet I was still a baby internally. My accomplishments were astounding to the unseen eye, living on my own with a full time job and, having intimate relations with a intelligent goddess of a school teacher who was old enough to be my mother; there was no way I was supposed to be living like this. I was supposed to be on the corner with my cronies playing the dozens, swinging yo-yos or studying to become a big time lawyer. Instead I'm wearing Kyle Tommy Moore's trousers, an abandoned father who left me when I was just an infant. Until this day I've thirsted for his love and guidance but, it has always been a shadow in my life. Why should I ever care? Olivia was always there and he wasn't, all the days of my life she was the best thing I could possibly come near. If my mother wasn't as strong as she looked she would be destroyed mentally. Probably snorting heroin like Janice or committed suicide like a dead-man-walking having no purpose in life. It felt like I been around the world once and seen it twice and haven't even begun to explore the existences outside of Camden.

The following Friday I returned home to what seemed to be a 7th street block festival of some sort that was filled with nothing but clamorous noise and excitement. My hands began to have this strange tingle, giving me a weird indication that all the chaos was coming from my residence at 2141.

"Stop the car, stop the car!" I yelled, demanding that Janice come to an abrupt halt. I hopped out in unison while the car was still in motion, racing in haste to my front door. I bumped, pushed and, slid through the crowd of tramps and hoodlums whom were full of partying bliss. I couldn't even hear myself think from the bass in the thundering speakers which screamed from my stereo system, while searching for Kyron who I was going to kill. The dime blue light bulb that had been changed impaired my vision as I looked high and low for him. And, the reeking of marijuana smoke and mugginess from people dancing did nothing but infuriate me even more.

I spotted Kyron as I approached the entrance of the kitchen, exiting out of the backdoor tailing some bimbo. "Kyron, what the fuck you got going on here slim," I exclaimed, as the brown skinned female looked on in disgust.

"Heeey Kyle, my main man…fifty grand," he answered, putting his arm around me, holding a beer in the other.

"Man, care to explain to me what the hell is going on 'round here with out my approval…ill, man get the fuck off me, slobbering' and shit." Kyron was beyond drunk or high he was numb.

"Kyle, I want you to me my pretty-young-thing her name is Tasha, she's my ghetto superstar," he said avoiding my primary question. "She fine as sharp cheese isn't she lil' bro'?"

"Slim you on some bullshit, I leave you in charge for a few days and this is how you repay me?" Kyron's state of mind had never changed even from grade school when he'd deviate and take matters into his own hands. I found the answer to his mothers' discharge and distance.

"Calm your ass hole young blood, today's E.B.'s birthday and we decided to throw him a little blue light special. Maaaaaaan, you should see how much money we made from this--"

"Fuck that money blood, what if my moms came here and seen this shit? We'd both be homeless, partying at other muthafukas' pads. You should have at least had the decency to inform me first," I retorted, heading back towards the backdoor.

My mind was boggled by everything that was taking place in my circumference; I had truly forgotten that Janice was out front impatiently waiting for me. Her Deville was nowhere to be seen when I came back out front to nothing but loud freeloaders. "DAMN!" I said to myself, heading back inside. I felt worse than Billy Ray Valentine (Eddie Murphy) did in the movie Trading Places when he had the party at his luxurious home; only difference was nothing was that priceless in my house to steal and there were even more cigarette butts of Kools on my floor.

As I made my way up stairs to secure the other rooms in the house, Big Tootsie, the DJ of the party had the sweet sounds of Marvin Gaye spinning on his turn tables. And every which way I turned there was horny muthafuckas making out all over the place. The bathroom was checked first, where Wayne was enjoying the tits of this watermelon chest slut named Michelle Patrick, blowing a joint in unison. In the corner room, adjacent to the bathroom, was where E-Bee had been being uncouth with Wayne's younger sister Booper; who wasn't even old enough to be at the party. Doubting that Wayne had mere insight to that awkward cohabitation and if he did, E-Bee would be amongst the maggots. And, just when I thought I seen all that I could see, there came a bleak situation in my foresight. Three of my aunts-Gracey, Sissy, and Debbie-were in my bedroom with my sperm donor - Big Kyle Sr. - snorting cocaine and plundering through my belongings; looking for things to steal, I guess to support there illicit habits. 'How the fuck did they of all people, get in my bedroom. Let alone the muthafuckin' party?' I asked myself, as I stared on in disbelief. They were so into their zone of deceit that they didn't even see me standing at the bedroom door.

The stench of piss, old spice, and ten day old garbage surfaced the room like spoiled air, giving me a sudden vomiting affect that was uncontrollable but I restrained my stomachs' pressure. Ignoring them for the moment, I went in to the hallway closet to retrieve my Louisville slugger baseball bat, which was smiling at me for a taste of action when I swung him across my shoulder; a brand new stick that was itching for a banging head session.

"You trifling muthafuckas," I exclaimed in rage, swinging the bat a 100 miles an hour after burst into the room, catching the four of them off guard. Coke debris surfaces the air like arson smoke, as the four of them tried to find a way to dodge the hard-stricken pain. All I heard was "Nephew pleases…And son not in front of company." They made me swing the slugger even harder with strenuous force. Implicating, "I'm not your fucking son and, the rest of you are nothing to me." Followed by an ominous demand of "Get the fuck out!" Prior to Wayne and Kyron pinning me to the floor and snatching the bat from me, I struck my dad in his knee cap with it; that was just a past pain release that I've always felt that was needed.

Next, came the busting of the blue light in the living room, telling Tootsie to stop the music and, for every single person in the party if they weren't out by the time I came back downstairs from retrieving my pistol, there was going to be a lot of wounded muthafuckas. No one called my bluff and I cleared house in the matter of ten minutes tops, except my aunts whom were trying to plead there innocence to me and begging me not to tell my mother. I didn't indulge in drugs or alcohol, so the dope fiend game that was being ran on me went in one ear and out the other.

"Nephew please don't tell my sister about this, okay…please," Aunt Gracey said, grabbing my shirt from a begging knee position. The three of them were well aware that my mother was there sacred back bone, when they ran out of places to go or options to execute; they all came to Olivia's grace for a better way. In my mind, what happened that night was the straw that broke the camel's back and taken its' last bounce with the illusionary ball-mentally-and I couldn't take it anymore. From the aspects of there drug habits, being irresponsible and when shit got thick they tried to wipe there asses' with someone else's clean hand. Well, since my hands had been covered in shit since my conception on this contaminated planet, I disowned them all but, in the process of doing so I told them one-by-one that they all owed me. I might have not needed a favor now or later but they owed me.

As far as the sperm donor went, there was nothing more I had to say to my reflection of a physical mirror but, "I guess it was written for our father, son relationship to have turned out this way. Maybe thing will get better in our after lives." He glanced at the younger version of himself before limping away, simultaneously giving me eye to eye contact and gave me a hearty response.

"You are my after life and I'm already dead son, just a walking spirit with physical features." He bowed his head in discuss. "One day you'll understand."

I stood motionless for a minute, trying to fathom this drug junky's conditions, who didn't care about himself, let alone me. Kyle was a waste of entity, not only to himself but, to whoever followed his walking shadow. Cocaine, dope, or any other powdery substance he chose to snort was the only thing that loved his ass; nothing mortal though.

After I cleared house, Wayne an I swept and mopped the place clean while Kyron sensually entertained his over night main squeeze in one of the upstairs bedrooms. Prior to me leaving with Ms. Tee to head to the shore, Kyron couldn't even squeeze his ass tight enough to shit a dime. Wayne knew, just as well as I that he had just met her at the party.

Tasha must have had the greatest sex because while Wayne and I furtively eased dropped by the cracked door, we could hear Kyron moaning like a bitch and the bed board pounds the back wall like a sledge hammer. We were on the floor in laughing tears from observing Kyron in action. He was in missionary position with his pants down by his lower ankles, rabbit stroking Tasha's sour flesh. What a fucking site to see, and I thought I was bad. The comical episode that Wayne and I shared was enough to put me in a snoozing coma until the following afternoon.

Exactly then, that afternoon I was stretched out across my bed with all my clothes on and, I don't even know how I got there. The last thing I remember was being in tears from watching Kyron's speed racing ass fuck Tasha. But, what surprised me was to see Wayne in the same place I'd left him the passed day, curled up on the hallway floor like a salted snail. As I tried hopelessly to get Wayne to awaken from the tiled floor, the bedroom phone rang giving off this alarming sound which made my ears ring a bit.

"Hello," I answered, going back to see if I could awaken Wayne once more.

"Kyle! Kyle!" The annoying voice screamed aloud, trying to get my attention. "This is Ahmad...Kyle you there?"

"Yeah fucka, stop yelling' in my damn ear, ya' dig?" He was a second away from being hung up on.

"Maaan, I got some bad news to tell you slim, E. B. was killed last night after he left the party about three-thirty this morning," Ahmad said, as if he never wanted to reveal the sad news.

"Don't be jiving me blood, now isn't the time," I replied in disbelief

"I'm far from jiving you my man." Shaviera, Ahmad's oldest sister really knew what happened to E.B. because she and E.B.'s sister Makeya were close friends. Shaviera picked up on another line of the phone, confirming the tough news.

"He's not lying Kyle, its true...Word is after he dropped Booper off home, and they went down to Luby's pool hall. His cousin Puba told me that they were shooting pool when a fight broke out on the dance floor. And, before they could make it out side, shots rang out. Puba was also injured, taking one in the leg."

I broke the bad news to Wayne who happened to hear bits and pieces, after hanging up with Shaviera and Ahmad. After reiterating what was brought to my attention about E.B.'s death to Wayne, my mind went blank. Wayne went and broke the painful news to Kyron. Instantaneously, all could think about was the film of memories that were once shared with us all.

I first met Ibraheem Townsend (Mr. Jumbo Ears), back in Mr. Henry's class, forth grade 1977. We both spotted each other in the school's playground during recreation. He wore this close cut afro that had more peas in it then curls and had these big ass elephant ears. I said to myself, 'God, that's a funny looking kid,' in a laughing manner. He was standing over by the fence swinging a yo-yo; I approached him in confidence like I'd known him for years. We exchanged names and the part of towns that we were from; he was from the Park Side neighborhood of the city; around the area of Luby's pool hall. E.B. was a transferee from Forrest Hill elementary, the only grade school that sat to the rear of Camden High school.

A few of the local toughs at school tried to chump him during his inception there but he managed to stand his ground and go hard on his own, he wasn't a pushover but he didn't fall for anything like most fragile minors. The funniest thing that we done together was ate about ten fried pieces of chicken that E.B. cut class to go and get for Kyron an I, to split in our seventh grade science class. E.B. was the dare devil of us all and if you didn't live on the edge with him you couldn't be around him.

Introducing him to Booper - Wayne's baby sister - was the best thing for him at the time. Raised in a dysfunctional household E.B. took to the streets early and only listened to his sister Makeya, but she was more like his guardian than his girl next-door. But, Booper who was just a couple of years younger than him, understood his and gave him a personal comfort zone that he never shared with anyone ever before. I just knew that they would be together forever, from the first time they kissed and he had a portion of sour-cream and onion potato chips still in his mouth; if that wasn't comfort I don't know what is. I think out of all of us, Booper was taking it the hardest because they were together like stars at night. I wondered would she ever love again.

The night after his funeral - five days later - was extremely bleak and lonely, in my eyes it was like God had taken the hood's only young Messiah. As I sat twenty feet from his pearl-white, gold trimmed casket, my thoughts were in deep reveries and my eyes were heavy and, also filled with gloom. Visioning my close friend lie dormant in his black, double breasted suit, as Kyron an Wayne - to the right an left of me - sat with there faces' drenched in tears. The truth of E.B's body lying in that motionless casket didn't really hit home until his oldest brother Jamie stood in front of his little brother's casket and began to sing "Stairway to Heaven," by the Ebonies. It was something about that song that put a move on my heart, painfully through emotion. I blew a few joints and poured sips from my bottle of dry Gin to the ground for my main man before me and the crew guzzled the entire bottle. In my mind, I felt in years to come that the love amongst my friends would change and E.B's memory would be the only love left for us to feel in the heart of the city.

# Chapter. 4

It was the beginning of 1985, a seventeen year old with a more vivid appearance than the year itself, having a Krush Groove style like that of the movie. Run-DMC wasn't only making a renowned name for themselves on the big screen, they were also blowing up the pop-charts with their powered singles "Its' like that," and "Sucker Mcs." The single by the young group New Edition, "Count Me out," was climbing the charts as well. But, that's how I was feeling, like no one could count me out this time around. It was like I had a premonition of what was to be expected of my life and I loved what was in my foresight.

Dipped in the latest fashion, I stayed with a resemblance of a Run-DMC b-boy, black derby brims, all kinds of Adidas nylon sweat suits, and various shells tops with no shoe strings in them. But, while my young ass was styling and profiling Wayne an Rasaan had went on to live out there hoop dreams until they hearts gave out, with basketball scholarships too the University of Maryland. While, Kyron was destined to fill in their footsteps he became the eyed blue-chip for the Panthers at Camden High school. Kyron was averaging 28 points per game, 12 rebounds, and 8 assist; 2 assist away from averaging a triple-double per game. Thanks to the Panther's basketball coach Calvin Turner for his science of the game, the Panther's gymnasium was giving birth to stars by the minute. And with lead man Kyron Owens at the helm, the Panther's remained undefeated and were on there way to an astonishing ninth straight Group IV championship.

Kyron was big time though, extremely larger than Wayne and Rasaan whom were in the eye of the elite since there freshman year. In just three years of high school, Kyron was being scouted to go straight from the amateur levels right into the big leagues. He had moved out of my place and in with this Fox named Deidra, whom he dumped the Bimbo Tasha for. She spoiled Kyron with a passion to do nothing else, but cater to his every need. And, he loved every bit of her parents' wealth being that Deidra's father was a doctor and mother was a sophisticated lawyer; if that wasn't some straight Cosby show shit there? But, as long as Deidra made the grades and Kyron scored points, they both wanted for nothing but at the end of the day, it was three against one. And, Kyron wasn't the one who was looking to strategize on an ulterior-motive.

In other depressing news, Dontae became a lost cause after he was fired from the shop for engaging in sex acts with Dena in the employees' bathroom; followers never learned. We kept in contact because of our friendship, and met up at Kyron's games often but, other than that Dontae was incognito to city he loved best.

Ahmad went into the navy after his hoop dreams turned nightmare and he had to have surgery on his elbow after he shattered it in four places in a dirt-bike accident eight months ago. He was hoping to live out his secondary dream of becoming a pediatrician in the near future.

I was the only one trapped in the forbidden struggle that everyone in my circumference had been excelling to more novel and higher dimensions. But, it was my idiotic choice to drop out of school in my sophomore year at Woodrow Wilson high; the books just weren't for me anymore. What an ignorant thing to say huh? Due too the lack of practice and dedication to my passion of baseball, I didn't even have the feel for the game anymore like when I was younger; besides our high school team was manure on the field. My old little league team was better than them, and besides, the skill an abilities that I had with the glove and ball I wasn't about to play with a group of scrubs. Situations like the ones I was having do take affect on your brain when you become arrogant and big-headed.

Working in the Rotti shop until sun up to sun down for Ted - who had two big NOW HIRING signs in the front windows-was far from motivational. Firing Dontae, suggesting that Dena not come around for a while and allowing Rose to come in an out as she pleased was Ted's way of saying "I'm your master now Boy." I was getting sick to my stomach from the smell of the joint, day… after day… after day. Rose had stop coming to work and around her daddy's grease pot about a month prior, I had no clue or assumed reason but, she could afford to live off the nigga P. S. expense. But, how could I complain when Ted's expense showered me with food, clothing and shelter?

$$\$ \$ \$ \$ \$$$

A group of females strolled in the shop around closing time one Thursday evening, as I struggled to get the remaining debris off the floor. "Aye yo' broom boy," The light skinned dame with the huge bamboo earrings called from the entrance door, as her crew followed her in toe. "Can we get some service or what?" Her tone was mellow but forceful.

"I'm not sure if the owner is cooking at this hour because where about to close in a minute," I answered, not even trying to give the Lena Horn faced cutie eye contact.

"Are you serious my man?" Her crew was also disappointed by my remark. "Come on…please." Her seductive facial expression got to me in one blink of her lash.

Ted came gaiting unsteadily from out of the back, wiping his greasy hands on his apron, chasing the attempt to render more customer service. "COM' on, COM' on wat is it tier huh? You ladies' hungry aye, looks like you've been on your feet all day?" His accent enticed them to the point of ordering more than they came for.

"We're closing and they want to place an order at closing hours."

"Well less feed them, shwan lose out on money? Spending money is gude money and no montey is bad mon-tey. Isn't that right ladies?" They all agreed in unison, still mesmerized by his annoying accent.

The breathtaking female whom referred to me as broom boy had to be about nineteen, no older than twenty-two. Short, around-about

5'5" inches tall, with a body that called like that of the-Wild! Her disposition enticed me to inquire into her vitals and whereabouts. As I stood behind the register collecting the money for their orders, Ebony was one of the females in the click that I spotted and knew from grade school days.

"Ebony!" I called, getting her immediate attention.

"Kyle...Kyle Moore?" She asked in awe, knowing it had been a long time since we last seen each other.

"Yeah... Who else would it be," I said as we embraced with a friendly hug.

"Its' been a while...you look different." I was flattered, but not convinced. "What has it been...? Eighth grade or so?"

"Yeah, 'bout that--"

"Lil' sis' you know broom boy?" Light skinned intervened, wanting to be in the know.

"Yeah girl, we go back since fifth grade... Bonsall Bear style." We shared a laugh about our old school symbol. "Kyle listen, I'm having a birthday bash down at Luby's pool hall this Saturday after the High's basketball game. You know I got to see my boy Kyron do his thing. Stop by if you get time?"

"Will do, I'm free on Saturday anyhow." Ebony was always the life of the party with her charismatic nature, and even though she was a petite, honey-brown kitten she could be taboo at times because she had this irate side that would make a muthafuka wonder if they had to put her out her misery, if they thought twice about it. In seventh grade, she intentionally disrespected a male school teacher by sticking her finger up his ass while he was writing an objective on the blackboard; the teacher had been pestering her all day long. I guess that exposed his true nature in manhood because everyone thought he was gay anyway, Ebony just had the courage to put her icing on his cakes.

But Ebony wasn't the alluring one to my fishnet eye; it was her sister with the feisty demeanor, covered in street glamour that enticed me. The light skinned vixen was the last to come to the register and pay for her food.

"You have a nice complexion," I said, collecting the money from her, knowing that line was a cliché too many that used it.

"I know, but thanks for noticing," she replied, sliding me the change, tipping my services.

"That would be rude of you not to share your name, wouldn't it?"

"Sharing my name with strangers is something I don't do and why you trying to get all familiar with me?"

"Familiarity keeps peace in the world." Now I felt like an idiotic philosopher, getting weaker and weaker at my pick up lines.

"No...What's your name?" her sarcasm put butterflies on my feet.

"I'm quite sure you heard your friend scream it out a while ago."

"I'd pay that no attention, and she's not my friend, she's my baby sister."

"You jiving' me, Ebony isn't you sis'," I stated, seeing no resemblance. Ebony was a shade darker and smaller in weight.

"What do I have to lie to you for broom boy? We have the same father, different mothers' corn ball. We get asked that all the time. Enjoy your night cleaning."

"Clown me if you may, but I still didn't get your name though," I pushed, with persistence.

"And the feeling is mutual," she retorted, heightening her sarcasm.

"Kyle."

"Lamaar, that's two A's, one R. now can I go, my boyfriend is expecting his food anytime soon." when I heard the word "Boyfriend," I stepped my game up even more.

"Hol' on... Hol' on a sec" I said, walking from around the counter. Lamaar came to an abrupt halt. "I hope you don't think I took offense to that boyfriend thing you shot my way? How you going tell me about a boyfriend when your standing in front of a boyfriend who wants to make you his girlfriend?" With her eyes behind shades, it was difficult to read her, to see if I got under her skin just a tad-bit.

"Because my boyfriend made me his Queen and until you can rub shoulders with him...which will probably never happen because of your occupational mishap? I will always be just that in your eyes a GIRL-FRIEND!"

I was ant size on the inside, a girl never turned me down to my face and made me feel like I didn't have nothing to offer the way that Lamaar did. But, plan B had already played out in my mind while talking to Ms. Hard to get; I just had to execute the move.

"Ebony let me speak to you for a moment?" I asked, needing to use her as a scapegoat.

"It's my sister right?"

It wasn't hard to tell that, because if it were Ebony, she would have known way back in the day.

"Okay, I'll see what I can do, I'm not making any promises though because you used to fuck with DaVita and that's Lamaar's befriends' cousin." That was my advantage point, due to girl talk.

"That was a puppy engagement with DaVita; I was only thirteen, besides she got a nigga too."

"Who, Kenny Morales? Please, he's only good for blowing digits on my sister and making her life miserable forms all the games he saturates her mind with."

"Come on Eb' do this one solid for me and I promise I'll make it up to you."

"Like I said I'm not making any promises, just come to my party Saturday night and we'll take it from there."

"Solid," I replied, with a smirk as she headed out of the exit doors.

Kenny Morales and I used to live on the same row in Sheridan Apartments on 10th street, but I didn't tell Lamaar that. This was back in 75'-76' when I use to live with my grandmother Ann and my Aunt Gracey; ironically my aunt still resides there. Kenny was a half breed - Spanish an black - who use to always come to my house and borrow some butter so he could make sugar on toast. He had to fine ass sisters, Keena and Latrelle, who use to baby sit for my Aunt Gracey all the time. I had a crush on Keena too, it was something about her dimples when she smiled that I enjoyed as a kid.

Kenny was a heavy competitor and, I didn't have the status nor the power that he possessed. He and Poohshaun were partners and the wire had him selling more sugar than he ate when he was a kid. With marveling thoughts lingering through my mind, I had not a clue of how I was going to clip the vivid dame Lamaar from his shoulders, with only fast food change in my pockets. I needed another hustle if she was going to be my Empress, because asking Ted for another raise wasn't going to do it. Besides business had been slow for us anyhow, every since some Chinese people opened up a take out place down the street on Marlton and Thorn Dyke street.

$$\$ \$ \$ \$ \$$$

Dontae, whose voice gave off a suspicious vibe, called me a few days later telling me that he had something big planned for tomorrow night; his words were succinct and he didn't reveal much. He asked one serious question, "You in or out." He's been my man since grade school, a hundred grand, how could I negate his offer. "Yes," was the only answer I knew?

The following night Dontae, his pops Dontae Sr. (Big D.S.), and his cousin Spring came through to see me in a black two-door Buick Skylark. Having the slightest knowledge of what was about to go down, I asked no questions because my mood shifted into me being down for whatever at that point. Dontae entered my house alone while Big D.S. and Spring sat out in the car. Dressed in all black attire and a black Pea-coat, I had this strange feeling that Dontae wanted me to do something illicit.

Making it sound and clear, Dontae explained the mission to the best of his ability, trying to convince me that entire plan was sweet and beneficial. He asked me did I have any black attire and a masked for my face. I had the attire but no mask. While preparing myself he threw me a skull hat, gloves and a bandana to cover up with.

"What's Spring doing tagging along on this move?" I asked for my own safety, having precautions of doing things with certain people.

"She's our decoy," he replied. "She's going to go in Ted's and make like she's places an order so we can--"

"Hol' up… Hol' the fuck up! The Rotti shop is the mission? No fucking way my man, count me out. I'm not wit that there." Dontae painted a clearer picture for me to vision once he filled me in on the reasons of such and act.

For the past twenty years, before Ted even opened the Rotti shop up, he used his vacant building to store huge amounts of illegal products for certain key men in the underworld; my uncle Muscles had been one of those figures. Ted use to be a great car driver who's virtuosity behind the wheel gained him lucrative mounts of money throughout the states. That's why when the time came for Dontae and I to stock the weekly food shipments, Ted never wanted us to give him a hand on certain trucks. He kept the kilos of heroin in a temperature area that was cool so the chemicals in the dope wouldn't dissolve and go bad.

There also was a metal ceiling safe embedded in the downstairs employees' restroom. "Well...I'd be goddamn," I said, in disgust. "All that time I'd been in and out of there and I never put two-an-two together to even look up at the ceiling. I guess it wasn't meant for me to do so." Dontae told me to calm down so he could finish explaining what else there was to know.

Ted and the nigga P.S. had negotiated on certain procedures that would keep them from losing any major money and to stay out of the eyes of authorities. Ted made an agreement with P.S. and these Dominican muthafuckas whom P.S. worked for, to be there personal loader and to import as much heroin that he could possibly transport twice a month until his casket was lowered six feet in the grave yard; he had a 25% cut from what made after both shipments were complete.

Rose-Mary was Ted's smoke screen of transporting the narcotics in state from Mexico. All she had to do was Keep the public's eye on her when she was in the presence of Poohshaun and those who had a hunch only could place P.S. wit Rose in or around her father's establishment. "That's why we were in the blind because Ted always would blow Rose's relationship with P.S. out of proportion. Making it seem like he was really in love with her and was sort of like her prince charming but in a stalking kind of way." A lot of past things that took place in front of our eyes started to make sense.

After I was fully advised about the mission and Ted's furtive movements in and out of the establishment, the four of us drove in the Skylark to make something out of nothing. Spring and I sat in the back seats, while Dontae drove and Big D.S. sat in serenity on the passenger side.

Nine-thirty p.m. was the approximate time on Spring's watch when we arrived at the shop on a extremely cool Wednesday night in February; a half hour before Ted was set to close. I felt like I was getting ready to execute the sequel to the gory Valentine's Day Massacre that happened back in 1929, between Al Capone and Bugs Morgan up in Chicago, Illinois. Dontae back the Skylark in the rear of the shop, off the side of Midvale Street. With the car's engine roaring tranquilly, the head lights got shut off and everyone's bandana went up.

"You know what to do," Big D.S. said turning in Spring's direction. "No room for mistakes, play ya' part." Spring got out of the car and leisurely gated up the alley like a model on a killing spree, every step was fierce and smooth.

"Aiight, you two there's no turning back," D.S. said giving us direct eye contact. "Ain't no turning back, let's hit this bitch and ride off into the cold winter night like John Wayne and the Sun dance kid, ya' dig?" Grabbing the shotgun from the floor's rear as he conversed to us what was to be done.

I trailed Big D.S. and Dontae, about five steps behind, who crept in the stores glass, revolving doors with two, fully loaded double barrel shotguns clinging to there shoulders' from under there Peacoats. I was in the lookout position, making sure no one entered or exited the joint and kept a vigilant eye on any patrol cars that made there way up and own the Pike; we had six minutes to get it all done.

The excitement thicken and there was no turning back, no soon as we entered Dontae put the doubled barreled shotgun to the front of Ted's forehead while his pop jumped the counter and did the same thing to Jamaican Jane. Before I turned the closed sign on the store's front door, I allowed Spring to head out and, I locked the doors back and remained posted.

Ted and Jane were gauged and taken into the basement to retrieve the goods. Dontae had his shotgun stuffed between Jane's thick thighs, with the top of the barrel grazing her pussy for a last time orgasm. If she dared to move the wrong way or scream in clamorously, he was going to make her vaginal canal become attached to her brain. Three minutes was all the time we had left before the fuzz came through and made their rounds.

Big D.S. emptied the freezer where the dope had been stashed and then beat the combination to the safe out of Ted's face, knocking his front teeth to the floor with the butt of the shotgun. In seconds the ceiling safe was completely emptied into one big, hefty trash bag which sat motionless over top of the toilet. I tied Jane and Ted up, they were completely unclad and then slid both of there crying asses into the below zero temperature back freezer. I felt a bit sympathetic while putting the act in motion; I was putting two innocent people whom gave me an honest opportunity in an icebox to freeze to death. As I watched them beg for mercy, I pleaded to God that I hope he didn't allow me to suffer in death like the two of them. After slamming the door completely shut, I headed back upstairs and out the front doors, vacating the premises just in time before the fuzz slid through.

"Hurry up lil' nigga," Big D.S. yelled from the passenger side window as I trotted to the car's backdoor. I had no time to shut the back door when Spring mashed the gas with her heel and, skirted down the back alley with increasing velocity.

Without one distraction or encounter with the law, we made it back to Dontae's pad safely. Big D.S. was overwhelmed in excitement from the sting that we had just pulled off.

"That's how shit is supposed to be done, in and out," He said, taking a few snorts of the heroin that we just confiscated from Ted's'.

It hadn't even been twenty-four hours before we could put the robbery behind us and D.S. was already killing his nose with that poison. Never get high on your own supply was a golden rule in the streets. I felt in my mind that the money and drugs wouldn't last long for them due to there redundant actions because they had no plans of gain for it.

"When you work together as a team, the job will get done

RIGHT!"

There were thirty keys of dope scattered around Dontae's wooden coffee table, we must have came prior to the delivery of the big shipment. Because Big D.S. said on Ted's worse day, he was packing at least a hundred at a time. Spring counted out three-thousand crisp, stacks of hundred dollar bills, which sat neatly stacked in front of me as well; the most money a young nigga such as myself had ever seen in his life. I was granted a fourth of the money and five keys of the blow. Dontae and his dad took a hundred grand a piece and twelve kilos for being the master mind behind it all. The remaining twenty-five Gs' went to Spring, who in D.S. and Dontae's eyes was a stand up rider but, in my eyes she was just a good girl going sour. The remaining blow, Big D.S. felt that he would use it for party packages; to turn tricks with I bet?

$ $ $ $ $

That Thursday, I received a call from my sickened mother, who had been out of work for the past two weeks because of the flu. We talked for a few minutes about her ailments and her needing any remedies or son's comfort to over come it all; she didn't need anything. She inquired about the episode that happened at Ted's, wondering how I was feeling and did I see it on the news or in the top headlines of the Courier-Post news paper? I stated that I knew nothing and didn't happen to see it on the news or in the papers. She suggested that I look for another job because Ted and his wife Jane had died. When the city detectives found the two bodies, they had been hogged-tied and frozen to death.

"Damn! That's a sin and a shame," I answered, feigning concernment. I didn't want to be reminded of that horrid night anymore, so I became discursive through a switched subject.

"So how's Niyah doing? Is she becoming a worse headache then before?"

"No, not really but I did have to smack her legs a few times because she want s to be a round electrical sockets."

"Oh yeah, she no that's a no-no." We conversed for a few minutes more, typical conversation from a mother who is always concerned about her son's well-being. Then she wants to drag other family member's circumstances and whereabouts into the picture; that's when I knew it was time to hang up.

After ten minutes of nagging on about the family tree, she gave me this number that my uncle left for me to receive so I could contact him immediately. "He's been back in town for a few days and he wanted to see you before he headed out."

"I can definitely dig that there, well mom thanks for the call and I'll be by to see you and my sister in a couple of days."

"Alright man, love you and stay out of harms way okay?"

"Okay mom, I will." Both lines disconnected.

My Uncle Lamont Muscles, now he was larger than the galaxy in the streets if there was ever one; this nigga had governor status in the state of New Jersey. The original "Dope man" himself, was a giant physically like Brutis from the cartoon Popeye and had big forearms like that of Popeye. He was a dark skinned complexioned man whom wore a neatly trim goatee. Uncle Muscles had been dealing drugs since thirteen, way before I was even a specimen in my pop's testicles; he was accumulating tons of federal reserved notes. In 1978, Uncle Muscles went to the penitentiary and was sentenced to six years for tax evasion. With the train smoke paper that he obtained, he just brought shit on general purposes and never gave the government a damn dime. But, his hedonistic, high life and heavy expenditures caught up with his ass. Uncle Muscles touched back down in 84', he's been home bought a year and I wondered what kind of plan he'd concocted for me to play a roll in.

When I was younger he use to take me out to stay at his home out in the tranquil, rural area of Williamstown, New Jersey; pure country life. His luxurious home sat on a few acres of land and he had a lot of expensive materials which embellished it and that flossed with value. His five foot swimming pool was my favorite place to relax and enjoy myself. As often as much, I used to wonder what it would have been like if he was my father, he was the coolest and most smooth guy that came into your presence.

I never wanted for nothing with him or even had to ask twice,

Uncle Muscles just gave to me willingly. I could remember the day he gave me Reggie Jackson's rookie card for my eighth birthday. He told me to never lose it because in twenty years it could make me a wealthy man; I was twenty years too impatient for that to happen. But, I still got the rookie card in a remote spot that I may have forgotten about but, it didn't matter I know that it's around. And that's all that mattered.

Materialistic bullshit didn't draw me close to uncle Muscles; it was his meek wisdom that strengthened my mind to grow in a different mannerism than one like he endured as a kid; streets raising him and no father figure! I guess he had to pardon himself for what his daddy couldn't do for himself. And, that was taking care of his responsibilities. He drilled in me to be a stand up, independent person that didn't need to count on anybody for a damn thing. And, to him, the terminology "Friend" didn't exist, because in a blink of an eye they gave you the dagger in the back. His perception of people was that no one cared enough to treat you like they would treat themselves and that everyone looked to get over on somebody for a better gain. No matter what it was, People hate you while you're here and love you when your gone that was his honest philosophy on how peoples' minds functioned socially.

"Silence would take you a long way, and walking alone would keep people from figuring you out." That was one of his golden rules of the streets and, the other one was "No matter how much trouble revolved around you and how severe the consequences maybe… NEVER RAT!" Those were the two golden rules that made him who he was in the streets but realistically, a lot of muthafuckas couldn't add.

True, his wife of many years was his success story, because he lived to die for her even if she wasn't true to their relationship or not; idiot. True was a human Barbie doll, I couldn't begin to tell you where my uncle found her at but she definitely was the truth. Her descent had to be of various nationalities, a mulatto, Puerto Rican, Hawaiian, and Jamaican; she was that gorgeous from the top of her head to the quagmire of her feet. She stood about six feet even - flat footed - with long, straight hair, slanted eyes, a honey skin tone and, was well built like a Jamaican jade stuffed inside of a soda bottle.

I was convinced that her beauty, not her brains had won my uncle's best interest at heart. Not saying that she was an incompetent woman but her appearance overwhelmed her intellect; just my opinion. I could remember True being in my presences when I was younger and my uncle use to point in her direction and say, "You see that beautiful lady right there and she's a diamond amongst diamonds. Always remember nephew a woman will never work for herself as long a she has the wit and certain tools that she can use to her advantage. So on your rise to the top, you use them to your advantage by making them work for you and sit back and watch the outcome. Only give them enough to be pleased with what they can't see and comfort them with enough security to make them feel as if they'll be protected from everything and everybody. And, they will definitely stick by you when you're at your own arduous cross roads."

Uncle Muscles also told me to never forget that woman are the key to a man's success but they're every successful man's downfall. Having no children, god-children, adopted children or dependents, the salacious dame True was his only concern and worry. "You can't be a hustler and a father at the same time," he would stress to me occasionally. And, he was right, how could a hustler run the streets day in and day out and be a full time family man? Evidently, the children who would one day grow to understand what had been taking place in front of their eyes, would eventually get turned on too the life and turned out in the life as well. No one couldn't tell me that Lamont Muscles wasn't an unadulterated genius who was before his life's capricious cycle.

# Chapter. 5

Saturday morning before getting myself ready to see Kyron in action against his arch rival school the mighty Wilson Tigers, I gave my Uncle Muscles a phone call.

"Hello," True said, answering the phone in a seductive tone, as if the ringing of the phone broke her beauty sleep.

"Hello True, how's everything going for you? Is my uncle around?"

"Everything has been just fine in my life, I can't complain. Hold on a minute, he's upstairs." True put me on hold to go and give him the phone.

"Yo' this Muscles," he replied, in a deep baritone.

"Hey now Unc', what it be like big guy? This is Kyle."

"Hey Marcus, I've been anticipating your call, where you been hiding at? You're a difficult guy to catch up with. I see you don't live with my baby sis' anymore?"

"I be around, yeah moms' left me the townhouse when she moved a few years back."

"I thought maybe you were living with one of those unstable bimbos out there?"

"Nah never that, you know my moves aren't that depressing," I answered, knowing that his lifestyle differed from mines in a drastic way.

"I can dig it, well what will you be doing later because I need to sit down with you and have a man to man. I can't really talk right now because I'm in the middle of something. So, I'll give you a call in the near future with a time and place so we can rendezvous."

"Well I'll be around, I'm going to see my man Kyron smash

Wilson later--"

"Who, that kid Kyron Owens? Man! He's a bad, young mutha-fucka with that ball."

"Yeah, my boy got skills… But after that I'll be free to rendezvous and elaborate on a few things with you until I head out to this party down at Luby's later on tonight."

"Liquor Luby still got that pool hall up and running with all them young knuckle heads? I can remember when I ran Luby's back in my day. After I went down and did that stretch, I know someone came and filled my shoes around that area. Because the game doesn't stop, people do. But, I'll call you after the game and we'll take it from there, okay nephew?"

"Solid, I can dig it." We both hung up in unison.

$ $ $ $ $

I managed to make it up to Camden High's gymnasium to watch my man Kyron dazzle the floor for the on looking crowd that would be in attendance. Dressed to impress, I hopped out the yellow cab with a million dollar glow. A white bucket Kangol, all white velour Adidas sweat suit and, a pair of white on white shells to make my attire run concurrent; I was looking like one of the hood's ghetto angel.

With the bleachers packed to its' capacity, the game hadn't started for another fifteen minutes. It was a blissful outrage how one young man could bring so much excitement and pandemonium to one place and there wasn't even any action to view. The fans chanted, "Ky-Ron O-wens is a K. O… Knockout. He brings the ruckus when he drives to the bucket."

Lames and dames were dipped in there finest splendor to view the young human highlight and, intrinsically the opposite sex. Woodrow Wilson was always great competition for the Panthers who undoubt-edly held the winning percentage by a slight margin. The Tigers had never been a lay down team in any categorical sport; they also had to outstanding blue-chips whom were fierce with the orange peel. Marvin Cubbage and Dawayne Earns were, if not equal to Kyron in skill and scoring. Marvin averaged 25.3 ppg. and 7 assist per game, Dawayne averaged 21.5 ppg and 4 assist per game. The Tigers back-court didn't consist of a one man army and their entire starting five were the cream of the crop.

The first quarter and been set in motion, the Tigers were in black uniforms garnished with white and orange trimming. And, the Panthers were in purple uniforms having yellow and white trimming. Kyron came out gunning like a solider at war, ranging shots from all around the court's perimeter. Every time the ball released from his palms, it was like painting a masterpiece, SWISSSH was the entire crowd heard and loved. Scoring the panthers' first thirteen points he really had the eye of the tigers.

In the second quarter the Tigers struck back, shooting 10/14 from the field and 4/4 from three point range. It was evident that they came to the panthers' house to show them that it was more than a game to play; it was a game of respect by any means necessary. Dawayne Earns quieted the Panthers' crowd when he came across half court and ranged and rainbow three pointer, amid the crowds verbal as the Tigers' fans chanted "OVERRATED," back at the Panthers' fans. They were directing their insolent remarks to the frustrated Kyron Owens who had only two-points that entire quarter. The Panthers went down by five at halftime, 55-50 to the underestimated Wilson Tigers.

A female walked up behind me and tapped me over my shoulder as I stood in the congested lobby to retrieve a beverage from the concession stand. DaVita, there she stood adjacent to me, blossomed like a ripe rose. I had to do a double take at first because I thought my vision was impaired; it had been four years.

"Heeeey, Ms. Mills," I said, amazed by how I thought she was returning back into my life, giving her a sultry hug.

"Oh my god, you got tall as ever," she replied, loving the new, improved me. We conversed for a few minutes before I headed back into the gym to watch the second half of the game. DaVita expressed how much she'd missed me over the years and hoped that one day we'd reacquaint; divine nature made it happen again. She knew times had changed but she wanted us to reconcile our friendship to keep in touch, which was fine with me. We exchanged numbers after I was asked if I was going to Ebony's party down at Luby's, I told her we'd hook up later.

Thoughts of conflict of interest began lingering through my mind as I made my way back to the stands. Reacquainting with DaVita wasn't a good idea when indeed I was after her girlfriend Lamaar. I wanted that old thing back but it was what I couldn't have which compelled me even more. My skin itched for Lamaar, who was very enticing to me.

The third quarter jumped off on the wrong foot for Kyron who shot only 2/5 from the field and was benched by Coach Calvin Turner, due to foul trouble. The fans directed aggressive "Booing," towards the referees who were blowing there whistles on every Tiger possession, like crossing guards.

Dawayne Earns, the enthusiastic sophomore continued to dominated the paint, following in the footsteps of the highly skilled mentor Marvin Cubbage. Dawayne was controlling the gymnasium; sinking three pointers like water he extended the Tigers lead by fifteen. The sold out crowd was quite like church mice while Kyron looked on from the bench, especially when Dawayne threw an astonishing alley-oop dunk to Marvin from behind the ark of the 3-point line.

The Panthers remained on the Tigers' trails, managing to keep the score close, trailing them by eight in the beginning of the fourth quarter. It was crunch time for the Panthers and do-or-die for Kyron who sparked the crowd with his amazing first quarter. Monte' Wayans the Panthers' senior point guard penetrated the ball through the Tigers' 2-3 defense with fancy ball handling and rigorous body maneuvers. Cutting the Tigers lead to three, there was still enough time for Mr. Owens to show the onlookers why he was the best high school player in the nation.

With eight minutes remaining on the scoreboard, the possession arrow pointed in the Tigers direction. "Defense… Defense," the fans ranted, cheering at the top of their lungs. Coach Turner yelled repeatedly from the panthers' bench "One on One… One on One." Changing the defense from zone from to man-to-man, Monte' was defending the on fire scoring machine Dawayne Earns and Kyron matched head on with Mr. Cubbage.

"Show me what you got... Com'on show me what you got," Monte' demanded as he pressed up on Dawayne like a defensive back. Dawayne threw an awkward pass in between two Panther defenders, which was intercepted by Baloue Scott, the Panthers' power forward. Baloue threw a speeding bounce past to Monte', who out of the corner of his eye observed Kyron accelerating full speed a head of him. Monte' lobbed the ball in the air, allowing Kyron to get a good vision of it and touch his hands properly so he could slam home the returned alley-oop dunk. As the crowd went bananas and the Panthers cut the lead to one. "Defense... Defense... Defense," the crowd continued to chant as everyone stood to their feet.

A Tiger player set a pick on Monte', detaining him as Dawayne drove around both of them and headed for the basket. From the Dawayne's blind side, Baloue jumped in front of Dawayne trying to prevent him from scoring. With force Baloue hit the floor and the referee blew his whistle as it brought the crowd to total silence, waiting for the official call. CHARGING! That was the ref's call on Dawayne who knocked Baloue to the floor.

With time winding down the Panthers slowed down the tempo of the game, Monte' controlled the rock and was waiting on the call from Coach Turner.

"Swing Ky... Swing Ky," Turner yelled. Kyron came running from the far corner of the court, swung around the baseline as one of his teammates set the pick on Cubbage. Patiently waiting in the other as Monte' swung him the ball, Kyron's form was together as he planted his feet properly and released the cannon from deep behind the 3-point line. "Oooooo-oop," was the crowd's roar as they watched the ball hit nothing but net, giving the Panthers' the lead.

From that moment on there was no looking back for the unbeaten Panthers who extended the lead as time winded down. With only three seconds left on the clock, the Panthers went out in style, Monte' threw another alley-oop form half-court to Kyron. Who dunked it backwards and hung on the rim and displayed that they were still number one with his opposite hand, holding up one finger. The final score was the Tigers 83 and the unbeaten Panthers 90, Kyron Owens and Monte' Wayans finished with a combined score of 55 points for the Panthers; Dawayne was the Tigers high man with 32.

$ $ $ $ $

Krystal's Lounge on the corner of 8th and Chestnut streets-Downtown - was where I rendezvous with my Uncle Muscles after the game. **Under 21, No Admission** - was the sign posted on the front entrance of the Lounge, since I was under age I wasn't allowed to enter the premises. But, due to the respect that my uncle had at the place, I was admitted off of his strength card.

Krystal's was an older crowd site, twice my senior, whose attire didn't quite fit my young standards; dress slacks and hard bottoms wasn't quite my twist at the time. Krystal's was the hottest spot in town, from Monday thru Sunday the place packed at least a average of seventy five people; majority of them were mainly woman searching for a come up. And, there were plenty of slot machine lames to come up off of in that vicinity. Rick - the D.J. - was this funky white boy who spun those oldie-but-goodie songs on the turn tables four days out of the week. Krystal's lounge was the hottest leisure outing in town for those mature persons who weren't to find of Luby's pool hall.

Cornered at the far end of the bar, my uncle and I sat a table conversing about a few unfamiliar things. "Tell me something good nephew," Uncle Muscles said, giving me a firm hand shake.

"We here Unc", it don't get no better than that," I replied, taking a sip of my glass of sprite on the rocks.

"I can dig it, same ol' shit just a different strain. But, let's get to the reasons of this sit down. I've heard a few things; I don't understand this quitting school shit… What's that about?"

"You know how it goes, everything isn't for everybody. A lot of shit just isn't meant," I answered, feeling like is disobedient child.

"I can't even begin to argue, you're your own man now and you're old enough to make your own decisions. Are you working?"

"I was until a few days ago, when some fools robbed and killed my boss down at the Rotti shop on the Pike." I felt the fabrication of story telling about to occur.

"You were slaving for Jamaican Teddy? That third-world, broken English nigga owed me a lucrative amount of gravy before I went in the slammer. I guess when you do dirt it comes right back to you. He deserved it. Your nose is clean from that shit right nephew? You didn't have anything to do with that play did you?"

I got a little nervous when he asked me that question; a chill so fierce hit my spine like I was lying on a piece of Alaskan iceberg that wouldn't melt. Giving him complete eye contact, I wanted to say 'HELL NO,' but this was a person I've never lied to before in my life. "Yeah, I was in on it." Nervously waiting on his reaction.

"I can dig it," he said, as if he wasn't too thrilled to have known the truth. "Were there other's involved?"

"Yup! Three others... My man Dontae'... His cousin Spring and his pop Dontae' Sr."

"Who? Apple head Dontae' from Park Boulevard? He's in me for about three hundred too, that sleazy muthafucka."

"I guess, he was the mind behind the plan and the turn out was sweet. We came off wit 30 keys of dope and three-hundred thousand in paper."

"That's it," he muttered, in a dissatisfaction way. "Ted's been moving tons of product out of that shop for decades and you mean to tell me that's all he had?"

"Yes sir, that's all that was there." I couldn't complain, that was a major come up for me, I didn't know why my uncle was so mad. I guess he wanted it all not some of the shit.

"And, what cut did you get off the top?"

"Seventy-five stacks and five whole ones just for watching the door." He didn't need to know the rest.

As we continued to converse, Uncle Muscles pulled a small, white piece of paper from his side jacket pocket. Just as he was getting ready to reveal it to me this brown skinned dame came and invaded our privacy with her watermelon cleavage.

"Hey Muscles, how's everything going for you over here?" she asked, leaning over his rear shoulder, giving me direct eye contact, with a smile that was to overwhelming for a picture. "Here's a couple of drinks on the house for use two... Enjoy," she continued, winking her eye at me in seduction.

"Thanks Dana," Muscles said, furtively sliding me a fifty dollar tip to slide between her pillowed melons.

"What's your name handsome?" she asked, gliding her hand gently across my face. Dana smelled great, I felt like sucking on all five of her fingers.

"Kyle." The bitch had me blushing and shit, I felt funny.

"Well as you already heard I'm Dana, I run the place. Anything that you need or want just feel free to ask, if it's not too much of a burden I'll be glad to provide it for you."

Prior to whispering something into my uncle's ear Dana winked her eye at me once more which implied that she was attracted to the young stallion. She was a fine pussycat, about 5'6", a caramel skin tone, petite with an onion to match those bazooka tits of hers and she had a perfect set of whites that would have made the sun turn towards Pluto. After she made my uncle laugh, she leisurely wondered back into her own atmosphere of professionalism.

"Did you give her the tip?" Uncle Muscles asked me, knowing it had slipped my mind. He pulled the white piece of paper out once more.

"Damn! I forgot she's fine as mink fur... She one of yours?"

"Nah slim bimbos like her aren't my speed, she's business for business. I'm business for a profitable gain. Enough about that whore though take a look at this here," He demanded, sliding the piece of paper across the table. The paper was a list of about ninety unfamiliar names, majority of them-females.

"What you show me this for?" I asked, very bewildered.

"That there is profitable gain nephew, all the names you see there are loyal clients."

"So! How does this pertain to me in any way?" I didn't give a fuck about names that made him who he was.

"You said you're no longer employed right?" he asked, as we both sipped our rum and cokes in unison. "Here's your stairway to a much greener heaven, it's a fast opportunity to turn that seventy-five grand into seven-hundred and fifty grand."

"By doing what?" I needed another double shot to hear the good shit he was spitting at me.

Uncle Muscles gave me a moment of clarity, by explaining to me who all the peoples were and what it was that they came to him for. Nothing more than buyers and customers who came for business or to get high, Lamont Muscles had it to give but not to test. Majority of the females whom were enlisted used blow and the other half worked for the small suppliers who copped from my uncle. The female names were used as a caution tactic, just in case heat and flames came from around the corner from the fuzz.

My duty would be to deliver the goods to the names on the list once a week and I would earn five grand in the process.

"That's it?! That's all I have to do?" I found that extremely hard to believe.

"That's it nephew, all you have to do is dump… Collect… Count the cash and make sure its all there." My uncle knew it was more to it, he was only giving me half of the story and the rest, I guess I had to fill in on my own.

"And the prices are?"

"Seventy grand when I'm in pocket and about eighty when I'm not in pocket." Could I handle the lucrative task was all I kept asking myself?

"Unc' that's a lot of money to be handling, I don't think the jobs for me," I said, feeling a bit nervous and I didn't make one move yet. "What if someone tries robbing me or one of them nasty whores try to set the kid up?"

"Not to worry nephew, this is a fishy game but let it get fishy and I'm gutting them all with this six shot .38. Oh and there's more to where that came from too. You aim correctly and you can knock a muthafucka on its' ass with one whistle. Ha!" Shit like that excited his soul.

"There are two things I ask of you, One… Never allow anyone to come in between family. Meaning you and me, we already have one strike between us because money and blood don't mix. Everybody wants to be apart of something that's fortified and they will say anything to get in your position or to be in my position. The only person that cares about you is you. Two, business and pleasure are like oil and water... They don't mix. Keep both of your heads where they suppose to be, your mind focused and your dick in your pants. You'll make out a lot better than a lot of people who've traveled down the road your going."

Sitting in an immobilized daze, very intoxicated from the two rum-an-cokes, I absorbed my uncle's philosophy as if my mind was an electrical tape recorder. Allowing it to play over and over in my head to prepare myself for what was to come. The position my uncle put me in was more than I expected, being a runner was worse than being a boss because everything operated and was transacted through the runner. If the in taker didn't receive his product the distributor didn't receive his money. The transactions was one big collection plate, product and money was going from one hand to the next only thing was the runner did all of the passing.

Uncle Muscles slid me a tiny package of his product and the stamp on it read - IN GOD WE TRUST.

"What's the meaning behind the stamp?" I asked, knowing that using God's name in vain was total blasphemy for come up purposes but, the government did it.

"Everyone loves money" the love, the smell as well as the feel of it and, what's the major standout statement on the back of every federal reserved note processed in America? In god we trust... Money's the root to all evil and these good ol' citizens of the United States will do anything for the love of money. So, I stamped my dope which happens to be money to these careless, psychotic muthafuckas after the only meaningful statement on a dollar bill. These fiends lives' are so fucked up from the addiction to this snow, they live day after day thinking that god is evil. When the product is good you have to give it a name that stands out. So with this," He implied, holding up the glassine sealed bag. "IN GOD WE MUTHAFUCKIN' TRUST..."

He gave the package of dope back to me so I could go and give it to Dana the lounge overseer. He gave me a suspicious look like she knew something I didn't; shaking his head in unison Uncle Muscles removed himself from the table and walked off. I approached Dana at the counter by the bar, where she flexibly was moving in every direction serving drinks and taking orders from other customers.

"Excuse me miss," I yelled, through the immense volume. She walked over towards me and said, "How may my assistance help you?" As the navy blue, satin scarf she had neatly wrapped over her head that brought out her mere beauty even more. Flashing the tiny sealed bag of dope in front of her eyes, she came from behind the bar and told me to follow her; as if she knew what was about to take place. We took a stroll upstairs to one of the lounges empty rooms, which looked like they were used for one night affairs.

Dana took the initiative of making the first move, asking no questions she began unsnapping the button on my Jordache jeans. She took a hit though before inserting my chocolate éclair into her boiling mouth. The blast drove her into an erotic trance, caressing herself passionately, she began squeezing her basketball tits, licking her fingers, and gliding her fingers gently up and down on her fury apple pie. Just from my clear observation I felt like I had already come all over myself; true tender dick.

Her ass surfaced the air like a hawk, having her back arched and down on all fours. Pound game was in tact, we were like two dogs stuck as I raced for sensational glory.

"This is the ultimate high baby boy," She said, giving me a run for my money. "Mmm... ITS'... ITS'... FUNKY BABY."

Now out of all the remarks she could have used she had to use funky? How ironic was it that her remark coincided with the smell in the room; a fish stench you wouldn't believe but the trim was outstanding. Ten minutes of relentless stroking pushed me to an emasculating climax but Dana was still going through sexual convulsions as if she wanted more. The episode was one and done for me, I got dressed and left Dana on the bed, where she was gently rubbing her clitoris to feel part two of orgasm heaven.

Laughing while checking the time on his watch, Uncle Muscles was waiting patiently by the entrance door. "That must have been some good pussy there nephew," he said, placing his indigo Kangol dude cap over his shinning bald head. "You were only up there for five minutes."

"It was like a box of lemon heads," I answered, humorously as we headed out the door. He might have thought I was jiving but I put my word on a stack of bibles and, if he could have felt what I felt the truth would have set him free.

$ $ $ $ $

Kaighns Avenue was cluttered in front and around Luby's pool hall. Before I exited my uncle's burgundy four-door Cadillac, he handed me a piece of paper with an address on it. Demanding that I meet him at the above address Monday morning for further instructions. After I stepped out his ride, I couldn't even plant my feet on the pavement and niggas were screaming his name like some renowned celebrity. "Yo Muscles... What's happenin' O.G.?... It's still your world cool," was all I could hear coming from the multiple amount of voices on the avenue. Uncle Muscles just took it in stride and continued strolling up Kaighns Avenue like he was the only person on the strip.

$ $ $ $ $

I went straight to Luby's kitchen and order me a chicken platter no soon as I entered the hall; I hadn't eaten since the game. As I awaited my platter to arrive, I sat at one of the back tables nearby the pinball, observing all things moving. Undoubtedly, the pool hall was loaded with lames, dames, and ghetto fames from all over the city. And, of course jive ass Poohshaun, Kenny Morales and, their crews were in the building as well. Kenny's fat, Cuban looking ass was over in one of the far corners hugged up with Lamaar, who seemed to be enjoying his company. She was dipped in her finest splendor, a cherry red head scarf, red laced blouse, a black pleated leather skirt and a pair of red leather Rocco boots, with a pair of red shades to make everything run concurrent. In lust of her beauty my mouth leaked saliva at the wrong time but, my attraction for Lamaar was fierce.

A few of the Wilson Tigers' basketball players came out in attendance, as well as some of the Camden high boys but, Kyron wasn't in the atmosphere; he was probably in some victory pussy after the

tremendous game that he had. Observing the hall with mere consistence, I didn't happen to see the party girl Ebony either. But, everyone seemed to be enjoying themselves, the dance floor was packed
and music trembled the entire hall. There were inexperienced pool
players at every table chasing the eight ball, smoking that good Mary
Jane and drinking Bodega; amid me devouring my chicken platter.

Tyrone, this smooth cat who I knew from junior high school had
whispered something into the Kenny Morales' ear and they both
parted from Luby's. Kenny leaving was my perfect chance to make
my presence felt in front of Lamaar. Removing myself from the back
table with a rum and coke drink in had, I made my way towards Lamaar who happened to be in one of the corners openly conversing
with her click. But, DaVita came from the clear winds and cut me
off prior to me reaching my destination.

"Heeeeey, chocolate girl," I said, with a wry smile.

"I assumed you weren't going to show up."

"You thought that because?"

"The party started over two hours ago and you were M.I.A." She
grabbed my drink from me and began sophisticated sipping.

"I been in here for a few, I was stationed in the back eating a wing
dinner," I replied, cutting my eye in Poohshaun's direction because
he was eyeing us like prey. "So did you show up alone?"

"No. I came with my around the way crew."

"Where's the birthday girl? Is she in here? I got a bone to pick
with her," I expressed, just so I could get away from her and handle
my engagement towards Lamaar.

"She's right over there." DaVita pointed in the direction that I was
headed in, right by Lamaar and the rest of the girls.

"Give me a second, I'll be right back." I wasn't even five steps
away from DaVita and I was distracted once more by the clamorous
calling of Poohshaun's voice. How ironic was it that he never said a
word to me since the first day I had ever seen him at my job.

"Aye yo' man," he called, waving for me to come to him. "Allow
me to get a second of your time."

"What's the word cool man, speak your mind to me pimp," I said,
not feeling the vibe. He came off as cocky to me and I got peeved

at shit like that.

"You're the young cat who use to work for my man Teddy Gram, right?"

"Yeah, I know you two were close and I'm sorry to here about the tragedy, Ted was good peoples," I expressed, in false sympathy.

"Aye man shit happens, I mean we all get our ticket to depart sooner or later right?"

"You never lied about that."

"But anyway I didn't call you to beat down about Ted. I wanted to know about the well preserved, dark skinned fox that you had up under your arm? I know you seen me watching use two?"

"Oh you talking 'bout DaVita, she's just an old friend from back in the day."

"So your saying' she's not a burden to you? Cause I did a social background check and your name kept popping up as her pleasure reliever." Poohshaun was trying to see what his eyes couldn't follow, but I allowed the fishing to continue.

"Nah my man, she's like a sister to me," I retorted, giving him the question mark look, wondering who gave him such information. Then again, Syrus was right; information blew through the windy streets like leaves in the fall.

"So, since she's like your sister and you two are real cool, what will it cost for you to get me acquainted with her?"

I glanced back at DaVita who had been eyeing us the entire time, and then I turned back towards him and said, "What about Rose-Angel? Aren't you two still an item?"

"I been canceled that whore's social card in my life slim a long time ago. Our relationship was like candy, good one day and sour the next." I already knew the true reason for the break-up between him and Rose; I just wanted to pick his brain a little.

"Listen, all I can do is put in a word for you, I can't make you any promises."

"That's good enough," he replied, giving me a firm hand shake.

I slid back over to DaVita who had an uneasy face then before, leaning up against one of the pool tables with her arms tightly folded.

"Prior to you playing match maker, I got word that you were checking for my home girl Lamaar?'

Lamaar who… What?" I played dumb.

"Yeah, now you want to play stupid like you don't know what I'm talking about."

"You can't be mad over some hear say," I said, knowing the truth.

"That would be foul Kyle, because you know how my feelings are for you?"

Feelings? I'm thinking how many feelings one could possibly have after four years of complete separation; besides we were kids. "Listen," I said, rubbing her shoulders. "Your friend Lamaar's style just was a big attraction to me that's all."

"So you do like her?" DaVita quickly answered, shoving me back. "Then whose next, Ebony or my cousin Tiffany? You just want to sling your seventeen year old dick in every pretty dame you come across?" So you are a whore, I eagerly wanted to say but I didn't want to make the situation any worse than it already was.

"Nah it's not even like that Veda but anyway… Listen, the cat P-Shaun's been checking for you for quite some time and he wants to acquaint."

"I know already, you're about the tenth person to relay that same message. I must admit that he's been persistent with his endeavors of trying to smell my sweet fish," She replied, looking over in his direction. P.S. winked and raised his drink in the air at her. "I don't have time for promiscuity in a person who's not ready to settle, I already have a lot on my plate as it is."

"It won't hurt to feel him out though; you might strike gold on your first shot. If not for yourself do it for me?" I asked, caressing the nap of her neck.

As DaVita headed in P. S.' direction, I rotated my eyes around the hall like an owl in search of Lamaar's person. Just as I went to make my move after spotting her, Kenny's fat ass was a step ahead of me. Ebony had found me as I made my way back to the rear of the place.

"Kyle… Kyle… Kyle," Ebony said, verbatim, grabbing my arm in unison. "I've been looking high and low for you for about a half hour now."

"Happy birthday," I replied, giving her a gripping hug before she started rambling off at the mouth.

"Thank you, listen my sister gave you a little feed back but it's not the best news you want to hear."

"What she say?"

"She said you were cute and all but you just don't fit her qualifications as some one she could sheet love with."

"Meaning?"

"Meaning that she already has a wealthy nigga that got his name written all over her kitty-cat and it's impossible for a person like you to make her meow-meow. She said them fast food checks won't cut her a slice of nothing and she brooded that you probably don't have a nice stroke game anyhow."

"Wow! What a way to misjudge this unread book boy," I uttered, feeling some kind of way about what had been expressed to me in a harsh manner. I glanced in Lamaar's direction with fire in my eyes.

My chance came once more when Kenny disappeared again; right there I knew it was my time to clean her perception of me. She was my focus and with every stride in her direction my implicit thoughts formed this structured articulation segment in my head. I felt that what I was going to say would win her over in a matter of minutes. Through peripheral vision, I observed DaVita and Poohshaun to the right of me getting acquainted and Kyron - who I hadn't seen all night - calling me from afar while rapping to a few honeys. But, my vision was paralleled to the appearance of Lamaar's curved shaped frame.

I came with an aggressive approach, rudely, interrupting the conversation that she was having with her girlfriends. "Excuse me," I said, very confident. "But I've been meaning to come over here the entire night and tell you how gorgeous you look in your outfit." Her friends all smirked at my compliment and began whispering to each other, giving me the "Who is this clown look."

"Oh really," she replied, pulling her shades halfway off her nose. "Nah, I keep it regular like you."

"Regularity constitutes popularity sometimes but, I just came over here to tell you that I received your vulgar message from Ebony. In fact I thought it was quite impressing."

"What?" I could tell by Lamaar's eyes that she was shocked by my response. "Your funny, I like that."

"I'm live and unique but that's not why I'm in front of you, can I offer to treat you and your lady friends to some drinks?" They all looked as if they were tipsy while asking.

"I think I'll pass on the offer, my girl's and I had enough to drink for one night."

"Well can I two step with you a little out on the dance floor then?" She turned and looked at her girls for an answer.

"Damn! Your very persistent aren't you," Kay-Nay added, liking my approach but was too envious to let me know that she was feeling me too. "L' go and work him girl, just don't let Kenny's ass see you wit him, you know how his insecure as is." Kay-Nay's chocolate complexion was fierce but the back burner to her hazel, poppy eyes.

"She's right, my boyfriend is the loony type, so I'm a have to rain check you on that too."

"One dance, that's all I need." I felt myself chasing for a dream come true. I guess it was my posture that got her to oblige me.

"Just one dance, that's it," she said, walking by me like she wanted to dance by herself.

Unfortunately, I talked myself in to a dance I solely would regret but didn't know it. As I two stepped to the Run-DMC cut and Lamaar's smooth body movement, I watched her go into a zone that she looked like she hadn't felt in years. In an abrupt motion, a hand came in a nanosecond flying across Lamaar's face, dropping her to the floor. All eyes were on us as the music stopped simultaneously, at that precise moment I felt for us both.

"You fucking whore," Kenny yelled, reaching towards Lamaar on the floor.

"Hol' on... Hol' on," I intervened, grabbing his arm.

"Hol' on? What muthafucka... Who the fuck is this?" he asked, shoving me back. "Fuck you." Kenny swung a wild haymaker and missed as I ducked just in time, as I gave him my hardest body shot.

The punch didn't even faze the heavy, chubby bastard of about three hundred pound.

A few people that I knew came to my rescue as Kenny reached into his side, pulled a pistol on me and put it to my face. "Hol'… Hol' Kenny," Tyrone said, smacking the gun down. "You way out of your element cool."

"Nah Ty, he's fucking out of control, he must don't understand what type of event this is or who the fuck I' am. I'm Kenny muthafuckin' Morales… You see my face?" he asked me, simultaneously waving the gun around like a Frisbee. "Never forget it nigga, because it just became your death certificate."

Lamaar and her friends were left to stay at the party after Kenny and his crew left the party at Luby's. I visualized the pain in Lamaar's eyes when I went over to aid her pain. Her feelings were hurt and it was my fault for chasing a dance instead of her truthful song of not wanting to go forth with my suggestion.

"I'm sorry," I said repeatedly, until she came to her senses of responding back to me.

"You have nothing to be sorry for, I brought everything on myself because I didn't want to go with my first instinct. Thanks for taking up for me though, most dudes would have just stood there and got suckered."

"It was the least I could do, you did give me an opportunity to dance with you. That was a coward man's act on ya' man's behalf, having too much power and being insecure doesn't mix together."

As time went on prior to me leaving the party for good, Lamaar and I got to know each other a little more during the course of being confronted by a lot of people I knew at the party, asking if I was alright. There really wasn't too much to converse about around the rest of the unseen watchers and gossipers, so we exchanged numbers and I told her that I would be in touch.

Just as I placed one foot on the side walk of Kaighns Avenue, this slim light-skinned guy name Garlin tapped my shoulder and pulled me to the side for a moment of his time. "What's up Kyle? Man, its' been a while," Garlin asked, giving me some dap and a slight hug.

"What's new G'? You know me, nothings changed but the weather round here."

"Solid. I can see that but let me put a bug in your ear before you roll." I inched a little closer to him as he began to speak in a whisper. "Lamaar, who you and Kenny got into it over?"

"Yeah, what about her slim goody?" I asked returning the whisper.

"She the reason why he put on for this city the way that he does, if it wasn't for her that nigga would be in the donut shop somewhere. He's afraid of losing her to another thorough cat such as you because if he does that then his trump card is won."

"And you tell me all of this for the benefit of?"

"Lets just say for a young cat, I been around the block to many times and I know when a nigga is do for his turn. And, I know a come up when I see one."

"So why you didn't you jump ship for the opportunity then?" I asked, feeling like Garlin was on some set of type shit.

"Everything isn't for everybody, you take care of yourself Kay," He implied, giving me a final handshake in stride.

From the first time I laid eyes on Lamaar that she was something special like precious jewels. Behind her rainbow lied Kenny's big pot of gold and I had to pick the master's mind to take both his treasures; I was the right leprechaun for the job. I was out to destroy Kenny and take claims to his fortune.

# Chapter. 6

A couple of months later, I was the early bird in the hood catching many worms to keep my dinner plate full of the strength of Uncle Muscles; everything was going as planned and in my favor. In a weeks time I was traveling to about forty drop points in the city, making deliveries. I was ranging in close to a half a million dollars a month for him, myself! With caution, I was riding a peddle bike in a pulverized atmosphere with packages of heroin in a black book bag; eleven thousand grams wasn't worth walking or driving in a car for the wrong kind of harm. Uncle Muscles purchased me a car but I was reluctant to drive into the wrong danger zone. My persona was to remain low key; I couldn't spell indictment let alone be investigated and placed in one.

I profited close to a hundred grand in two months of errand runs, a hundred and seventy-five thousand to be exact. I felt like a mobile train that was fiercely in motion and to rewind me back wasn't even an option. The heroin packages were being moved like cartons of cigarettes in corner stores, either by the gram, an ounce or a whole one, it was getting moved. I invested my own product into my uncle's fortune for insurance of a rainy day; the five keys from the robbery went to Muscles and even my hundred and seventy-five grand as well. Being a runner was my position but being the boss was my long term goal.

Terry, my uncles' side dame taught me the fundamentals of how to cut, measure, and bag the heroin myself. One of the estates she owned in the city was their operation laboratory, called the "House of Chemistry." If I wasn't out making drops, I was in the House of Chemistry observing, learning, and asking questions. Billy Bad Ass, my uncles' partner in crime and best friend since childhood, was an experienced chemist with the product also. Billy and Terry used to test the heroin themselves to make sure it could give and take what the customers wanted from it. I called Billy "Chopper," because he sat in one spot all day with a few deck of cards, chopping dope into a thin powdery substance.

I had the slightest clue of where my uncle found such beautiful woman from but, Terry was fine her damn self - close to True but not fine as her - and was tall as a light post. I could tell that it was Terry's cerebral intellect that impressed my uncle because she was always reading into something or analyzing something common to turn it into perfection.

"Why Terry over True?" I asked, one day pulling him aside. He replied, that brains went further than beauty on any given day, Plus, Terry's mission was nothing less than money and that aligned with his life cause he felt that he was born to make it anyway he knew how. Terry was his strategic rider and vicious gun slinger; quiet as kept she was about action.

My second mission was orchestrated and executed by and with Terry, who felt that she had been violated by some guy she had met on a night out on the town nine months prior. Chucky was the targets' name and he rubbed or caressed Terry the wrong way on the dance floor at a highly dined restaurant; forceful kisses and fingers up her dress was a no-no in her eyes. She kept all that happened to herself and got the drop on him a few months later when a mutual friend revealed his vitals and numbers; even the names of his children and spouse.

Unknowingly, one restless night Terry rung my phone and told me that we had a funeral to attend. I read between the codes and suited up, for some reason though I felt comfortable going with Terry as if we had dealings for years. She came and got me in a stolen, navy blue, Chevy pick-up truck and told me to be the designated driver. A seventeen, unlicensed driver who had no real steering control, gassed the pick-up truck like it was Bigfoot.

The nigga Chucky was slipping more than a virgin dick in some old head pussy, 'cause I was directed right to his location; the drop was cake walk. He was double parked across the street from Krystal's Lounge, reading some papers or something as an anxious whore sat on the passenger seat irking his nerves. I hit the lights about a block up but left the truck running. Before I could put the car in park, Terry was already out the truck and on the move.

After catching up, we both squatted and tiptoed along side the parked cars on 8th street; behind Chuck's van. Terry pointed just before we got to the van, directing me to go to the passenger side of the van. The bitch on the passenger side screamed for mercy when she seen the grim reaper looking down her tonsils. The whore's scream didn't override the sounds of the four Taurus 9 millimeter that were playing laser tag with the van's windows. After all clips were emptied in the van, Terry and I skirted up Mt. Vernon's one way street with the lights off.

Up until now, I still have no idea of who the female was in the passenger seat of Chucky's van; not that I really cared. The news paper had her marked as Jane Doe because the thirty-two shots that I emptied into the van, detached her face.

$ $ $ $ $

I seen no sort of hate or envy in dudes my age that weren't moving how I was moving because I respected the game and I was really looking past other people's lives. Besides who could fault this seventeen year old, correct card playing, big move making opportunist from achieving the one goal that everyone with a career sets there mind out to obtain--BEING THE BOSS!

I had monthly tabs at every store I ate or shopped from, that was quite of a plus for a skinny kid who rode around on a ten speed, hook barred bike, appearing broke, having no money in his pockets, dropping of major weight of heroin. Even though my mother was still paying bills at the townhouse she left me, I decided to move towards something better and purchase this deluxe condominium in these two-building edifices in North Camden called the Northern Glamour Towers 1 & 2. They were way better than what I seen on television from watching the Jefferson's sitcom for years on in; former legislator of the political democratic party, Walter Rand even had an entire floor to himself in the elegant building. You had to be a resident there to roam freely, it was like US Customs when entering and exiting the plush view. I barely stayed there though because I was constantly on the move, it was just a piece of mind atmosphere and a spot I kept all my fine materials and linens. Uncle Muscles was the only person that knew about the place, he made a few propositions with the owner to get me in there.

I would be lying to myself if I said I didn't purchase the condo to impress Lamaar's hedonistic lifestyle. In my eyes every queen needed a kingdom to roam but the bad thing about it was that she didn't even know about my place. Nevertheless, our foundation of friendship matured over the months of on an off communication and a few dates. But, Lamaar didn't give in based on the fact that she still was in love with Kenny. It was her fear in Kenny that kept her intimacy from being shared.

Lamaar was the closes thing to a shared partner which I hadn't had in years, I was still single and fraternizing with no regards of settling, unless it was with Ms. Green. Contrarily, I got hardheaded and reckless with my testosterone and didn't take heed to what my uncle explained about business and pleasure not mixing. I began having sex with five of the fourteen customer's bimbos that I was dropping off too, per week. Most of them married with a few kids, they lured me in with there physical prowess which overrode my reasons of handling business.

Tahwanna, Malika, Jennifer, Marie, Tamyra, Myesha, and Michelle were the five customers that I delivered to on Mondays. They handled and set up meetings for there significant others or boyfriends that were out in the field of operations taking care of other task; these ladies sold from the inside out. Mondays were my days on their busy schedules, they welcomed me into there places of comfort with open arms, sexy lingerie, or totally unclad; knowing what enticed me best. Instead of me saying no, I chose to dick think my way around my uncle's money.

Shakana, Ebony, Donna, Zankeya, Belinda, Neeta, and Daneen were the females I dropped off to on Wednesday. Now these seven go getters worked for themselves, they were purchasing anywhere from a quarter of a key to a key and a half of heroin. They weren't your average city, in the project, go to there house and ring the doorbell type bitches. They had me coming to there jobs, meeting them in supermarket bathrooms, bars, and exquisite restaurants to do transactions. Meeting these flat back, money flippers in business bathrooms, exchanging dope for dollars then getting my rocks off was a great two for one play in my eyes.

Ebony was probably the only one that I never had sex with, our respect level overrode it all. She was running errands for her father - Jahee "Ty" Green - who happened to own Shimmy Shine car wash on Mt. Ephraim Avenue. Furtively, the entire family was damn near underworld prone; their infrastructure was set up well. But, I didn't understand the reason of why Ebony didn't do any business with Kenny's fat ass for her father? After every re-up Ebony gave me re-up money in advance, that's how much she trusted me and wanted to be the first to get hers off top.

Ebony was who I made my last delivery to on Wednesdays, only because she was my eyes behind my head and other ears to the streets. By weekly, I got debriefed about certain heavyweight just so I could be aware of what was occurring around my uncle's crew. Ebony knew practically everything about the fakers and makers, who was doing what, who was doing who, and what was doing what?

I wasn't too concerned about half the city buying from my Uncle Muscles, what worried me was the other fifty percent who were fucking with the Dominicans and guys like Kenny Morales and his team, P.S. and his crew and Big D.S. and Dontae; who crossed over and started dealing with the Dominicans after the robbery sting. Ebony revealed that the Dominicans - whoever they were - were trying to corner the entire city with there product and lock the muthafucka down. Once they heard about the product "In God We Trust," and how it was saturating Camden's street corners, they were reaching for my uncle's throat.

"Black Death," was the Dominicans high-potent street stamp, which came out after my uncle's stamp. And, it had fiends in the street dropping dead after one lick, and hustlers from all over getting rich with in days. Ebony said, fiends who snorted gained instant nose bleeds and those who life revolved around the needle were in deep nods for hours or they just didn't wake up. Their biggest advantage over my uncle was that they dropped their prices ten-thousand dollars from the actual retailed street price which was seventy-thousand a brick. The Dominicans conducted business out of this to story building on 10th and Ferry Avenue called the "Two ways Inn." Ironically, the place had one entrance and exit, my mother use to go there to a have a drink or two when she got off work on occasions.

Kenny Morales managed the joint, the distribution building for the Dominicans who made Kenny apart of there organization when he was about twelve. Ebony didn't even know who these Dominicans were herself, they were mere phantoms of the devil that didn't want Camden to know they existed physically; Kenny was all the physicality I needed though.

$ $ $ $ $

Days later, my uncle and I, along with Terry and Billy sat at the round table to discuss the situation involving the Dominicans and there vicious street dropper Black Death. From there succinct details, it seemed to me that they knew what the Dominicans were up to. Their conquest was to rule the city with an iron fist and diminish my uncle's clientele because of past disputes which they deemed a severe technicality.

Prior to my uncle doing time in the penitentiary he use to do heavy business with these two Dominican brothers by the names of Mikey an Richie Munez, two lucrative snowmen who distributed more snow in the city than the North Pole. Having straight dealings with them since the age twenty, they were the brains in his eyes and of course he was their muscle.

However, Muscles had a strong team of his own while buying from the two Dominican rebels who arrived off a boat out of Peru in South America. Billy "Bad Ass," Big D.S., Jamaican Ted, and my pop was the awesome foursome that made my uncle's street empire the integer of the hustling game. And, even though my uncle had the money and power to be wealthy on his own, respectably he brought his friends in to share the life he possessed; his retinue was untouchable.

Back then, Ted's pizza-turnover spot was used by Mikey and Richie for weekly shipments that were coming in from Mexico. They made Ted a lucrative offer of a hundred-thousand dollars a month for every shipment successfully made. After the shipments came through Mikey and his big brother Richie distributed majority of the product to Muscles and Billy. They were like the only two grinders in the game that knew the fundamentals of heroin at the time; they cut, weighed and packaged the dope themselves. Muscles and Billy supplied the runners (Big D.S. and Kyle Sr.) who sold at a major street level to the city. Everyone was considered an equal in the fierce seven man flock, no amount of money made one person better than the next it was just that Mikey and Richie were the connect.

The Dominicans had a smooth five year run, dealing with Muscles, accumulating a hundred and fifty million dollar drug cartel. This was the year Joe Frazier defeated Muhammad Ali at Madison Square Garden for the heavyweight title; all seven of them were in attendance. Contrarily, in 1971 the competition was full force and decreased Muscles and the Dominicans' profit. Not from some local drug rivals either but, from two highly vivacious woman whom were very street intelligent named Shannon and Sabina Smith; old dames of Big Kyle and D.S.

Two sisters preferably known in the game as Shake & Bake because of their sassy, yet adorable features. Shake (Shannon) and Bake (Sabina), started out purchasing clips of dope at a time from D.S. and Kyle, who were going to see them every other day when they first started out. Clips were single, tiny bags of dope that were being sold for twenty dollars a pop and Shake an Bake were buying five bundles a piece until they made enough money to purchase a half a key in weight.

Within two years time, Shake and Bake managed to hustle enough money to buy two kilos of dope. Their clientele came in innumerable amounts and they had enough street credibility to start their own retinue. Muscles' sisters Gracey, Debbie, and Sissy were good friends of Shannon and Sabina; they all were neighborhood friends once upon a time. The triplets became apart of Shake and Bakes' franchise after helping them work there way up to Power status. Muscles' didn't approve of his sisters being in the game let alone be apart of his organization because he thought that they were a successful man's downfall. When word got to him that his sisters were going hard for theirs in Shake and Bakes circle force was executed and talking was not an option; they were looked upon as bait into the game as well.

Terry, was once upon Shake and Bakes' crew, until signals got crossed and they got flipped so she felt going with the opposition would help in more ways then one. Terry was the one who handled any frivolous feuds that conducted its' way into there form of business. She was the enforcer and backbone of Shake and Bakes' firm.

By 1972, business was on a major up rise for Shake and Bake, so major that they opened up a night club called "Club Shakes," and had the streets chasing for there explosive stamp "Pussycat." Terry was the creator of the name because she said "It was the key to a man's mind and wallet." With that quotation phrased, Terry's words deemed to be true because they were making so much money off of Pussycat that Muscles started to send his runners to cop from his little sister. But the cross came into play when the Dominicans started serving Shake and Bake, all the while maintaining their distributable ties with Muscles. They figured that they didn't owe anyone anything, not even loyalty, so why not have the best of both worlds?

As time past, unknowingly, Mikey and Richie cut ties with Muscles without informing him or anyone in his organization. Situations became so bleak for Muscles that his long time friends - Big D.S. and Kyle Sr. - even went astray and turned against him; they two joined forces with Shake and Bake. Billy was his only true rebel who stayed true no matter what money or situation that approached them. He hugged Muscles after the storm and told him that "Money couldn't buy love." Which happened to be true in their eyes, ironically for Kyle D.S. and the Dominican brothers, money brought them an entire new family.

Muscles went incognito in the game in 1973 and, Pussycat became the prominent street stamp in Camden and the Tri-state area. They made Mikey an Richie so much money that the brothers decided to give everyone out of Shake an Bakes' organization their own supply of heroin on consignment. But, it was intervened and thwarted by the sisters before it got to out of hand.

A meeting was orchestrated by the sisters and played out with Dominican brothers, and the brothers were told by Sabina that if they tried to divide their family, that it would be casualties of war. Shannon, Sabina and, Terry stood firm in what they believed was true family and was thinking longevity. But, the triplets, Kyle, Big D.S. and other peons crossed over, thinking of themselves they agreed to greed not longevity. By mid-73' it was all out war and Terry was doing majority of the head hunting.

Kyle Sr. who was groomed and grew up in the wars of the streets wasn't in fear of what Terry and the two prissy sisters were coming at him with. He became the head of the third segment divide that the Dominicans took a part in breaking up. While D.S. and the triplets became the muscle for him. Their first fulfillment of friction was the burning down of Club Shake's and, with the help of the triplets, managed to rob Shake an Bake for fifty keys of dope and a half a million dollars after taking that severe lost Terry and the sisters decided it was time to move on, so they white flagged their claim as a trio of a certain power and status.

By the end of 1973, Kyle Tommy Moore was the man to beat and be dethroned from the undisputed game of street contamination. The Pussycat stamp was overridden by the newest acquisition "Top Dawg," in the matter of months; it was the novel snow flake in town. Kyle was the man who supplied, who supplied, who supplied everyone. Known to most as the "Great One," because he did it his way and stood alone, having the mentality of a lion and the heart of a gorilla. He fucked with nobody if they didn't fuck with him, a true street loner.

Word on the wire was that Muscles had resurfaced in town a little while after the marketing of Top Dawg started to expand and The Great One became the new HNIC. Kyle didn't fret; he gave two fucks about a sissy who surrendered his way of life to a bunch of whores, giving a bad name to the game of hustling. Muscles knew that his time had run short and the glory of reigning at the top was a long way from his heyday; he came back in peace. Unquestionably, having a seven figure status quo, Muscles had changed for the better of self improvement. He'd married his long time girlfriend True and was exercising his duties of being family oriented. Billy contacted Muscles a few days later to enlighten him about prevalent issues that were crucial. Being as low key as they could, they met around the time when no one lurked the streets, way after reasonable hours of being awake. Billy warned him that it was a million dollar bounty over his head, priced by the Dominicans and Kyle. They wanted him out of the picture because they knew that Muscles had plans on returning with a fierce chess move and attacking them in return. Billy also received a call from a source who knew a source that Kyle was getting high on his own supply because there was nothing else to do; Tony Montana style. And, that he planned on executing a triple cross by robbing the Dominican brothers for a hundred keys down at Krystal's Lounge. The meeting was scheduled for the following day, and once the smoke cleared, having the Dominicans out of the picture. Kyle would reign supreme as the new snowman of the underworld.

At the crack of dawn, the heat was on and the plot was already in effect as Big D.S. and Kyle packed four guns into two stainless steel briefcases that were holding about three million dollars in cash. Richie an Mikey weren't that blind to come to a huge deal like that themselves, so they sent a few expendables who had the slightest idea of what was about to go down. The expendables were told to deliver the hundred bricks in a tranquil manner, make no negotiations, no promises and, to bring the money back safely. But, everything didn't quite go in that easy tune, truly a good plan turned sour.

Unannounced, three unidentified mask men arrived just as Kyle was making the transaction with the no-nothings, shooting their way towards the keys and money. One of the mask men fired a pump shotgun a few times in the direction of the expendables, dropping both of them like rain. Another headed for the money aiming and firing at both Kyle and D.S., as both parties played lazar tag with each other. As Kyle headed for the dope, firing low, two bullets met his chest first before he could reach out and grab the briefcases. He stumbles back, knocking over a few tables before hitting the deck while D.S. came from behind the counter shooting with consistent itchy fingers at everyone in the place. He was the only one who made it the gun massacre without a scratch on him, along with the mask men who skated off with everything, money and drugs. Who was the mole was the real question?

Billy and Muscles arrived late to the honeymoon that was blocked off with numerous squad cars, forensics and yellow tape. From a distance they watched two bodies be pulled from the lounge in body bags and Kyle got lifted on a gurney into the back of an ambulance van. Situations got no better after the shootout robbery; Kyle was placed in critical condition and put into a coma for about a year. And, months later Big D.S. went up state on a nine year bid for holing up a liquor store owned by an elderly white man. He got away with two-thousand dollars in cash but when you do stupid shit like rob a spot with no mask, how far do you think your going to make it?

Big D. S. had to resort to the triplets taking over the business for him and Kyle; they tried keeping the network functioning but it just wasn't the same. The thought of them being the next Shake, Bake, and Terry was just that - A thought! So after they couldn't profit money like there gaining mentors, my aunts then became addicts to there product; snorting more powder then Johnson & Johnson. Kyle's hustling stature and money sunk in haste like the great Titanic ship.

By 1975, the entire city was without poison in the streets, dryer than the Sahara desert there looked to be no hope for Camden's street market future; it was similar to the disastrous stock market crash of 1929. There were no connections, Richie and Mikey were amongst the missing every since the hundred key sting and there were no signs of the three unidentified mask men neither. No runners or suppliers in birds eye view to lock down the streets, the sun had rose on the east for many pillars in the city's underworld but was overshadowed by a severe hurricane blast which washed away the hustler's hope and pipe dreams.

But, the hustler's poster child - Lamont Muscles - resurfaced the underworld and allowed it to blossom again from the roots of the street corners, with the help of Terry and Billy. Terry detached herself from Shake and Bake after they didn't retaliate in the one way street war and dropped there crowns without being defiant. The money that was left over after they were robbed for the lucrative amount could have lasted the gals an enjoyable decade. So when Shake and Bake got tired, Terry took her cut to the table with Muscles.

They met at a resort down in Florida while on vacation, there bumping into each other was a coincidence; it was mind detecting mind for what they both knew best - A connection! But, Terry had just what Muscles was looking for, one of her long time friends a guy by the name of "Chocolate Bippy," was a mainstream socket to many electronic accounts and product based sites. Mr. Snowman himself told Terry whenever she was in need to contact him immediately.

Moves were being made, after Muscles vacation and Terry came from seeing her mother in Jacksonville, the two along with Billy met with Bippy to conduct business. With an offer neither party could refuse, the proposal was settled on a firm hand shake and smile. Two hundred keys for 1.4 million dollars and another two hundred on consignment for the same price, was nothing more than motivation to get more for Muscles.

Instead of doing business with Ted for the shipments, Bippy had his own traveling crew; all Muscles needed was a drop point. Luby was the only person that Billy could think of with a delivery truck and was trust worthy enough for the job. Liquor Luby, who was stigmatized with that name from a past habit of drunkenness, had known Billy Bad Ass since grade school and was willing to back an old friend. Billy enlightened Luby on the entire drop point process and a few under the table moves that were agreed upon by only those two. Luby knew who to contact if anything went wrong.

By the summer of 1975, the big three had Camden's drug market under control once again but this time with enough brain power to wipe out a habitat of elephants; all the right connections that could build an indestructible foundation. Flooding the city's streets like rain, they were selling fifty keys of dope a week. Their street price stayed the same even when a drought fell upon them, just so they wouldn't have to sit on anything else once prices dropped. And, the suppliers who brought from them didn't have to wait to move backed up product that was not salable. The quicker the flip, the faster the profit was their motto.

For three years the streets were reined by Terry, Billy, and Muscles, until Muscles had to go upstate for tax invasion in 1978. Billy and Terry managed to maintain the business while Muscles did his time. They both promised to take care of True while he was enduring cruel and unusual punishment. Every two months, Billy and Terry were giving True fifty thousand dollars from Muscles cut of there profit. True smuggled so that Muscles business behind the wall operated normally in the slammer. She also kept him informed about his multi-million dollar operation and what it was that Billy an Terry were doing to increase the products value and keep the customers happy.

In 1980 a man by the name of James Fidell, known to most as Jimmy extorted his way to a piece of Muscles business through Terry and Billy. Opening up drug markets and putting product on every corner and area that Billy and Terry operated in. The tall, high-yellow yet vicious Jimmy Fidell had a motto of "Get down or pay now," procedures in the streets. Terrorizing the streets, he began holding people for ransom notes and killing anyone who whispered his name; Jimmy was destined to be the next sovereign one.

Along with Jimmy came entire heartless mongers who had his same intentions and goals of conquering the streets. Vinnie Parker, one of Muscles and Billy's consistent buyers, and Fletcher and Morris, two partners who ran with Vinnie. Randolph Patches, Lonnie Jerry and a bunch of others that had either money, power, or respect became buyers to and close friends of Jimmy. Once everyone recognized Jimmy's power and the respect respectful icons in the game were giving him, Camden was his; the new town drug bully.

Terry and Billy cleared the way and fell back once they visualized Jimmy, the problem that was itching their hands for war. Vanishing from the game once more wasn't a bad idea, so they thought, just so they could scrutinize things more carefully; Muscles also thought it was a wise decision if they got out for a while and watch the snakes slither the grass.

Just as fast as Jimmy Fidell came and took over the game he was murdered even faster by an unidentified suspect who caught him coming out of his ignited car. Word on the wire was that it may have been the persons who killed Richie and Mikey's men and brutally injured Kyle but no one really had direct evidence on the real suspects. Jimmy brought everything he deserved on himself. Because when you're dealing with gangsters us like yourself in the game the odds are definitely stacked against you. Playing the bully, and having different strokes for money against different folks who live just like you; will definitely leave you stiff in a pine box.

Observing Jimmy competition with meticulous eyes, Billy and Terry decided to get back in the game, since he wasn't no longer going to be a problem to their everyday solution which happened to be money. Jimmy's ridiculous purchase price was set way out of range at ninety thousand a key when the market was super low in stock. Terry and Billy gained back all of their clientele after cutting the street market price back thirty grand. No wonder Jimmy was lying dormant so quickly because he was drying the streets out of work with out of range prices.

Terry and Billy got all but two of their supreme clientele buyers, Kenny Morales and Poohshaun Britten who had adamant loyalty for the Dominicans organization and didn't believe in accepting Billy's offer of sixty thousand a kilo. Poohshaun had a sit down with Billy, not to negotiate but to forewarn him that the Dominican brothers were back in business themselves. The Dominican brothers sent one request to Billy and Terry, not to cross paths in sales. The minute Mikey and Richie got word that Billy was trying to play cut throat on clientele, war would be waged.

Truly in disbelief of what was verbally sent to him, Billy wanted to have a sit down with the Dominican brothers to discuss differences but Poohshaun thwarted the idea before Billy thought everything would go in his favor. The Dominicans had everything to lose and nothing to gain in the catastrophic streets and it was beyond their boundaries and character to meet on unfertile land. So, Billy tried to give Poohshaun a contact number so the brothers could reach him but Poohshaun had no sound interest in accepting it. He took and dropped the ripped piece of paper towards Billy's feet as if his pride had taken over his power of reason. As he turned and walked away, Billy smelled war but he didn't want to play their game but he did so anyhow just so his organization and revenue could remain operating and earning more.

$ $ $ $ $

"I'm not quite understanding the minimized story that you all just ran down to me," I said, knowing there were three sides to every story and I was looking for exact truth and facts. "Something's missing because you mean to tell me that the Dominican brothers have been supplying major figures and many of your buyers for the past several years and they've been camouflaged to the streets like shadows in the dark all this time?"

$ $ $ $ $

The three of them remained mum to my questioning as if they didn't have the energy to explain another rendition of the summarized edition of the city's drug underworld tyrants and schemes.

"So as far as you three know, Poohshaun and Kenny Morales could be filling the Dominicans shoes and are the connection themselves?"

"That's impossible," Billy said, as if he knew something that we didn't. "Two of our buyers, Fletcher and Morris, who know Mikey and Richie very well say that Poohshaun and Kenny are nothing more than errand boys for them. Using them for deliveries and pick-ups and, to find more reasonable connections. They are really not factors, the pretense got those who don't really have no power or influence over them, fooled. "

"So what about Shake and Bake or them three mask muthafuckas who've been just poppin' up robbing and killing major figures?" I asked, trying to put more of the pieces together.

"Shake and Bake relocated and went west to St. Louis somewhere after someone dropped the dead bodies of their boyfriends, James Riley and Eddie Domino, off on their mansion's lawn one morning. There was a note attached to one of the bodies that had a message written inscribe, Your next if you continue to the stamp know as Pussycat throughout Camden and the towns orbited around it. They were in contact with me for a few months after they packed up, and wanted me to come with but I refused," Terry explained, downing a glass of water. "And as for those three nocturnal assassins, no one can suspect who they are or when they will strike again."

"This extreme, unsolved drug mystery has you three in a position to a point if you make one false move, one of use could be next."

"You Think? We play the game just as well as they do, we've been doing this for a long time. It's like teaching old dogs new tricks," Muscles added, slamming his fist in the palm of his other hand. "That's why their igniting controversy and flooding the streets with the Black Death stamp. They want us to bite the bait so we can war over stamps but if we start unnecessary killings and just dropping muthafuckas it fucks up the flow of business. So the best strategy for now is to move out of harm's way and keep our positions locked so the Dominican brother's can keep on guessing--"

"About futuristic plans that we already would be executing and how we're going to annihilate them without being clumsy through chaos," Billy filled in, speaking over Muscles.

"So the next move is?" I asked, being a combustive force to the problem.

"We follow their lead," Muscles retorted. "Make our product just as well as theirs, uncut, and change our stamp to Black Death. And, double-up on their runners to push our product through them. That way they'll be thinking that they conquered the city and our clientele as well. But, really we'll be taking money out of their pockets. Once they catch on to what it is that we've done, they'll be picking their brains trying to find the mole or another plan to wipe us out. By then we would have made enough money to present a war with them and their allies."

"Uncle you're really trying to start a war?" I asked, hoping he changed his mind due to the fact that our army wasn't big enough.

He turned facing me, with eye-to-eye contact and said, "If they want war then war it's going to be." Muscles was great at being combative and putting out heavy competition but, I never knew him to war with anyone in his life. I guess to be the best you have to defeat the best and since my uncle felt in heart that he was the best at turning white to green and, vice-versa for the Dominican brothers who had the same mind state. It was time to bring the best of the best out of the best. Forcing his hand with only twelve months back on the contaminated streets wasn't the brightest ideas but isolated time turns a person's character into that of a renegade.

# Chapter. 7

The scorching summer of 85' rolled around and the weather's temperature wasn't the only thing affecting the city and the citizens in it. Bullet shells, domestic violence, robberies and murder also kept the wrong heat aligned with the daily summer forecast.

Muscles plan was a success story to a successful disaster, after putting his product under the Black Death stamp the war erupted immediately. We began warring with the entire city, there was a leak somewhere that caused it all but, the shootouts were constant fire work episodes. I shot at one of the Dominican Bothers' soldiers for so long one night, chasing him up a dark alley in Cramer Hill, I had to beat him to death with my gun and a belt buckle from my pants because I ran out of ammunition.

A couple of weeks after the open discussion at the House of Chemistry, Billy bumped into Vinnie Parker - one of his top buyers - down at the Blue Saloon. The Blue Saloon was a local eatery down by the Ferry avenue train station that was known for their delicious rib platters. Vinnie was playing both sides of the fence, trying to cut side deals with Poohshaun to get in closer with the Dominicans.

Pretty Vinnie was in awe when he observed Billy enter the Saloon and approach his table. Vinnie tried to greet Billy with a hand shake but in return Billy stunned him with a stiff fright jab to the face. Simultaneously, he whipped his gun out and aimed it at Poohshaun, being two steps ahead of Billy; he had already had his showing. The customers that were seated had run out of the place in fear of their lives, only three remained.

Flashing and pointing guns at each other, Billy told Poohshaun to walk head high with caution and to ride with every car window down because the war was that serious. "Bring it nigga," Poohshaun answered, having no intentions on lowering his pistol as Billy backed his way out of the Saloon.

As I continue to make my rounds in the thoroughfares of the city, I changed my pretentious appearance as much as I blinked. Dressing as a junkie, or a salesman in a suit from time to time, even dressed like a lady wearing a wig a and heels a few times. Obtruding out like a sore thumb, everyone who was apart of something or being someone in the streets knew who I was and what it was I was doing and, who I was doing it for. Muthafuckas were after me as well, so I disguised myself to keep the lurking eyes to a minimum.

The disguise thing worked for a few months but it still didn't stop me from getting robbed for a brick and a half of dope and sixty thousand in cash. And, a shot away from everyone who knew me, sitting at my wake weeping tears, screaming BASTARD! Myesha Parker - Vinnie's baby sister - who I delivered to on Mondays was getting drop offs four times a month from me for about five months. I never came to think twice about whom her peoples were or who it was she was copping for. That was due to me committing foolish acts, dick thinking.

A couple of weeks after Billy's outburst down at the Blue Saloon, I never knew that blows were exchange to the point that I would be put in harms way. My main concern was getting the job done and I was doing it to the best of my ability. Around a quarter-to-nine in the morning I arrived at Myesha's front door, as usual the plan was to make the transaction and be on my way. But things didn't go as planned on this particular morning. As I counted the last of the buy money, making sure everything was there, Myesha crept behind me and gently began caressing my shoulders and kissing on my neck. I resisted with might but she was very persistent like a mass of bees from a honeycomb.

Myesha was on her feetless twos blowing me before I could even finish counting the rest of the money or put up a fight to calm her horniness. The twenty five year old ghetto diva's lips had a mind of their own, freezing my resistance. Truly stuck and off point, we managed to make from the kitchen's table into the living room floor. But that's the furthest we mad it before my erect stroke stick was in between her moist cum sucker.

Straddled over top of me, giving me direct eye contact, Myesha had my mind lost saying to me in gyration mode, "You love it don't you... Don't you love this pussy?" I was only seventeen, what teenager wouldn't love some older pussy? But like they say money was the root of all evil, in my eyes pussy was its' replacement.

The bitch whipped my own pistol out, directing it clean in between my eyes but still was riding me like the whore girl she was. Pulling one of DaVita's stunts - so I thought - playing with the gun in front of my face as if we were roll playing. But, this wasn't acting and the gun was fully loaded, having me right where she wanted me, half naked with my pants down on her living room floor in an immobilized position. Her loser brother Vinnie and two of his flunkies came rushing from behind the basement door like a surveillance team anxious to make a drug bust.

"Get the doe and snow," Vinnie commanded, to the other two airheads. "You never expected this smooth shit to be happening to you did you lil' man?" he asked me this time, kicking me in the gut simultaneous.

Vinnie kneeled over top of my head while his sister still had grips on my dick from the straddled position, with the gun in my face. "Tell Billy the coffin he lies dormant in after I'm through with him is going to look like a Jamaican fitted cap when I'm done and also let your uncle know that it was nice doing business with him... No hard feelings." As he walked away Myesha added, "Sometimes good pussy is bad for your health," before smacking me over the head with the burner.

$ $ $ $ $

After waking up and regaining my consciousness I was lying around a bunch of fetid garbage and old news papers, ass naked. The impact from the gun blow to the rear of my head must have knocked me out instantaneously. I was lucky to be unclad in the summer time because if it was winter I probably would have frozen to death. I was in the land of the lost, I seen no pedestrians on the streets, cars weren't moving on the roads and there were no buildings or row homes to go into for some help. My vision was impaired from the deep gash I had over my right eyebrow but from the looks of the atmosphere around me, Vinnie and his crew had dropped me off in the country where some farm owner grew crops for a living.

It was scorching hot and the time had to be around 3 p.m. because the sun was at its' peak and there was no shade, not a pinch of air and I was very dehydrated, lying on the side of the dirt road looking like a orphan. As time moved and the sun smiled in my face, a van finally pulled along side of the road - Finally! These two young white guys hopped out of this white appliance van and aided my feebleness. They were in their early twenties, no older than twenty-five; one of them wore glasses and had this long ass ponytail hanging form his backside. The other dude had a low hair cut with a pointy nose, they both were slim physically but ponytail dude was taller.

They both helped me into the van, laying me across some sturdy boxes which were holding heavy items inside. My body temperature dropped rapidly once I was inside the air-conditioned vehicle.

"Here cover up with this until we can get you to the hospital or something," The pointy nose white boy said, with a joint hanging from his lip. "So what's your name dude?"

"Kyle," I replied, in a battered voice. "And yours?"

"Oh I'm Keith and this dork here is Derrick. I have no fucking clue as to where his mother conceived him from."

"Fuck you dude," Derrick answered, as the two of them threw a few playful punches to each other. "So what happened to you? How'd you end up naked, on the side of a dirt road out here in Westhampton, with a big fuckin' wound over your eye?" We were out in Mt. Holly somewhere, ten minutes away from Rancocas state park.

I started to act like I had a bad case of amnesia due to them being strangers and all. There might have been a couple of badges under those plan clothes that they were wearing. But, I had a change of heart because they did take time out to come and rescue me from Mother Nature's devastating heat wave.

"I really can't remember, all I know is that someone was trying to rob me," I answered, giving them half the story.

"So where ya' from?" Keith asked, as he dodges through traffic.

"Camden. The bottoms which make you feel like your on top."

"CAMDEN!" They both exclaimed in unison as if it were hell or some shit.

"Your 'bout an hour away from your county dude," Derrick added, as if I was in another state or something.

"I know a little bit about your hometown my man, its' narcotic central for damn near the entire east coast line. Drug fuckin' heaven, I done a research paper back in high school on notorious cities and Camden was my top choice--"

"That's because the dumb fuck never been outside of New Jersey's state lines." Derrick intervened, clowning on his boy.

"Fuck off loser... But Kyle like I was saying, the paper was titled Camden's Candy. Man, more drugs are smuggled into that small city than the coast of Miami. That's what some analyst and investigators say anyhow."

"No way Dude."

"Yes fuckin' way," Keith retorted, snatching the joint from Derrick's mouth. "Kyle you want some my man?'

"Nah, I'm straight bunny."

"The nine square mile city had been supplied by these two Cuban or Dominican tycoons named Rich and Manny Munez, I forget there names but it something like that and these muthafuckas became millionaires over night - LITERALLY! Back in the early sixties they were like the only two mongers with smack. Federal authorities and D.E.A. agents had been watching them for more than fifteen years but could never pin them with anything due to there discreteness to major Cuban links and their family's discretion to strangers. They never got caught doing anything illicit."

Saying absolutely nothing and paying close attention to familiar details, I just lied across the boxes in complete silence. I had a gut feeling that one of the two was more educated than I when it concerned other environmental areas in Jersey, knowing more than their average peers. And, I'd been living in Camden all my life and Derrick knew more of what was going on than I.

"You ever saw them before dude?" Derrick asked, referring to

Richie and Mikey.

"Who Me?" I asked.

"Yeah, Rich and Manny?"

"No, those two jokers were before my time in the streets."

"Aye dude Rich and Manny have been dead for almost fifteen years now."

"What!" I exclaimed, loud enough that a sharp pain shot through my brain, they both looked at me in a weird way; like they knew both knew I knew something.

"Yeah dude, their deaths have yet to be solved and the suspects are still out there enjoying the glory of their cold case files. The media, news analyst, and the underworld can't even figure out what happened in their mysterious deaths. When they found their bodies on the front lawn of one of their girlfriend's lawn, the news papers had them burnt to a crisp like wasted turkeys' dude," Keith joked with in a chuckling manner. "The coroner had to identify them both by dental records, what a fucking way to die huh?"

Evidently, the Dominican brothers weren't in existence or the main connect to Camden's underworld. Well then who was, was the question? Someone or something has been using their names to keep a certain status quo or to reach one for that matter. But, no one seemed to know who was playing Casper the friendly ghost behind the Dominican's fortune. Or who those three dark men were who just been popping up on major connections and suppliers when deals went down, annihilating them. I began connecting the pieces to the mysterious drug frenzy little by little.

I was back in Camden County in no time thanks to Derrick and Keith and the profound conversation about Camden's drug economy. They got off the 130 Interstate exits via Kaighns Avenue so I could go to the emergency room at Our Lady of Lourdes Hospital. They helped me into the emergency room and waited until I got treated by physicians there and then my two cool white boys drove me to my condo in the Glamour Towers; I hadn't been home in months. I invited them up for a resting spot before they headed back north but, they refused because they wanted to beat traffic at rush hour time.

Keith handed me his business card which read, O'Keefe's Electronic Appliance Company on it and, told me if I needed any home work done from house wiring to television sets, to give him and Derrick a call. In return, I gave them a contact number at my other pad, letting them know that I had connections as well. And, if they needed anything, anything at all, no promises was guaranteed. But, I could find away to make a dollar out of fifteen cent. They both promised to be in contact in the near future.

$ $ $ $ $

The situation with Myesha and her brother Vinnie landed me completely in the shit house with my uncle. Muscles found out what happened to me before I could even go to him and explain. He, Billy, and Terry came to my house days later in an upset manner due to my thoughtless acts. I was sitting in their presence with fifteen stitches across my eye, looking stupid. Muscles then gave me a long, chastising tirade about not listening to him and, thinking with my dick. Everything was rhetorical, my side of the story was on deaf ears. My services to them were no longer needed from that point on, Muscles advised me not to play the streets at all, until things calmed down. They wanted me to sit back and think on my reckless actions and what it was that I jeopardized. The way my uncle cut me off, felt like I lost everything and wasn't going to gain anything from that point on. It was back to square one again, no job, no sort of steady income, and no sense of direction.

Two days later, Muscles came back to the towers alone, not to talk or show any kind of remorse. But, to drop off the money that I had earned while running for him. In seven months of working I made an immense amount of money; about $400,000. But, after I got robbed for the $250,000 dollars worth of goods, I was only left with one hundred and thirty thousand dollars; keeping the five keys of heroin that I invested with him in the beginning. I felt fucked all a crossed the board but that's how the game was played when you made mistakes.

An entire week passed without me stepping one foot out my front door, eyes still were in pain, mind filled with stress and the state of depression that I was in had me trying to figure out a new way to hustle so I wouldn't get caught. I was in bed sleep, trying to escape my own stupidity when the phone rang clamorously like music at a party.

"Hello," I said, in a raunchy voice, not wanting to answer the phone. The operator clicked in and told me that I had a collect call from Dontae Watson. After saying yes to accept the charges, Dontae said hello to me like he was on vacation.

"Hello, Kyle."

"Yeah it's me, what's up slim?"

"Listen daddy, I'm in a serious jam my man."

"How serious?" I asked, hoping it didn't concern a life or death situation.

"I'm down here at the county jail waiting to be processed."

"For what?" Now his situation was life threatening.

"I can't go into to many details right now but I'll be sure to fill you in as soon as I get out of here. My bail is set at five-hundred thousand cash or bond. I'll be sure to reimburse you when I get out with interest."

"Alright slim, give me 'bout a half and I'll be there to post it for you, okay?"

"I appreciate it blood," he replied, before hanging up the phone."

I slammed my head back on my pillow, discussed because my sleep had been interrupted. I sighed wondering what it was that Dontae had gotten himself into to get his bail set at five-hundred grand. Following behind his pop, he probably got into some deep shit.

I called in a favor to my cousin Wadeelah, to see if she could go and post his bail for me. I asked her to meet me on the corner of 3rd and Mickle Street, downtown, across from City Hall; she agreed, asking no questions. I had to cab it to the destination because my uncle repossessed my vehicle from me also. I never drove it anyway but that was besides the point, I might had of needed it for an emergency like the one I was engaged in now; he probably trashed my bike that was left at the house of chemistry as well.

"What happened to you" Wadeelah asked, standing by the phone booth on the corner of 3rd and Mickle Street when I pulled up and stepped out the back of the cab.

"Oh, this," I said, touching the bruise on my face."I got into a little scuffle down at Luby's last weekend."

We walked across the street to the county clerk's office, where bails were. Wadeelah services were needed so she could sign off on the bail receipt, because I wasn't putting my John Hancock on any documentation that could be traced back to me. I was a low key dude, and fifty grand without any occupational insurance was deemed to be questioned. But, Wadeelah was covered all around the board, making a five digit a year salary as a teacher's aid and, she worked as a receptionist at an auto mechanic place too. I didn't consider myself as a criminal but I was a miscreant to the streets and I was severely under employed.

The fifty grand was confiscated by the clerk's office and the paper work had been signed and processed to the county jail for Dontae's release. Wadeelah and I sat patiently inside of Broadway Eddie's steak shop which sat on the corner of Broadway and Mickle street; a few blocks away from the county jail. Wadeelah and I sparked a conversation about her whereabouts, progression, and how the rest of the family was doing since I kept my distance most of the time.

My Aunt Gracey had went into a rehabilitation center for ninety days, hoping to get her drug addiction under control. In my eyes, three months wasn't enough time for her to even get any rest. From all the drugs she done tampered with, she needed at least a year and a half of cleansing. My Uncle Muscles wrote off a twenty-thousand dollar check For Wadeelah's college tuition on her birthday. I was proud of her because she deserved it since we were in grade school she always made the honor roll and kept her mind on her studies. Ironically, I felt very stupid because I could have been receiving the same rewards and achievements but, I chose to do things my way. And, that was the hard way that took a left turn in life.

After eating and sharing laughs over our childhood, Wadeelah and I headed back to City Hall to see if Dontae had been released. In deed, he had been, just as we approached 3rd street he was exiting the county jail's gate. He approached us with the look of haven't slept in days and smelled like an infested basement. Wadeelah hugged him, and I shoved him because I didn't want any of his bad luck to rub off on me.

"You looked like you were in there lying with ghost," I said, looking into his livid face.

"A slim, over there in that building, behind those walls," he replied, pointing in the jail's direction. "It's a jungle inside, that's no place for humans."

Wadeelah told us that she would be in touch and pulled away in her two-door Ford Focus sedan. I went back down to Broadway Eddie's to get another bite to eat and pluck Dontae's brain to see why he had been arrested. Dontae was my childhood crony but I didn't trust him, I seen to much of his father in him to do that and that nigga's blood was flooded with cross and a dagger.

Over a large, cheese pizza we sat in Eddie's and conversed; I could see in Dontae's eyes that something or someone had pushed him to the limits of revenge.

"So, what happened now that you and your psychopathic pops got into but can't get out of now that the laws on ya' ass?"

"Nah slim, its' not Big D.S.'s fault on this one," He said, with a disappointing look on his face. "It's my cousin Spring."

"Spring?" I whispered in a low tone. "What about Spring?" The connection had me lost for a minute.

"Man, homicide detectives came to my house and arrested me around nine o'clock, prior to charging me with robbery and murder. I was in the police administration building sitting in this tiny ass room for hours. I was nervous, had to shit real bad and my heart was racing faster than Jessie Owen doing the hundred yard dash--"

"Dont' not to cut you off slim but get to the fucking point." I didn't need blow by blow fucking details; I needed the exact source and issue with the source.

"Alright... Alright. The night we robbed Ted's for the money and drugs, Spring hit the cash register for the money inside the till before you let her out of the store. Did you see her making any unofficial moves?" I gave him a convincing look as to say 'Nigga are you serious.'

"If I would have seen it, your bail wouldn't be five-hundred thousand dollars now would it?"

"You have a point, but the detective Rolan Fisher showed me the forensic lab reports from the scene of the crime and the match are positive to Spring's prints.

"So she told," I stated, knowing that I was next to be prosecuted. "I'm next I know it."

"I doubt it, because she never mentioned your name. The criminal investigation reports that I read and from what Rolan disclosed to me, Spring only gave up statements on my dad and me. She told homicide that we forced her into making the move with us."

"I told you... I told you that night we went to handle that mission, she wasn't to be brought along. I guess because I was the amateur nobody wanted to listen to me."

"That was my dad's stupid idea to do so."

"So where is she now?"

"Either at her mom's house or in a remote location somewhere hiding out until it's time for her to testify on the state's behalf."

"And your pops?"

"He's probably on America's most wanted top ten wanted fugitive's list by now, homicide has a APB out on him as we speak. They told me if I'm found guilty on both charges I could face life in prison."

"So how are you going to go about the situation from this point on?"

"Man, there's only one way to go about it, I have to off Spring but--"

"But my ass! She's trying to off you, listen slim I know how you feel about her being family and all but that should give you an even bigger reason to make her amongst the missing." I could see the fear of killing Spring was affecting him, he was truly scared. In my eyes it seemed as if Dontae wanted to kill himself. "Always go with your first instinct, never second guess it because that can get you caught up. I got a better idea, since you're my man fifty grand and all. I'll handle her for you, just find out her location and get as much information as you possibly can and I'll take care of it from there."

"Kyle, I appreciate everything your doing for me, you've always been the strongest branch from the crew's tree."

"Yeah, yeah... You just find out where Spring is before you find yourself shackled up the river for the rest of your life."

$$\$ \$ \$ \$ \$$$

After Dontae and I finished discussing Spring and how we were going to settle the score, I went seeking for more information from him about the mysterious underworld and who was the masterminds behind the franchise of the Dominican Brothers. I knew he knew more than the average no nothing because his dad talked about what he lived in his heyday.

Dontae opened my eyes even more about the suspicious trails which followed behind the Dominican's fame. His pops told him years back that some lady named Terry was the cause of a lot of mischief that took place for years and she was the one who put Big D.S. up to kill my dad, when he was the driving force of the underworld. And, the night they planned on stinging the Dominicans for those three-hundred kilos of dope inside Krystal's Lounge, that's when Big D.S. was suppose to shoot Kyle Sr. and make it up out of the lounge safely without being harmed; Big D.S. was next to take over. But, D.S. claimed that things never went as planned after he shot Kyle and got away, he never got his fair share of the pie and he never heard or seen from Terry after that.

Prior to Big D.S. and Kyle showing Shake and Bake how to grow and survive in the drug business, Terry was already a major piece in there world of fame and glamour. She was the one who brought Shake and Bake in with the Dominican brothers and took her three high school friends - Gracey, Sissy, and Debbie-and brought them into the family too. The triplets already knew how to maneuver in the game because coming up as teenagers Muscles taught them how to rob and steal from other hustlers.

After Shake and Bake progressed in the game D.S. an Kyle Sr. took them to meet with Lamont Muscles not just for business purposes but, to become apart of his family of future fortune. But, Terry foiled that planned after going behind Shake an Bakes back, telling Muscles that Kyle an D.S. were only using the girls to knock him out of business and consume all of his wealth; Muscles turned them down and cut Kyle Sr. an Big D.S. loose all in the same breath.

To maintain their positions in the game after Muscles terminated their team card, the two of them began conducting business with Shake and Bake and the mighty Dominicans. But somehow Terry's conniving mind brought their bright idea back to being just pipe dreams. She made Shake an Bake dismiss the two partners-in-crime because she told them that Big D.S. was putting the triplets up to steal from them; by delivering bulks of heroin to Kyle Sr. then saying that they had been robbed for them. It was all concocted by Terry who masterminded the schemes herself. She was sexually engaged with Kyle Sr., making the triplets steal from Shake and Bake, and having Big D.S. plunder them so they could stray from the game like Muscles did in 1973.

Terry was the helm to Kyle's status quo in the underworld due to her delving information, intimacy and letting him know Shake an Bakes' every move. With the help of Terry and the assistance from D.S. and the triplets, Kyle Sr. managed to retrieve fifty keys of dope and a half million dollars in money out of Club Shake's and then set it ablaze. Shake and bake gracefully bowed out and disappeared like two shadows in the dark after that.

When the smoke cleared, Kyle became the new HNIC and there was no one for miles of the underworld to combat his tyranny. Conclusively, Dontae unveiled that his father never explained to him the real reason for him shooting my dad. But, as far as he knew there was more than enough information to the mysterious drug puzzle's facts that only certain key players knew about. Information that kept me guessing and assuming the truth that only Terry and those around her knew about; I was another step closer though and I just got intrigued.

Once the pizza had been devoured and our conversation ceased, we both went our separate ways. Dontae promised to return my bail money to me in days and with all his brain power, Spring's location would be sought even if he had to force his way through certain family members; that I didn't see him doing though.

# Chapter. 8

On every newspaper in town, Dontae and his pops were the cover story behind the Rotti shop massacre for weeks on in. I began seeing Dontae's face so much after our talk in Broadway Eddie's that I felt as if I had killed him myself and he was prancing around haunting me for revenge. The fuzz had his pad under surveillance twenty-four hours a day, all day. I'm glad my money was brought to me the following day or wouldn't receive it for months due to him being followed and watched.

The summer of 85' was the worse summer I'd experienced and it was far from over. I lost an illicit, low key job that paid more than a doctor's salary, not to mention I lost my uncles trust and loyalty. Everything was over lustful thoughts and some nasty whore who seduced my mind for her brother's own personal gain. And, just when I thought I was back to my own safe haven, I received a call from the young beau Lamaar Green. Her voice was in pain when I answered the phone and like a dummy being very concerned, I hopped out of bed in the middle of the night to comfort her troubles.

Lamaar sadly expressed to me that Kenny had beaten on her for no reason at all but, I knew better to believe that; because there was two sides to every furious story. She said that he had taken some personal issues out on her, which were eating him up inside. She packed a few clothes and some important credentials and called me immediately. I gave Zakeya Perry-the receptionist-a call, letting her know that I was expecting company and gave Lamaar my address as well.

The time was a quarter after one in the morning when Lamaar arrived at my house of comfort. The bruises that Kenny left behind her black Gucci shades and the pain which streamed through her tears made it tough for her to ever love him again. I filled my Jacuzzi with bath water so she could relax and retrieved an ice pack for her eye.

During the half an hour spent bringing calm to her thoughts in the Jacuzzi, she elaborated on the inception of her and Kenny's relationship. And, how it started off with clear skies and sunshine, then ended in dark clouds and rain. Lamaar met Kenny in junior high school (Morgan Village), a few years prior to me graduating from Bonsall elementary. Always pretty and having a little class even before she hooked up with Kenny, the only thing that changed was her maturity level. Lamaar had four older brothers-Dave, Bubbles, Magoo, and Itchie-who always looked after her and kept her head in the books. Itchie, the third oldest, stayed in her ass the most, telling here that she never needed a man for nothing. If she needed anything at all, to count on him because he was he only man. Ironically, Itchie told Lamaar that the young boys growing up only wanted her for one thing and that was the fish between her legs.

However, Lamaar didn't see it Itchie's way, she and Kenny became a couple in the 7th grade, and she rolled the dice to see if shit stunk for herself. One thing lead after another and Lamaar and Kenny became an official item. Always being the jealous type, Kenny was very insecure about the female that he was courting around with. He began to get beside himself as time went on, inflicting domestic violence whenever it satisfied him to do so; even around company.

Lamaar's brothers would go on a hunt for Kenny like he was their prey on days that he and Lamaar missed school or wasn't fighting over something petty. They would literally go to the school and pull Kenny out of class just to smack him around a little. Telling him if he was caught around Lamaar they were going to make him amongst the missing; typical brother controversy. The love wasn't that easy to let go for Lamaar because of what her brothers insisted on, it was Lamaar's sassy disposition that made him head over heels for her like a psychopath having no mental treatment. Kenny couldn't shake her; it just came to a point where Lamaar's brothers just gave up on keeping them apart.

Once Lamaar's brother's got past the fiery desire of alienating themselves form Kenny and welcomed him in as part of the Green family, Lamaar brought him into her family's wealth of the drug game. Lamaar stated the given fact that it was her who brought Kenny in with her father and brothers to rise in the underworld. Kenny knew nothing about the basis of heroin, let alone selling it until she showed him the light of it all.

Lamaar learned the game from her three older sisters - Pam, Janell, and Naytomi -who all aged her a bit. When her brothers were making moves they never allowed Lamaar to get a slight glimpse of what they were doing because what they were apart of wasn't for her. So in turn, she would inquire about things through her sisters and learn different aspects of the game. All her sisters use to maneuver the way I moved for my uncle, delivering packages and picking up buy money. They also set other hustlers up to be robbed for tangibles that made them who they were. And, once Lamaar acquired all the right fundamentals to the game, she effectively used them to her advantage.

Lamaar started out stealing from her father Jahee to get Kenny a push start in the game. Taking a few ounces at a time, risking her life for the love she had for the airhead Kenny. Watching Kenny's back from sun up to sun down on corners while he pitched clips of dope. Selling weight to customers out of town and having intentions like her sisters did, of being the downfall to the next hustler who was on top of his status quo too. She would give niggas a little pussy only to get in their pockets in return, and robbing them all by her lonesome just so her man could be the next big thing. A true rider, his Bonnie, the one who did all of his dirty work for him while he sat back on his fat ass and got large.

When Kenny got enough money to play with the big boys he became affiliated with the almighty L.S.D. crew; a hustling click that Lamaar's brothers ran. The L.S.D. name came from the street where the money came and the customers were consistent-Lake Shore Drive! Along with the strip name came a few older heads that were before Kenny's time, two guys by the name of Bobby Muse and Ike Ewing. They were the connection to many connections in the underworld, mainly the L.S.D. retinue. Barry Webb, Tyron Baylor –Kenny's right hand man, Leonard Mitchell, and Jermaine Cones were the men amongst Bobby, Ike, Kenny, and Lamaar's brothers.

$ $ $ $ $

In 1977, L.S.D. was the name to beat and the environment was the best competition around, only until federal authorities came in and began spoiling there meals. Everyone in the L.S.D. crew went up state to do time except Kenny, for drug trafficking and conspiracy. Jahee, his four sons and Lamaar's two older sisters - Naytomi and Janell - joined the circus also. The Feds even apprehended Kenny's two sisters - Keena and Lavell - who were making transactions for guys out of the organization.

After the fall of his sisters, Lamaar's family and the almighty L.S.D. crew, Kenny wanted to abscond himself from the game. He felt that he would be the next to go if he stayed and played fair ball with unfair familiars. But, Lamaar wasn't trying to give in that easy, she had a family to support now that she was Queen of the household.

In the process of paying homage to her family and friends in penitentiaries all over jersey, Lamaar took her experience in the game to unimaginable heights. She got connected into the great Lamont Muscles through her father, who happened to be one of Muscles close friends. And, Kenny began doing business with Joe Riley and Eddie Domino, two men whom mingled with Shake and Bake.

"Kenny doing business with Riley and Domino?" I had to intervene and cut off her explaining to find out more of who these two guys were, "Who were they? Where were the so called Dominican brothers at this time around?"

"Who!" She asked in a loud voice, as if they never existed. "Lamont Muscles was the sole controller of the streets when my family went away. He was doing business with my father before I was even born. Muscles was like family and I tried to keep everything the same when my dad went down. Through letters from my father was how I got in contact and put sock drawer money into effect. When I went to Lamont I was empty handed with nothing. And, Kenny's fat ass gave me no money at all to keep the ball rolling due to fear of steel bars. So after explaining myself to Muscle about my situation, and indigence with no way of taking care of my family. He gave me a hundred-thousand dollars out of his pocket for the love and respect he had for my father Jahee. Fifteen at the time, I used a portion of the money to support my mother and little brother Vance. And, there was no one to hold the glory of Lake Shore together and Kenny's scary ass got a job at the A & P food market, working the deli department. So I had to take matters into my own hands."

"He was that scared?"

"Petrified as a lost kitten. So I took a risk and jeopardized my freedom by putting Muscles' product out on Lake Shore with the help of my sister Pam and a few friends... Tiffany, Bay-Bay, Pookie and Tameka went on the grind with me. The six of us brought new life back to Lake Shore Drive and the entire Fairview neighborhood."

Meticulously, I continued to listen carefully to Lamaar but in my own thoughts I was tying to reattach the underworld's broken glass. After Muscles went to jail in 1978, Lamaar fell short of a main connection, so she took the money that she made to a man by the name of Poppa Smurf. Poppa Smurf was like an uncle to Lamaar, he was the mate of her sister Pam. Smurf wasn't a big time figure but he had a lot of connections and made a lot of moves. Lamaar dealt with Smurf for about six months before he went to prison for selling to a couple of undercover officers; he disappeared from the game in 1979.

After two and a half years of grind struggles to keep a consistent operation on Lake Shore, jumping from one connect to another and taking care of her imprisoned family, Lamaar got discouraged. Her indolence towards everything and everyone around her was what she began to take pride in. She became so stressed, after surviving a gun chase in her vehicle by three unidentified mask persons, who gave chase for blocks. She managed to get control of the vehicle and escape the scene and, the mask persons who were probably the same people who robbed the Dominicans. And, put Jimmy Fidell out of his misery back then.

Once Lamaar put her homicidal destruction and hustling troubles behind her, she became so afraid for her own life she gave up the streets to find a better her and, gave up on friends and family too. Her venting process was truly needed but, I still didn't understand how Kenny began doing business with Riley and Domino, when the so-called Dominican brothers were the best thing since Al Capone to control the streets. And, how did her fat fucking boyfriend become so feared and powerful in the city of sin, when in deed he was working in a sandwich shop. She had my mind lost and traveling after all the filling in the blanks was done.

Lamaar reiterated the fact that there were not two people by the name of Richie and Mikey controlling Camden's streets when she dedicated herself to the hustle of bringing dope back to Lake Shore Drive. It was Lamont Muscles who helmed the streets and saturated them with snow, even before the drastic sweeps, droughts on heroin, and the lost of major connections due to the murder rate skyrocketing from 1973 to 1975.

Kenny got acquainted and became cool with a young thunder cat named Poohshaun Miller at the beginning of 1980. Poohshaun was an errand boy for Riley and Domino at this time, who happened to take over from where their dames - Shake and Bake - left off from. Poohshaun had a tab in the A& P food market, and use to get special orders made from a few employees there. This is how the two acquainted; Poohshaun never knew Kenny on a personal level but would catch him in stride moving with the L.S.D crew from time to time.

Kenny and Poohshaun had the opportunity to engage on many social encounters and bonded with visions on a money level. As time went on and Poohshaun felt comfortable, he then introduce Kenny to two of the dope game's finest suppliers - Joe Riley an Eddie Domino. Instantaneously, Riley and Domino offered Kenny a position he couldn't refuse, making him and Poohshaun interact on the same level. Riley and Domino cared less about the moves the two boys made on the side, just as long as they handle what was primary first.

Lamaar continued addressing the fact that once Kenny got in big with Riley an Domino, she gave him every penny that she had ever accumulated from the Lake Shore strip; all but the hundred grand that she wanted to pay back to Muscles. In the mist of moving for Riley and Domino, Kenny added his few ends from hustling with the substantial amount that Lamaar brought to the table. He took it to Riley in return of purchasing his own product and reopened the Lake Shore strip with the potent - snort dropper.

Kenny was putting his hustling tactics down harder than he ever did prior to being put on by Lamaar's brothers. While Jahee Green and his family, along with Kenny's two sisters and majority of the legendary L.S.D. crew awaited their day to touch grounds, Kenny was blazing the streets with product. His silent partner in crime - Poohshaun had an operation running on Liberty Street, off of Haddon Avenue, directly around the corner form Luby's pool hall. The beginning of 1980 was a success for the two solid, young men who had nothing to fear as long as Riley and Domino had authority to command.

Like a casting spirit, fell a man named James Fidell who had an intense grudge on his shoulders like every hustler in town owed him start up money. Jimmy was as raw as they came, gorilla pimping his way to the top Like Frank Lucas but, had to much might and not enough intelligence. He literally pistol whipped mongers, killed in broad day light, and held major figures for ransom notes. Jimmy even tied Kenny and Poohshaun up ass naked and took them to Riley and Domino, demanding twenty keys of dope and for them to gracefully bow out of the game. Or they had no other option but to lie cold in a river of streaming blood.

$$\$ \$ \$ \$ \$$$

Riley and Domino didn't hesitate to meet the demented Fidell's threatening proposal, giving up the twenty keys for the sake of Kenny and Poohshaun's life. They got caught with their feet up and their guns down by Fidell who approached their territory prepared and ready. Jimmy's motto was to disrespect the game and have no remorse for anyone in it. Intrinsically, he took it upon himself and strolled in the Total Elegance -unisex hair salon and put a gun to Terry's head. He demanded that she take her organization and business out of the city and Network it in a different environment. Or, her only other option was to float in the Delaware River too.

$$\$ \$ \$ \$ \$$$

Fidell had the streets all to himself by the summer of 1980, appearing all over town as if his body was made of Teflon and, selling bricks of dope for outrageous; a lucrative bounty was placed over his head though. Hustlers in the streets of Camden froze like roaches on the wall when Jimmy would pull up. But, since a tuff guys destiny never lasted long, Fidell's rise in the game slowly waned, the tougher he became.

Lamaar's sister Pam use to court Jimmy's father - Old man Chucky - who was one of the largest number runners in the Northeast. This is how Jimmy got to be a major threat, from the power his pop possessed and, the respect that all hustlers and old-time O.G.'s had for his father. People that didn't know a thing about the underworld or who Jimmy really was, would come to Chucky and tell him horrific stories about his son. Asking could he please place him under control and talk some sense into him but, the spoken words of Chucky went into one ear and out the other to Jimmy.

The wire had it that, Terry walked up on Chucky at Daddy Ghost's number spot on Sheridan street, where slips were turned in and she pulled a gun on him while he shot craps. Telling him to relocate his son or he was dead meat and a two for one was twice the fun. But, in return Terry got nothing from Chucky but a laugh in the face, as if she was nothing more than a woman's joke. Then he smacked her with a back hand, knocking her to the ground and in unison his crew backed him with their guns.

Someone's bluff was called and Jimmy's dance with the devil became even more severe. A dark cloud precipitate over his head and it started with the kidnapping of his daughter DaVita Mills on her walk home for school. She was held for a ransom note of 1.5 million dollars, no exceptions or dollars short.

"Jimmy was DaVita's father?" I asked, very perplexed and amazed at the same time, I couldn't believe my ears.

"Yeah" Lamaar replied, "She's Chucky Mill's only granddaughter, he named her when she was born."

"And how you know that?"

"Because me and her cousin Tonya are best friends and we all grew up damn near in the dame households."

I then saw where DaVita got her aggressiveness from and how mentally grew faster than her peers. So, it was Jimmy who pulled the gun from his car window and pointed it as I came walking out of his front gate.

Jimmy paid the 1.5 million to get DaVita back and once she was safe, he moved his family out of Camden in 1981. But, that didn't stop his problems from getting worse than they already were. Mysterious phone calls to his establishment and home began to happen, and he would be followed in his travels like the fuzz was his protector. But, that didn't stop him from showing his face in town, it was like he didn't his death to be a secret to his killers. He wanted people to bear witness to him being murdered.

On the night of May 5th, 1981 as he came out of a friend's home in the McGuire Projects in East Camden he got his just due. Kenny told Lamaar that Terry approached him after she heard what Jimmy did to him and Poohshaun; this was a couple weeks before Fidell's murder. Words were exchanged between the two, as he exited Ali's barbershop in Park side, on Haddon Avenue; asking Kenny if he wanted to partake in the mission of killing Jimmy. Kenny was a bit nervous because he never killed before, so he rain checked Terry's idea and said that he would get back to her with his decision. But, Kenny's timid ass never got back to Terry; it was Poohshaun who pumped him up to call her back after Kenny explained the situation to him. Kenny told Terry that he wanted in and that Poohshaun wanted a piece of the action too. But, before the three of them could move out on Jimmy, they were beat to the punch and Fidell's head was already knocked off.

Approximately 11:30 p.m., on the night of May 5th Jimmy was on his way to his car which was parked on Westminster Avenue in the McGuire projects. When an unidentified person wearing all black popped out from a bunch of parked cars, adjacent to Jimmy's and put sixteen close range shots in his body; from head-to-toe. Jimmy was D.O.A. before the cops and ambulance even arrived.

When Jimmy's coffin was lifted off and put into the ground, it was a hustler's rejoice to the underworld. The contaminated streets celebrated, having parties and enjoying Fidell's needed demise. There was no sympathy, remorse, or bereavement process for the vivid but aggressive, light skinned bully. Local business owner came back to open their establishments after Fidell's funeral because when he was in existence he was reckless with his aim. Majority of his target practice was at guys who sat in eateries, bars, or Luby's pool hall.

"So how did all of those events affect you and Kenny's relationship?" I asked, needing the core situation that made them both turn in opposite directions towards their feelings.

"Kenny got careless once Riley and Domino came back into play after Fidell died and he and Poohshaun began seeing tomes and tones of cash. He began giving me the cold shoulder, not coming home for weeks on in, smacking me with money like I was his whore, and disrespecting who I was as his better half in front of company. He was even trying to fuck all of my friends, including my sister Pam and my best friend Tonya. He doesn't know I know these things. And, he was even having a sexual romance with Muscles' silent partner Terry while he was in prison. My sister Pam use to do Terry's hair years back and she told me. She said Terry would gossip to her on personal subjects that weren't even suppose to be reflected upon. Terry never knew that Kenny had a girl and my sister never told."

"Damn, he treated you like that? I guess the distrust makes it difficult for you to ever love again?"

"Yes it does," She expressed, tearing heavily once more from all the agony Kenny put her through. "I even hid in the trunk of his car one night just to see what it was that he was really doing on nights that he didn't come home to me. Terry was really giving sheet love to my man; he picked her up that night too. I didn't pin-point the actual location that they were headed in but I heard a lot of bags rattling in the back seat of the car... could have been money or something? He spoiled the bitch and she was already being catered to, Muscles was her wealth and she governed his throne while incarcerated. And, I even heard him tell her out of his own mouth that he was falling out of love with me because I was beginning to come in between his money and time with her. After those honest words Kyle, my heart's been cut deeply every since then."

"So, why'd you stay around? Why didn't you just run with another man and leave him lonely?"

"Easier said than done, my love, time and dedication to him was up for grabs and I wasn't about to allow no spare of the moment pussy come between that. Everything that constituted Kenny's well being and all of the merits that he's cherished happened because of me... I made that fat fuck," She cried, weeping from her tears. "But, what put the icing on the cake and crushed my spirits was when my sister Pam was killed early in the year out in front of Krystal's lounge. She was sitting in Chucky Mills van when someone killed both of them and left a note on the front windshield that read... You're down three to nothing... Game over! It was written in red lipstick. Kenny didn't even bother to come to my sister's funeral or try to comfort my suicidal tendencies which raced through my mind for weeks after my sister was buried."

Sitting in extreme guilt, I didn't even want to hear anymore of the story after Lamaar opened up to me about her sister Pam's death. Chucky was the cause of Pam's tragedy and know that she was Lamaar's sister, it started to affect me to a point of killing Terry myself just for getting me involved. Pam was the third innocent person I put to rest for the sake of someone else's black heart and fatal way of thinking. The relationship between Lamaar and I didn't even have enough time to go sour and, furtively, I was already on her bad side. Intimately I wasn't in love with her but I loved her and the personality she possessed, she was very broad minded. I could never face her and confess that I partook in murdering her sister. Apart of her soul was numb because of me and we weren't even committed to cause separation, all in one breath.

Lamaar's hurt for her lost love in Kenny and my guilt of her sister's death, cause us to embrace and make passionate love. In the process she whispered, that she wished someone killed Kenny Morales. As her deadly words circled my brain in the mist of our passionate intercourse, I wondered, while giving her the best stokes form my manhood was her intentions of having her boyfriend killed a fantasized thought? Because of the new comfort zone that smothered her heartaches and pain, or was she speaking the truth due to what he put her through?

My eye's widened like the Incredible Hulk's and my heart race a million beats a minute when I heard those horrible but needed words roll from her sultry tongue. Because I really wanted him to sleep with the fish in the sea, so I could rest on my fears that kept me frightened in his presence. Reality was the way of the world and I was destined to deal with what was real within it.

# Chapter. 9

September came into existence, it was a few days before Labor Day and if I was still enrolled in school I would have been entering my junior year. But, that was all history now just like the summer, the only thing I was preparing for was the changing of the weather.

Lamaar and I became an item after months of getting a better understanding of each other on a mental level; she now resided with me in the Glamour Towers and even found a gig with my mother at the Dayton Manor nursing home. When she wasn't working she was always home doing her duties as my better half. We were both scheduled to attend my family reunion on Labor Day that was taking place at Cooper River Park. But, that didn't meet the fact that I still didn't tell her that Lamont Muscles was my uncle. Being the secretive person that I was, I felt wrong in a way but everything wasn't for everybody to know.

I tried reaching out to my uncle, not to see if he was attending the reunion but to see how he'd been holding up since the last time we spoke in person. I hadn't heard from him since he cut my chances of being an up and coming boss such as himself. The house of chemistry's phone never got an answer on the other end and no one answered Terry's phone either. Billy's phone services had been disconnected and, my mother told me that she hadn't heard from her brother in a while either. I became worried at that point because he and my mother were to close beyond comfort; my uncle always kept my mother in tune with his whereabouts.

Luby didn't even know where my uncle was after I went through there on a few occasions to see if he'd stopped by. I inquired about the shipment process that Luby was doing for my uncle by way of Bippy but, far as Luby knew nothing was effective because there wasn't a shipment in about a month or so. The last transaction that was executed had gone sour and no one could explain what went wrong or pin-point how their system was figured out. Luby didn't go into much detail; he just said that my uncle lost an enormous amount of money on a beautiful proposal that turned out ugly.

Strangely, the pool hall began to get random raids on a daily bases by local authorities. Nothing that explicit had ever taken place in his home of work in the past thirty-five years he'd been there. Benny Smalls, a lieutenant for the Camden police department and a familiar resident in the neighborhood, told Luby that his subordinates were getting anonymous tips that minors were running narcotics from the pool hall. Also, during school hours a lot of teenagers and students were hooking the classroom. But, Luby's didn't open until 2 p.m. in the afternoon on weekdays and 11 a.m. on the weekends. Somebody was whispering to the fuzz and was setting out to diminish his business operation.

$ $ $ $ $

I finally got in contact with my uncle later on that evening at True's residence, I had a slight hunch that if he wasn't roaming the city streets or at one of his permanent destinations, True's home was where he resorted too. But, I thought nothing of it because he and True hadn't been on the best of terms since he was released from the state pen; he probably was trying to rekindle an old flame.

"Yeah," He said, as if he had a sad heart.

"Hey Uncle Muscles… This is ya' long lost nephew just given you a call and checking in on your status because I haven't heard from you in a few months. Just trying to make sure everything is alright with you." I felt the need to lift his spirits if he was in a disappointing mood.

"What's the verdict with you young blood? Continuing to stay out of harms way?"

"Of course, nothing too much is happening with me. Still beating the streets up in finding work in this everyday struggle. Other than that isn't too much happening Captain."

"I hear that solider but listen I need to talk to you about a few serious things which can't be revealed over the phone. Hopefully I'll see you at the family reunion and I'll beat my gums up for you then. There's a lot that's been kept in the dark for so long and I feel the need to confide in you because I see that your aptitude for the hustle is relentless. I've been out of sight for a while trying to figure something's out. "

"I've needed to talk to you to because there's some under the cover information that I think you need to be debriefed on. Have you heard from Terry and Billy lately?"

"Billy and I chatted briefly last night and Terry's been missing for I don't know how long nephew."

"Yeah I know," I replied, nodding my head in disbelief that it could be Terry that's contaminated and the one who made my uncle take that extreme loss. "Well I don't want to hold you up O.G. so I'll just see you in a few days."

"Take care young gangsta, later."

My uncle was on to something or Terry for that matter, he probably was sitting back planning a way to wipe her off the planet. He was more strategic than forceful and it was very difficult to read him or figure his next move; he stayed mum. But, the heat was on and we weren't the ones who were going to get burned.

$ $ $ $ $

The following night I received a phone call from one of my childhood cronies - Lu-Kay - whose family owned a grocery store (Greenies), directly across the street from Kenny Morales' money spot and night, hot spot - Two Ways Inn.

Since the days of spinning tops and being a snot nose kid ripping through Centerville projects, Lu-Kay and I grew together. And, even though he was a few years my senior like the rest of my crew whom grew with me, Lu-Kay was always around when needed. When I got word from my eyes in the street - Ebony - that the Dominican brothers and Kenny Morales had the club directly across from my man's store, I enlightened Lu-Kay on to what it was I was trying to benefit from. Also, to meticulously watch everything that transpired in and out of the night club.

$$\$ \, \$ \, \$ \, \$ \, \$$

I got abrupt call weeks later from Lu-Kay as Lamaar and I lied in bed, telling me that Kenny was alone inside the Two-Ways Inn. To me, it was a divine sign and blessing in the skies because the club was always packed to capacity, even on a slow night. Kenny never walked alone or was caught off guard by himself in any place or at any event.

As I dressed, Lamaar awoke from her rest or at least broke it to see what it was I was doing out of bed at that time of the morning. My fibbing response was that I had to go and pick up one of my uncles from the transportation center, downtown- Broadway, that was coming in from Atlanta, Georgia to attend our family reunion. After kissing her on the forehead, I grabbed her car keys and headed out the door. My mission apparel had already been placed in the trunk of Lamaar's black Saab, buried under the spare tire.

As I drove to meet up with Lu-Kay I had a bad case of neurosis, I felt I still was a amateur in the field of work, my hands weren't ambidextrous when it came to the use of certain artillery; from a distance my aim was inaccurate. Having no Terry, Big D.S. or someone there that was adept in that area, I was bound to cause an error. Life itself was about that though, taking chances and making risk on your own. Palms were sweaty, knees even heavy, and I carried more butterflies in my stomach than caterpillars once I arrived at my destination. 'Get in, get the shit, don't hesitate, and get the fuck out Kyle,' I whispered to myself as I hit the lights on the Saab. Lu-Kay told me to beep the horn once to assure him that I was in position behind the store.

Ambling slowly, Lu-Kay trotted to the Saab, opening the door without warning, scaring my heart rate, I didn't even see him walk up.

"Man, what the fuck cool! You scared the shit out of me," I exclaimed, as my heart entered my butterflies. "You were in the bushes or something?"

"Nah, behind the dumpster," he relied, shaking my hand. "What's the word though?"

"You tell me I-Spy, you're the one with what I need to hear."

"Kenny's in that muthafucka all alone and all we have to do is squat and wait until he rolls."

"And, the time on that could be hours from now?"

"What time is it?" he asked, observing the time on his wrist watch. "It's two-forty-five, Kenny should be coming out in approximately fifteen minutes. He and his flunkies usually come strolling out about this time or a little after three almost every night."

"If he isn't out in fifteen minutes, we're in ya' dig?"

"Oh most definitely."

As we kept our eyes focused on sight for Kenny's departure, Lu-Kay begin explaining how he assumed Kenny to have a lot of issues that he couldn't possibly bear.

"Kyle, I'm telling you slim, Kenny isn't up money like everybody proclaims him to be."

"And you say this because?"

"Because when he and black ass Poohshaun renovated, remodeled, and opened the joint seven months prior. They packed the joint everyday of the week, vehicles cluttered Ferry Avenue... Almost the entire tenth street as well. Now you can tow a car away from this muthafucka."

"So you're saying that he might not have any loot crawling around in there?"

"Oh, believe me he got something in there because I sent my moms to case the joint for me one Saturday night. And, she told me that she mistakenly walked into an unauthorized money spot... Thinking it was the restroom. The bathrooms in the club are located on the second floor along with another bar and TV. Lounge. Kenny and a few of his flunkies were circulating money through money machines when she accidentally peeped in. She only got a quick glimpse due to the body guard in position on the other side of the door. The body guard pushed her away and told her that she was in the wrong area to use the lady's room. Plus, there's still a lot of clientele running in and out of there in chase of that Black Death snort."

"I thought that was off the market?"

"It may not be, but whatever their selling has them seeing more than enough dead presidents... I'll tell you that much."

"Yo'! Kenny's on the move," I said, shifting the gear into drive, pulling away slowly.

Kenny was backing out of the establishment's parking lot when I cut him off with the hood of the Saab. Kenny hit his breaks with force and exited the driver side door with aggression but Lu-Kay was already out of the car before I even could slam the gear back into park.

"Get the fuck back in the car... Get the fuck back in now!" Lu-Kay yelled, with a commanding voice through the black bandana that covered his face.

Fear and nervousness garnished Kenny's face and eyes as I went to pull him back out of the car. Having a look of shitting himself, he begged for mercy, as he cried out, "Please don't shoot me... Whatever you take just don't kill me."

"Shut the fuck up," I insisted, pushing him to the entrance of the club.

As I anxiously waited for Kenny to open the club's doors back up, with the burner to the side of his melon, Lu-Kay stood behind us, guarding the premises and on alert for anything suspicious. It was as if Kenny was reading our fucking minds once we made our way inside because he directed us straight to the money spot. The room Lu-Kay's mother mistakenly observed was definitely the jackpot. With every key on his ring, Kenny was trying to open up the padlocked door but was hesitant like he was stalling for time.

"Just give me a minute?" he asked, like what we were doing was a legal duty.

Impatiently, I smacked him over the head with the pistol because time was of a short period and I couldn't give up a second more. I dropped him right where stood, and shot the lock off the door myself. Lu-Kay dragged Kenny's body in the room, for the sake of him trying to flee. There were two duffle bags of money sitting directly in bird's eye view of the room; the room didn't even have to be ramshacked, because the pool table in the center of the room possessed it. It had to be a coincidence to Kenny that someone might sting him for doe sooner or later, so he left a dummy stash out in the open.

Closing both bags, I threw one to Lu-Kay, strapped the other one across my back and was on my marry way. Forgetting all about the chubby, mixed chump, Lu-Kay had to grab me and point towards the floor.

"What the fuck are we going to do with him? He can't stay in here unconscious."

$ $ $ $ $

Giving Lu-Kay direct eye contact, I paused, thinking… thinking, I didn't want to kill Kenny because I had got what I came looking for. But then again he did put a gun to my face down at Luby's in front of a crowd of people, telling me that he was my worse fucking nightmare. A lot of fear was instilled in my heart after that night and to top it off he hurt the most precious thing that meant everything to a man who didn't deserve her.

"Fuck it," I said pointing the gun towards the floor where Kenny lied, unconsciously. DOOM-DOOM-DOOM-DOOM-DOOM! Five fierce shots penetrated Kenny's body and I didn't even have the courage to look.

As he gasped for air, I bent over and looked him into his eyes, as he took his last few breaths I said, "Recognize my face," pulling my masked down. "Who's having the nightmare's now?" In saying, I backed up and clapped to more shots into his chest, sealing the deal.

As Lu-Kay and I made out way out of the club into the parking lot, a squad car was cruising in our direction. From about fifty feet away, I froze when I got a visual of the cop car. The police officer grabbed his walkie-talkie, hit the wailer to the sirens and began to speed towards us. Lu-Kay started shooting at the cop's front windshield, screaming, "Get the fuckin' car… Get the Car!"

While Lu-Kay covered for me I sprinted towards the parking lot, the cop and Lu-Kay began having a shoot-out similar to Wild West, under the clear night sky but the only difference was the officer had on a vest. Backing the Saab up in reverse, I positioned the rear of the car towards the cop and stepped on the gas, in full throttle, aiming to run the cop over. But, in return he fired a couple of shots into the back windshield and dove to the side before I could get close.

Simultaneously, I pushed the gear in drive and opened the car door for Lu-Kay to get in but he was still banging of shots at the cop. The cop recovered from his dive and raced towards the driver side of his squad car. But before the cop could get into full stride, I raged like a NASCAR driver and hit the gas once more. It was a Kodak moment when I hit the cop, flashing lights were everywhere, and he froze in mid-air before I hit him. After driving over him one time, I just knew the cop was dead but, just for reassurance that he was, I backed the car up and drove over him again. And then rode over him a third time before Lu-Kay exited the vehicle and put two fiery metal shells in his anatomy. In turn we skirted off in high velocity down Ferry Avenue with two duffle bags of money and two homicides too run concurrent, without looking back. And, just that quick I had forgot what had taken place.

Lu-Kay and I went to my spot on 7th street in Chelton Terrace after we disposed the guns and clothing evidence. We sat in the house counting money and we were about four blocks away from the murder scene. Evidently, Kenny an Poohshaun had to be selling twenty dollar bags of smack because all the stacks of money that were counted to be recounted had nothing but Andrew Jackson faces.

Angrily, under my skin I was burning more than a raging bull, due to the fact that we only wounded up with $560,000 dollars after all of the plotting and scheming Lu-Kay and I did to get to this point; and only $280,000 was my cut. I felt like going back to the Two Ways Inn to shoot Kenny's fat ass a couple of more times.

"I told you... I told you Kenny wasn't in pocket like everyone thought he was," Lu-Kay said, confirming his assumptions. "But, what should we expect from a middle man who played puppet to the Dominicans? That's who we need to be getting, them different language bean eating muthafuckas."

"Slow down Lu, one thing at a time Pa', besides the Dominicans wasn't who Kenny was working for."

"What! And how you know that?"

"Let's just say I was the man who set next to the man, who sat next to a bunch of men that validated Kenny's slave man's position."

"So who's in the position much higher if it's not the Dominicans?"

"Two cats by the names of Riley and Domino."

"Riley and Domino… Riley and Domino," Lu-Kay muttered to himself. "Nope, the names don't ring a bell."

"Remember the saying, the greatest trick the devil ever was making the world believe that he didn't exist?"

"Of course because that's me and I made the statement up." Lu-Kay humored himself.

"Well other than you Mr. Funny man, that's Riley and Domino the two ghost of this underworld money."

"So without Kenny in existence Riley and Domino are worthless to us."

"Not quite my boy because there are a lot more ghost floating around behind the two enormous spirit's haunting seasons. That a lot of the drug underworld has yet to see or hear about. You know in this secret society no one can be trusted."

"So how do we catch them?"

"By playing Pac-Man, get as much information to this unsolved puzzle as we possibly can… Chase nothing and allow everything to fall into place and come to us. Then we go after everyone but first we must play by ear."

"Who do we start with first now that Kenny's out of the way?'

"Kenny's man Poohshaun, he's our main target."

When Lu-Kay and I finished discussing our future plans about getting to Riley and Domino, it was the crack of dawn. I was extremely tired, feeling like I had a bad case of insomnia that happened to back fire on me and emasculated my soul. Right before I headed out to take Lu-Kay to his destination, I called Lamaar to see if she needed anything before I took it in for the remainder of the day. But, before I could say one word Lamaar hung the phone up in my ear, it was obvious that she was mad at me for staying out half the night.

"Lamaar… Hello… Lamaar," I said, hoping my mind wasn't playing tricks on me.

"Man, I know you didn't just call Kenny's Dame after just killing the muthafucka?" Lu-Kay was perplexed by the endeavor, as I kept trying to call back.

"Of course, why shouldn't I? She's been my misses for months now, the girl and the gold is how I move. I want it all not just some of the shit."

"You jiving' me my man, you fucking Lamaar Green from Fairview? I find that hard to believe."

"Well believe it slim like you believe in the man upstairs or you can call her for yourself to get validation," I said, opening my car door.

"I've wanted some of that trim since '73, nigga you scored big time… Damn! Since six grade, I was chasing that lucky star." He had the serious look on his face that said, nigga I'm jealous but I envy you for now.

Lamaar was just leased pussy in my eyes, we weren't married and she wasn't my sweet cattle or nothing, I was just her handsome young thing. Besides there was no harm in Lu-Kay's freedom to speak on his past feelings of infatuation. It wasn't like Lu-Kay was screwing her… Then again?

"So you always had a thing for my redbone huh?" It was time for me to manipulate the situation.

"Hell yea daddy-o I was a sucker for that pretty face, playing fool in front of the boys when she walked through with her crew. She took all my lunch money."

"All of it?"

"All five dollars worth of it, she was that fine in my eyes."

"Blood since I respect game I'm a return the favor for a favor… Here take this." I gave him my house number. "I've known you too long to let some whore come between us."

"Kyle, man nah I can't take this," He said, feeling awkward, trying to hand the number back to me. As I focused on the road ahead, I pushed the paper back to him, making my point concrete.

"Give her a call," I said, thinking of one of the oldest tricks in the book, hoping Lu-Kay didn't fall for it and hurt my pride. "Let's see how honest and true the whore really is, she hasn't shown her true colors to me yet. Everything is still in dog vision right now. If she bites the bait, then we gut the fish."

"And if I do get to bone her, then what?"

"Then you'll have your wish come true and I'll be the fool next time who fell for the pretty face, ya' dig?"

"My man," he replied giving me a pound as I pulled in front of his residence.

"Call between the hours of two and four o'clock, she's always home then."

"Solid. I'll be sure to do just that but you just let me know when you get something on those two unknowns, Riley and Domino," he stated, shutting the car door as I waved him off in unison, pulling away from the curb.

$ $ $ $ $

Later that night, I awoken to a clamorous television, having all of my clothes on, after falling asleep on my cream leather sofa; I don't even remember going into the living room after I got home. It felt like my mind was playing tricks on me because it sounded like strange noises were coming form the kitchen.

"Lamaar... Lamaar!" I yelled, hoping that she was upstairs in bed but I got no response.

The numbers on my watch displayed a time of 7:15 p.m. and, half of my day went by through the cause of me sleeping. While checking the messages on my answering service, my shower water ran in mist of steaming the bathroom. The first few messages were from Lamaar's girlfriends who called more than bill collectors. As I undressed and skipped the unimportant ones, the last message that came in was marked urgent. It was a message from Dontae...

"Kyle this is Dontae, I hit the jackpot on her number and the location. Some nigga she's been dealing with for a while across town in Sycamore Court apartments... A few blocks from Krystal's lounge. His name is Johnny Price and the Address is building G, apartment number 4. If your going to make a move it has to be quick, my first court date is scheduled for next week... Later!"

The location I knew exactly. My Aunt Laura and her daughter Stephanie lived in a house in that vicinity on Mt. Vernon Street; which happened to be a block over. Instantaneously, I picked up the phone and dialed my Aunt Sissy's number. She picked up on the first ring, like she was running a fast food business or something.

"Aunt Sissy," I said, calmly after she answered.

"Who Dis'?"

"Kyle, mama."

"Oh, hey nephew what brings you to call me this time of the day?"

"Damn! What's all that noise in the background?"

"My company, playing pinochle with the radio blasting, but what's up though? You need me to hook you up with some of my girls on the track?" She laughed a little to her own humor.

"Remember that favor I told you I would need from you and your sisters a few years back?"

"I suppose so, boy you know my brain is fried past a boiling point from all the drugs I done used, so just remind me of the favor."

"I need you and your twins to meet me down at Krystal's lounge tomorrow night around eleven o'clock."

"Now you know tomorrow's the reunion." My Aunt Sissy was extremely family oriented, she was like a grandmother, sister, mother, and cousin enwrapped in one when it came to our family.

"I no that but I'm talking 'bout when the reunion is over."

"We'll talk tomorrow at the park, I have to go nephew I got this damn food on the stove and I don't want it to burn. Come by and get a plate."

"Aiight then, I might stop by... Later."

I called Dontae after I hung up with my aunt and reiterated the same message that I told my aunt. In an unhesitant response, Dontae told me that he would be prompt and wouldn't miss it for the world. The nails were intact and if everyone played their position, everything would go smooth.

While the steamed, hot shower water relaxed my muscle tissue, I stood under the water in deep thought. I'd become one of the devil's angels over night with mischievous thoughts of harm, lies, stealing, and killing all for the wrong reasons. I sold my soul to him for no apparent reason or I guess to conquer what made others superstars in the game - Money! Or, maybe it was to take the easy way out in life because I was just that lazy and afraid of working hard to achieve success.

"Ugh!" I said, frightened from the feel of Lamaar's cold hands caressing my chest.

With closed eyes, I could hear her weep and moan cries of hurt, I had no idea why she felt this way. I turned to face her and held her agonized face in the palm of my wet hands. I seen the tear's of Kenny Morales' death stream down her face, as she held me close. Truly speechless, I didn't want to feel her pain, or let alone say something that I didn't mean for the betterment of her well being because that nigga had to go. I was the master mind behind Kenny's death, the cold hearted guy that she fell in love with. I wanted badly to say, "Why cry, you got what you asked for, Right?" But that would just have made matters worse and I would have been showing my ace in the whole then.

"Love is so crazy, and it can in many mysterious ways that we'll never come to understand. It really doesn't take effect until after the person is no longer with you."

Lamaar cried out to me like a newborn baby as if she lost her first, her last, her everything. There were better days to come, then again maybe there wasn't any for her to gain because in heart they came and went with Kenny. I mean for me, by the minute, I knew my days were numbered and deemed horrific through every breath I took. Because of the love I dishes out was a mere potion of evil and, slowly but shortly it was destined to haunt me. 'Cause what went around came back around twice as hard as the first blow.

# Chapter. 10

The yearly celebrated day of hard work in America rolled around, and I felt that the holiday should have at least been honored once a month because citizens of America have been putting in laborious efforts since the beginning of time. Ironically, all of my hard work was done in the wicked streets but it was still some type of labor.

The sun was shining giving the atmosphere the feel of bliss, and the air's aura was smooth giving of a nice breeze of spring down at Cooper River Park. The family reunion jumped off to a great start, many of my little cousins was playing joyously, and the adults were talking like they were at a stock market convention. Slouched back on one of the pick-nick tables, I was enjoying my barbecue rib plate with macaroni and cheese. Too reticent for anyone's conversation, I didn't have too much to say, especially to the family members I only got see once a year. When there weren't any type of family events or funerals to attend, none of my family members were in contact with no other family member; even in case of an emergency. The triplets and my Uncle Muscles were exceptions to the family's rule because they were always available to any person in the family's needs.

$$\$ \$ \$ \$$$

My grandmother Ann had ten children whom she raised through many labored days on her own. My mother's other siblings were my other three aunts, May-May, Arlena, and Carole who were Baptist cultured. The three of them were very distant, especially my Aunt May-May she traveled and moved more than a person in the service. I never got to see them as much but it was wise because half of my family was impractically disordered. My Aunt Carole lived in the area of Cooper River Park, the Pennsauken environment where the cops were deemed racist and didn't too many blacks reside.

I had two other Uncles whom also were twins (Will and Lovell), whom resided in the Atlanta - the mother land of black people. They came back home more than they needed to like they were scared of the southern culture that the Peach state hade to offer.

"Hey son," My mother said, taking a set next to me. "I haven't heard from you in a week or so, what's been up?"

"Nothing too much mommy, just been taking it easy," I replied, playing with my little sister Aniyah.

"You found a job yet?"

"Com'on Livy not right now!" I really wasn't trying to hear the ethical tirade.

"Yeah ok, you aren't going to be nothing but a bum just like you daddy." What a way to denigrate my character before I even reached the firm stages of adulthood. I guess she figured since I lived on my own I had no other choice but to be as I lived.

"Well if you were with the bum I wouldn't be following suit, now would I?"

"Boy don't get your damn teeth knocked out all over this park... And where's Lamaar? I haven't seen her red ass in about a week either. "

"Who knows, every since her old boyfriend got murdered her mind hasn't been right since."

As we continued to converse, I finally got up enough guts to asked my mother why she and my pops weren't together after all these years? She retorted that he was to busy living the fast life and indulging himself into crime and drugs; she couldn't be bothered. She deplored the fact that she even introduced my Uncle Muscle to my pops before my conception in her womb. Because they probably would have still been together, she even told me about his cheating and deceitful ways through affairs with my Aunt Gracey. I always wondered why she and my aunt rarely got along or even spoke half the time they were in each others presents.

My Uncle Muscles and True showed their faces at the reunion, as always they both became the center of the reunion's attention.

While all of my other family members inundated his space, I didn't even bother to confront him. I made my way back to the cooking grill for some more of those savory ribs that my Uncle Will was saucing up.

"Damn Nephew, if you eat any more ribs your not going to have none your damn self," Uncle Will said, jokingly as he flipped burgers on the back grill.

"As long as you keep them coming like this, the ones your cooking will protect me."

"Ahahahahahaha." His drunken ass couldn't help but laugh as he downed a can of Old Milwaukee beer.

After I finished throwing back three more of my Uncle Will's tender ribs, I gathered up my aunts to discuss and layout the mission that was going to take place later on. The four of us walked over to the brink of the Park's lake to communicate.

"I need the three of you to meet me at Krystal's tonight," I said, in a whisper as we stood in a close huddle.

"For what? What's going on?" Aunt Debbie asked, unaware of what I told my Aunt Sissy.

Elucidating the entire situation to them, I told them that I need a move handle tonight because my life was in jeopardy. I told them to meet me at eleven o'clock sharp and I would fill them in from there, we all agreed mutually to what was proposed about the arranged mission.

I played a few games of pity pat with my three cousins, Wadeelah, her brother Mobart, and their little sister Malika who was ten years old. While the rest of my family enjoyed the exuberance of being together before the silent season of autumn arrived.

"Hol' four, seven," Mobart said, throwing out the seven of club.

"Hol' seven dirty four," Malika retorted, as it was on me to pluck. I plucked into a wild deuce, and threw a queen.

"Ha, Deuce! Take this nasty whore."

"Hol' nasty whore, I'm out, "Wadeelah said, gleefully. While shuffling the cards Wadeelah revealed that she saw DaVita at the Pennsauken Mart up Rt. 130, inside the Eric 5 movie theater a few nights ago. Telling Wadeelah that it was urgent that I contacted her,

DaVita didn't explain why I needed to get into contact with her, she just needed to talk to me.

"Did she give you a number or some sort of contact information so I could do so?"

"Nope, Nothing. And, I didn't bother to ask." Go figure, I thought, how bright of her not to, it must have been insignificant anyhow. My Uncle Muscles walked over to our table as we continued playing cards.

"What's up Uncle Muscles," Everyone said, in unison and kind manner.

"Nieces and Nephews," he answered, giving everyone hugs and handshakes.

Uncle Muscles stayed with us and played a few hands of pity-pat before secluding himself from the table, to enlighten me on unsettled issues that he'd been running into; we went to his car to converse.

"So you and Auntie True are back together again I see?" I said, wondering what went wrong between him and Terry.

"Yeah, we finally settled our differences."

"I thought use never went wrong in the first place."

"We definitely did due to my carelessness of playing both sides of the fence. I committed and bonded myself to one of True's relatives prior to meeting True, and the relationship didn't turn out how I expected it too. Plus, I was flippant back in my younger days of courting and now my past has caught up with me."

'So, you still haven't heard a word from Terry yet?"

"No not yet, I'm really not looking forward to talking to her, she's become one of the biggest misapprehensions to me and my illegitimate business. She's been hireling me to get ahead this entire time."

"I knew it, I fuckin' knew it," I expressed, angrily. She's been the problem, but how did you discern the mysterious problems?"

"When you've been in the game since age fifteen, you begin to speculate preposterous situations. But, the entire time I was in the penitentiary Terry was my blind eyes in the streets."

"But, wasn't she giving True insight on--"

"Terry only told True what she wanted her to know, so it couldn't benefit me. Terry's a very phenomenal intellectual and been in the game long as I have... She knows the game like no other."

"So what about the fifty thousand dollars that she and Billy allegedly gave True a month, of your profit?"

"I came to find out that that was a bunch of lies, I had no profits or incoming money on their behalves of the streets when I was away. Because we had no nexus to gain or earn nothing from. Bippy and I arranged a few deals and agreed to put our business on hold until I touched back down. Now what Terry and Billy did on the side didn't concern me at all. But, Billy told me that he was giving True ten-thousand on the here and there so that her needs wouldn't become insatiable. Out of his own pocket, he offered it to True. Billy had enough money to last him the entire six years that I was away, he didn't have to interact with Terry at all. His affluence went beyond Terry's greedy influences."

So that was one of Terry's reasons of becoming interrelated with Kenny Morales, to leech off of his necessities.

"So what, was Terry broke or something?"

"I don't know nephew, when I was behind the wall though she use to write me letters stating that she was struggling and she needed me home so she could stabilize herself again. When I came home she was so fucked up that she had moved back down south to Florida with her mother. But, I called for her to come back... Brought her a six bedroom home out in Moorestown and gave her the house of chemistry, along with three-hundred thousand to easy her pocketbook pain. Blew a half million on her alone and I wasn't back where I needed to be yet."

I sat on the plush leather interior, tranquil, listening and envisaging everything he was explaining to me.

"I know she blew her money on materialistic things, trying to maintain her hedonistic way of living and probably was snorting that blow in the same tune. But, that's a woman for you nephew, the key to success but every successful man's downfall."

"So how did signals get crossed between you and Bippy?"

"Terry! She was nagging me about some sweet deal that Bippy had in store for us. Instead of thinking twice about what it was I was about to get myself into, my thoughts became inured and I just reacted. Thinking we were going to get over some how and it was going to be a major come up. All in all, I was the one getting fucked and Bippy came up a squandering one point two million. So, after the move went bad for me, Terry moved along with it. I'm so disenchanted with myself for being so careless, I got to get the whore smoked before she comes with a more diminishing idea."

"Just say the word uncle and I'll leave that whore in tomato juice, ya dig?"

"It's dug nephew, enough said," he replied, slapping me some skin.

Malignant to the streets anyhow, murder had become my new fetish and my trigger finger itched terribly to put gun powder in Terry's melon. As I opened the car door, maneuvering to exit, True was approaching.

"Hey chocolate," she said, smoothly gliding the back of her hand across my cheek.

"Gulp," My throat replied, I became reticent and my mouth just wouldn't open to release a single word. "He-hey auntie True." I stammered in speech but that was the first time True ever touched or came that close to me. She was even more voluptuous up close. She was the epitomized black Barbie of the 80's; Phylicia Rashad before Clare on the Cosby show.

"Lamont," she said, fluently, leaning over in the car's window. I eased my way back towards the barbecue as they began to converse.

"Later nephew'," my uncle yelled, tooting the horn to seal the deal. I glanced back, threw my arm up in the air with a closed fist as I strutted on.

Five hours or so in the park, things started to seem repetitive, talking to the same person twice, saying the same shit over and over like I was in rehearsal; I was truly bored and tired. I paid my last respects and regards to my grandmother Ann, my mother, and a few other relatives. I had to get out of the park before the liquor took its' toll on my relatives and their intoxication went from pervasive language to violent flurries.

There was a fiesta frenzy taking place down at Krystal's lounge when Dontae and I arrived around nine-thirty. The dance floor was very energetic, people's feet were mobilized by the oldies, and the bar was flooded with a lot of overwrought foxes, whores, lames, and original gangsters. Dontae and I were by far the youngest two in the joint, but due to the respect and strength of my Uncle Muscles, I was able to enter most of the over twenty-one, after hour establishments in town.

Dontae and I copped a spot at the bar and began talking about old times over a few shots of cognac. My Aunt Laura, my grand-mother's sister from my pop's side, sent a few drinks to us that were on the house; they came in oodles. I was taking the shots down like glasses of tap water. Three shots in and my mind felt like a lingering heaven, my mood altered into elation.

"Yo' slim your eyes are glassy then a muthafucka," Dontae said, giving me a gawking look. "It looks like you smoked a nice spliff of that green rhino."

"Get the fuck out of here nigga," I said, gazing around the bar to see if I seen the whore Dana. "I'm Chinese, but I like chins on knees... Get it?" Dontae burst into an annoying laugh, from my corny as joke. I didn't see what the fuck was so amusing to him, I guess because the joke was on me.

"I wonder if the hoe of beauty Dana still own this joint?"

"Who?"

"Nobody my man, talking to myself," I retorted, taking down another shot of the sweet taste of ginger flavored brandy. "I'll be right back, going to take a piss."

'Watch your step, don't trip into no chins on knees," Dontae replied, jokingly.

Speaking of the devil, just as I was making my way into the men's bathroom, Dana and I crossed paths.

"Heeeey Dangerous," I said, very drunk founded from the potent liquor that my aunt offered. "I just was whispering your name." Dana gave me a ogling stare from head to toe, without saying a word she kissed me and then whispered in unison, "You can have this pussy anytime you want it," Softly in to my earlobe. I smirked at her passionate statement and returned the whisper, "And so can you, fair exchange isn't a robbery in my eyes."

I turned and entered the men's room; the urinal seemed to far away so I almost pissed on the floor. Until, Dana gripped me from behind and said, "Allow me to control that for you daddy." She held my dick in a firm position while I pushed yellow water.

Dana then put the lock on the bathroom door, and in haste our freaky natures took over. In fierce passion, I slammed her back up against the bathroom wall, dropping my pants and simultaneously she lifted her black, rayon fabric dress above her stomach and locked one of her legs around the edge of my back. Once the permeation process was in full effect, Dana moaned in soft whispers of gratification.

"Mmmmm," Dana sighed, resting her head upon my shoulder. "Keep me dripping' daddy... Um-Hmm." My mind was elsewhere's, I couldn't even respond to her lustful statement if I wanted to, I had wonderland reveries of butterfly tingles as I watched a million unclad Dana's dance around me. The liquor was talking to me but my dick was walking for me, between Dana's sultry peaches it was hard for me to concentrate.

"Umm, what do you know about these two jokers name Riley and Domino?" I asked, gyrating inside of her.

"Ri-ley... Ah, aaaaah... Riley and Domino are two... Invisible, underworld drug lords to these streets. They own... Ah! Own a lot of lucrative businesses, auto shops, grocery stores, and the Two Ways inn night club. Their biggest investment is the Glamour Towers."

My pace in stroke slowed drastically once I heard the Glamour Towers roll from her tongue, my uncle was doing business with them bastards and didn't even know it. It was Terry who brought the condominiums to me and Muscles' attention. "What else do you know?" I continued, putting my tongue in and around her ear.

"Their relatives to Lamont Muscles dame Te-eeerry." I couldn't stroke no more after I heard Terry's name, I paused and held Dana as firm as I could.

"Thank you," I said, kissing her cheek."I appreciate all of you even the information."

"No Chocolate," she said, "I appreciate all of you and I render my sincerity and my pussy to you willingly." Dana slid her fingers across my lips, placing the scent of her sweet nectar under my nose.

Dana fixed he black scarf above her head, pulled her dress down and walked out of the bathroom like nothing ever happened. I, on the other hand splashed a few sprinkles of water of hot water over my face, trying to awaken my mind to sobriety.

"Damn! What the fuck slim did you flush your head in the toilet or something?" Dontae asked in a chuckling manner. "You've been in there for about a half hour

"Nah, my man I flushed it somewhere else... Did my aunts arrive yet?" I downed one of his drinks.

"Yeah they been here for about a half hour now, waiting on you to finish up with Foxy Brown over there," he said, pointing towards Dana at the bar. "There over by the jukebox."

$ $ $ $ $

Dressed for a dirty mission my aunts looked as if they were going to rob the joint, their game faces were on and they were dressed in all black. As I approached them, signaled with my hand for them and Donate to follow me outside.

We went to the rear of my car which was parked on a side street next to Krystal's, I popped the trunk and handed each of my aunts a pair of gloves, a ski mask a piece, and three brand new Louisville sluggers.

"Here's the address," I said, handing my aunt Debbie the piece of paper. "She's in apartment 4, building G in the Sycamore complexes. Make it quick, clean and remain sullen when its' over. Knock that tattletale bitch out the park."

"Nothing but homeruns nephew," Aunt Sissy said, smacking her hand with the bat.

"Grand slam that hoe," Aunt Gracey retorted with a smirk.

"Look! Just get in and get back here, so I can destroy the evidence."

Dontae went back into Krystal's to get a fried chicken platter, and some more cognac with a few brews. I remained in the car, seat slouched back, air-conditioner blowing, as thoughts of my aunts getting the job done roamed through my head. I prayed to myself, hoping that none of them were high or had cataclysm syndrome, because they were known for fucking up. But, I swore on my own soul that, "I loved my aunts with all the oxygen in my body." But, if they so happened to fuck this one up and, somehow got caught or questioned about Spring's murder. The three of them were dead meat, because pressure burst pipes and when a person's back is up against the wall, matters worsened; especially with a female. 'Please God, don't let me have to do some thing to my aunts,' I thought to myself with my eyes closed.

Dontae returned to the car with two, quarter glasses of brandy and two Miller Light beers. I wasn't too fond of drinking beer so I tossed the two Lights in the backseat. Extremely inebriated, we continued reminiscing on the good ol' days of our childhood together. Laughing at the times he use to chase me home from elementary school, and how I made the big payback in the third grade; I beat him up. After that we became closer than most brothers and sisters were growing up under the same roof.

"A slim," Dontae said, shaking my hand. "Through it all you showed me nothing but respect and, don't let anyone tell you otherwise." He hugged me with every piece of vim in his body; it was an emotional moment for the both of us, and tears began streaming down my face as if I just lost someone close to me.

An abrupt knock came up against the driver side window; it was my aunt Debbie, whom scared the life out of me. "Is it done?" I asked, leaning up against the car.

"Yeah mission accomplished," Aunt Debbie said, in confidence.

"Grand slam nephew just like I said earlier," Aunt Gracey add.

"You all didn't leave any traces of evidence to where it can incriminate any of you right?" I asked, scrutinizing their safety.

"Nope, none what-so-ever," Aunt Sissy replied, in her own honesty. Taking all of the dirty evidence and placing it in the trunk of my car.

My aunts told me exactly what took place in building G, on the second floor in apartment 4. They allowed my aunt Gracey to elucidate what transpired, since she was the loud one of the three. Gracey reflected that when the three of them arrived at the apartment, Aunt Sissy unscrewed the hallway light by the staircase. So that no one in the other apartment complexes could recognize them. Without looking through the peep hole, Spring answered the door like she was waiting for someone who had just left out, to return; elusively avoiding the presence of strangers. With medium force aunt Debbie smacked her across the forehead, only to knock her unconscious. Aunt Sissy dragged Spring's body from the door into the living room, while Gracey and Debbie groped around the apartment in the dark, checking for any other roaming bodies. Evidently, Spring was home alone and, in twenty second flat she was beaten from head-to-toe, Mob style. Aunt Gracey grabbed a sheet from one of the beds in the house and neatly coved Summer's corpse with it, prior to exiting the apartment how they entered - meek an quiet.

"Smooth, very smooth," I said, giving them hugs. "I'll call you all tomorrow."

"Sure thing," Aunt Sissy replied, as the three of them headed to her car.

Dontae and I hopped back in the Saab and pulled away from the area of party and crime. "It's over baby, now I can get some fucking rest," Dontae said, taking the last guzzle of his beer.

"So you still haven't seen or heard from your pops huh?" I asked, wanting to take him off count as well.

"Nah, the dirty muthafucka hasn't crossed my path in a while, I don't even remember the last time I seen him. A slim pull over by that alleyway up ahead." He pointed to one of the day trenches near the row homes on 9th street, near Atlantic Avenue.

"Where right here?"

"Yeah, it don't matter, I got to piss like a race horse," he said, quickly exiting the car.

"Yea, me too," I uttered, silently cocking the handle back on the 9 millimeter handgun I had stashed away under the seat of the car.

Dontae was so in tuned with the concentration of his urination process; he wasn't even paying me any mind. I crept around the back of the Saab and tiptoed behind him in the dark alleyway. He didn't even have the chance to face death; I just put the hammer to the back of his head and squeezed off two shots. Instantaneously, opening up his cranium.

"Sometimes love hurts muthafucka," I said, spitting on him before I jumped back into the Saab, skirting off down 9th street like I was on a high speed chase with the fuzz.

I couldn't leave one without the other; Dontae was already hot as fish grease, famous to the media and local newspapers in town. When homicide found his cousin Spring's body, eventually the police would have charged him with her murder because she was their informant. Three homicides and a robbery dangling over his head, who knew what his capabilities would have turned out to be after them damn federal agents would have been throwing basketball numbers in his face. I was conspired to both unlawful acts, if he would have told on my aunts. It was probable that they would have drug me in as well. And, going down for conspiracy to 1st degree murder and robbery, I couldn't afford it; my time was about flipping dead presidents. My time was borrowed and I was trying to live life lavishly like there was no tomorrow.

$ $ $ $ $

I received a very unusual phone call the very next day, it wasn't a complete twenty-four hours since the last time I'd been up and the damn phone kept ringing and ringing; making me so infuriated.

"Hel-lo," I answered in a tiresome tone.

"Kyle we have to talk," The unusual voice said, on the other end.

"I'm not talking to nobody that I don't even know over this jack... Jack! Who am I speaking with, might I ask?"

"This is DaVita."

"DaVita!" I exclaimed, looking over my shoulder to see if Lamaar was still in bed but, luckily she wasn't there. As I wonder where Lamaar crept to, it was marveling to me how DaVita retrieved my phone number.

"How--"

"I got the number from Lamaar a few days ago so I could contact you," She said, being a big dictation to my conscience. "Is she home? If you don't mind me asking?"

"No, she's probably at work."

"Oh okay, but moving on, I'm starting to regret the fact that you compelled me to acquaint myself with fucking Poohshaun."

"Why would you regret such a thing? He does not own up to his manhood?"

"He's a very insecure and derange person, he's going through some kind of disarrangements or something. He doesn't allow me to move, picks fights all the time, locking me in the house and even putting guns to my head. I snuck out the house to make this phone call, he's like my own personal watch dog or some shit."

"Call the fuzz up," I answered, having no better advice to give her.

"Kyle, I don't do the untrue blue thing, that's so beneath me."

"Well, what do you want me to do?"

"Can you talk to him for me, beat him up... Just do something. My feelings for him have become very adverse and reluctant; I'm scared to leave him though because he may kill me or something."

"You got him like that? He's just pussy whipped that's all."

"Please, I hardly fuck his chubby ass, I wish my dad or pop-pop was still alive because he would have been an unsolved mystery."

Questioning DaVita about Jimmy or Chucky wasn't in my intentions of the conversation; as if I didn't already know. I didn't want to prolong the conversation no more than I had to.

"Shit. Scare him with a gun like you did me years ago."

"I was only playing with you, besides I don't even have a gun."

"Steal one from him... Look! When I run into buddy I'll talk to him, okay?"

"Alright... Kyle."

"Yes DaVita." I was becoming annoyed.

"You know I still have feelings for you right? Even though I know that you with my friend and all, I still want that perfect relationship with you."

"We do have a relationship… A platonic one as friends."

"I want more than a common friendship--"

My line click, interceding DaVita's mysterious truths and feelings about me but, bad as I didn't want to click over and accept the other call; DaVita was becoming a nag. I placed her on hold and click over to the person on the other line.

"Hello."

"Nephew this is your Aunt Sissy, I'm calling to tell you that your Uncle Muscles was shot last night." I was at a lost of words, completely silent on the other end of the phone. My legs trembled with nervous tension and I caught an instant headache.

"Is he dead?" Tears rolled down my face from the horrible news.

"No, but he's listed in critical condition and they say he might not make it."

"So what hospital is he in?"

"He's at West Jersey Hospital and majority of the family is already there."

Unintentionally, through the rage of frustration I hung the phone up in my aunt's ear. It was ignorant of me but I was in a rush to get to the hospital. The phone rang with consistence as I made my way out of the door, I kind of figure it was DaVita calling back but she just had to leave a message.

Most of my family was in the hospital when I arrived at the emergency room, near the corner of Mt. Ephraim and Atlantic Avenues. They all were in a serene but disappointing manner when I walked in. My mother and aunts were trying to calm my grandmother Ann down, as I tearfully made my way toward them.

After emotionally overcoming my hurt with everyone in attendance and, sharing feelings of pain with my grand mom, Billy and I took a walk outside to discuss the situation. "So what are they saying happened?" I asked, hoping that Billy had some type of information on what had taken place the night before.

"Word is, is that Muscles and True were coming out of Internationals, the corner bar that sits on Chase and Persian streets--"

"Yeah I know where that is." I cut Billy off because I didn't need the location; I wanted to get straight to the point.

"And it's said that two muthafuckas hopped out a car and start shooting at both of them."

"No description on the car... The model? Was True shot too?"

"There was no make on the car or who the shooters were and True was wounded also," Billy said, fixing the crease on the top of his tan brim hat, as his five-foot-three frame looked up at me to converse. "She was hit twice, in her left shoulder and once in her hip. Doctors said she was hit with two four-five rounds and, your uncle was hit in the back with a twelve-gage at close range."

"What you think, Terry's work?"

"If the shoe fits."

Billy and I continued conversing, through devised plans on how we were going to retaliate on Terry, if found. She was the malignant bitch behind the inscrutable mask of drug underworld harm. Every time something rigorous happened, she was incognito but the cause to a lot of fatal mishaps. We both felt that if we were mistakenly wrong, Terry would be just one person we would have to grow without as life moved on.

I went to the main lobby to get a hospital pass from the lobby's secretary so I could go and visit True on the six floor. There was really nothing to talk to True about; I just wanted to pay my sincere respects. The observation was unbelievable when I entered True's room and seen Ms. Thornton in tears by her bed side.

Truly in doubt, I was perplexed as I slowly ambled over to True's bedside, Janice's face was very much marveled when she seen me enter the recovery room. Behind the tears and agony, I felt that Ms. Thornton had some doubts of her own and, speculated on the unknown about True and I.

From a distance, I observed True reposed in a peaceful sleep; the tragic incidents didn't phase her mere beauty one bit. She still looked like God's guardian angel that was in my presence a day prior.

"Let me speak to you out in the hallway," I said, motioning my fingers towards myself, in front of Janice. She sat her belongings on the chair and trailed me into the hallway.

"What are you doing here? I asked, very confused.

"What I'm doing here has more sustenance than your own reasons for being here. So, why are you here?"

"For my uncle, but I came up here to see how his wife was doing."

"Your uncle!" She exclaimed, loud enough that the entire patient floor could have been disturbed by it. She then covered her mouth prior to observing both ends of the corridor.

Down the end of the hall, away from True's room sat another small waiting area where Janice and I went to finish our puzzling conversation.

"Let's start from the beginning?" she asked, needing confirmation, I guessed. "So Lamont Williams also known to many as Lamont Muscles is your uncle?"

"Yup, he's my grandmother's oldest boy of ten, my mother's big brother. So in turn I ask again what are you doing here and who is True to you?"

"When I heard that True, my baby sister... Had been shot, I cam as quickly as I could to be here for her." Carefully, as I scrutinized the situation at hand, I picked Jackie's brain a bit at a time, I needed to know all that I was blind to pertaining to the connecting dots; not just some of the shit.

"A couple of years back I truly recall you going through a stage of depression. Frantically, out of aggravation over your husband, you were using illicit drugs such as weed and dope to calm the anxiety. When you expressed your feelings to me, I really couldn't fathom the situation myself. It never took that much of an affect on me because it wasn't my problem to begin with. So, what I honestly want to know is whether True and my Uncle were the two individuals you were referring to a couple of years back at your summer home?"

"Yes," She replied, putting her palms over the streaming tears of a clown.

"There are still a few things that are throwing me for loops at a time and missing form this picture. If you married my uncle back in sixty-four and ten years later he marries True in seventy-four, how come its' just being brought to your attention a couple a years ago?"

"Muscles and I were never legally married, I just claimed him as my husband back in 1964. At that time my baby sister whom was all of sixteen began having a fling with Lamont but, this situation was very blind to my knowledge. I never pin-pointed the silent affair between the two because True lived in Vineland, a huge distance from me. Unaware of the fact that he and True shared a duplex home down there and, he was always on the go or in the streets. Muscles only had time for me when he had time, if you know what I mean? Our relationship was in the palm of his hands... On his time... He was the sole controller of everything."

"And your two daughters are by another man I suppose?"

"Yes, my twin daughters Janaya and Jazmine were through another man three years prior to Howard's acquaintance. But, in the same breath he was truly playing both sides of the fence. The situation became conclusive to me after he went to jail in 1978, True and I both were bumping heads on separate occasions trying to see him in that cold hell. He made visits for us on different days, but how I found out about him and True mingling with each other. He mailed True a birthday card and by accident put my address on the envelope, instead of hers. That's how everything began to unfold and go south for him."

Janice and True sat down and discussed the entire situation after everything was out in the open. True confessed, that on days Janice wasn't home or was working late, Muscles would furtively come to Janice's home to see True. They would partake in intercourses in Janice's bed, giving away her virginity to Lamont Muscles. There after he moved True out of her sister's home and to his residence down in the country; only to avoid trouble and for True to have her own privacy.

In the mist of the affair, Janice found explicit photos of True in their summer home out by the shore; where Janice tried committing suicide. Through an agreement, Janice and True went to see Muscles together after hatching out their frivolous feud with each other. Janice thought it was best if she kept her distance from Muscles and not be available for him or True. Scrupulously, Janice gave the both of them the cold shoulder, only to alleviate her pain.

On the other hand, True wanted a divorce, she felt entirely wretched for what she had done and the damages she caused to the relationship that she and Janice once possessed; she had to let Muscles go also. Muscles had been living in a state of oblivion for almost a year and a half prior to him being released. No visits, collect call acceptances, mail, nor was there a Janice or True there to worship his hard times. It was evident that the relationships he built from the bottom-up, with hopes of great prosperity, did nothing but become a putrid apple.

"So the stock broke title was the throw off for what Muscles was really apart of?" I asked, having more to say.

"Yeah, kind of, I gave Muscles that title after he helped my grandfather build his grocery store and cleaners from the ground up, which is known today to everyone as Young's grocery store. On the corner of 8th and Vanhook streets, parallel to Carl miller's funeral home."

"Mr. Young is your grandfather?" I asked, completely astonished.

Young's Grocery store was a prominent business in my neighborhood, old man young was this cool light skinned dude, who wore all kinds of dress hats, and held a toothpick in his mouth at all times. He was a very broad minded man about how his business operated. He had no enemies, even the thieves, beggars, and knuckle heads whom started trouble out in front of his store at times, respected Mr. Young for his principles of reasoning.

"He's my father's father."

"It's definitely a small fucking world I tell ya'."

"Majority of the money that Howard profited from the wicked streets of Camden was invested through me into certain business. Just so he could have some sort of legal income and wouldn't be broke at an old age. Part of my duty was to launder dirty money for him; he has about six-hundred thousand of legal assets covered in stocks and bonds under my name. "

I truly understood what Janice meant by having everything to lose and nothing to gain, she was the backbone of all that my uncle possessed and played a stupendous part in helping him build his drug empire from a pebble to an unreachable mountain. Genuinely worded, the women he used for his own personal gain were main keys to his success.

"Before concluding the conversation," I said, having more to unleash. "I don't know if you are or were aware of this but, the man you shared a fling with out of reckless temptation due to Muscles' carelessness, happens to be my sister's father."

"I was already aware of that fact," she implied, tearing even more from her own truths.

"I had this uneasy feeling, knowing that you were related to Donald or were close to him. Because as I reflect back, the house that I dropped you off at that night, was that same house Donald had taken me too during our fast affair."

"And, that was your reason for leaving that night that I got out of the car, when I went to go and see what type of chaos was taking place at my home? And, every since then you purposely loss contact with me."

"So true, plus I don't know if you and your mother know about this or not but Howard introduced your mother and I before. Back in our younger years of fun, I never met a face and the day she busted in the room with that bat in hand. I really couldn't believe my eyes and all the trouble I had caused. This entire tragic accident is because of me, if I wasn't so domineering and arrogant towards True and being such a priceless bitch, she would never be going through this," Janice muttered, crying over my shoulder, as I held her close.

After calming Janice's emotions and concluding our inscrutable conversation about True and Muscles amid her circumstances, I paid my respects to True once more. She was still at rest when we both returned to the room; I kissed her over the forehead before leaving her at peace. I gave Janice a new contact number where I could be reached just in case something else happened or if she just needed to vent a little. As I made my way off of the hospital floor, I hugged and kissed Janice goodbye and told her that we'd meet in the near future.

Billy was the only one left in the waiting area when I exited the elevator and came back into the lobby. Only to inform me that my uncle had made it through surgery but went into an abrupt coma. Billy Holmes was hurt on the inside, the pain garnished his face all to well but he maintained his composure externally. He and my uncle had been best friends since third grade; they thought as a pair and produced results as a team. He wasn't only my uncle's best friend and partner in crime; he also was my uncle's mentor at heart. Helping Muscles break his way through drastic trials and tribulations. Billy stated the fact that he and Muscles made their first million dollars from an ounce of heroin back in 1963. After linking up with Richie and Mikey, the tyrannized but departed Dominican brothers, Billy and Muscles never looked back.

Billy said the reason that everyone respected Lamont Muscles and loved him dearly was because he never denied anyone a piece of his fortune. If ever desperately in need, Muscles was the helping hand; "No," wasn't in his every day vernacular. "I'll try" or "I'll see what I can do," were positive words he would use to keep people's hopes up. The word "No" to Muscles was like denying people their own lives.

Billy expressed that he was through playing the cards that he was dealt as a teenager, in the game. Dealing with so many problems and sacrificing his life just to end up lying dormant in a coffin wasn't for him anymore. Especially since the person he looked and seen himself within, put niggas to rest for, and would die for, lied painfully in a coma. But, he said he couldn't remove himself from the game, like the champion he was until he accomplished one last mission. And that was putting the fierce dame Terry out of her misery. Backing his every word, I supported his decision one-hundred percent.

# Chapter. II

Proceeding along a week later, in contrary form I stood over Dontae's casket at Carl Miller's funeral home. All by myself at his viewing, my memory bank was completely vacuous about all the good and harsh times we shared. Extremely stuck on the fact that I put him out of his misery and disappeared off into the night as if he wasn't apart of my deficient discomfort of living. With no feelings of sarcasm, I blamed everything on his spirit flying cousin Spring, whose coffin was solemnly placed into the dirt days prior. As I glared at the marbled-brown coffin, I truly misapprehended how a whore came between us. Solicitously, in the serene atmosphere I said a prayer to God over Dontae's somnolent corpse; Asking God to forgive me for all the pain I'd caused.

In my eyes, Dontae was better off in heaven looking over me or in hell keeping it warm because life wasn't made out how everyone expected it to be. Felony after felony, robbery and murder in the first degree, life in the penitentiary for Dontae would cause him to commit suicide. Being erased and living in exclusion was best, for the both of them; matters were more at ease this way.

$$\$ \$ \$ \$$$

My pop Kyle Sr. appeared through the funeral's smog with in a blink of and eye, from out of nowhere. Jumping out of fear, my heart dropped as he put his hand over my shoulder from behind.

"Surprised to see me Marcus?" he asked, looking like the grim reaper, dressed in all black. "I'm quite sure you are because its' been a while since we've been in each others presence."

Wondering to myself, who or what brought him out of his inde-

149

cent cave to enter Carl Miller's funeral home and how did he know I was here? Kyle resembled an old orphan, a lost soul that deserved to be in Dontae's place. Badly, I wanted to ask him why wasn't he dead yet but I remained tranquil and allowed him to talk on.

"Let's go take a seat in the back of the funeral home so I can talk to you about a few things," Kyle said.

"Man are you crazy!" I exclaimed, in an intense volume, pushing his hand away from my shoulder.

"Shhh," He replied, placing a finer over his lips.

"I'm here going through a bereaved situation and you come in here wanting to talk in the back of a spooky ass funeral home. We can go outside and talk in a minute."

"Let me pay my respects to D.S.'s son and I'll be right out there."

"Hurry up because my time is limited." I stood out front for a few minutes before Kyle came over towards me with a bottle of liquor in his hand.

"What's the bottle for?" I asked, ostensibly concerned.

"It helps me get through my retrospective pain, something you don't need to do when you get my age. It's a very bad habit to get rid of," He implied, taking a swig of the poison.

"So what do you want to talk about, I don't have all night?"

"Let's walk."

"I don't need to walk I have a car."

"Come on Marcus let me just have ten minutes of your time."

Swallowing my pride, my pop and I strolled across the street from Young's grocery store to the Isabel Community Center - Known as the Pool - on the opposite corner of 8th and Vanhook streets; we took a seat on one of the cemented tables.

"Son, I understand your reasons for killing your home boy Dontae," he said, as I gave him a curious look. "I know your quite amazed about how I know, just know that it's not hard to connect the dots in a mysterious maze when you lived in the maze your entire life. You come from my testicles son, you have my genes, and we're A-A likes but two different entities. You think how I done already thought, doing what I already did many years ago."

The gibberish language that Big Kyle was talking went in one ear and out the other, one of my aunts probably told him the Spring situation and, he linked it to the Dontae issue; he was connecting dots from someone else's hearsay.

"Since I've been destroying myself in these horrifying streets for the past thirty odd years, I've seen a lot of my friends leave here unwillingly. Not from old age either, but from wretched materials which happens to be priceless in this blind world. Money, jewelry, flaxen clothes, cars... You know shit people appreciate with merits but, when they're gone the valuables that they once possessed are left here. Now I know you're wondering where I'm going with this but listen son if you going to cherish that omnipotent dollar more than you cherish you're morality, you're going to lose in this here life. Cherish you're temple because nobody is going to take care of you like your going to take care of yourself. Be smart, don't take the horrific road that your old pappy done traveled into, it's nothing but a death trap."

"Man, the shit you're saying, I done learned already on my own terms but, now that I'm grown up you want to offer some kind of fuckin' guidance. I think if you took a minute to hear yourself talk, you maybe more fortunate than you already are. Guzzling that waste--"

"Hey! Enough got-damn-it," Kyle exclaimed, in aggravated tone. "Now you may think that you're grown but you're still a boy to me... My boy and I am still your father. Now I know it may seem that I was a disappearing act in your life and I do apologize but son," He said, before taking another pop of the bottle. "I was there, there when you were born, when you took your first steps. I was the one who put that bat and ball into your hands because I seen something in you that no one else could vision... A winner! I felt that day would come when you brought the glory home for the family. But now it's like you've become what I already was, a fucking waste. You're out here wasting potential to the powers of poison in these fierce streets that are becoming worse by the minute."

"How the fuck would you ever know what I am or what I've become? Fuck you nigga, you don't know shit, just what you hear and that shit can get you killed."

"When you're dreaming in your sleep, I'm the last eye out like a fuckin' owl, seeing things that other people can't see. Like that nappy headed gal' you're messing around with--"

"Who Lamaar?"

"Yeah, the luscious piece of beauty that got your nose open, she got more game then pimps in Chicago."

"What you mean by that?" He was starting to confuse me.

"This is what I mean," He replied, finishing up what was left in the pint of liquor. "Whores use their quantities and qualities to gain in life. This happens to be their bodily features, beauty, wit, charm and, their number one money maker... Pussy! Pussy is the root of all evil, not money, the terminology Money over Bitches has been being said for ages. And there's not a paper chaser that I ran with whom became successful because a whore was always their downfall. Take a good look at your strung out, fiend of a father, I'm living proof. Your Uncle Muscles is living proof and there's many more where we came from that never made it through the pussy that we spend a life time chasing after our nine months of birth. They use us to be another good fellas down fall, the new terminology should be P.O.M... Pussy over Money! Women shall forever rule the world by using a man for bait, taking all of his strength to become as powerful as they once were."

Big Kyle explained to me clearly, what he meant by being living proof to the powers of the P.U.S.S.Y! Prior to my conception to this here life, my mother introduced Uncle Muscles to my dad. Big Kyle stated that before the even met Muscles in 1960, he was indigent at the age seventeen. He maintained his way of living by being a shoe shine boy and living off the expenditures of his godfather Willie Johnson; who at the time was a genuine number runner. Willie ran with the notorious number pack crew, Chucky Mills, Marshall Mellows, Pop Ghost and many others.

Big Kyle's father Khalif wasn't the father my dad proclaimed him to be or worth a damn to his up bringing. So, to help his family survive to make ends meet, he and his childhood friend Dontae (Big D.S.), began robbing and looting. Certain stores, laundry mats, and banks kept Kyle's family from the depth of starvation. The money he stacked from plundering and the extra ends that was given to him from Willie had all went to Muscles. Muscles and his best friend Billy were already in pocket, slinging quantities of marijuana for these two tycoons by the names of Timmy Tange and Lance Whop.

Before the Dominican brothers had a name, Timmy Tange and Lance Whop controlled Camden's streets. Muscles, along with his retinue, Billy Bad Ass, and the Holmes brothers (Stevie, Howe, Spider, and Haas), operated this spot called the "Deli the on Dime; on 10th street, off of Vanhook street. The name came from this grocery store that was positioned at the top of the block, across from the Branch Village apartment complex.

The Deli is where Kyle progressed in the game, in a years time he mastered the game of hustling and began climbing his way up the drug ladder from 1960-61. With the help of the Deli crew and the guidance from Muscles, Kyle managed to make a $100,000 dollars from the $6,000 dollars he came to the table with. Quote-unquote, Muscles told Big Kyle, "Before he was done in the game, Kyle would be a millionaire," and, indeed Muscles kept his word.

$ $ $ $ $

In 1964, the Holmes brothers all went down for the carelessness of illicit maneuvers. For the love of money the Holmes brothers would do anything to possess a rich man's nature, they were a ravenous group of brothers that had selfish desires beyond reason. The cause of greed had them selling masses of heroin to the Feds, causing them to split 30 years a piece in the slammer. But, before federal authorities could get a hold of Tange and Whop, the brothers closed down the Deli operation and fled the state; going out west.

Things didn't seem to promising for Muscles and his team who had mere visions of longevity in the game. After the rise of the Deli had taken a sour fall for them all, the hindrance caused their progression to go back to square one. On the same note, Kyle was robbed for more than $70,000 dollars in cash out of this apartment that he and Big D.S. only knew about. The last of the hundred grand he had to his name purchased an automobile and a home for his girlfriend Olivia. Without question, Big Kyle still believes that D.S. stung him for the money in the apartment but, undoubtedly, D.S. denies having anything to do with the foul transition.

Forecasting more ways to hustle, Kyle's bright days began casting more dark clouds, his godfather Willie had been indicted as well. Willie went up state for aggravated assault for shooting one of his number clients, after confuting over some money that was owed. The victim was shot four times, twice in the knee caps and twice in the clavicle area. Willie was sentenced to fifteen years in the slammer after the guy testified in court. There after, Kyle's propensities for drug money began to decrease, going back to shoe shining other than robbing was one of his tendencies.

That's until Muscles got his big break by running into the Dominican brothers at a car lot called "Choices," that the brothers owned in East Camden. They all were acquainted through a purchased car and recognized as heavyweights from the enormous amount of cash that was being spent. Richie sent word to his older brother Mikey about the two black guys and, coincidently the Dominican brothers were the men Muscles and Billy were looking for.

Muscles and Billy started out buying a few ounces of dope at a time from the Dominican brothers for the sole purpose of reopening the Deli on the dime. Only to get up enough money through rebuilding their clientele in Camden's worn down neighborhood. Having a reconstructed team, everyone's position was filled and the Deli boys soon became the "Jelly boys," because the more money they stacked, the more their pockets began to jiggle like jam.

With a two and a half year run Muscles went from copping portions of dope at a time, to becoming a third partner with the Dominican brothers; requesting that his retinue share tides as well. The Deli was still the number one distribution winner but some how the guys seen more gold at the end of there grinding tunnel; they expanded their network. In doing so, they saturated frosted flakes throughout the entire town; Muscles wise decision became a remunerative outlook for everyone.

In retrospect, Muscles always stayed low-key, unlike Tange and

Whop who loved the spot light; Big Kyle recalled being just like them. He and Big D.S. were the vivid hoodlums who were always apart of something or in extravaganzas that didn't even concern their nature of business; true rodents to the streets of Camden. This is how Big Kyle became familiar with the two young ladies named Shannon and Sabina at this night club called the "Red Carpet." The Red Carpet was stationed on the corner of Broadway and Chestnut streets, about a quarter mile from the bus terminal and Broadway Eddie's.

Big Kyle and D.S. mashed some guys head in that night after he threw a drink in my Aunt Debbie's face at the bar. Shannon and Sabina were present with Debbie that night; they were the ones who stopped Big Kyle and D.S. from killing the nigga. Before the fuzz arrived they all removed themselves from the night club scenery. Aunt Debbie introduced they four of them to each other and after hearing that they were lieutenants to the tyrant Lamont Muscles, Shannon and Sabina affirmed themselves as the woman of Kyle and Big D.S.

Shannon was on the arm of Big Kyle, who happened to have a deep fetish for darker women of color and, Olivia had been put into a secondary position; which wasn't the brightest decision for Kyle to make. He was playing both sides of the fence with Shannon and Olivia amid distributing masses of marijuana through the city for Muscles; making him feel untouchable. Shannon and her older sister Sabina - Big D.S.'s dame - wanted in on the action too. Big D.S. wasn't too fond of the girl's decision of partaking in the illicit field but, Big Kyle's arrogance and unwise thinking made them feel that the idea was good.

Shannon and Sabina came in the game with only a thousand dollars, refusing to be dependents to anyone that they did business with; including Kyle and D.S. who had substantial wealth. The sisters started out buying small amounts of weed and began selling it themselves on the corner of 8th street and Central Avenue, in the Roosevelt Manor project-complexes.

Shannon and Sabina made a local name for themselves by the end of 1964 and, because of their hoyden behavior they changed their names to Shake and Bake. Also, they formed their own entourage of females having similar qualities and called them the "Rush Girls." The Rush Girls consisted of, Gracey, Sissy, and Debbie and this rough tomboy by the name of Terry; who happened to be a paper chaser herself.

The Rush Girls were loyal and more than trustworthy and devoted their time to Kyle and Big D.S. And, with their impressive actions and commitment came higher positions and more money; so they all thought. Bringing them to Muscles attention, Kyle thought it would be wise to have them apart of their six man organization. All the Rush Girls had to do was bring their prophecy to the round table, so Muscles wouldn't have to work as hard. However, Muscles denied the girls a better future in his line of business and turned Kyle's hopes of a bright future back into pipe dreams.

Muscles, who was already infuriated due to Kyle and D.S.'s engagement with the bimbos on a business and personal level, knew his two friends were trouble prone. And, above all his triplet sisters were caught up in the Rush Girl's unknowledgeable circumstances. Muscles told Kyle to ditch the whores and focus on a hustler's primary goal, accumulating money and, his own whereabouts before they got him caught up. Contrarily, Kyle thought Muscles was talking gibberish, so he refused to listen and kept on continued to interact with the dames.

$ $ $ $ $

Shake and Bake envied Muscles, not because of what he had but, because of what he didn't give them, a chance. A little while after Kyle broke the news to the girls, strange things began happening, making matters worse for Kyle and Muscles. Kyle and D.S. started getting robbed for lumps of marijuana and enormous amounts of cash -$30,000 and $40,000 dollars at a time - and their cars were being set ablaze. Also, their homes were being broken into, someone even tide and gauged Olivia to a chair in her home, demanding Kyle's money. Kyle's mind became so anguished that he almost became eccentric to those around him, rolling down hill once more, going from a six figured Joe to being flat broke like chipped wood.

But, it was Muscles valor which saved Kyle's diminishing downfall once more, after giving him the benefit of the doubt. Muscles paid the Rush Girls a visit in the Roosevelt Manor Housing Projects, with a large retinue on stand by and heavy artillery. Demanding, not asking through questions that they remove themselves from the game or situation would turn bleak. Instantaneously, with out a slight fight the girls waved their white flags and vanished from 8th street and Central avenue with no hopes of returning.

In the beginning of 1965, things really looked promising for Kyle and the six man team. Muscles and the Dominicans brothers came up ten times more from the hierarchical potions that they sat upon. Plundering seven hundred kilos of heroin from these four zillionaires by the names of Cuban Pete, his younger brother Eric Enos, their cousin Jose, and their long time Ace in the whole Kool Kirby; who all resided in Florida.

$$\$ \ \$ \ \$ \ \$$$

Two out of the four drug lords were murdered - Cuban Pete and Kool Kirby - and Eric and Jose managed to escape the fierce gun battle. Consequently, the Dominican brothers and Muscles forced a personal vendetta and didn't even know it. It was extremely idiotic to kill two made men and leave the other two alive to seek revenge.

The Dominican brothers wanted nothing more than to take over the world in 1965, being the captains of the ship of heroin, having more to offer than any major figure on the East Coast. Richie and Mikey wanted Muscles apart of their franchise, the side deal cut arrangement would have affectively edged Billy and the others. But, Muscles stood firm, not biting the Dominican's bait and speaking in strength to them by saying, 'Their my family, we started from nothing and when its all said and done we're going to end with nothing.' Once the offer was turned down, Richie and Mikey turned the other cheek.

Instead of partners the Dominicans became nothing more than the connections, plain and simple but, in the same token Muscles had no way out. He had to survive droughts and was wished well on his success of moving whatever quantity that was given to him. But, Muscles knew just as much about how the Dominican Brothers operated than they knew themselves and the only way that he could get out was to cash all in or get found in some sailor's fish net.

Taking the Dominican brother's statement into consideration, Muscles came to the table with every scent he and Billy ever made - $900,000 to be exact - and the team he quarterbacked. A fifth man was even added to the round table, a man by the name of Teddy Soledan, known to Muscles and friends as "Get away Ted," due to his valor behind the wheel of a car. Since Ted was a superb driver and was a local that was starting up a business on the side of town that was familiar to the Dominicans. Richie and Mikey thought it was wise to use Ted as their driver and his building for the shipments that would be transported in from Mexico to the South Camden loading docks. In return, the Dominican brothers was willing to Ted a hundred thousand a month and take care all of his business assessments if everything went according to plan.

Big Kyle said he touched so much money from the beginning of 1965 to 1970 in the filthy streets of Camden that he completely took the money for granted. He took vacations two and three times out of the month, brought luxurious cars, and blew crazy digits on diamonds. Every time he blew a hundred thousand on worthless things, another hundred thousand was being collected. Money was nothing to Big Kyle and it was like it grew on trees for him and the organization that he was apart of; becoming a seven figure drug rich over night.

Big Kyle admitted that while he was living life at the top his illicit extravaganza, he was still in love with the two women that he couldn't escape. Olivia - his passionate rider - got fed up with the irresponsible actions that he produced towards his son (Me), while being an altruist to Shake's every need. The tick-for-tack became redundant to Olivia who wanted Kyle to make a decision and, without doubt he chose Shannon. Shannon was all for what he was producing at the time and, the streets had him not being what Olivia needed him to be for her son, a genuine father.

After he ran away from me and my mother's comfort, his success turned to turmoil and his stardom began to fade. He was held ransom for a half-million dollars and Muscles had been bamboozled out of $560,000 from Big D.S., who said that his money spot was empty due to careless spending. The money was given to Bake all along, she pacified his penis to a point of him making love to the devil to satisfy her every need.

Shake and Bake managed to eased their way back into the drug game somehow, being very paternalistic, Kyle took Shake and Bake to Muscles again. Only, this time the misogynistic Muscles lowered his pride of distrusting women and, gave Shake and Bake some lead way. Becoming their connect, Muscles supplied them with whatever they purchased and gave them the authority to conduct business in the Manor projects under one condition, not to contaminate his business.

Shake and Bake brought two keys and were getting two whole ones on consignment from Muscles, the sisters were going through four birds in two days. In six months time, by November of 1970, the two business vixens made Muscles and Billy so much cash that Muscles decreased their price of purchase to fifty-thousand a key; twenty thousand under the original sale price and whatever they purchased Muscles doubled on consignment.

Kyle's foolish interactions fucked up everything with the sisters, even the trust Muscles had for them. Constantly, thinking with his dick Big Kyle began cheating on Shannon to sleep around with my Aunt Sissy and Gracey for his own gratification. Things weren't that pleasing after Muscles stopped dealing with Shake and Bake and, cut Kyle and D.S. loose due to Terry's envious feelings towards Kyle and Shannon's relationship. She told Muscles that Shannon was using his sisters to bring him down so that Kyle and Shannon could be more prolific in the game.

$ $ $ $

Contrarily, Sabina wasn't feeling the entire situation of earning for Muscles and sacrificing their womanhood in the streets just so he could see a profit and, turn them loose like some wild untamed bitches. Sabina caught Muscles coming out of Jock-A-Moe's tavern on the corner of Vanhook Street and Mt. Ephraim Avenue and, put two guns to his cerebral area. Bake whom was distressed and anguished through tears had told Muscles to cut her and Shake back into his organization or he would find his mother in a pine box. Allowing Muscles to know that situations were severe, Bake shot him twice, once in the hip and ass. She didn't want to kill him, only scare him into believing that she would and that he was playing on grounds of fire with no extinguishers.

Prior to 1970 closing its yearly chapter of going on into the next, someone had followed Muscles to his home in the country around early December. Whomever it was had doubled back a few weeks later when neither true or Muscles were home. Evasively, looting his home for $460,000 dollars and a vast extent of jewelry. Assumingly, Muscles tried to point the finger at whom he thought did the crafty work but really was clues with concrete evidence.

1971 was the year of the woman through the hustler's prediction in the streets and the Chinese calendar couldn't go into detail like the streets of Camden could. Richie and Mikey vanished into thin air after cutting a side deal with Muscles' rivals (Shake and Bake), behind his back. For the purpose of keeping their affluence on an up scale by being a consistent distributor to both parties. Customers and prominent figures started losing out on enormous amounts of cash due to the Dominican boys' missing people's stunt.

Muscles and Billy were to busy looking for another connection wile Shake and Bake were controlling the streets but they lost out on a lot of money and clientele also. Muscles gradually began to fall behind Shake and Bake after drug consumers became accustom to their potent product called "Pussy Cat." Shake and Bake had the triplets administering their entire operation in the Manor projects and also in the Branch Village apartments which was paralleled but on the opposite side of 9th Street. While Terry handle the logistic side of the business, in motto of selling cheap for a quicker flip that would keep a consistent flip with the supplier.

Kyle and Big D.S., on the other hand were making wise decision plans, investing and laundering most of Shake and Bakes dirty greenbacks into legitimate businesses. Such things as a night club in a renovated hardware building, downtown on Market Street; what use to be Crawford's Supply Inc., directly across the street from the main City Hall building.

Club Shake's became the most popular and talked about gala in town, once it was commenced in the spring of 1971. People from all over - inner and outer stators - made their presence known at the luxurious night club. Even a few big celebrities came to party, Dean Martin, Richard Pryor, Pam Grier, and even Reggie Jackson himself came out to have a good time. The three story, two dance floor establishments that was decorated with a live Jazz band and a huge bar, pack in people ever night of the week. Complimentary drinks were free after midnight and vital dishes of soul food were accommodated.

$$\$\,\$\,\$\,\$\,\$$

Also, the two flamboyant hoodlums opened up a bakery establishment, far north of the Dominican brother's car lot to increase their business market. Sabina's bakery on Federal Street created everything from cupcakes to wedding cakes. Sabina's bakery was the first and only bakery to open up in the city of Camden.

It wasn't long thereafter that Shannon wanted out of her relationship with her long time friend and mentor Kyle Sr. due to the fact of hireling him for her own personal gain; needing his assistance anymore due to her wealth. Plus, she was tired of him living off her expense and giving her the time that he volunteered without expecting any compensation in return; to his old dame Olivia and his son.

Strategically, Terry went behind Kyle and D.S.'s back and told Shake and Bake that the two of them were mendaciously deceiving, having a problem with their arithmetic. Having the triplets steal kilos at a time from them and giving them all to Kyle and D.S. as if they had been robbed. Shake and Bake turned the triplets loose without informing Kyle or D.S. and, not telling what Terry told.

Shannon then allowed her silent friend - whom was kept behind closed doors - Eddie Domino to fill in where Kyle left off at. Terry introduced the two of them during the time Shake's night club was getting renovated; eight months prior to the club's grand opening. Eddie was this tall, bronze tone, construction worker who had a brother named Joseph Riley. Joe was light skinned, medium build dude who began mingling with Sabina after his brother got his foot in the door with Shannon.

The love that Shannon lost for Kyle emasculated his mind to the point of him crawling back into Olivia's arms, hoping that she would accept him back. Evidently, it didn't turn out how Big Kyle expected it too, Olivia turned that smile-of-a-day into a reluctant frown; his dreams of being with her again were just that - dreams. Kyle even lowered his courageous pride and went back to Muscles and Billy, begging for their forgiveness. Sympathetically, Muscles and Billy, whom were low key due to Shake and Bake's fame on the throne of the streets, accepted the two pleaders back into their money cipher; under a few conditions only. One was to destroy Shake and Bake's multi-million dollar enterprise just how it was built and offing the poisonous rattle snake Dominican brothers.

Prior to their acts of espionage on the dangerous, Diva sisters, their hard work came to them on the account of Terry. Willingly, she came to Kyle seeking advice to aid her depression. Also, elucidating to Kyle that since Shake and Bake got ahead in the game and acquainted with their new Knights - Riley and Domino - who were helping them shadow Terry's appearance of being the ultimate trio. As if she wasn't the primary factory of the Rush Girl's rise to riches. Shannon was disgruntling Terry's character to the Rush Girl's and other crime figures in the underworld, to denigrate their friendship entirely. Terry felt far from the loyal one that was living off of the sister's livelihood but she felt that the sisters had it embedded in their minds that they made Terry. Terry even overheard Shannon and Sabina depreciating her as a friend and business partner; plotting on ways to kill her.

$ $ $ $ $

Strategically, Terry came to Kyle assuming that, since, Kyle and Shannon were no longer together, she could use his helping hand to diminish the distinguishable sister's reputation in the underworld. Coincidently, Terry didn't know that Kyle needed her for that and more because he was trying to corner everybody in and take over.

For an entire ten months - since the end of June 1972 - Terry became Kyle's decoy while playing her steady position as a Rush Girl. In no time, Kyle was getting so much significant information from Terry, that he even knew their vacation schedules before they were even devised. Muscles told Big Kyle to worry about Shannon's necessities because he wanted Sabina all to himself.

With the help of Terry and assistance from the triplets, Big Kyle got the drop on Shake and Terry coming out of a remote money spot, carrying fifty keys of dope and $500,000 dollars; in two hefty trash bags. Sissy smacked both, Terry and Shake over the head with the butt of the gun, while Gracey and Debbie dragged Terry into a dark alley. Sissy and Big Kyle took the trash bags and placed Shannon in the trunk of their vehicle with the goods.

Terry's plans were a success, after Kyle deliberately left her in the alleyway to regain her consciousness. The only person that stood between her and her authority of being the only queen of the underworld was Sabina. Unconsciously, Sabina's limitations on the survival clock slowly ticked by like blinks of a human eye. But, prior to finding Sabina Big Kyle connived Muscles and Billy, stealthily keeping the money and product that he looted before taking Shannon into their presence.

$ $ $ $ $

Shannon depleted information that would allow Muscles to find her sister directly before she was murdered. With a loquacious tongue she began telling Muscles and Billy everything just so she wouldn't exit into her own after life. Shannon's information and tips wasn't enough to save her from death, they wanted her soul. Billy took Shake for a lengthy ride, somewhere in Pennsylvania, where he shot her in the head twice and dumped her remains off in a river; her ankles were chained with a heavy device so her body wouldn't wash ashore.

Two days later, Muscles got the drop on Bake strolling into her lofty mansion in Voorhees, N.J. as she put the key in the door, Muscles put the gun's key release to her head. Telling her if she sneezed wrong that her mucus was going to be all over her front door like pea soup. Billy and Muscles did Sabina the same way Shake was handled, tied and put into a trunk and taken to Delaware. But, instead of killing her instantaneously, Muscles wanted to watch her body go through some rigorous pain. After Billy untied Bake's wrist, Muscles shot her in each of her hands, both forearms and, in both thighs. As she cried out for mercy, she was kissed on the forehead and dropped off in the Delaware River.

It was over an hour of explaining his side of the truth and I still couldn't fathom how a female became his downfall. Intervening, I had to ask him, "When was he going to get to the point?" Because I was getting tired of listening to his verbalized motion picture. His response was, "I was concluding my story before you rudely interrupted me in speech."

$ $ $ $ $

After burning down Sabina's bakery and detonating Club Shake's simultaneously on a cold winter night in February of '73, Kyle paid these two young, ruffians by the names of Sidney and Knotty $15,000 dollars a piece to off Muscles and Billy. Big Kyle was tired of being their shadow in the sun, he wanted to be the primary act in the city. But, Big Kyle's plan wasn't a success story and Sidney and Knotty's mission backed fired, making them into his - Muscles - story.

Fretfully, the two boys cringed to the power and respect that Lamont Muscles and Billy Bad Ass carried out. Instead of following the order and going back to receive their other half of the money, they went to Muscles and Billy and told them who they were and what it was that Big Kyle wanted them to do; even handing over the bounty money to them. Being the brainy act intellectual lion that kept him king in the drug jungle for many years, Muscles took the goons' words into consideration. But, it didn't stop him and Billy from settling Kyle's differences.

Sidney and Knotty were hanged from a noose, from a tree in the back of Farnham Park on Park Boulevard; directly across the street from Camden High School. Their deaths were caused by being anonymous figures with perfume information and for all they knew, the two ruffians probably went and told Big Kyle the same exact thing. Thereafter, Muscles notified Big Kyle through a note that was mailed and delivered to his front door. Reading inscribed:

If you want me dead then be a man and come and do it yourself.

All you have to do is check out the scenery in the back of Farnham Park

If you think I'm bullshitting, never send insects to do an animal's job.

$ $ $ $ $

Big Kyle never seen or heard anything from Billy or Muscles after that note landed at its destination.

Buyers, suppliers, runners, fiends, lames, and dames came to Big Kyle asking common questions about Shake and Bake. Where they were, and what happened to the analgesic product known to the sniff and bangers as Pussycat and, why wasn't the smooth, pain reliever on the streets anymore? Big Kyle's vacuous mind only could give everyone the cold shoulder because he had no answers to give anyone and if he told the truth there was no point in him living either. Shannon and Sabina were major distributors in the game at one point, Big Kyle's connection as well. Having an astonished mind, Big Kyle had not one promising idea of how he was going to come across a major connection. There were no Dominican Brothers, Tange or Whop, Sabina nor Shannon, or Muscles and Billy around to hold fort Camden down through the street corners.

Kyle went on a hunt immediately, traveling north to New York

City, browsing for a main distributor up in Harlem. He was in search for two, tranquil guys by the name of Boo and Simmons; two of Big D.S.'s chums. Boo and Simmons were two brothers whom owned a lot of small businesses in Harlem and were internationally connected.

Boo and Simmons were found in a small area between 8th and 9th Avenues off of 139th Street, in a development called "Strivers' Row." It was an aristocratic street for wealthy individuals and certain clientele who happened to endure the soulful atmosphere of the Sycamore Café; that was owned by the two brothers. After explaining who sent him and the reason he had traveled miles on in, Boo and Simmons welcomed Big Kyle into their house of service. Over plates of delicious soul food and Italian dishes, the three men discussed certain propositions. But, however, since Boo and Simmons underworld days were behind them, the two mid-aged men made a few important calls for Big Kyle to more prominent figures that they knew out in Jersey all to well. Boo put Big Kyle on to one of his close relatives named Timothy Freeze, another heavyweight whom also played ghost in the game.

Kyle felt that he'd been sent on a wild goose chase, driving back and forth through New York's state lines into New Jersey. But, Boo and Simmons stared Big Kyle correctly into the hands of Mr. Freeze, who owned a penny candy store on the corner of 8th and Spruce streets, in downtown Camden; a few blocks up from Krystal's lounge. Tim wasn't a difficult person to spot, standing 5'10" inches with the complexion of a beetle. He and his crew sat out in front of Frazier's Candy store throughout the majority of the day; reminiscing and shooting craps.

Big Kyle was frisked and questioned by one of Tim's big men, named Scotty Lee, before he could even converse with Tim himself. Scotty Lee was this brown skinned, Hulk of a man who looked as if his entire life had been nurtured through the sound gates of prison walls. Big Kyle felt violated after he was stripped ass naked and told to bend over and cough for scrutiny of any wired devices taped to his body. Tim's organization moved with caution and they didn't trust the faces on money, so it was hard to trust anyone who wasn't apart of their circle. Tim's own personnel had to go through the same stripping process before they resumed their daily positions and did any work in the field.

Big Kyle and Mr. Freeze sat in an empty room, upstairs inside the candy store for some hours compromising and negotiating different deals and prices that would benefit the both of them; before coming to a legitimate agreement. Forty-thousand a key was the final proposal and in order for the price to go below the actual retailed price that was set, Big Kyle had to buy ten or more kilos.

With the laborious help from this guy named old man Sonny, who was an expertise in the field of the dope game, Big Kyle and D.S. put this fabulous snow together named "Top Dawg," to embraces the drug corners of Camden. Following Suit of Shake and Bake's late brisk Pussycat, Big Kyle and D.S. created the name Top Dawg after finally earning their right to be majesties to Camden's drug throne; also having the grandeur heroin in the palm of their hands.

Ninety days after the meeting with Tim Freeze, Big Kyle and D.S. ran through the fifty keys of dope that they extorted Shake and Bake for as if they never had it. They sold nothing in weight, chopping up every bird and slinging it through the city streets like fliers. They made close to ten million dollars, enough money to last their children in death. The S & S boys were off to a great start in the summer of '73, they were running through twenty keys a month from the chemically pepped Top Dawg. The money became too outrageous from their sales in weight, quantities and, lump some from other buyers and suppliers that the need of slinging Top Dawg in small portions wasn't even necessary. The faster they flipped Top Dawg in weight, the slower it was for them to sell in the streets.

$ $ $ $

Terry, who became Big Kyle's misses after putting him where he needed to be, thought it was best if they labeled the kilos of dope top Dawg. It was a brilliant idea but if the feds got a hold of it, organize crime would be the indictment. But, Terry's witty mind had come up with another clever idea. She took a few thousand dollars and opened up a concession - food and fruit - stand at Farnham Park; selling a variety of beverages and sandwiches. But, at the same time she sold dope in bulks to decoy the attention away from her partners and, since she was selling food anyone who wanted to purchase the Top Dawg had to use the codes Terry invented. Hot dogs were the main code because it sounded just like Top Dawg but was spelled different. Terry knew whom to sell food to and whom not to sell product to, Big Kyle and D.S. had a hand full of major clients and the rest were street level junkies. Terry's hotdogs and sausages came with a special, never selling frankfurter individually. So the people who were buying the food didn't get the wrong impression and she wouldn't screw herself over.

Big Kyle admitted the fact that if it wasn't for Terry's keenness, he and Big D.S. would be doing eternity in the penitentiary due to their blatant nature while offing the Top Dawg product. Big Kyle and D.S. were close to a global connection, traveling to different state to meet drug consumers from Northern Jersey, out to Chicago and, down South to Atlanta, Georgia. Big Kyle and D.S. were so ravenous for dead presidents they even took a huge risk of strapping twenty-one bricks to their bodies and getting them through customs in a Chicago airport. This major player named Dollar Ken who supplied most of the windy city's streets requested the invite for Top Dawg. Due to the vacancy of dope and the drastic drought in the Northern region, the keys were sold for $90,000 a piece; a two-million dollar come-up.

From the summer of 1973 to the summer of '74, Big Kyle and D.S. made Tim Freeze so much money, for the sake of his well-being Tim disengaged in doing business with them. The results of how fast the money came and how it accumulated, froze the mind of Mr. Freeze and scared him to the point of backing out. The tall, bronze toned, full bearded Timmy Freeze was a high intellectual who was already ten steps of the game. And, after the lost of their mainstream importer, Big Kyle's mind became drenched in frustration over his paper chase in the game. Terry and D.S. couldn't even talk sense into his thick skull of attempting to leave the underworld alone for a while. The tall, Dominican favored hood rich go getter stood adamant in what he wanted to achieve - The Game, Chico! With distress surfacing, he knew but one other way to relieve his personal tension and that was to get high on his own supply. Because he knew that it would be hard to trust and find another irreplaceable connect like Tim and his organization.

Situations got no better for Big Kyle who rapaciously had an insatiable sense of greed for the thin, green, flammable Federal Reserve Notes. Two of Big D.S.'s associates in the game (Magoo and Itchie), Lamaar's older brothers introduced the S & S brothers to Bobby Muse and Ike. Two smooth, low-key money makers who were very reticent in the underworld and the people that orbited in their surroundings. Bobby and Ike had a great habit of whispering to people when they conversed, in their eyes life's fortune was secretive and everything wasn't for everybody.

$$\$ \$ \$ \$ \$$$

Money ran its mouth for them and a person's bullshit was just that - BULLSHIT! It was obvious that Big Kyle had what they were looking for and they were what he was searching for in return. Keeping their conversation to a minimum and being concise with Big Kyle, Bobby and Ike arranged for Big Kyle to purchase fifty kilos of heroin at a reasonable price. Big Kyle, who only copped ten to fifteen while dealing with Freeze, had another opportunity for a big come up and a easy way out, just in case he had to go hunting for another connect; he still would be in pocket.

Evidently, things didn't go as expected for the impatient heroin chaser, he'd been hoodwinked out of two-million dollars by two of Bobby and Ike's stunt dummies, in exchange for fifty fresh packages of flour. Being amazed by their bravery and guts that it took to pull of the hideous act, in an assailant manner, Big Kyle drove through the Almighty L.S.D crew by himself. Numbed from inhaled heroin, he shot up the entire Lake Shore Drive community with a machine gun. Carelessly, aiming at young children and women and, anyone who was in the vicinity at that present moment. Big Kyle even pistol whipped his childhood chum - Big D.S. - for acquainting him with

Bobby and Ike.

Big Kyle was so furious with that matter he reached for the un-thinkable, one of the most crucial things that any human being could do to another person in the street life. Big Kyle made a call to the local authorities on Bobby Muse, Ike, and what was left of the L.S.D crew. He figured since they were out to ruin them, why not take them down as a whole too.

$ $ $ $ $

In September of '74 the dope game's quick sand started inching his body in faster than he could grab a hold of his turning life to find a safe way out. A few weeks after taking loses to Bobby Muse and Ike, Big Kyle was hospitalized. Almost overdosing on his own product, Terry rushed him to Cooper hospital's trauma unit. Where he could have died if it wasn't for sacred attempt of taking him out of the cold Jacuzzi that he made as a death bed. At his recovering side stood Big D.S. and Terry, the triplets expressed their condolences too through a dozen roses and balloons. Muscles and Billy tried to pay their respects after hearing about the horrible accident but Big Kyle turned them away. Not out of any hate but, because of the love that Big Kyle destroyed between them and the neglect that was ensued to make him realize that he fucked up genuine love that was unconditional. Telling Terry that he would rather die in his sleep before he patched things up with his old friends due to his own deceitful nature.

Big Kyle's fortune in the game finally sunk in November '74, even after his unstable injury he still wanted to be the crowned ruler of the underworld. But, while lying in the hospital bed for over a month, he had his thinking cap on. Trying to delve ways to find another thorough connect like Mr. Freeze, he made it clear to Terry that he was going for broke; wanting the underworld to be controlled by the palm of his grimy hands.

Being very prude towards Big Kyle, showing that she had extraordinary abilities of being that helping hand, Terry became Big Kyle's human modem. Making calls to people whom knew people so that

Big Kyle could be effective once more. In the process, Terry came in contact with Joe Riley and it was evident that Riley and Domino took the reigns of Shake and Bakes' fortune after they went missing.

Face to face, Terry explained Big Kyle's situation and how desperate in need he was of getting a consistent nexus. Riley wanted Big Kyle to reach out to him and his brother when he was stable and able to communicate on his own; business would be there for him. Kyle had been informed about what Terry had executed for him and as he lied reposed in patient comfort, he felt blessed to have another opportunity to come knocking.

But, Big Kyle wasn't patient enough, time was money and he was living for it in the minute not the moment. Kyle entrusted Terry with closing the deal herself due to her endless effort to get him in with Riley and Domino. Willing to spend three-million dollars all she had to do was get them to agree to his devised proposition. The deal was put into effect and once he was released from the hospital the move would transpire.

The proposition was to give Big Kyle a hundred kilos and fifty on consignment for the three-million. Riley blessed the proposition by giving Big Kyle a stupendous bargain, two-million dollars under the original street price and an extra forty keys.

Big Kyle planned a double cross after Terry got the confirmed word from Riley that financial standards were met. Killing two birds with one stone, the plan was to purchase the hundred keys and, take his money back to complete a round robin. But, little did he know Riley and Domino were already aware of what he imposed.

At the crack of dawn, things didn't go as expected for Big Kyle, Terry and Big D.S. at the meeting point of Krystal's Lounge. Two of Riley and Domino's pawns were sent to cop and slide without exchanging any verbal information that could lead to something fishy and cause for the point of no return. Having two chrome handguns under the money in two stainless steel brief cases, Kyle was ready to do business.

The two pawns allowed Kyle to sample the product to make sure it wasn't artificial before exchanging dope for dollars. Big D.S.

couldn't resist taking a sample as well, but he only did it for his own personal mood so when the temperature rose in the room he wouldn't have no remorse about any ensuing blood shed that was about to occur. After D.S. gave Big Kyle the signal that the blow was a hit, they both bust the latches on the brief cases. Simultaneously, the two Hispanic pawns began conversing in Spanish lingo and started to unzip the bags that the heroin was being carried in.

Big Kyle gained a nervous reaction instantly, unsure of what the boat cruisers were communicating about, he then looked in Terry's direction as if she put them up to what ever was about to take place. In return Terry smirked suspiciously and whistled abroad, sliding a pump shot gun from the sleeve of her white, quarter length coat. And, before Big Kyle could blink another eye, Terry took and blasted off two intense shots, smashing both the Hispanic pawns.

Out of the mist of nowhere, three unidentified persons, garnished in all black attire, jumped the counter of the bar and began letting off shots at both, Big Kyle and D.S. Unable to grab the guns that were inside the brief cases, D.S. was the only one that returned fire and that made Big Kyle feel that it was a double cross.

Big Kyle got low with the brief case in toe towards the exit doors, but he was stopped in his tracks by two fast, striking bullets to his abdomen. Big Kyle went into an unconscious state and remembered nothing after that point.

"So it took you an hour and a half just to tell me that Terry had something to do with you getting knocked off your feet? Un-fuck-ing-believable!" I said, in disgust to the immeasurable amount of time that it took for him to get his point across.

"I needed you to get the full understanding, so as the picture became clearer to your knowledge of your own view point, I wouldn't be misapprehended. The what, when, who, and how's would have came into play if I gave you a summarized version."

But, the how's still lingered in my thought of unasked questions because there were quite a few things that kept me guessing.

"How did your verbal movie pertain to any of Lamaar's whereabouts?"

"I'll be on my merry way after I fill you in on this here," he stated, pulling the hood from his coat over his head, to block the cold air that surfaced towards us. "The whore is conniving and sneaky just how Terry use to be and she's dealing with one of those two brothers, Riley or Domino. I don't exactly know on what kind of level but I caught her a few times creeping with them on separate occasions. The in between is something that you have to figure out on your own to understand her mysterious contaminations. Always remember, fear no man for whatever reason and trust no whore that you feel is a loyal asset."

Having nothing more to say, my pops turned and walked off into the cold, clear night; with no intentions on looking back he vanished immediately like the grim reaper that fulfilled his duties for that night.

$ $ $ $ $

And, the more I found out about the mystery that lied with in the underworld, the more I thought that everyone that knew an infinitesimal amount or had dealings within. Were advocating false information to my unknowledgeable eye, as the icing was slowly being put on the cake. More people's name were being mentioned and more tragic events had taken place; leaving me in the blind, not knowing who to believe.

# Chapter. 12

A month and a half streamed by like Niagara Falls water flow - fast and consistent - and I hadn't seen or heard from Big Kyle since our talk down at the Isabel Community center. But, I did manage to get my hand on some noteworthy credentials that described who Riley and Domino really were. My Caucasian duo - Keith and Derrick - gave me a printed copy of their vitals, after we went and bugged one of Terry's homes out in the Pennsauken community.

Keith and Derrick were very crafty when it came to hi-tech technology, with the help from their technical prowess we managed to set up cameras in Terry's living quarters, bedroom, and tape her phones. Derrick and Keith had some kind of device that connected the surveillance from Terry's home into their appliance store. They had unlimited recording like a security system that would spot Terry, who had been missing every since she bamboozled my uncle for some millions, like a hawk in the sky.

The documentations that I had on Riley and Domino had been significant and mere, their entire life history was astounding. James Riley and Edward Domino were apart of this drug organization and multi-million dollar empire down in Miami, Florida. The crime figures Mob was known as the "Silent Sons of Escobar," S.O.E. for short. The name was originated from the great guru Pablo Escobar who along with the Medellin cartel was superior in Columbia.

James and Edward were two, malicious gun slinger and hit men for the S.O.E cartel. Originally from Jacksonville, Florida the boys had been placed in everything from shelters to boot camps all over Florida's geographical region; their names were in the correctional system. Two unruly miscreants who stole cars and committed robberies like throwing newspapers.

The two brothers did six years in a state penitentiary in 1963 for innumerable violent crimes. While serving their time, the two men got acquainted with a Cuban guy by the name of Kirby Rios. After helping Kirby get out of debt and bringing some sort of peace between him and brothers from the Muslim nation. Riley and Domino became made men and put in positions which marveled their fantasized thoughts. In 1969 when the three desperados were all released from prison, Kirby Rios welcomed the two waif strolling men into his notorious crime la familia.

Cuban dapper Don, Peter "Cuban Pete" Cabrera and his brother Eric Cabrera were the heads of the S.O.E crime family, along with their cousin Jose. The three men were internationally known from the boarders of South America to the United States and beyond. Once the missing link (Kirby) which formed their four horsemen foundation was back in the company of the familia, the restart button was pushed and distributed business became the main agenda.

The four men were importing infinite loads of opium from the boarder of Costa Rico for the price of nothing. One of Kirby Rios' family members named Raymone "Rican Ray" Montanez, worked on an opium field in San Jose. Rican Ray picked, processed and manufactured the addictive narcotic drug and, once every six months Ray would meet the S.O.E. boys at the drop point in Costa Rica. And, by the boat load Pete and Eric would transport the drugs pass the Coast Guard base and bring it in too Miami.

The S.O.E Cartel possessed so much heroin that they could have formed a ski resort with it all. Cuban Pete and Eric had a tandem scroll of names in sequential order that were chief clientele to their lucrative franchise. In damn near every state on the East Coast the Silent Sons of Escobar had at least three people in every major city buying from them directly.

This is where Riley and Domino came into play, Pete and Eric made the two brothers a part of the gang under two circumstances:

One, to kill anything and anyone who came in between their organization, business, and profits. Which alone grossed a stupendous $200 million dollars every six months?

Two, to never break their promise or code of being apart of the most fierce organization in America. Their duties were simple, to handle the risky missions and dirty side of the glamour and glory.

Through agreements, the brothers aggrandized the murder and homicide rates to and all time high. Since their release from prison in 1969, more bodies went amongst the missing in Florida alone, simultaneous links of murders throughout the East Coast started connecting back to Homicides that took place in the frenzied state of Florida. Three-fourth of the homicides that happened on the East Coast from 1971 to 1976 was all related to each other. Men, women, and children that were murdered had similar autopsy reports and being wounded form the abdominal area-up; and burnt to a second death.

America's East Coast became a national holocaust for every race, over a war on drugs. After Cuban Pete and Kool Kirby were gunned down and burnt to crisp skeletons, the other one hundred and eighty bodies were found. Riley and Domino were dubious to Eric and Jose about Cuban Pete and Kool Kirby's death. And, Eric and Jose, both, had a gut feeling that Riley and Domino partook in the heroin lords killings. When Riley and Domino got word that Eric and Jose were hot on their trails, the brothers vanished immediately and made a detour back North.

I began second guessing myself once again, wondering if the Dominican Brothers put Riley and Domino up to do the hit on Pete and Kirby so they could be well off. Or if Eric and Jose were just trying to off Riley and Domino so they both could reign in their family's position after they were taken out. Remaining clueless, my mission was to find Riley and Domino and, try to get in contact with Poohshaun; including the whore Terry.

$ $ $ $ $

Two weeks after, Keith, Derrick, and I bugged Terry's domain and I received the vital information on Riley and Domino. I bumped into fat Poohshaun down at Donkey's Steak Place on the corner of Liberty Street and Haddon Avenue. Donkey's was a local eatery but served the best seasoned steak with onions on a sesame seed roll that

I had never tasted.

$ $ $ $ $

Donkey's was another hangout joint where Poohshaun cared to relax and stuff his belly with their finest meals. Having an intriguing scheme, my plan was to get as much information about the tyrant brothers - Riley and Domino - but, first I had to open Poohshaun's mind up to something different and make him feel a little comfortable. Asking him about his shallow relationship with DaVita was the kicker because I helped orchestrate their bondage. And, my only abrupt reasons of conversing with Poohshaun was because I spotted his green, two-door Mustang parked in Donkey's restricted parking lot. I was heading down Haddon Avenue, on my way to attend my baby sister's birthday party.

Surrounded by a few members in Poohshaun's retinue, he was sharing laughs and grubbing simultaneously when I approached the table.

"How's everything today Pooh?" I asked, pulling a chair up to his table. The two men whom were already stationed at the table pulled guns on me before I could even take a seat. On the verge of complete defecation, I stood motionless when I felt the two, black, steel guns striking my temple and forehead.

"Tarantula and Dre!" Poohshaun exclaimed, pushing there arms away. "Put the guns away before Antonio sends the man through here." Tarantula and Poohshaun's ace Dre pulled backed and tucked their guns under their shirts.

"Is everything cool over here guys?" The slick back, dark haired Antonio asked, removing his toothpick. "Pooh-Pooh I don't need any static today from you capeech? You know my place of business is already hot from all your other nonsense."

"I know Antonio, but there are no problems,' Poohshaun answered, sliding Antonio two, crisp fifty dollar bills.

After Antonio went about his business, Poohshaun told me to pull up a chair and relax before we conversed on different levels.

"Tarantula and Dre, leave us be for a moment to talk in private--"

"You sure fat cat because I don't trust this muthafucka," Tarantula implied, giving me a horrifying stare. In pure serenity I sat silent, giving Tarantula a very naïve look as to say "We shall meet on unfertile land once again." Simultaneously, I sat astounded, wondering what person in there right mind would named them Tarantula? Then again, he was quite a hideous species, having a face uglier than something in the Night of the Living Dead. Tarantula stood about 6'2", very dark skinned with an overbite that made his lips seem even bigger up close.

Dre was similar in height but had a contrast complexion, light skinned with a head the size of a pineapple. He was calm faced, which made me even more leery about him than his partner because he was too quite.

So what's on your mind Kyle?" Poohshaun asked, biting into his steak sandwich. "What brings you to my neck of the woods?"

"Well you know since the death of your right hand man Kenny Morales, you've been incognito to the town's atmosphere of business and chaos. I wonder why? But on my way to my destination, I spotted your Mustang out front."

"I understand but I've just been trying to stay out of harms way, being that it's a lot of suspicious things going on around us that we don't fully understand."

"Indeed so," I responded, nodding my head gently.

"I'm trying to watch my own ass, because the dark side maybe out for me as well."

"What dark side? Who?" I asked, trying to figure out what he knew that I didn't know.

Poohshaun gave me this frigid look like the information he was holding within emasculated his way of living.

"You have this fretful expression on your face, does some one have you cringing from there power? What about the Dominican brothers, are they the problem?"

"Kyle man, there's no such thing as the Dominican brothers existing, Riley and Domino have been living off of their affluence and eminence of Richie and Mikey Munez for decades. The two domineer brothers have been deceased for a long time now.'

"But, you're still part of Riley and Domino's retinue?" I asked, trying to juice him for every piece of information that he could possibly spare.

"I dealt with them every now and again but nothing to major, after Ted's joint got robbed Riley and Domino started straying away from Kenny and I. I guess they were having doubts about me and Ted's murder, thinking maybe I ordered the hit. I was out of town when that entire scene happened and, now I have doubts about them getting at Kenny. They told me that they would never do such a thing, but I know Riley and Domino, their bloodlines are contaminated with rattle snake in it. They will Cane and Abel muthafuckas if situations become to severe and bleak.

"So, what would make them kill Kenny, he was a pretty cool dude?"

"Cool but foolish!'

"Foolish? What makes you think that of him?"

"Every since his secret affair with Terry who happens to be Riley and Domino's younger sister. Once the relationship got too conspicuous back in 81-82', our loyal scale with Riley and Domino had subdued drastically and the trust went out an empty window."

"So Kenny was fucking Terry and what? Riley and Domino didn't see Kenny as being humanly fit for their little sister? What does she have to do with their business and were they concerned if Kenny dicked her down or not?"

"Some how Terry was plundering her brothers out of enormous amounts of cash through Kenny, and making it seem as if Lamaar Green was the master mind of all deals gone sour. And, the buy money not being there when Riley or Domino came to collect. You know Lamaar was the matriarch of her father and brother's money spot at one point and time.'

"Right, Right."

"So around that time when Lamaar was putting up heavy numbers, Kenny tried to get her killed. So that Riley and Domino would think otherwise about me, Terry and him. And, make it seem like Lamaar was the cancer but Kenny's intriguing scheme didn't follow through."

"So what happened afterwards?"

"Lamaar escaped death and was a bit demented for a while, fearing for her life. So she secluded herself from everyone and everything. But, somehow she found out about Kenny and Terry, then addressed the issue to Joe Riley one day they coincidently bumped into each other. After they both told their sides of three stories and aligned what seemed to be their own truths, they became paramours on the contrary to Terry and Kenny's situation."

"That's it?" I asked, looking for a legitimate conclusion.

"Slow down slim there's more to it," Pooh replied, pushing his hand towards me in a yield like motion. So after stabbing each other in the back the truth finally came out. Without Lamaar being in the presence Kenny, Riley and Domino scene for themselves how mendaciously conniving Kenny and Terry were being. Money was still disappearing without having Lamaar to be the fall girl. So instead of Killing Kenny and offing their sister, they allowed them to roam at their own free will."

"Free will?! What do you mean by free will?"

"They treated Kenny like a slave, making him run unusual errands with no funds or compensation. Starving him basically."

"So Kenny was really broke then?"

"Not necessarily empty do to the survival kit that I and the L.S.D boys made deposits into. But he was no where near rich or in pocket like when we first collaborated."

"And what about Terry's assets and wealth?"

"From what I visualized she lived off the land, never known her for having vast amounts of cash. But, in conclusion to the matter at hand, prior to Kenny's death, Kenny tried offing Riley after Domino gave him insight on Lamaar and him being and item. Kenny went to kill Riley and the gun jammed and Riley fled the scene. Then Kenny disappeared after he beat Lamaar half to death. Only I knew where he was and where it was he planned to be but instead of leaving the state for a while until things blew over. Kenny did some implicit shit once more, being greedy he tried going to get the rest of some money he had stashed at the night club and somebody got the drop on him and a cop. Knocked my boy's dick in the dirt and got away with his cash but, I told him to leave that whore Terry alone. But, you know other than some money, pussy is the key to a man's heart and mind."

"You ain't ever lied about that shit," I retorted, downing some of the coke soda that was sent over by Antonio. "So you've been moving discreetly in the hood because you feel that you're the next one to be the unusual suspect?"

"Not necessarily because of my fear of Riley and Domino because niggas bleed just like us and we all breathe the same air. But, it's due to be being under close watch by the Feds."

"The Feds! You've been vacuumed by everyone else's heat."

"Yeah and these three, dick head agents wipe my ass when I shit … Vincent O'bryant … Willy Petite … and Norman Frisby. Then I got fine ass Tracey Smalls the cop and her entire task force harassing me. But there investigating my crew, Riley and Domino, your uncle Lamont Muscles, Terry and mongers all around us. They got everybody and their kids under surveillance, pictures, and phone taps having reckless conversations. Your face is even upon the drug's underworld board, sketched and linked under your uncle's organization.

"My Face!" I exclaimed, at such a high pitch that everyone in the steak house turned and looked in my direction. "What'd you mean my face?" My tone came to a whisper.

"Listen young blood, the Feds are like insects, they fly and move in silence but at the same time observe everything that moves in their atmosphere and field of study. So even at times the tiniest modicum of evidence becomes remunerative to their entire bust operation."

Between my loins, there my heart lied right in the middle of my sack while sitting uncomfortably at the wooden table. My questions about DaVita's whereabouts became a faded picture because the Poohshaun's insight was a crux and I need more confirmation.

"So how long has this operation been effective?"

"I can't exactly pin-point that but its' been some years now."

"So why haven't the Feds made any bust or arrest yet? If they so called have so much edification on the drug underworld and the Camden kingpins?"

"Because they can't catch those that are being watched doing any thing illicit. Plus no one has become gainful to their leads or needs of whispering or getting fed cheese. That's why I'm low as can be because the Feds are like herpes, once they got you, they got you forever."

Out of the mist of now where came these brisk and invigorating sounds of sirens and tire's skirting out in front of Donkey's place, as if the spot was being robbed. Just my fucking luck, those boys were on their way inside to either do a Q&A or apprehend someone. Scared shitless, I had no where to run and Poohshaun's cover was blown.

"Pooh-Pooh here they come," Antonio yelled from the font counter. "Either clear house or their going to do it for you."

Shots began to ring out in front of the Steak house, everyone in Donkey's place fell to the floor for cover as the fierce frenzy got more intense outside. Poohshaun's fat ass hopped up from his seat, flipping the table in unison.

"I promise you that I won't be handcuffed today," he stated, pulling two hand guns from the level of his waist line. "Something's telling me that they had this spot bugged and if that may be the case, the conversation we were having will be held against the both of us. How you want it may man, in some cuffs or a bag? Their gone to take us one way or another." He offered me one of his pistols.

While Tartanula, Dre and a few other guys from Poohshaun's crew covered his ass, in high pursuit of a stand of with the police in the mid-afternoon on the busy thoroughfare of Haddon Avenue. I was very hesitant about making a move and second guess whether or not I should get involved but how ironic was that the authorities already had me involved. If only and I knew I shouldn't have's began lingering in my thoughts. I didn't possibly know what type of bullshit I got myself into but I was in to deep to step out of it.

Instinctively, I disrobed the top half of my body, taking my t-shirt from under me and tying it around my face ninja style. In a simultaneous manner, I threw my coat back on, zipped it and then grabbed the gun from Poohshaun. There were sixteen anxious little footballs in the clip and one ready to be released from the whole. Once I let the first one out, tandem the others would go. All I had to do was squeeze first and, trying to escape my troubles. As I closed my eyes to say a brief prayer, all I heard were fireworks and Poohshaun's heavy voice saying, "Where going to meet up one way or another, either here or the other side in hell. But, I refuse to surrender to these muthafucking political figures for all my sacrifices in the struggle."

Once Poohshaun exited Donkey's steak place, I was right on his ass when I got out and raised my arms high in pretended submission. There were so many authoritative forces in the middle of Haddon Avenue, it seemed like an Academy ceremony for first time recruits or some shit.

There was no strategic communication or walkie-talkie movement when I began to ring shots off from Donkey's small parking lot. Only wild uproars form the heavy artillery that surfaced around the cops and criminals. Tarantula and Dre, both, were banging of these two Mac-11 machine guns that had majority off the police officers running and ducking for cover. Three other guys, assumingly apart of Poohshaun's crew were side-by-side, triangle style, giving up shot after shot from three pump shot guns.

Police helicopters surfaced the air while camera men and news anchors stood from a far, putting the action on film. Wishes of being a sniper came to mind as I made my on to Liberty Street for a clean get away. But, my wishes couldn't avenge the reality that was happening in front of me.

There was no way out, the fuzz even has the back of Liberty Street blocked off with a flock of mindless cops. The only way out was death and with no bullets left and now where to run, I wasn't to far from it. As I observed the area for another escape route so I could break free from the bloody gun massacre, I spotted a tiny alley-way in the middle of these houses on Liberty Street's right hand side; I slowly backed my way towards the alley.

Instead of wasting my seventeen shots to shoot and miss at the police, I should have aimed and dumped all of them in fat Poohshaun's Mellon just to secure myself from the investigation. Before he was caught and brought all those down who appeared in photos on the bulletin board at the prosecutor's office.

Poohshaun and his men had to be full equipped with heavy

artillery, ammunition and bullet proof vest because they were having a fierce stand off with about fifty officers and no one was dropping. I was approximately twenty feet away from the clamorous shootout that was similar to Wild West, ducking behind this grey Chevy pick-up truck. Poohshaun and his entire team took off running in quick strides and they were heading in my direction. Evidently, they had to run out of ammunition but what had me confused was I didn't know where they were all running to. Because directly behind me were nothing more than squad cars and agitated cops sending shots in the direction they all chased to get too.

Poohshaun's crew scattered out in different directions like army ants, I guess they figured that there own directions were best. Darting through abandoned houses and the only alleyway around, I had no choice but to follow suit. Running through the crevasse that I had my sights on from the beginning, I was determined to lose the trailing police men. My intentions were to strip down of all my clothing and lose the gun because they never got a visual of my face.

With the slightest idea of where I was running to, I just ran for clearance from the chaotic scene. The faster my velocity had picked up the closer the sirens and helicopter came near. After sprinting as fast as I could through the forever and a day alleyway, I came upon a tandem row of gated backyards. In an acrobatic form, I started hurdling over a bunch of metal wired fences which stood before me. Dogs began barking and running from places unseen to my eye's periphery. Tripping over my own feet, I was very nervous not from the acoustic sirens or helicopter noise but from the untamed dogs.

Prior to me reaching the last yard in the alleyway, I spotted a squad car from a distance heading my way. I paused... Two second styles, glancing around like a chicken with its head cut off for yet another quick escape route. I tried my luck in the backyard as the squad car gained on me from about a football field in distance. I headed for the backdoor.

Still masqueraded ninja style with my gun in palm, I gasped for an immense amount of air as I leaned up against the anonymous backdoor very exhausted. The kitchen's silence aligned with its emptiness as I observed the entire space within. I assumed whomever lived there was either at work or out on the town at the time of my unintentional break in.

Just as I was on the move to search the entire house, this short, caramel toned female headed towards the refrigerator in the dark. In haste she glanced in my direction but never eyed me, so I thought. By the time she went to double take in my direction, I had the gun resting on her temple, gauging her mouth with my hand.

"Uh," The lady said, wanting to scream but was too scared to do so.

"Shhhh," I replied, waving the gun towards me so she could walk in my direction. The female got in arms reach of me and I gently gripped her by the nap of her neck and whispered, "I'm not here to rob or harm you." She shook her head agreeably to my every word.

"I was being chased by the fuzz and ran out of routes and places to hide, so unknowingly I tried your back door. Ironically your door happened to be unlocked."

$ $ $ $ $

I released her neck and turned her towards me then reached in my pocket and pulled out all the money that I had. Having about seven-hundred and fifty dollars, I gave the female two-hundred and fifty of what I possessed, for all the trouble I caused her and whoever was in the house. I then asked her to tell me her name and asked her was there any more people inside the house? She told me that her name was Limboo and that her sister Nanoo was asleep with her boyfriend Kylie Belle in one of the upstairs' bedrooms.

Grabbing Limboo by the rear of her bra strap, trailing her in a slow manner upstairs to the room her sister Nanoo was in, I peeped around the corner of the wall to see the bedroom door slightly open. As I continued to hold on to Limboo, I reached over her shoulder and pushed the door open as slowly as I could with the tip of the gun. Nanoo and Kylie were reposed to the bed serenely and nude like the cause of some ruff sex put them both under for the night. I shook Nanoo by her ankle to awake her from the endless sleep she was having.

"Later Kylie," She said, motioning her hand towards her foot, simultaneously rolling over on her stomach.

"Nanoo... Kylie, get up!" Limboo yelled, shaking the sheets on the bed. She shook the sheets intensively causing Nanoo and Kylie to jump up in complete paranoia.

"What's wrong?" Asked Nanoo, visioning a mask man behind her sister. "Oh my God--"

"The muthafuckas going to kill us all." Kylie implicated, reaching for his pants on the floor. "Listen man, whomever you are or whatever it is you're here for, I only have twenty dollars and an identification card."

"Wa-Wait a minute Kylie and Nanoo," Limboo yelled, over top of the two loquacious voices that were in a loud, discursive manner.

"Wait What?! Wait for what? Where being robbed and this whore is talking about wait and shit--"

"Whore? Who the fuck is you calling a whore? You brown skinned dwarf."

I cease all three of their denigrated speeches towards each other instantly, I was one of America's most wanted fugitives and the addition of their rackets was making my matters worse.

"Hey, hey, hey," I said verbatim, waving the gun in the air. "Enough got-damn-it, I'm not here to rob or kill your asses. Explain it to them for me Limboo." I poked Limboo in the back with the hammer so she could finish my reason for being there.

"He was being chased by some cops, ran out of places to go and, with the strike of luck found our back door to run in. He even gave me a hundred dollars for all his troubles."

"A hundred dollars?!" Kylie asked, as the baritone in his voice changed. "Well let me get one of those crispy Jackson's so I can go up the street and get me a pack of Newport's."

'A hundred dollars.' I thought to myself, Limboo was getting over but, then again if I would've opened my mouth about what she really received, she probably would have called the police on me for fucking up her hustle.

"Well if he's not trying to harm us why does he still have the black t-shirt covering his face and the gun pointed to your back?" Nanoo asked, covering her naked body with the sheet on the bed.

The three of them started staring at me awkwardly as if they knew me from somewhere or seen me before after I removed the shirt from my face and tucked my gun.

"So what's your name handsome?" Nanoo asked, ogling my appearance. I wanted to ask her why? Then lie and give her a fake name but she seemed pretty cool.

"Kyle," I responded, leaning on the pearl-white dresser that was stationed in the bedroom.

"Kyle... Kyle what? You do have a last name don't you?" Nanoo began fishing.

"Moore... My last name is Moore." I thought she was trying to be sneaky for some reason on some set up shit, but I remained cool.

"Moore... Moore... I know a few Moore's," Limboo said heading towards the bathroom.

"Kyle Moore," Kylie mumbled to himself, in thought. "You're not a relative of the great one himself, Kyle Moore from North Camden are you?" I was hesitant in answering Kylie's question, because I never told anyone that didn't know that Big Kyle was my father, that he was my father. I deprecated his character all my life because he was never there for me.

"Yeah he's my pops," I said, reluctantly.

"All man, your pop Big Kyle was a smooth fuckin' gangsta in his day, around when I was a teenager but I knew the streets all too well, Dig it?"

"So, Kyle's your dad huh?" Nanoo asked seductively, blowing smoke from her cigarette. "He definitely was a lady's man back in the day, whatever happened to him?"

"I have no idea," I replied, trying to cut the conversation short. "He's around somewhere."

After acquainting myself in the right perspective and getting a little comfortable around Kylie and the other two ladies, they allowed me to chill for a few and gather my thoughts while flicking through every channel on their basic television. I was trying to catch any breaking coverage news but nothing was on channel 6 or 10. But,

Channel 3's Eye Witness News had coverage on what went down at Donkey's steak place.

From what the Eye Witness News displayed, there was no exposes information on whether or not Poohshaun and his crew were apprehended or, what charges they faced. But, the Lady News anchor did go into specific past history that the malignant boys had in different criminal files. Eye Witness News showed coverage on me running with a gun on my waist up Liberty Street but they had no leads on the suspect at large; I was considered armed and dangerous.

Nanoo and Limboo treated me as if I was a long lost relative or distance cousin or something, offering me food and beverages and out of curiosity they asked if I needed a shower. I was too through after that question, I knew I had to find a way out the house and deter situations before the ladies had other outrageous tendencies to throw at me.

The only thing I needed to use was the phone to contact some of my peoples for a ride; all the other offers were irrelevant to my use of need. Limboo gave me the okay to use the jack which was upstairs in the bedroom.

$ $ $ $ $

I dialed every important person and memorized number that I could possibly think of so I could escape my troubles quietly. Because I damn sure wasn't going back in front of Donkey's place to retrieve my car, I'd prefer walking before I got caught in that burning vicinity.

My strumpet girlfriend Lamaar never answered the phone at the house, I kind of figured she wasn't home but just the thought of checking didn't hurt. My final call was to my mother's domain, I knew I could count on somebody at her house to come get me in their vehicle because there was a party going on there for my sister Aniyah. Necessarily, I didn't want Olivia to answer the phone because she was going to give me this long tirade about me not being on time for my baby sister's party and I really wasn't up for that shit.

Luckily, my mother didn't answer the phone due to my cousin Wadeelah picking up. My conversation with my cousin was concise and to the point of getting me to my permanent destination. I told her to find someone that was at the party with a car, to come and pick me up from Mechanic and Louis Streets. Wadeelah told me to hold tight and she was going to send someone right over to get you.

After I hung up with Wadeelah, I sat up on the side of Nanoo's bed with my palms over my face, in deep thought; just trying to get myself together. In my state of a slight daze, I stumbled across a bunch of used heroin bags filled with residue on the gray rug.

$ $ $ $ $

Out of curiosity I picked up one of the tiny glassine bags to see if I recognized the stamp of any kind of competition of my uncles. The debris of chemicals inside were very strong, it was like the bag had just been used minutes prior to my notification. Obviously, I concluded Nanoo and Limboo to be weary eyed and talkative from the bags of heroin.

The stamp wasn't an ordinary one that circulated through the streets; in fact the logo was new and original. The dope bag was garnished with a yellow happy face; I began guessing what the name of the dope was. Happy Days, Happy Face, Joy, Sunny Smile, et-cetera-etcetera. Then it hit me, the thought of Riley and Domino changing their dope could have been the case to take the heat off of their old stamp that was being used prior to Kenny's murder.

Kylie came back in the room while I was analyzing the stamp, drying his hair with a towel; he was in the shower the entire time.

"What's happening captain?" He asked, drying his face with the towel. "What you got there?"

"Just a few used bags of happy face dope that was lying all over the floor when I came to use the phone."

"Them damn whores forgot to throw that shit away, trifling bitch-es," He replied, scooping the used bags up from the floor with his hand. "Where are they? Limboo... Nanoo!"

"They left about twenty minutes ago, saying that they were going to the store."

"They aren't going to a damn store, they went looking for that happy fix."

While Kylie dressed, I stood on the other side of the door - in the hallway - asking him questions about the happy face bag that I found on his floor.

"So it's a new brand of dope floating around in the streets I see?"

"Yeah, its' been on the streets for about a month or so now." After my first question there was no reason to ask another because Kylie told me everything there was to know about the stamp, willingly.

He elucidated that the product could be purchased anywhere in Centerville from the corners of 10th and Vanhook Street (Branch village), to 8th and Central Avenue (Manor Projects). The product hours varied, but whoever was running the operation had a two shift schedule; six days a week and were closed for business on Sundays. On the contrary, they had a work ethic similar to God's creation of the heavens and the earth.

The brand of dope was called "Smiley," and the reason for the name was self explanatory too Kylie, as well as myself. Smiley was operated and moved through Centerville by this maleficent retinue known as the "Good Wood Boys." Kylie stated that this group of young muthafuckas was vicious, they played no games when it came to money. They would literally kill a nigga's family if he came short of a dollar.

Marveled by the information that Kylie shared, I was a bit bewildered about the information he knew so much about. That's when he told me that he use to run for his two brothers - Chucky and Bud - who administered this raw powder spot off of 7th and Chelton Avenue. Directly across the street from the Stanley Park Playground was a flow in the area that I was raised in.

$ $ $ $ $

Chucky and Bud turned Kylie loose after finding out from a connection of theirs, this sleepy, one eyed gambler named Pee Wee Franklin, that Kylie was getting high off of dope. But, Chucky and

Bud were two debonair old heads who'd been in the game since the late 60's, early 70's. Who showed majority of the hustlers that came of age on the street corners of Centerville's plantation, the fundamentals of the game and how to get money.

As bad as I wanted to learn more of what Kylie experience with Chucky, Bud, Pee Wee Franklin, and the Good Wood Boys, my ride had intervened on the session; beeping the horn repeatedly. I gave Kylie my regards and thanked him for looking out for a stranger, I also gave him my phone number to keep in touch with me.

Making my way towards the black, four doors Buick that sat in the middle of Mechanic Street, I covered my head with my t-shirt so I could remain anonymous to the area. I had a gut feeling that those boys in those two-thousand dollar shoes were still in the vicinity investigating the crime scene.

Wadeelah was in the back seat with my other cousin Alesha, who was sitting on the passenger side next to this honey toned, baby face brother whom was driving. Respectfully, I spoke to everyone to cease any tension that may have been in the car for the cause of not wanting to pick me up but came out anyway to do so. Alesha was my Aunt Sissy's youngest daughter, she took the initiative of introducing me to her boyfriend, the driver.

$ $ $ $ $

In the process of Alesha's boyfriend and I shaking hands, I voiced my name and in return he told me that his name was Jingles. His name took me by surprise as soon as he told me the weird nickname, truly flabbergasted I wondered how he acquire Jingles as a name. Noticeably, in the flow of us shaking hands, it wasn't hard to miss this enormous gold ring on Jingles' pinky finger. The ring was designed in a two letter form, having the initials "GW" embellished with so many crushed diamonds, I could see my reflection sparkle off of it. Out of curiosity I asked Jingles what did G.W. stand for? He gazed at me through his rearview mirror, having a slight smirk on his face and answered, "It stands for a great world."

I concurred to the meaning of his ring by just a shake of my head, but in thoughts of irony I knew wasn't shit great about the world of Camden which we dwelled upon. As I focused on what was ahead through the front windshield for anything suspicious, I glanced at the rearview mirror a second time and watched Jingles watching me. He winked his eye and smiled cinematically as if he knew that I knew something about him, or knowing that I knew that his ring stood for another meaning.

As we made our way down Louis Street toward Kaighns Avenue, we were cut off by two unmarked squad cars, which blocked the front and the rear of the Buick from escaping. In a nervous manner, my two cousins and I began to worry even though they were unaware of what was going on; I was waiting for one of the detectives to snatch my black ass out of the back seat and apprehend me. Shitting bricks in the back seat, I just knew that Poohshaun got caught and they got a description of my person.

$ $ $ $ $

Jingles told us that everything was cool as he rolled down the driver side window, as a white detective wearing black shades pointed a shotgun at the passenger side window. Wadeelah and Alesha began to cry and tremble out of fear of the guns, I on the other hand sat mum, peeking through my t-shirt that was halfway on my face.

"Mr. Johnson," The brown skinned, baldhead man, wearing shades and a suit said as he popped off some chewing gum. "I see that you and your Good Wood gang are still at it, being mongers to my community amid this huge drug sweep in Camden's city."

"Look man I don't know what you're talking about," Jingles replied, scratching the back of his curly head.

"You hear this shit Vincent?" The baldhead man asked, tapping his partner that sat in tune on the passenger side.

"Yeah I hear him Norm but I'm not fuckin' listening," Vincent retorted as they both burst into laughter.

"Look you Hawaiian Looking muthafucka, I got you and your fuck boys under heavy surveillance... Twenty-four hours around the muthafuckin' clock. I know when you're pissing bitch, stop trying to follow in your father's footsteps because you're going to end up getting him involved in your bullshit."

"Tell old man Willie Meeks that we'll be to see him tonight at one of those local gambling spots to play a few numbers," Vincent said, as he and Norman laughed even harder.

"Get the fuck out of dodge," Norman said, waiving his hand up and down in Jingles' face, pulling away from the Buick slowly.

Jingles pulled off in a calm manner as he kept his cool behind the wheel and recollected his thoughts, with the same smirk that he had when I first glance his way. Wiping Alesha's tears from her face with his right hand, he told her and Wadeelah to stop crying and relax because there was nothing to worry about.

If Jingles was upset for being put on the spot by the detectives or scared due to the investigation that was brewing, his facial expression didn't show it one bit. His calmness made it seem as if we never got stopped in the middle of Louis Street by them dudes in them two-thousand dollar shoes.

Jingles dropped us all off when we arrived at my mother's house downtown on 4th and Walnut Streets and, then pulled away instantaneously. He either was going to warn his crew about what had happened or had another serious mission to handle. I, on the other hand had similar troubles that worried me, not as severe as Jingles' but I, too, was being watched. And it was either by the same muthafuckas that pulled us over or other unfamiliar faces that mingled amongst me in the streets. Even if I tried to escape or get away, I couldn't because I was in way to deep and I had other missions to handle that would be centered on another investigation anyway. But, I was determined to get to the bottom of what kept every one in the drug underworld head hunting for each other's power and riches. Before we were all brought down by the law and the laws of the land were thrown in our face for connecting the dots themselves.

# Chapter. 13

Later that night, after having a splendid time at my sister's party, I walked from my mother's place to my residence in the North Glamour Towers. Ambling at my own pace, I needed to relinquish a lot of distressful thoughts that were eating me up inside. And, the slow walk to the North side of the city was the best way I could clear my mind of the entire situation that were affecting me at that time.

My Uncle Muscles not being able to move the bottom half of his body while lying up in West Jersey's Hospital very unstable was just part of the massive issues that boggled my mind. Everyone and everything in the drug underworld's perspective of past and present kingpins, wheelers, and dealers all were deceiving dimensions to me. They, whom lived illegal and committed illicit acts for a gainful out come, had venom spitting bloodlines. My conscience was eating away at me severely; I came to think that my two clever white boys were working with authorities. With the cerebral areas and technological minds to participate in that field, no one could fault me for feeling the way that I felt.

It was a little after ten when I arrived at my condo, and I was exhausted from the nice, long walked that I needed to cope. A hot shower was calling me to relax and then hibernate like a bear in my bed. The entire apartment was pitch black when I entered, without turning on any lights I groped through the apartment and headed straight to my bedroom, undressing myself along the way. My bedroom was similar to my entire inside, dark and gloomy like a frigid attic. Even with the empty gun piercing my waist, I was still a little scared. Up until Lamaar moved in, my spot had never been as dark as it was but, doubtfully I began to suspect that she was up to something sneaky; lately she'd been acting strange. Staying out all night at times, taking the phone off the hook at night and, making the house dark. She was already fucking with no of the most feared brothers in America, and I was residing in his edifice of wealth. So what was my conscience telling me? Kill the whore before she had me killed.

Tripping over a boot or shoe when I entered my room to reach for the light switch, I tried to break my fall but twisted my ankle as I fell upon the bed.

"What the fuck!" I screamed aloud, feeling a couple of bodies in between my sheets."

I jumped up off the bed as quickly as I could, grabbed the empty gun from my waist and hit the light switch on the wall in unison.

Of what lied before me, I couldn't believe my fucking eyes, "Muthafucka!" I shouted, seeing my main man LuKay and my hoe fucking in my bed.

"Kyle baby it's not what you think," Lamaar said, backing herself into one of the room corners, with her hands in the air in a pleading manner. "I'm so sorry, oh my God."

"Whore shut the fuck up," I retorted, waving the empty gun in both of their directions.

"Kyle my man can you please put the gun down before one of us gets hurt?" LuKay asked, grabbing for his pants.

"How the fuck do you know my name? This whore told you my name?" I asked, grabbing Lamaar's hair with a tight grip. LuKay sat mum while Lamaar pleaded and denied it all.

"No, no, no I never told him your name... I swear."

Unintentionally, I smacked Lamaar over the back of her head with the burner, dropping her across my bed. It was the frustration of not knowing literally that she would execute her deceit, and I was hurt.

"Damn slim," I said, with both arms obtruding toward s him. "The plan was for you to fuck her, but not in my hut."

"I know daddy but the strumpet never told me anything about you living here. Plus, I never asked, I thought she lived here on her own."

In aggravation, I watched Lamaar lie unconscious, but I wanted to get grimy and pop her and frame LuKay with the killing; he was the one fucking her. The motive would have been pure jealousy, that's how niggas get when their dicks are tender and they can't get enough of that sour pus'. But, gangsta's didn't roll in that manner and I had to strategize different.

"So cat daddy, now that you know the whore is untrue do you want me to get rid of her?" LuKay asked, feeling no remorse.

My ego was saying, "Fuck it Kay kill the disloyal bitch," but I knew she couldn't go just yet, she had some important information that I needed to be unveiled.

"Nah Lu we can't get rid of her just yet."

"Why not?"

"Because she's our meal ticket to Riley and Domino's wealthy fiesta of federal reserved notes."

"How do you know?" he asked, in an inane manner, needing to know everything.

"Damn slim! Are you going to ask a million questions or are you going to go with the flow," I replied, hugging him around the neck with a tight grip.

Contemplating on whether or not LuKay and I should go ahead and pop Lamaar, we tied her to one of the chairs in the dining room area, ass naked. Just in case she regained her consciousness and tried to flee, immobilized to a chair was best until I got what I need-ed. And, out of spite, I made LuKay strip and tied him to a chair next to her, so the plot wouldn't seem as obvious. LuKay was scared I could see it all over his light face; he knew I was up to no good. For no apparent reason LuKay wasn't going to get hurt because he never done anything to harm my life. Plus he'd been my ace boon-coon since my snot nose days as a tender adolescent. I said the same thing about Dontae's ass but I hoped I wasn't contradicting myself a second time.

Lamaar regained consciousness after I tapped her cheek a few times, after being knocked out for at least a half hour. "Wha-What happened?" She asked, being a bit woozy, trying to move her arms but noticed that she was tied to a chair. Her eyes widened when she seen the position she and LuKay were in and, peeping me kneeling down in front of the both of them with my gun in palm.

"It is fact and truth to believe Ms. Green that you have been a very disloyal figure in my life. And for reasons that are irrelevant to my involvement in our relationship,' I stated, in a calm tone.

"No Kyle, baby never… I would never do anything to hurt you, you're my--"

"Shhh," I said, putting a cease to her uttering gibberish. "So you wouldn't do anything to hurt me huh? Ha haaa, you really are joking me right?"

"No baby I --"

"You're still intervening while I'm talking." I slid the empty tool across her chin. "See the man sitting next to you? The man that you were having a heated bed affair with." Lamaar cut her eye at LuKay then gave me a puzzling stare.

"He and I know each other very well, if I'm not mistaking I guess it's been since second grade right LuKay?"

"Something like that," He replied, looking in Lamaar's direction.

"And I know you're startled and shocked by the news but, I had to use someone that was beneficial so you can open up to see the disloyal person that you really were. Now that I'm clearly aware, I need some imperative information that will also be beneficial. I think this will even things out between us after I talk to your furtive lover boy Joe Riley." Lamaar damn near swallowed her tongue when she heard Riley's name roll off my tongue.

Questioning was a big subtraction for me once I began to pick Lamaar's brain, all I was looking for was a succinct elucidation of the truth or nothing but the truth or Lamaar's identity was going to be made false.

$ $ $ $ $

Lamaar's tale of and affair with Joe Riley and why she was being sly and deceitful in our relationship came to calm and smooth like morning air. Stating the fact that after the first night that I brought her into my comfort zone after she was allegedly beaten by Kenny because she and Riley were found out. She had continued on seeing Joe Riley and was dealing with him for as long as Kenny had been involved with Terry. She kept the situation away from her family because she knew how her brothers would have retaliated if she had told them what had been occurring. Sympathetically, her father had been ill and she didn't want her family going back to prison for nothing foolish.

Unexpectedly affected, I too was marveled when she told me that she had dealings with Poohshaun when all the stabbing and snaking was taking place with her, Riley, Terry and Kenny. Poohshaun went behind Kenny's back and informed Lamaar about his partner's fling with Terry; that's how their affinity was unveiled. Poohshaun's feelings became so profound for Lamaar; he disowned DaVita and wanted to terminate his friendship with Kenny by killing him; Only to have wanton Lamaar to himself.

Poohshaun's name should have been Pooh-Bear after telling Lamaar about who was out to kill her. He admitted the night the mission occurred he was present but he wasn't with it at first. He went along with it anyhow because he didn't want Terry or Kenny to suspect anything or doubt his tough side of a goon. Poohshaun was the driver that night that Kenny and Terry were shooting at her with two shotguns. As I listened, I figured Poohshaun wasn't as gangsta as he depicted himself to be, a true sucker in my book that was in love with a voluptuous floozy. Never the one to misjudge because I fell for Lamaar myself but by no means was I going to spill my guts about significant street matters, for the sultry tissue in between her legs.

I'd heard enough about Poohshaun for an entire lifetime, I really needed to understand why she started being conniving and untrue towards me. Was it me or did she simply have a passion for going from one nigga to the next?

Lamaar froze up when I started to discuss her faults in our relationship, and in a verbatim aspect, she kept reiterating that she was never out to hurt me or our relationship. It was Riley and Domino whom were out to ruin us and take down my Uncle Muscles. I truly understood the brother's vengeance for my uncle and apprehended the fact of them wanting me because I was involved.

Before revealing the truth through a sound mind, all Lamaar could do was shed tears and cry out of pain that she caused. Expressing that all the years that her family had done in the penitentiary was because of my pops Big Kyle Sr. I already knew my pop's side of every story that he revealed but, I assumed she had another version with another twist to it. Lamaar's wording was painfully expressed in a nervous manner as her legs shook constantly; she unleashed her true feelings pertaining to everything.

Before Big Kyle thought of being in the ranks of Camden's underworld, he transported blow for doe to anonymous customers for Lamont Muscles. In route of delivery, he would make drop offs to Ty Green. Now Ty and his sons brought from Muscles because on the contrary Bobby and Ike were crooked businessmen and weren't to be trusted. Bobby and Ike would get a regular customer to buy from them, get their customer's customer to do the same thing and then would plunder their customer and their customer's customer for everything. Once they were comfortable enough to get everyone comfortable and do business with them for a while, getting a two for the price of one sting. Bobby and Ike got their scheme off on a few inner-city mongers but mainly their missions were done on out of town guys in different states - Virginia, Maryland, Chicago and Tennessee.

Ty Green never informed Muscles and his crew about the intriguing schemers because he figured Muscles would have eyed their dispositions from afar. Beside Muscles was like a son to Ty and he didn't have to worry about being bamboozled by Muscles because didn't have a problem revealing his trump card.

After Muscles wet low key in the game ant the money queen's - Shake and Bake - disappeared, Ty shut down his entire operation also. He had no nexus to trust and do simple business with. So when Big Kyle and his courageous partner - Big D.S. - took over Camden's heroin throne in 1973, Itchie and Magoo began doing business with Big D.S. through a mutual friendship the three guys share prior to there acquaintance in the streets.

$$\$\$\$\$$$

It was Itchie and Magoo who put Big D.S. and Big Kyle onto

the Bobby and Ike's schemes and Dreams of robbing the hood to keep their chips stacked like connect-four. Big Kyle and Big D.S. came up with a plan of their own to raze the two fraud men stratagem. While dealing with the prominent Tim Freeze, Big Kyle use to send Big D.S. to do business with Bobby and Ike through Itchie and Magoo, only to keep them close.

Prior to Tim Freeze cutting Big Kyle's distribution card Big D.S. began fraternizing with Bobby's dame, Missy Amour. Big D.S. was out to ruin Bobby and Ike, and the best way to do that was through their woman. Once D.S. hooked Missy like a fish he manipulated Missy to get Ike's whore Princess Pooh, a young, genuine college girl. Princess Pooh attended Camden County College, downtown Camden and had been a three year student whose course of study was sociology. The plan was for Missy to get her friend Pooh to acquaint with Big Kyle.

Princess Pooh didn't bite the first line of bait that was thrown her way by Missy via Big D.S. For obvious reasons Pooh didn't incline to the desires of Missy's game because she had Ike's money and his love. What more could a girl want or ask for? Big Kyle on the other hand didn't give up to easy, he loved a whore that put up a tough fight and secured themselves from a nigga's bullshit.

After a luxurious Chinchilla fabric coat, a pearl necklace enhanced with a three caret diamond to complete it and, two dozen roses specially delivered to her place of employment for two weeks straight. Princess Pooh gave in like a culprit that couldn't handle the pressure of taking her crime to the grave. Whores would do anything for the love of another nigga's money, the life of his luxury, and the fine expenses of what he offered through materials. Especially, when his merits and valuables were charitable to their needs.

Having no speculation, Bobby and Ike continued to do business with D.S. through Ithcie and Magoo. Having the slightest idea that four of their associated people were being used to destroy them. Missy and Pooh used espionage tactics to gain confidential insight on their men for Big D.S. and Big Kyle to use against Bobby and Ike; who their next victims were, the deceptive maneuver, the destination and cost of the mission.

Off of the strength of their muscle, the S & S boys brought in the cerebral Terry to complete their missions. And even though Big Kyle and Terry were and item, he titled Terry as his younger sister around Pooh and Missy, so everything could go according to plan.

Missy and Pooh struck an immediate attraction to Terry once all were acquainted; it was as if they knew each other for years. But, with other ironic intentions of being malevolent, Terry had the two women right where she needed them to be.

Regular sessions of girl talk was what gave Terry leads on where Bobby and Ike were holding majority of their money. While the S & S boys had Princess Pooh and Missy Amoure spoiled with and in so many splendors, they weren't even expecting the unexpected. Missy and Pooh were being put in some what of a crucial situation and never realized it because of the way the S & S boys expenditures had them sitting on top of a glamour girl pedestal. Whatever Bobby and Ike priced for their misses, the S & S boys doubled the women's pleasure as a kick in the face to their foes.

The relationship for Missy and Pooh became so fortunate from the S & S boys, Big D. S. and Kyle brought the two dining Ladies an all you can eat buffet restaurant and, named it Missy Pooh's. Princess Pooh went from a studious college student to writing checks with her gold digging friend in tow doing the same thing.

The S & S boys and Terry tripled the profit of what they invested into Missy and Pooh, for the sacrifice of their lames fortune in 1974. They seized an incredible fourteen-million dollars worth of jewelry, other tangibles, and money from the two set-up artist.

Expeditiously, things changed for the worse and really back fired on the S & S boys after losing their mainstream connect. And, even though they were well off with out Mr. Freeze they couldn't leave the game alone because the cupidity of having even more cash called for them. Being satisfied wasn't enough but having more was what they lived for.

Ironically, having more slowly devoured on a decreasing scale, due to Big D.S.'s fatuous act towards Itchie and Magoo; the S & S brothers found themselves in a shit house. Instead of Big D.S. giving Itchie and Magoo their cut of what they all plotted and plundered from Bobby and Ike. Big D.S. pocketed Itchie and Magoo's portion of the money without informing Big Kyle and, kept Itchie and Magoo dubious to the turnout of it all.

Without any notification or warning, Itchie and Magoo took matters into their own hands. Unusual things began happening to Big D.S. and Kyle, their girlfriends were kidnapped, held for ransom and, the delicate restaurant Missy Pooh's had been torched. Big Kyle and D.S. had no more than five hours to get the money that was taken from Bobby and Ike to Itchie and Magoo or Missy and Pooh would have felt the repercussions.

Without out a touch of fear, Big Kyle and D.S. told the two disguised voices over the telephone prior to the five hour passing, to suck a dick and to do whatever they felt was best for the wretched whores. Also, with a touch of sarcasm, the two brave hearted muthafuckas told the voices to give them a call back after they knocked off Missy and Pooh. Kyle never was conscious enough to see that D.S. was the cause of all the intensifying heat. Up until Missy Amour and Princess Pooh were found slain to death in their homes with particles of the heroin Top Dawg scattered on their bodies.

Prior to the women's murders, Big D.S. was tossed from the Tacony Palmyra Bridge; he managed to survive the high sky dive and was rescued in Pennsylvania, suffering a few broken limbs. A few days after D.S. was thrown from the bridge, Big Kyle was almost ambushed and blown from Missy's yacht that Big D.S. had purchased. Big Kyle tried absconding himself from the mysterious tension but evidently he'd been found and, he was fortunate to have escape death before it totally reposed him.

Kyle had just made it off the yacht into the Delaware River after numerous shots from the dock was flying rapidly in his direction. The large amount of bullets had wreck the deluxe thirty-footer and three strikes of dynamite subsequently followed the shots. Blowing the boat into tiny shreds and sent five-million dollars in cash to burn in the smoke and flames. The hunt of Red October and the men behind the term didn't have enough of Lucifer's angels to annihilate the S & S boys for good.

A few weeks prior Pooh had contacted Terry, before she was killed and explained what Itchie and Magoo were trying to do to her and Missy. Off of D.S.'s technicality of not keeping his word of payment. In return, Terry told Pooh that she would dead the entire situation. Terry then went back and enlightened Big Kyle on the situation, advising him that Itchie and Magoo were the wolves savoring his flesh. After concluding that D.S. pulled a fast one and kept the money, Big Kyle wanted to cancel everyone he had dealings with from his livelihood; including Big D.S. He came up with a marvelous plan to do so as well.

$ $ $ $ $

The plan was to get Big D.S. to purchase $2 million dollars worth of blow from Bobby and Ike, make Itchie and Magoo kill Ike, Bobby, and D.S. for the $2 million dollars and the blow. Get his cash back and then get the authorities to bust Itchie and Magoo with all the drugs. A great plan turned into a bad mission after Itchie and Magoo crossed back over and forewarned Ike and Bobby on Kyle's scheme. This was similar to what Bobby and Ike did to their customer's customer to get rich.

Bobby and Ike allowed the deal to go through, sending two pawns to meet and deliver fifty keys of blow to D.S. in a remote location. In exchange for the product, D.S. forgot to test the product and gave the two pawns the money. The surroundings petrifaction must have made him rigid from the lingering death wish that trailed his heels, that he rushed the procedure without making sure his product was pure.

Big Kyle and D.S. both got fucked dry; Big Kyle lost out on a lucrative amount of cash in return for fifty fresh packages of cooking flour. And, his brainless partner lost as well but took a rigorous ass whipping in the process for being so careless. In a time frame of two weeks, Big Kyle and D.S. lost out on $7 million struggling dollars, trying to con cons and got swindled.

The S &S boys dreams of being eminent in the underworld was covered in pure excrement once Homicide Detectives snatched them for Missy and Pooh's deaths. Glenn Sunkett, Craig Pease, and

Lavar Hicks Questioned Big Kyle and D.S. for an entire month about the murders and its motives to commit. If it wasn't for Big Kyle and D.S. being pulled over on a traffic stop and checked for warrants on the night of Missy and Pooh's throat were cut from ear to ear. The two first degree murders would have buried the S & S boys under the prison system.

The product of Top Dawg that was sprinkled over Missy and Pooh after they were murder wasn't even dope. When the forensic drug laboratory's test went got back to the homicidal unit, to see if the two murders were drug related. The results came back negative and the white substance happened to be cooking flour.

Thereafter, Detective Glenn Sunkett notified Big Kyle about the test results and explained the procedure in detail. Sunkett told Mr. Moore that whoever committed the murders was trying to set someone up or thought they had something to make Missy and Pooh's murder seem organized. Whoever it was that caused the tragedy didn't know what the fuck they were doing, so Sunkett thought. But, what Sunkett didn't know was that Big Kyle already knew who was behind the powder situation. Bobby Muse and Ike tried framing the S & S boys with the murders by putting their adhesive label in with the flour. Making a joke of the disastrous event and trying to sent them a questionable message.

The joke wasn't on Big Kyle for long though, what turned out to be funny to Bobby and Ike became an ironic situation for them and their entire L.S.D. crew. One humid afternoon in July of 1974, there was tow heat waves disturbing the L.S.D crew's premises. Unknowingly, while shooting craps with a few of his men, Bobby Muse never seen the man disguised in a Jamaican hat with dreadlocks and a pair of black shades appear in Fairview's quiet environment; driving a Mr. Softee's ice-cream truck.

The theme music from the truck awoken the neighborhood, residents and children came crawling form under rocks unknown when they heard the tunes form the blue and white vehicle. But, what they didn't know was that the driver wasn't coming to sale ice-cream or banana splits. He came to deliver a few tiny projectiles that were made of carbon and iron.

Bobby Muse and his crew were so into the dice game, they never recognized the ice-cream truck or the dread inside. All the kids and adults who crowed the truck for service started becoming impatient, wondering what was taking the guy so long to open the window. The kids and neighbors that stood on the out side of the truck creating a fuss started making their way back to their homes and other areas. T.J. one of the L.S.D. members walked over to the ice-cream truck and demanded some service for the other people in the neighborhood. With force T. J. banged on the truck's tiny glass window with intense forced that caused the glass to crack.

The Jamaican man slid the driver door open and fired two shots directly into T.J.'s helmet, ceasing his tough actions immediately. Everyone in the vicinity began to scattered for safety, but Bobby Muse and the other guys that were being entertained by the shaking an rolls of the tiny, red cubes. Dropped everything in their possession and unloaded a multiplicity of shots back in the ice-cream truck's direction.

From fifty feet away, Dread stood on the driver side of the truck and fired tandem shots at whoever opposed him. Out of nowhere another arm came out of the tiny cracked window and started to fire rounds as well. Simultaneously, as the arm continued to pour shots like Liquor, Dread hopped in the driver seat and skirted down Lakeshore Drive in high velocity.

$ $ $ $ $

Four females were killed, two children were hit and labeled in critical condition and Teon Johns - aka- T.J. had been brutally murdered. There was a six thousand dollar reward at the time for the person who found the Mr. Softee truck and the light skinned victim with blackish brown dreadlocks. A month later, the ice-cream truck was found by the Camden police department in an empty vacancy by the Walt Whitman Bridge. There were no leads on the dreadlock suspect who cause the shooting and, one of the child victim's that was critically injured in the shooting happened to be Lamaar's niece Safiyah. The seven year old Safiayh was paralyzed from the waist down and confined to a wheel chair.

By the spring of 1975, A.T.F agents and federal authorities were receiving anonymous tips that pertained to the Almighty L.S.D crew from an informant by the name of "The Great One." The Feds and A.T.F members had so many leeks and accurate information on the L.S.D organization, they knew the times when they all exited the house in the morning and when they took it down at night like clock work. Consequently, the L.S.D organization was put on around the clock surveillance for two and a half years before authorities apprehended every member that had been investigated.

Rodney "Bobby" Muse, Ike Ewing, Barry Webb, Tyron Baylor, Leonard Mitchell, Germaine Cones, Jahee "Ty" Green, David Green, Bernard "Bubbles" Green, Janelle Green, Toni Green, Keena Morales, Lovell Morales, Lavar "Little Larry" Johns, Donald "Don Juan" Smith, Joey "J-Rew" Alvarez, Charles "Chunky" Miller and a few others were all apart of a $600,000 dollar a month drug trafficking network for a couple of decades in Camden's city.

Itchie and Magoo winded up getting more time then any other member in the organization after being apprehended with more than two pounds of dope in labeled packages called "Easy River." They both were charged with organized crime on top of the other offenses that were issued in the investigation. They were convicted and sentenced to thirty years imprisonment.

Lamaar was informed by someone undisclosed that her family and friends were set up and snitched on by my pop Kyle "The Great One" Moore. A few years after her peoples were confined to a cell, Lamaar's father Jahee "Ty" Green sent her all the cooperative information that was in his discovery entailing who did what for what and why?

Ty was diagnosed with lung cancer in 1983 after serving six years in prison and was extremely ill. Prior to, Jahee never smoked or used illicit drugs, he was in healthy condition. The finger was pointed directly at my father by Lamaar for her father's ailments. After sitting through her wicked congregational fable about her family and what it was my pop had done to destroy them, I still misapprehended how my troubles took affect on Lamaar and why were the tyrants, Riley and Domino out to hunt me down.

Adducing her verbal explanation about my situation with her, Lamaar addressed the fact that I was the son of the harmful coin flipper Kyle Moore Sr., and the nephew of the sovereign drug lord Lamont Muscles. She wanted me to suffer for all the drastic pain and suffering that she and her family went through. Since Big Kyle was inexistent to her knowledge, I was the closes thing to him that she could ruin and feel proud about destroying Big Kyle's offspring before I had the chance to fully blossom. So she figured since Riley was going after Lamont Muscles, she could get him to kill two birds with one stone.

Lamaar hit me with a verbal low blow once her truth about me unfolded, I wished upon a star for just one bullet to be in the empty chamber that I palmed. LuKay would have thought that I was out of my mind for pushing Lamaar's mind out of hers and leaving her brains looking like a hot pizza topping on my rug. The way she felt had me furious to the point if some had taken my temperature it would have read boiling point. I was truly irate and aggravated for falling for Lamaar. And, even though my pop wasn't worth a damn, his words or wisdom for the qualifications of beauty to get quantities of luxuries was factual.

What made the situation even more vague is that I put Lamaar before myself at times; I would have starved myself to take care of Lamaar's necessities. It hurt me to know that I was being faulted for another person's actions. The term "Blood is thicker than water," had more then one interpretation to it.

"Why'd you kill Kenny Kyle?" Lamaar asked, in a calm but up-setting tone.

"Kill Kenny?" I retorted, with a perplexed facial expression. "I didn't kill Kenny, what makes you think of such of thing?"

"Don't play stupid Kyle your so-called buddy over here," Lamaar implied, nodding her head in LuKay's direction. "Told me every-thing."

"He did what," I said, turning toward him.

"Kyle, blood don't believe that miserable bitch, she's lying," LuKay said, trying to maneuver his way out of the chair. I couldn't believe my fucking ears, LuKay pulled a Poohshaun move for un-known reasons right under my nose.

"What made you...? I know this whore's pussy wasn't calling for you that much?"

I backhanded LuKay in the face with the burner, knocking him to the floor simultaneously. Tucking the gun, I made my way to my bed room to retrieve my aluminum baseball bat from the inner closet. While searching high and low for it, the strangest shit happened, all the lights went out in the house.

$ $ $ $

After finding the bat, I made my way back to the dining area to see what had transpired during the short time I had gone. I started to think that the blackout came from an electrical problem in another area of the Glamour towers. And, hoping at the same time that Lu-Kay and Lamaar didn't get loose to get on some Alfred Hitchcock shit.

Just as I turned the corner to head in the direction of the dining area, two extremely loud gun blasts shredded my front door, from about forty feet away. I froze as I observed Lamaar and LuKay scream to the moon, my intentions was to try and turn them loose before the unknown gunman entered, and tried to kill us all. But, that would have been one big contradiction because I was going to kill them myself.

Concerned about my own safety, I left Lamaar and LuKay right where they sat, making towards my bedroom so I could escape through the back fire exit. Getting to the door was a big inconve-nience because it happened to be locked, which was ironic because I never locked the fire door. I pushed, pulled, and kicked the mutha-fucka, still, nothing seemed to happen for me.

As I looked for a place to hide and escape my troubles, the gun-man inched towards me in haste. Having no other option I just knew I was dead meat and, in a flash the gunman stood before me. But, I wasn't about to let this grim reaping muthafucka get the best of me and give up on myself at the same time, so I chanced him. Not trying to be a superhero but trying to dodge the devil's angel one more time to see another day of my short lived life. With about a three step start from the bed to the rear balcony, was quite a distance.

What the fuck! I had nothing to lose, either way I looked at it I was a dead man anyway. Thirteen stories away from escaping death, ten feet from the rear balcony, and the other fire escape that was embedded into the wall's platform. I would have been filled with bullet holes all over by the time I reached the window.

As soon as I acted the gunman reacted to my taking off in his face, hearing nothing but gunfire as I leaped twice across my king sized bed; my main focus was reaching the balcony. Having my arms folded to protect my face I emerged through the sliding glass door with every piece of energy that I had left. Dizzy and weak, I managed to make my way down the laddered fire escape as the gunman continued sending bullets my way, leaning over the balcony.

In the back of the Glamour Towers sat nothing but large, horizontal dumpsters that accumulated garbage. I had made it all the way to the fifth floor's fire exit before turning myself loose like a leaf to fall into one of the three dumpsters that had a pool of garbage inside. With firm consistency, the gunman fired to the gun couldn't back no more. I assumed the muthafucka would of stopped after he seen me render my self to the air. I dug my way to the bottom of the garbage to secure myself from the rain seeking bullets that were landing between the all the trash.

As I lied under the fetid waste from about twenty minutes until the rapid fire ceased, wondering if the malicious grim reaper was in route to finish me off and leave me smelling awful like the garbage. My mind was racing a million thoughts per minute wondering who, assuming who, where, and how did the muthafucka get up to my apartment without addressing the receptionist Zakia. And, bypassing the two front security men. Something was telling me the night Dana informed me that Riley and Domino owned the Glamour Towers, I should have packed my shit and relocated.

Once I felt the coast was clear, I crawled out of the dumpster and staggered my way to the front entrance for someone to get me some medical assistance. My right arm felt dislocated, and I had been shot twice in my right thigh. I passed out in seconds of people coming to my rescue and remembered nothing from that point on.

# Chapter. 14

I was hospitalized for two months to a bed in Cooper Hospital's Medical Center, on Haddon Avenue. Two days after I was admitted into recovery, I regained my consciousness and was informed by Lynette Bennett, one of the nurses that assisted me daily. Informed me that I was brought in the emergency room by a man driving a yellow cab, and told doctors that he found me on the curb of 7th Street in front of the North Glamour Towers.

The past incident that happened to me on the cold winter night of November 20th 1985, was inscrutable to me. Assumption after assumption, assuming it was Riley, Domino, or Terry who shot at me from thirteen stories up. Only because the thirty-one story edifice was owned by the two disembodied brothers and their vicious sister, subsequent of trailing their deceptive maneuvers. I definitely grabbed a forged check that my ass couldn't cash, but wanting to be on a hundred moves all the time. I popped up at the wrong killer's crap game because every chance I got to roll, I done hit their number -Seven; to many door blows and I wasn't even beating for my safety on the side.

While awaiting my release but getting the right medical treatment and therapy from different doctors, I received sad news, bad news and more bad news. I read an article in the Courier-Post Newspaper, in the B column of the South Jersey section about Luther Kane "LuKay" Johns' death. The rhetoric stated that when homicide detectives found the twenty-one year old man who reside at 112 South 10th Street, in Centerville's Branch Village Apartments. He was tied to a dining chair with the back of his head blown open like a cracked watermelon. A spokesperson for the Camden Police Department told officials that a group of children found the body floating in a creek behind Cooper's Point Middle School, in North Camden. Sympathetically, LuKay was murdered due to my troubled circumstances, I probably should have let him finish his business with Lamaar then he wouldn't have been in such a terrible position. But, then again if the gunman didn't pay us a surprise visit, I'd probably had beaten them to death with the bat anyhow.

The article never mentioned Lamaar's name, not even in one sentence or even mentioned her whereabouts. Or, elucidated whether or not Luther Kane Johns was with another individual at the time of his murder. I wasn't bypassing the fact that Lamaar was lying in an unauthorized area smelling awful as well but her body was probably amongst the missing.

February's tales and news in Camden's deteriorating city was stunning to know about, having a censorious twist. A few suspect's from Poohshaun Miller's retinue were brought up on charges for being involved in one of the biggest drug investigations in Camden's history, which happened to be called Operation Sundown. Operation Sundown is a high qualified, tactical team of all forces from New York, Philadelphia and New Jersey to diminish a multi-million dollar drug ring. That's been flooding the Neighborhoods of Camden, parts of Philadelphia and Maryland since the early 1970.

Terrell "Tarantula" McGriff and Andre "Dre" Downes were just two of many names from one of the fiercest heroin blocks in Camden that were arrested for being caught with more than a million dollars worth of packaged dope. Inside a vacant, luxurious domain out in Merchantville, N. J. News officials said the two guys were apart of a million dollar a year business and in charge of a six digit a month dope distributing corner on Liberty Street, off of Haddon Avenue.

The Channel 6 news also said that Operation Sundown wouldn't be leaving the city until every dealer was apprehended and removed from the streets. Investigators told the news that there was over a hundred suspects under investigations. I figured Poohshaun was one out of the hundred suspects that Operation Sundown was anticipating to shackle. But, if they were planning to bust ninety-nine muthafuckas in the gloomy underworld, they better had put more brisk energy into their duties. Because their arrest clock was winding down, due to drug lords taking other drug lords into illegal custody and leaving them dormant.

While I lied absent minded in an unstable position trying to perceive or figure out my strange surroundings, contrarily, Poohshaun was somewhere hiding while Big D.S. remained amongst the missing. And, Terry's anonymity from the city, probably became an acclimation to a new environment. Due to the respect of my Uncle Muscles' position in the game and his pain in a wheelchair, there was no way I was going to give up on finding a solution to the Loyal's disloyal. I sacrificed my life for a bunch of lies and twisted stories but felt that I was getting close.

Over the course and time I spent rehabilitating myself in Cooper's Hospital, I was fortunate to talk to my Uncle Muscles twice a week, encouraging each other's spirit. My grandma Ann and a lot of my other family member - including my mother - catered to my uncle's dismalness regularly. Progressing well, he told me that he was going to therapy twice a day to strengthen his legs. Billy took time out of his busy schedule to pay me a few visits while I was in the hospital. He'd been my uncle's side every step of the way, producing as many results as he could to undermine any excuses that he even attempted to have lingering in his mind.

Billy and I conversed for hours about numerous things pertaining to his street life in general. His hands were washed thoroughly to what was current in the contaminated streets, twenty years of sacrifice was too much for him to lose. Based on the disloyal ways of the new breeds, sacrificing was even hard to come by in his eyes. In the late 60's, early 70's a hustler's hustler was well respected. No worries, or leery looks over your shoulder in the direction of another hustler that was getting paper to cut your throat for the money you struggled for. Situations were ironic if a person wasn't into nothing and they were hungry. Back then, anyone who stepped foot into the illicit swing of things got a piece of what was employed in the underworld.

Things drastically changed for the worst for Billy who strived to make a better living for himself as a monger in the national street affairs. Legends started to cringe to the steel walls of penitentiaries, due to the survival of eating the government's cheese, once the three brothers - Superior, Supreme, and Federal Courts - began giving out time like basketball scores. Back then, if a Hustler's hustler sensed a nigga out to rat or heard people whispering in the game, they were handled by whoever struck first. If a muthafucka knew that pressure would bust his pipes and force him to turn against the silent majority, he should have never entered the depression tunnel of the illegal pharmacy.

Billy's intellect to the streets were similar to my uncle's train of thought, giving me significant advice and encouraging me to be the best at whatever I had a passion for. Quote-unquote, Billy told me to "Respect the three L's on my rise to the top," which were Life, Love, and Loyalty. Without human existence there would be no use, without someone you could turn to for a helping hand there would always be adversity and, without a firm crew that lived by a certain creed I was prone to death before my time was up.

Financially, Billy maintained his stability to open up a grocery store on Marlton Pike, called Cousin's Food Market; a few blocks down from the old Rotti shop. He also, invested money into a vacant building to open up a Martin Luther King daycare center with my uncle. Billy told me that as long as he was in pocket I was in pocket, but it wasn't optional to take his kindness for weakness.

$ $ $ $

As the day went on it got better with time, my two Einstein minded white boys came to visit me also. We had been out of contact in a few months mainly because I was hospitalized. I introduced them to Billy prior to leaving them alone for a few to attend my therapy session with Nurse Bennett.

When I returned the three guys were conversing profoundly as if they meshed for years. But, since we all wee in each other's presence and all had intentions of being a derogatory supplement to

Terry's disloyal reputation. We were in the right atmosphere to discuss plans and strategies of capturing her.

Prior to going into depth of the issue at hand, I had to bring to light that I had this weird feeling that Keith and Derrick were part of the law, some kind of preppy, intern prosecutors or two fresh meat under covers. Keith and Derrick jumped completely out of character before I could explain myself. Once they calmed down I had to apologize for judging two books by their covers.

Keith and Derrick had been best friends since high school, two brainy scholars who took education as jokes and did nothing but smoke pot. And, scheme, scam, and swindle people out of money. They never graduated from high school, due to being expelled for breaking and entering on the school's premises and wiring cameras in all of the girl's bathrooms.

Derrick grew up a Mr. Fix-it, learning from his father who fixed cars and wired and rewired technical devices. He used mechanical circuits as a study guide to master electronic components.

$ $ $ $ $

Keith on the other hand was an average misfit to his environment, who stole, looted, and scammed his neighbors out of their hard earned money. Disguising himself as a boy scout as a smoke screen to pay rent at home, he would travel his neighborhood selling cookies. One day he really needed cash to support his pot habit, so he went door to door in his neighborhood and whoever didn't answer, he found a way in and robbed them for everything that could be sold. Keith even did two years in a juvenile detention center for plundering an entire hardware store, using a stolen U-haul truck. Truly convinced, the succinct summary of my two psychotic hippies life's history overrode my harsh thinking, about them having dealings with the law. Ironically, if they were under cover, inspector gadget muthafuckas, they had the dictation of my conscience greatly confused.

The taps that Keith and Derrick allegedly put into Terry's phone the night we bugged her phone were having some sort of technical difficulties by sending mixed signals. Any calls that were connected to transpire had given off a clamorous beep as if the company was testing the phones or Terry had them disconnected. All the rest of the planted device that were in Terry's bedroom, bathroom, and living quarters were up and running. But, Terry herself was no where near the environs of her home or in the town of Pennsauken for any matter.

For the past four months from sun up to sun down, Keith and Derrick had fast forward and rewound tapes that were studied to trace Terry's maneuvers. Billy even enlightened us about Terry's house of chemistry, the entire place was vacant like it was up on the market for sale and renovation. If Terry was suppose to be a bold vixen type, what was the purpose of absconding herself? Billy also gave us insight on Terry reaching out to my Uncle Muscles back in December. Revealing her spill about her happiness of his ceased superiority to the streets and she wished that death would have been the main result of the attempt. From Terry's verbal abuse, my Uncle Muscles went into slight cardiac arrest, and what was expressed through Billy from Terry froze my mind as well. Because my uncle's pain was my pain and her words revealed a true sense of hate.

So we all agreed that if Keith or Derrick came across any imperative information, they would notify Billy immediately while I was still confined to a hospital bed; and vice-versa.

A week before I was scheduled to be released from Coopers, I received three unexpected visits from my Aunt Sissy, DaVita, Wadeelah, and my older cousin Alesha. My Aunt Sissy was the first to stop by with the latest news and updates on my demented family's affairs.

Over a vast amount of soul food that my aunt brought for me to devour, she sat and poured her heart out to me from a retrospective view point, wishing things were different. Aunt Sissy expressed that if she had listened to my Uncle Muscles back when she was a teenager, she wouldn't have struggled the way that she did. And, indulging in drugs would have never been a carefree option of hers. But, wanting to be a fast ass and smell her own vagina she wanted to follow in the footsteps of her other half (Gracey). Muscles made sure that all seven of his sisters were stable and had financial means.

At seventeen, the triplets all lived together in a three-bedroom condominium, with separate cars, attending Woodrow Wilson High School in 1967. Sissy, began smoking marijuana, snorting cocaine, and was the first to get pregnant. Once hooking up with her around the way girls (Shannon and Sabina), and the distant tabby Terry; who use to commute from Florida every summer to stay with her grandparents. The girls became flamboyant foxes to the city's streets. The six girls formed a click called the "Rush Girls," because everything they did or planned on doing was always fast paced, and they didn't hesitate or second guess nothing. Once they all came to an agreement about something that they wanted to do or get, they went after it expeditiously.

The late Shannon and Sabina introduced my three aunts into the world of the heroin. They knew bits and pieces about the drug but never indulged until they linked up with Shake and Bake. Shannon and Sabina who learned the game from there uncles - Timmy Tange and Lance Whop - who controlled the city of Camden's street corners with tones of marijuana in the early sixties. Had both made ends meet by selling modicums their selves to aide their needs and wants.

Shannon and Sabina, who were three years older than my aunts, started out selling in high school. Sabina was two years older than her sister Shannon and they both were making a cash flow off of three dollar joints back in 1963, when my aunts were only thirteen. Sabina was the mother in a sister's form to the four gals, who were spoiled in the fun life of amusement parks, movies, and lunch money after walks to school.

Terry, who was a sister to them all, came around occasionally, or when she wasn't back at her mother Fu's residence down in Florida. She was the middle child of three girls and was spoiled rotten by her father Keith Quarters, who happened to be a detective for the Camden Police Department. Later on became a D.E.A agent for the state of New Jersey, and was killed in the line of fire in 1961.

Terry who went on to pursue a career in college down in Florida after her father was killed, came back to Camden to hook up with her girls in 1967. Shannon and Sabina as well as my aunts already had their hands in the game when Terry returned. But, Terry didn't only indulge her hands in the game with the girls, she put everyone's feet in also. Allowing her crew to understand that it was more to hustling than making money, Terry schooled the girls to watch everyone and everything around them. Because the closes friends were the ones with the venom and she taught them how to play cards by their opponent's hands. Allow their opponent to force their hands, never their own and Terry also taught her girls how to shoot guns and people.

My aunt told me that Terry made her shoot her first and long time boyfriend Wesley, who she met while attending Woodrow Wilson High School. Wesley was very jealous and insecure and didn't want anyone talking to Sissy if it wasn't him. He was very abuse and hands on with my aunt, if he even thought she was subconsciously thinking of another guy. My aunt would always cry over her sister's shoulder after Wesley beat on her or, would got to Terry and Sabina for help; with black eyes and busted lips from time to time.

Terry got tired of Wesley's abusive tolerance towards Sissy and one courageous day they went duck hunting. Terry and Sissy caught Wesley strolling in his home early, one morning as Terry sat in the car and watched my aunt run up on her abusive lame. Sissy squeezed four shots into his body with a .38 revolver and until this present day Wesley walks like a pimp but with a cane and a limp.

On the Rush Girls' rise to the top, signals between them all, slowly got crossed and unnoticeably flipped once they became matriarchs in the underworld. Shannon and Sabina whom were courting with the S & S boys (Big Kyle and D.S.) prior to Terry coming back from Florida; were purchasing small amounts of heroin from their boyfriends to sell in Roosevelt Manor housing projects; which undoubtedly happened to be Lamont Muscles territory.

Lamont Muscles didn't care if Kyle and D.S. supplied Shannon and Sabina with heroin, long as they didn't move it through his turf. Shannon and Sabina were furious about Muscles not wanting them on his turf because they felt that it was their turf too; they were born and raised there. Terry stepped in and told her girls not to fret because she was going make her understanding understood to Muscles. But, even Terry's reasoning and propositions couldn't move Muscles into being slightly convinced. He was already aggravated by the fact that Shannon and Sabina had his triplet sisters involved with their illicit activities. And because Big Kyle and D.S. were mixing business with pleasure.

With the intellectual instinct from the domestic cat Terry, the Rush Girls took matters into their own hands; since they couldn't go to Muscles they brought Muscles to them. Big Kyle, who had a super crush on my Aunt Debbie while engaged in a relationship with Shannon, would have done just about anything to smell her body scent. So, without informing Shannon or Sabina, Terry made the triplets, separately, deceive Big Kyle out of Three kilos of heroin that belonged to Lamont Muscles. And, it was all in a disguised form of pretending to be Debbie just for a little peaches and cream.

Simultaneously, Terry had Shannon and Sabina extorting and plundering all of Lamont Muscles' dealers and runners that roamed the Manor Projects. Muscles' Manor Crew whom was known throughout the city and Centerville community as the O.B.S Boys (Orange Bag Squad) because they sold tiny orange bags of dope. Cringed to the feet of the Rush Gils once they got a taste of some steaming artillery. Making it known that if they couldn't do business in Roosevelt Manor, then Muscles couldn't either.

With promptness, Lamont Muscles and his retinue were retributive after receiving word about how intensifying the Rush Girls came at his corner boys. Muscles and about fifty of his soldiers caught up with Terry, Shannon, and Sabina at Sophia Café, which was their main rendezvous on the corner of 7th Street and Central Avenue. Made them exit the establishment in a peaceful manner then took them around to the rear of the building and they strip naked. One of Muscles' soldiers on the front line took a gun and pistol whipped them all and tossed them into one of the accumulated dumpsters.

Terry flew back South after the altercation, Shannon and Sabina went alienated themselves, Gracey and Debbie continued to roam loose and My Aunt Sissy became pregnant with my cousin Alesha. My Aunt was extremely emotional as she began to talk about her pregnancy. Her tears had me a bit astounded because I never seen her in an emotional stage before. I felt that her past history of being a Rush Girl wasn't the cause of her being emoted. Something had boggled her mind to the point that she had to allow her roiled anger profuse from within.

Consoling her feelings in comfort, I asked with a verbatim tongue, "What was bothering her?" She began to weep even more a she stood over my bed trying to explain to me what I was anxious to hear. She made me promise and swear that I wouldn't tell a soul about what she was about to unveil. I swore and promised on everything that I thought I loved but, you can bet your ass that I had all my fingers crossed.

Sissy finally got up the courage to tell me that my cousin Alesha wasn't only my cousin; she was my fucking sister too. My heart paused and I blacked out for about five seconds, ironically I blacked out on my aunt too. The issue marveled my mind to the point of me using verbose language; I didn't believe one word as I called her every fallacious liar and untrue muthafucka in the book of reality.

It took two 500 milligrams of acetaminophen to calm me down, once I was back into relax mode I needed to know when, why, who, what and how the incident became Alesha. I didn't consider my Aunt Sissy as Family anymore, she was just plain ol' Sissy Williams to me but, she stood by my bed side with a tight grip on my hand. Drenched in tears she explained the situation with a moment of clarity.

After the Rush Girl's split up in 1964 and Sissy became pregnant, she went to Big Kyle for help about the matter. At fifteen back then, my grandmother Ann would have killed her ass if she found out and, Muscles would have devoured Big Kyle. So she kept quiet about her pregnancy, only Big Kyle knew. Consequently, he told her to flush it down the toilet and send it up the Delaware River. Twenty-one at the time of the incident, Big Kyle was to busy birthing the streets of Camden with narcotics. He was married to the game but a kid with it would have been a major setback because Olivia wouldn't have took that too well.

Sissy decided to keep the baby after Big Kyle's declination of it all and, waited a slow seven months to tell my grandmother Ann, so she wouldn't have to abort it. Ann understood her plight but disowned in the process because Sissy lied and told her that she didn't know who the Father was. Only for the reason of mot being disowned by her sisters and judged as a trifling whore. But, Grandma Ann had already considered her just that - A Whore!

In the spring of 1965 she gave birth to Alesha Moore, as she continued to live in the three room condominium with her sisters. She managed to take care of her baby girl with the help of her twins. Gracey and Debbie were still dealing with Big Kyle and D.S. on a business level, so whatever extra money they made, it went directly to Sissy. At sixteen it was arduous for young Sissy to raise Alesha but she managed to adapt, getting a job at Krystal cleaners down town on the corner of Newton Street and Broadway.

When Alesha was three and the Rush Girl's reunited once more in 1968, my Aunt Gracey had become pregnant with Wadeelah in June of that year. Three months after my mother became pregnant with me. Sissy delegated for Gracey and filled her position until she was well and able to move with the crew again.

I vomited after Sissy told me that my Aunt Gracey had got pregnant by Big Kyle too. My Aunt Gracey never told a soul but how Sissy found out that Big Kyle was the father, she found her twin in the bathroom one morning with slit wrist. That's when Gracey explained to Sissy the situation, but just like Sissy, Gracey smoke screened who was the biological father and blamed it on her ex-boyfriend Clifford. Clifford accepted Gracey's pregnancy without hesitation and promised to be there for the baby Wadeelah.

Until this day, Sissy told me that no one knows the exact truth except for Gracey and me. The chaotic disorder would crush the family and destroy my mother's heart. Sissy wasn't thinking about my feelings or how it would affect me; I guess I was one of the strongest in her eyes. I wanted to tell her that she had to leave but that would have anguished her mind even more, so I allowed her to continue...

$ $ $ $ $

On the Rush Girl's rise to the top, Shake found out about Big Kyle dealing with both of my aunts. That's the real reason a lot of corruptive things were happening to Big Kyle and D.S. The Rush Girls solemnly swore to each other when they first joined forces that they would never let no man nor woman come between them. Promises were broken once Big Kyle and D.S. visualized how the woman operated, since Shake didn't want nothing to do with Big Kyle after she used his street smarted mind to gain in the game. Big Kyle found numerous ways to bring confusion between Shake, Terry, and the triplets by telling them all, on separate occasions what the other didn't say. Just to break up the loving friendships that they all shared with one another.

Debbie and Sissy quickly caught on to what Big Kyle was doing and wanted to do something to quell the He say / She say that he flared between the crew. Sissy said that every since she had Alesha she worked hard at doing something rigorous to Big Kyle. A few years after my sister Wadeelah and I were born, Sissy admitted that my Aunt Debbie poisoned his drink one night down at club Shake's.

$$\$ \, \$ \, \$ \, \$ \, \$$$

The poisonous liquid didn't really affect Big Kyle the way the triplets wanted it to because he never finished his entire drink. He sipped on it a few times then left the glass at the bar. Over the years Sissy said that Big Kyle's mind would wander in an amnesia state, as he forgot a lot of things. By the time he reached the drug throne in 1973, he was downing so much medication it was as if he'd become human medication himself. Having side affects of weight loss, blurry vision, and the loss of teeth.

The triplets wanted more than what he went through to happen in a more severe way but after he was brutally shot at Krystal's lounge, they all felt that their missions were accomplished. Big Kyle's been a dead man walking every since he came out of his disabled coma a couple years after he was shot.

As Sissy concluded her sided story, my eyes were filled with ocean tears because my family, too, had major flaws. Knowing for a fact that Sissy and Gracey never made an attempt to explain to Wadeelah and Alesha that they were sisters and that I was their brother. My family was pure water in my eyes as I scene the dishonesty from a far and blood was suppose to be much thicker.

Sissy was speechless after seeing my tears; she just kissed my forehead and left me in the hospital room in a full daze. I began to see the resemblance that I and my sisters shared once the black and white family picture was imbued by Sissy. Wadeelah and Alesha were both light skinned, having their mothers and Big Kyle's complexion. On the other hand, I was blessed with Olivia's smooth, chocolate complexion. We all were tall, except that I was a bit taller. We had the same muddy eyes, noses, and facial structures. I felt like a fool for not perceiving the situation a head of time and I felt that it was also my duty to explain the aged secret to Wadeelah and Alesha.

$ $ $ $ $

Two days later I received yet another visit, this time it was from DaVita, who I hadn't seen for months on in. She was still looking like the innocent angel that I got with back in 1980, just a tad-bit mature. My mother was the one who had enlightened him about my accident and told her what hospital I was in. She just stopped by to wish me well and to say her farewells before she left the state for Florida to stay with relatives. It was definitely something about Florida that had a lot of Camden citizens relocating down bottom.

Not very concerned but out of spite, I asked why Florida? DaVita grandmother was ill and she wanted to spend some time with her before she passed. She asked me did I get any updates on Lamaar's whereabouts or any leads to where she could have disappeared to. There were no leads and I had the slightest idea where she could have been, all I knew was that my boy Lukay had been tied and killed in Farnham's Park.

In return, I asked her about Poohshaun's whereabouts and why was he being badgered by the Feds so much? DaVita elucidated that every since the day she rang my phone about six months ago about Poohshaun's abusiveness, she hadn't seen or heard from him. That was another reason DaVita was heading south because she was tired of being watched and pestered by authorities concerning Poohshaun. She couldn't even use the bathroom in peace without them knocking at her door. DaVita had no idea of why they were after him the way that they were but it wasn't to arrest him. Because if they wanted to apprehend him there had been plenty of opportunities for that.

DaVita sat by my bed side, rubbing my hair and caressing my left hand, telling me how much she missed being with me and wished we could become more than friends again. I truly didn't understand the big attraction I drew on DaVita, we had a relationship five and a half year ago that didn't even last long. What was it that she seen in me that I didn't see in myself? I was clueless, but I knew at that very moment DaVita became the allure of my hormones. Was it the tight fit Calvin Klein jeans, her bamboo earrings and all her splendor or, her just being in my presence?

I'd been out of sexual contact since my strumpet ex-girlfriend wanted to tap the waters of dishonesty. But, as I ogled DaVita's smooth, dark complexion I couldn't hesitate in asking, "Could we take it there?" DaVita sighed, with an expression of needing to hear them words come out of my mouth for a very long time. At a slow pace, she went and locked the door, which wasn't that much of a problem because Nurse Bennett had given me my timely medication prior to DaVita's visit. DaVita hit the light switch on the wall and headed toward me as she disrobed in movement.

DaVita's matching pink panty and bra set savored my taste buds, wanting to rip them off with my teeth. Smelling like a freshly picked fruit basket, she mounted over me and started giving me passionate four-play. She sucked and licked me from my earlobes to the middle of my tender phallus. As she breathed around my loins I felt myself getting ready to explode a volcano, I truly was lacking dick control. Once inside of her succulent mouth, every nerve in my body went frigid. All I saw was clear blue skies, colorful rainbows and blossoming flowers as she continued to work magic with her lips. The sensation got even warmer, as DaVita inconspicuously penetrated me inside of her sultry goods. She took my hand and placed it on the rear of her full cotton candy round.

She caressed her C-cups like squeezed oranges as she gyrated her hips while speaking in tongues. Saying things to keep me stiff inside of her, but what excited me more than the sex itself was that she was fucking me with her panties still on. She reached her climax and milk from her breast squirted out in sprinkler form as she bounced harder and harder to the uncontrollable feeling. The orgasm emasculated her to the point that she had to lean over and lay on me to regain her energy.

As I put effort into seeking her same feeling, DaVita gently started to bite on my chest, which definitely was my spot. When touched right, my chest remained tender for days. Slowly, I whispered "I'm comin'," repetitively in her ear as I brought her towards me and clutched her body close to mines for support. In haste, DaVita pushed my hands away, replaced her pussy with her mouth for a second time and slurped after the remains.

After the intense gurney romance, I lied calm in bed watching the hilarious sit-com "What's Happening," while DaVita freshened up in the bathroom. I was awoken by a kiss on the cheek from DaVita whose time was limited for unknown purposes. As bad as I wanted her relentless company at that moment the time ceased without notice. She handed me a piece of paper that had a few numbers where should could be reached if ever needed. Before heading out of the room she took the pink panties she wore during the sexual escapade and sat them on the nightstand, telling me to smell them if I ever forgot what her passionate touch felt like. A forehead kiss sealed our time together and I felt that that would probably be the last time that I seen DaVita. Because my chances of going to Florida were slim and how I blundered, her number would have been lost in no time.

$ $ $ $ $

The following afternoon my sister-cousins, Alesha and Wadeelah stopped by to see how I was doing. I was a little weary eyed from earlier but I maintained my composure in front of them both. Before

I could finish my hellos they tagged teamed me with what was going on in the everyday world of street gossip about what, who, this and that.

There was a big article in the Courier's Post about Wayne Weston and Rasaan Money, the two All-Americans who played for the University of Maryland. Allegedly, the two impact players were arrested and charged with breaking the NCAA rules, by accepting gifts and money from certain agents and clients in the sports world. Wayne was also charged with three pounds of marijuana, which was found inside the boys off campus apartment. He was apprehended and taken to the Maryland County Jail but released on a $50,000 dollar cash-bond. No court date had been scheduled for the two nincompoops who thought they had it made in the shade.

The news took me by surprise at first but then again Wayne and Rasaan always tried getting over on people. I know they were kicking themselves in the ass for fucking up something that was laid out for them. All they had to do was play ball and attempt to make the grade because they were that skilled. Now, with bleak situations brewing, their meal tickets of going pro were slimmer than a kitchen table's toothpick.

Things got no better as my sisters went on explaining about my man Kyron Owens. I knew Kyron didn't have all his marbles since we were kids, when he put a dead bird in our third grade teacher's - Mr. Avant - desk drawer. I was just hoping that he didn't pull any illicit stunts like his other two dummy friends. Apparently, the high school All-American senior was expecting a baby. Wadeelah found out the news from his girlfriend Deedra who was in her trigonometry class.

Deedra was three months pregnant before she broke the news to Kyron, the nations top basketball prospect. Deedra said that Kyron wanted her to abort the baby because it was going to interfere with his chances of going to college. Deedra made a wise decision by telling Kyron that she was keeping his first child, with the help of her parent's affluence she didn't need Kyron at all. Since he's found out the news, Kyron has fouled out of three games and missed a week of practice.

I thought it was simplistic to deal with the bimbo in the first place. Prior to him moving out of my place, being with Deedra was going to raze his basketball career. But, I guess he didn't want to listen to a friend who flipped hot pizza turnovers. Deedra ironically wasn't the culprit, it took two to tangle and she knew that the baby was the key to Kyron's pockets if he made it big. Three guys who I respected and looked up to growing up were sliding down razor blades into alcohol rivers.

The shocking news that I was struck with was no where near as severe as the news I was going to make them aware of. We were sharing nothing but jokes, laughs and smiles inside the invigorating room but, internally I felt the aura in the room about to change once the mega-tom bomb was dropped on there parade.

Being blatant as possible with the sad/good news, I came straight out and said what my ego told me to say without having to cut any corners. "The two of you are my sisters." They gave me these fatuous looks, chuckling as if I was playing but they didn't know that I was serious as my heart beat. As I reiterated myself the baritone in my voice deepened, having a facial expression of despair. A breeze of silence overcastted the room's happiness once they scene my seriousness.

As I went into detail about the situation I seen two wild animals come out of Wadeelah and Alesha. There Q & A process overrode my explanation process; I caught an instant headache from all of their fussing and babbling. Situations had gotten so out of hand; I had to call for Nurse Bennett to calm them down.

After two 500 milligrams of Tylenol and Ms. Bennett's help of restraining my sister's mood swing, I explained everything to them the way Sissy gave it to me. The fling Big Kyle had with Gracey and Sissy, the depression of Big Kyle wanting them to be aborted, and how the triplets poisoned Big Kyle. I felt it was wrong for me to be doing Sissy's dirty work as I addressed those issues.

Alesha had her mother on the phone calling her every vulgar name in the book of profanity after I filled them in. I don't think Sissy got one word out to justify her secrecy to her daughter. After she finished she slammed the phone down, sat back in the chair next to

Wadeelah and poured tears of agony. I thought that the way Alesha came off was harsh because Sissy gave her life but could have flushed her out a long time ago.

Wadeelah on the contrary just sat across from me very relaxed with her legs crossed but in a deep daze of bitter sweet reveries. Probably trying to figure out why just like Alesha and I. Her face was heavy, I could see that she wanted to pour tears of a river but she was either trying to stay strong for me and Alesha or the issue didn't take effect on her as much.

The issues made the day seem so long and dreary, my sisters stayed the night with me. I guess they were to hurt to go anywhere; it wasn't like we just got reunited after so many years. We'd been around each other all our lives and had enormous history together and the issue had shaken them up. I tried cheering them up by reminiscing on a lot of things that we did coming up. In the mist of it all, the three of us promised to always stick together and stay loyal to one another, unlike some of our family members who were very deceitful and dishonest.

Three sisters was a heavy burden to carry because they were more of a concern than the demographics I was trapped in. The more I tried to ease my way of living, more bullshit came into play and through it all I felt that I was the bad guy. I felt that it was truly time to say good night to most of what lied in between.

# Chapter. 15

The day I was released, I went home the way I came in, in a yellow cab but I really want to walk to put pressure on my leg. But it would have taken me and my one crutch forever and a day. Plus, I wanted to see how much damage the mysterious gunman caused in my condominium. From all of the multiple gun fire, I knew I was either gone to be evicted or have to renovate the place over again.

I was approached by two female clerks as I entered the lobby at the Glamour Towers, as I made way back to my apartment. Their names were Ericka and Tina; they had to be new at the job because I'd never been stopped for anything on my way to and from my pad.

$$\$\ \$\ \$\ \$\ \$$$

Before I came out of character or began to confute with the two ladies, I asked to speak to a supervisor or someone with a higher authoritative position. Ericka, this short, redbone with a petite figure picked up the desk phone to page her boss. I really wasn't paying Ericka any mind because her co-worker was the one with my undivided attention; she was trying to see if my name was on the residence list. I gave Tina, both, my apartment and extension numbers to my place of comfort (1331 and 8168). But, the funny thing was she still had no listing of me being a resident there. Having a fiery disposition, I dropped my crutch and snatched the clipboard out of the whore's hand, to check for myself. Simultaneously, after I got hold of the clipboard, this short, light skinned man with glasses approached me at the front desk. "Hello sir, my name is Eyeball Jenkins," He said, shaking my hand. "I'm the owner of the Glamour Tower, how can I be of some assistance to you?"

'Owner?' I thought to myself. 'When the fuck did that become effective?' The information truly startled my mind. "You're the owner?" I asked, scratching the back of my neck. "So what happened to Riley and Domino?"

"Who?" Eyeball retorted, like he had no idea of the names. "These Towers were sold to me by the original owner Mr. William Holmes."

William Holmes didn't ring a bell; I didn't know who to believe or what the fuck was going on. All I knew was that I had $25,000 dollars invested into my apartment and, I was getting hassled by a midget and two coo-coo birds. I was willing to show Eyeball my proof of purchase and the transaction statements that came with the voucher and deed.

Eyeball spared me the hassle of going through with the procedures and went into his personal information cabinet to pull my file. "I told you," I said, pointing to the file. "I knew I wasn't crazy."

"Calm down sir, I never doubted your truth," He said, examining my file with his bifocals. "Mmm Hmm, I see," He continued, as he flipped a few pages.

"Is there a problem of some sort?"

"I believe there is a problem Mr. Moore," He imposed, turning my file towards me.

There was a big void sign stamped in red marker on the original copy of the deed. "Void?!" That's impossible because my place was paid in full with cash... No check or credit cards. The receipts right there in your face."

"I see it Mr. Moore," He said going back into my file. "You were in apartment 1331, right?"

"That's correct."

"Well the problem is sir, here at the Glamour Towers violence and harm to residents and visitors are not prohibited anywhere in this building. Take a look right here," He continued, pointing to a statement in the policy. "It says on the above date of November 20th 1985, apartment 1331 was assailed and wrecked."

"Someone was trying to kill me."

"I can understand all of that, but neither I nor any of my staff were here to verify the incident. I'm just following policy guidelines."

"What fucking guidelines?" I voiced, smacking the file out of his hand. "Well get Willie Homer or whatever the fuck his name is, on the phone or get my twenty-five Gee's before the both of these muthafuckin' towers go up in smoke."

Eyeball must have seen the frustration inside of my pupils because after I started raising hell, he pulled me into a back room - behind the front counter - and was willing to compromise. Out of the kindness of Eyeball's heart and the $25,000 dollars that I put into the building's treasure, Eyeball offered me another apartment. An even bigger duplex, fully furnished, having three bedrooms and two and a half bathrooms. Since I wasn't stable enough to travel back and forth up the long flights of stairs or walk to and from the elevator, he made sure that the duplex was on the first level of the building. All I did was sign a few documents and he threw me a set of keys and, told me that he would take care of my other housing needs.

Prior to us both heading out of the back room and me going to observe the new place on the 1st floor. I asked Eyeball did they move a new tenant into my old apartment. And if he did, could he give them a call to see if any of my belongings were still inside. He checked the residence roster and some had already filled the slot at 1331, a woman by the name of Kelli Browning.

Eyeball dialed Ms. Browning's extension to see if any of my belongings were up on the 13th floor. He wanted to get approval from Ms. Browning to see if it was appropriate for me to go up and retrieve them. She must have given him the okay because as he continued to converse with her, he winked his eye at me and gave me a thumbs up to proceed. As I departed from the elevator and made my way towards Ms. Browing's apartment, my mind envisioned her as some grumpy old lady whom fussed all the time.

Before I could even knock at Ms. Browning's door, the knob turned and the door opened like I was entering a haunted house. I truly couldn't believe my eyes and who stood before me when she greeted me at the door. Kelli Browning was far from grumpy and old, she put the B in beautiful and the G in gorgeous. I hadn't seen anything that breathtaking since the rainbow on a sunny day.

Kelli's skin was light toned, her face pure, paced with a cinematic smile that belonged on the front cover of Cover Girl Magazine. She had long, jet black, curly hair and stood about 5'9" barefooted and weighed about 130 lbs., naked. Her appearance startled my voice box and immobilized my speech.

"Is there something you would like to say?" She asked, as I stood stiff, blinking my eyes faster than flashing lights.

She took the imitative of introducing herself to me, extending her hand in my direction. Snapping out of my daze, I then responded, "Oh! Hi my name is Kyle," extending my left hand because my right one was in a sling. I felt nothing more than cotton when our hands touched.

Kelli invited me into her newly, refurnished apartment and asked me to make my self comfortable as if we fraternized for a few months or so. She conversed with me while walking back and forth through the apartment, telling me how the condo had been renovated prior to her moving in and how they left my furniture and covered it with white sheets. Management never told her that someone lived in the apartment prior to her moving in; she assumed that the furniture was an accommodation.

$ $ $ $

Kelli's disposition had me a mental head lock that I could care less about the furniture, all I could think about was furnishing her; I really wanted to know her on a personal level.

"You can have all of the heavy things," I said, trying to make her understand that I was generous. "The leather furniture, bedroom set, all I need is my clothes and personal papers and I'll be out of your hair."

$ $ $ $

Kelli thanked me by shaking my hand once more, saying that that was the sweetest thing that a man has ever done for her. She must have been reading my conscience because before I could delve into her vitals, she beat me to the punch. She inquired into everything from my birth place to my employment status. Of course I lied to her a little, even though she was fine as freshly picked peach, she was still a muthafuckin' stranger. I gave her a little of a lot and portions of my lifetime with out hesitating.

"I'm twenty years of age," Lying straight through my teeth because I could tell by her physique that she was in her mid-twenties. In reality I was only eighteen but I had to round my number off to the nearest tenth if I wanted a slight chance. "I'm also the only boy of four children."

"You're groomed very well to only be twenty years of age," Kelli replied, as she gathered most of my belongings.

"Thanks."

"Well I'm the youngest of two; I have an older brother he's in the army."

"Oh! That's what's' happening, one of my friends... Ahmad is in the Air-Force. I don't mean to pry but what is it that you do to survive in this cold world?"

Kelli paused for a second, as if she needed time to make a lie about her career field. Giving me this dubious look as if she didn't want me to know any of her personal credentials.

"I'm a county clerk at city hall... Downtown," she answered, neatly placing my clothes in a plastic bag. "I've been working there full time for about six years now, since graduating from Woodrow Wilson."

"You graduated from Wilson?"

"Yeah, why do you know people that attended the school?"

"I was a student there at one point until I dropped out at the end of my sophomore year."

"Why'd you drop out?" she asked helping me up from the sofa.

"Family issues, money needing to be made and food needed to be on the table. You know how setbacks are?" I had the slightest idea as to why I keep lying to Kelli, I didn't know whether it was her beauty, or me, trying to stay level headed with her so she wouldn't think otherwise of me.

"I understand your circumstances completely, I too have had some struggle run-ins. But, I learned that when you take your time in getting situated and handle your responsibilities with patience, everything falls in its proper perspective."

The aura that lingered between Kelli and I felt as if we shared a platonic relationship that never soured. The way that we conversed with each other was surreal but, it was like I could talk to her everyday in a depressed state and she would help me see my way through. And, by the way that she expressed herself, I could tell that Kelli was truly mawkish on the inside.

Kelli and I shared a few more laughs as we continue our conversation towards my apartment on the 1st floor. I damn near fainted when she told me that she was single and had no children. My relationship stock, with her, went up ten more points from the previous elaboration back at her apartment. Simultaneously, my dreams were a bit shattered, Kelli had just gotten out of a three year relationship with her ex-boyfriend Allen, which she depicted too be turmoil. Stating that Allen wanted to have his cake and eat it at the same time and that wasn't her way of being an item to another. Shit, she was second-to-none in my eyes and for her to tell me that was to say that Allen had to spit in her face with no remorse. Her focus wasn't into a sheet romance; Kelli was trying to establish a career. A man and a relationship, if on passed her by would definitely be a secondary option. But, a nigga like me was willing to wait; she wasn't the only person that had some sort of patience. Just as long as she lived at the same residence as I, I'd play the secondary position around the clock.

We exchanged extension numbers after she helped me down to my apartment; I also gave her my phone number to my pad in Centerville just in case she couldn't reach at the condo. Kelli, then hugged and kissed me on the cheek and told me that she would definitely be in touch. Right at that moment, telling her I loved her in a serious voice was all wanted to do. After she left, I lied across my tepid, terry cloth sofa with her on my mind until I fell asleep. Her beauty boggled my mind so much that I didn't take my jacket off or inspect my furnished domain.

$ $ $ $ $

Later on in the week I went to my Aunt Carole's home in Pennsauken to attend this family meeting that was orchestrated by Wadeelah and Alesha. I sensed what was going to take place and it was the first of any family meeting that I ever attended. It was obvious that my grandmother Ann as well as my mother wanted nothing more than to get to the bottom of the triplet's deceitful secrecy pertaining to Wadeelah and Alesha.

The household felt as if they were all awaiting my presence so that the meeting could get under way. All of my aunts, my two twin uncles (Lovell and Will), Alesha and Wadeelah, and my mother and grand mother were staring at me like I was the culprit when I arrived. The living room was tranquil and everyone remained mum to the issue that nobody seemed like they wanted to open up and discuss.

I didn't get the chance to take off my coat and get comfortable before the confuting began and, it was Alesha who raised hell like a saber tooth tiger in the middle of my aunt's living area.

"All I want to know," she said, looking in her mother's direction as Sissy sat tranquil as a cat, next to her co-defendant Gracey. "Is why you never told me or the family that Kyle or Wadeelah are my brother and sister? After all these damn years you should have just took it to your grave."

$ $ $ $ $

Everyone's attention shifted towards Sissy and Gracey, patiently waiting for a response and honest answer. "I was scared back then," Sissy expressed, with heavy tears trickling down her face. And, pandemonium overcastted the room from my aunt's moderate answer, the entire family knew that she was full of bullshit. Even Gracey, her ride or die bitch gave her a suspicious look.

"Oh, that's bullshit and you know it," My mom exclaimed.

"Sit down Livy, let her finish explaining herself," Uncle Will said, grabbing her by the arm.

"No fuck that Will, that bitch know what she was doing, she wasn't scared. She just didn't want anyone in the family to disown her whorish ass."

The street romance between Sissy and Big Kyle was a major issue that my mother never had knowledge of and was truly marveled by such information.

"So you were fuckin' Kyle before Gracey?" Olivia asked, as the astonished questioning kept everyone in a perplexed state.

"You want to know the truth," Gracey said, jumping up from her seat.

"That's why we're all here so we can mend this situation," I added, so the process could pick up.

Gracey was like the President of the United States as she spoke articulately while revealing the dark truths. Everyone was tuned in on the breaking news, having no interruptions.

"At the time of Kyle and Olivia's relationship, Kyle was also dippin' on the side with my girlfriend Shannon. Olivia knew and we kept telling her to leave his ass alone because he wasn't right for her. Me and my twins had a sit down with our big sis' and explained the mendacious ways of Big Kyle. But, Olivia didn't want to listen, she thought we envied her for what she and Kyle shared. So the twins and I let her deal with the situation the best way she seen fit. Some time passed and Kyle and Shannon were still seeing each other. I approached Shake myself and told her about the relationship that he shared with my sister. Shannon took heed and was willing to turn Kyle loose but the entire time I tried getting Shannon and Olivia to open up there eyes to him, he was trying to tap Debbie"

Everyone's attention shifted once more, from Gracey directly over to Aunt Debbie, who was sipping on a glass of water.

"I can't believe this shit," Olivia said, patting her eyes with some tissue. "All three of my baby sisters back stabbed me like that--"

"I never fed into Kyle's bullshit," Aunt Debbie retorted, slamming the glass of water on the table. "I always put my family first even when I was immature, I never thought with my legs. Kyle tried his hardest to manipulate me with money and all kinds of materials so I could fuck him. The real truth is that Sissy and Gracey had sex with

Kyle pretending to be me so they could swindle him out of money and drugs. For the mere purpose of achieving a goal for our crew the Rush Girls. We were trying to dissipate our own brother and his team for our own gain in the game. Because Muscles was treating us like an enemy and didn't want us anywhere near his territory. Obviously, Sissy and Gracey got caught up with the hedonistic life that Kyle portrayed and couldn't get enough of what he offered. Just like he had Shannon and Livy at one point, he entrapped them with his pimp hand too."

The truth was divulged but everyone still wanted to know why did Sissy and Gracey stealthily keep the matter of Wadeelah and Alesha from the family's attention? Sissy made it clear to everyone that she truly was scared and didn't want Olivia and her other family members to disown her and alienate themselves. Sissy and Gracey, both, admitted that they never induced termination of their pregnancies; abortions to them were like murder in the first degree.

$$\$ \, \$ \, \$ \, \$ \, \$$$

Both situations was wrong, either way the family looked at it or Sissy and Gracey perceived it to be. The family began comforting Sissy and Gracey's emotions, first through forgiveness and then with sympathetic hugs and kisses.

Gracey and Sissy, had a personal sit-down wit me, my mother and my sisters to get a stark understanding of their wrongs and how they would make it better for us as a family. In a profusion of tears, Sissy told me and my sisters to always stick by each other no matter if she and her two sisters never forgave each other. And, Gracey stated that it was bigger than forgiveness and that God wouldn't have forgave them for the damaged they caused to everyone.

As time passed, the atmosphere of cries and voiced pain cleared with a mere festivity. Everyone sat around hot dishes of soul food, joking and reminiscing about the good ol' days. It always took some sort of wrong doing to put my family back on the right track, at times it discouraged me because I grew up apprehending that blood was thicker than water. But the irony of it was, I knew there would be a time of more furious issues to come and that would put my family back through adversity, causing the water to dilute the blood.

$ $ $ $ $

That night, after spending half the day with my family the day with my hysterical family, I took a cab to my townhouse. I hadn't been there in months, but I went for three reason, too get a piece of mind, see if my utilities were still on and to check my money spot. This held an enormous $410,000 dollars in cash in the safe.

Prior to me going to my safe which was safely embedded inside my floor, under the bed, I checked the missed calls on my answering machine. There were more missed calls from my mother and bill collectors than any other person who had my phone number; well over twenty five calls between the two. DaVita called a few times letting me know that she made it to Florida safely and was looking forward to me returning her call. The last two calls were from Billy and my two wizard white boys.

As I sat across my bed remunerating my stacks of money, I tuned in close to the two recent messages. Keith and Derrick's message was a few days old, they both called to tell me that the mission was complete and that they didn't want to get into to much detail over the phone. Billy called them and kept his explanation brief, saying, "That the Rush had been put on the girl," whatever that meant. They didn't come and tell me in person because their van was in the auto mechanic shop.

Billy's message confused me even more, he confidentially spoke in codes, saying, "The blood in the cloths had been washed and now I could rest well." The message boggled my mind so much; I didn't waste anytime to analyze it, because I went to sleep. The devil must have sent me an angel in my dreams because I woke up in the middle of the night, drenched in sweat and dehydrated. The weird thing was, I didn't even know what I was dreaming about I just went into the bathroom and ran some water in the sink. I threw some cold water over my face so I could gather my conscience and become more aware of what it was that I dreamt.

I took a long stare in the mirror, thinking, brain racing, thinking more until I finally read between the enigmatic codes that were left on my the machine. Terry's blood was washed, meaning that she was dead and the mission was over. In a way I was glad that the deceiving, disloyal, conniving bitch was handled. But, in a way I wasn't because I was left with only half the mystery to the drug underworld's puzzle. And, Terry was the lead to the other half of the puzzle. I wanted nothing more but to have her in my presence to get the other half of the unedited version of what really took place in the underworld. The chances of that was never a chance and I had to get over it and move on with the rest of the life I had.

# Chapter. 16

The following month, in April I was back on my feet maneuvering slightly, my leg brace was removed at Dr. Blynn's office on Mt. Ephraim Avenue, across from West Jersey Hospital. Dr. Blynn had been my personal doctor since I was pushed out the womb; he told me to try an exercise my arm and leg twice a day. So I could put the feeling back into my muscle's tissue and his physician prescribed me these big analgesics, orange horse pills to be take twice a day for the next month.

$$\$ \ \$ \ \$ \ \$ \ \$$$

I hooked up with Keith and Derrick after my brace was removed to go car shopping. I didn't want anything too luxurious, just something to get me from point A to point B. They took me to a compatriot by the name of Mike but was known to them as "Big Hustler." Because Mike would sell his children if he had to just so he could pay the smallest bill. Keith, Derrick, and Big Hustler grew up in the same neighborhood as adolescents but parted ways when Mike's parents decided to move to Pennsylvania before his freshman year in high school.

Through the years they all managed to say in contact with each other and stay close by. My two white boys had the low quantity, good quality hook up with their pal Big Hustler Mike. Sort of a favor for a favor thing, Mike had the cars and Keith and Derrick had the appliances. However they compromised and worked out their own propositions wasn't any of my concern; I was just looking for the right deal.

On our journey to P.A. they gave me more insight on Billy's phone call pertaining to Terry. Billy called them around 3 a.m., he tried reaching me first at the hospital but they told him that I had been discharged days prior. But, he told them to blow the power on the surveillance at Terry's home because she was watching us in spirit. He didn't go into any further details, he just told Keith and Derrick that everyone could go back to their normal lives and handle more important business. In ending he told them that he was going on a long vacation, having no idea where but he was absconding himself from Camden and the entire New Jersey state.

Keith and Derrick reviewed the tapes one more time before they disconnected their installments. They wanted to make sure that they didn't bypass any important clues or skip over Terry's shadow but after the review they still came up empty handed.

Once we arrived at Mike's Hustling Car Convention, I got binocular vision instantly. My eyes widen to the enormity of cars that were on display. Mike had to have about three acres of old and new cars of all varieties. After being introduced to Mike I seen why they called him Big Hustler, he was a big country white boy, standing about 6'5" and 300 plus pounds. He made my Uncle Muscles look like Olive Oyl off of Popeye the cartoon and his hand sat like dumbbells like he lifted logs for a living. His appearance would make an unsure customer change his/her mind about buying one of his cars. Because I damn sure had doubts after being in his presence for more than ten minutes.

"Looking for anything specific?" he asked, grabbing hold of the suspenders on his trousers. I wasn't looking for anything too particular, just something clean and fast. I yearned for fast cars; if I wasn't into sports as a kid I probably would have stole cars for a living.

After about an hour and a half of browsing and test driving a few of the cars that Mike had at his auction, I finally came across an automobile that fit my character. A brand new, 86' Celebrity Classic four-door sedan, gray, fully equipped and went from 0 to 50 in 9 seconds. I had to have it, not even caring how much Big Hustler priced it at, the Celebrity befitted a young celebrity such as me and the lanes were fit for her.

Since I was a friend of Keith and Derrick, I was a good friend to Mike the Big Hustler also. Mike gave me the car for eleven grand, straight cash - nothing more, no less. Mike sealed the car with two temp-tags, handed me the title of ownership with the keys and told me to enjoy. He told me that if I needed to borrow or rent a car for any reason don't hesitate to ask or give him a call.

On our way back into the Garden State we decided to take a detour in to Pennsauken to Terry's home just to observe the scenery. It was around ten o'clock when we arrived in Terry's old neck of the woods. The neighborhood was serene, only street lights and crickets dwelled the atmosphere as we stood out front in profound contemplation. Terry's entire home was vacant, we could see straight through her windows through the other side of the house, similar to the visual at the House of Chemistry. Keith wanted to kick in the door but it was bolted shut with three big padlocks.

We were astounded, wondering how and when did Terry have the time to empty the entire house and vacate the premises. When Keith and Derrick had around the clock surveillance on the spot. The mysterious situations that were beginning to take place began to scare me in more ways then I could imagine. The underworld's puzzle started going from clues to horror. Someone had to empty the place after my boys disconnected their wires.

Besides the sturdy, wooden For Sale sign on Terry's lawn, sat a metallic mailbox. On the inside of the mailbox were stacks of papers and letters dated to the above addressee, a guy by the name of William Holmes. This was the same guy who once owned the Glamour Towers, now owned by the nigga Eyeball Jenkins.

"William Holmes!" I exclaimed, as Derrick and Keith, both, looked at me strangely.

"What about him you know him or something?" Keith asked, grabbing the stack of mail out of my hand.

I elucidated the issue about who William Holmes depicted himself to be, Keith and Derrick were shocked when they heard the only story that I knew about William H. and the Glamour Towers. But, William H's circumstances weren't adding up to any of us because we all knew that Terry was Riley and Domino's sister and they use too own the condominium spectacle. But, what was inapprehensive was we didn't have an idea of where William H. came from and what ties he had with Terry and her spirited brothers. Before parting ways I asked Keith and Derrick to see if they could delve some information up on William H. and to get back at me.

$$\$ \ \$ \ \$ \ \$ \ \$$$

Instead of me driving to Centerville, I decide to go out North Camden and be nosey around the condominiums premises for a while. Just to see what clueless material lied beneath the towers so the trouble could stay ignited? Tina, the brown toned bomb shell was working the front desk when I entered.

"Hello Mr. Moore," She said seductively, biting into a banana.

"Hi Tina," I replied, opening my mailbox with the key. "You working alone tonight I see?"

"Yeah, Ericka's out sick and Eyeball left early to handle some personal business and my shift is just about finished in another fifteen minute. Twelve o'clock... Maybe I'll stop by before heading home," She said with a smirk that enticed me as she bit into her bottom lip seductively.

"Maybe you will, maybe you won't but I suggest that you do so," I hinted, grabbing my mail as I headed towards my apartment and winked my eye at her simultaneously.

No soon as I got into my apartment I headed straight for bathroom and ran some water in the tub. As I undressed I checked the answering machine while breezing through my mail. There were only two messages on the machine and they were from my mother and Kelli. Kelli had been so busy working that she couldn't reach out to me, only on her free time. She decided to give me a call just to let me know that I had been running through her mind since our first encounter at my old pad.

Kelli's message touched me a little but not more than the mysterious letter I'd received from my old dame Lamaar Green, who I thought was roaming free in spirit up into this point. From the way that she inscribed her feelings to me, it was evident that she was alive and well somewhere anonymous. The letter had no address and the postmark was too vague to read but it read:

*Dear Kyle,*

*I know by the time you receive this letter you'll be truly surprised and wondering all kinds of crazy things at this point. But I just wanted to tell you that I survived the shooting that night caused by the robbing bastards that were out to harm you. All I could remember was waking up in a cold, vacant house wearing nothing but my underclothes. I had a gash across my forehead that caused me to receive twelve stitches. The gunman must have knocked me unconscious after shooting at you and must of took LuKay some place because I was left abandoned alone. I know the both of us are probably nonexistent to you and you wouldn't give two thoughts about our whereabouts. But, Kyle you have to understand that I've been through more turmoil than one could possibly bear. A horror movie since a teen and, I've given you a brief summary of how I've managed to escape thus far. It's all irrelevant now and behind us both but I was just writing you to make you aware of my well being and that I'm far away from what has contaminated my soul my entire life. This is probably the last time you will hear or receive a letter from me because I'm never returning to the end that you dwell upon. Never forget that as long as you're in the game, ironically it is a game and just don't be a fool for to long and get caught up! We shall meet again on the other side but for now live life.*

*Love Always,*

*Lamaar*

My chest had tightened and I was out of breath from Lamaar's notation, feeling like my ribs were touching. I was almost dead meat, LuKay is dead meat and she's the only unharmed survivor. It was something definitely wrong with that picture and I came to conclude that it was a set up and that Lamaar was apart of the mysterious game. I had a gut feeling that there was more to Lamaar's letter, then what I read. Out of the blue, why would she write me and not leave a return address or any kind of information to where she could be reached? She was definitely a valuable piece in the game herself and I was going to unveil her true identity if it killed me.

Undoubtedly, Lamaar dealt with Terry's malignant brother Riley but, no one seemed to get a visual on them but my shallow mined sperm donor. Lamaar's letter definitely put the icing on the cake; I was tired of thinking, putting together all the wrong clues that seemed right. I was tired of being sick and tired, so I took Lamaar's letter, burnt it over my stove and flushed down the toilet.

I played Kelli's message back just to hear her sensual voice one more time so it could wane my frustrations. But, I wound up dialing her extension for the hope of her anticipating my call. After receiving no answer I headed for the bath and just as I stepped my foot into the water some tender tapping came at my apartment's door.

"Who is it?" I asked, looking through the peep hole, not wanting to answer but I answered anyway.

"Batina, is Kyle home?" she replied, as I put the extra lock latch on the door, opened it and peeped through the crack in unison.

"Was Kyle expecting you?"

"Yeah, but if he wasn't would my being here be a problem?" She asked, in a flirty manner.

"Yes it most certainly would," I answered, as we both shared a laugh.

Batina wasn't as attractive as Kelli but she had this aesthetic appeal that would catch an unseeing eye any day of the week. Standing about 5'7", very petite, my eyes weighed her in to be 130 lbs. give or take. She had the definition of the Coke bottle with a long, braided ponytail that flowed off of her caramel skin. Her teeth were pearly white, straighter than two parallel lines; she must have flossed and ate apples on a daily. But what enticed me more than whatever I noticed was her voluptuous breast size, her knockers were nice. Forty-double D's bounced on her small frame and she wore them back pain free.

There was no beating around the bush with Batina, far from the shy type she got right to the point of whatever she was engaging into. Once I finally got the opportunity to relax in the tub, Batina followed suit. I was shocked a little because we barely knew each other but I flowed with her.

"I know you maybe looking at me in a whorish way, thinking things are moving kind of fast," she said, turning the hot water's knob. "But I'm very promiscuous and whatever I have a fetish for I go after." Chocolate men in tubs, what a fetish!

Batina closed her eyes, reposed her body between my legs and relaxed her mind as she rested her head upon my shoulders. We talked a little while pouring water down her neck. She summarized how she grew up, and what made her so carefree to life. Her entire twenty-three years were spent in North Camden's part of town; 8th and Vine Streets was her sanctuary. Her mother abandoned her when she was just an infant, leaving her grandparents to raise and nurture her. Due to indigence she dropped out of school in the tenth grade and worked her physical prowess to get what she needed to survive. She admitted to being a running rebel prior to landing the job at the G.T.C.

At the tender age of fifteen she began exotic dancing at this local spot called the Black's Den in South Camden on the corner of Sheridan and Norris Streets. She said she only performed and never indulged into any sexual favors. Her first love Shan, who took her virginity at nineteen, had he doing robberies and shooting guns at seventeen so she didn't have to strip for cash. An idiotic move to do, she was placed under pressure and even risky for her but for some reason the shit made her pussy wet.

Shan was a monger to the streets of North Camden, selling any drug that was profitable for his pocket. In the beginning of '83 Batina's street romance with Shan closed in a fatal ending when she turned twenty years old. Shan was shot twice in the chest after exiting Tony and Ruthy's breakfast spot.

Batina explained that she put blood, sweat and tears in her three year relationship with Shan. And, being single for the past three year without him hasn't been the same but the ill will has made her more adventurous to life. As I continued to pour water down her neck and massage her delectable breast she left some advice on my brain to burn. Telling me to never second guess my decisions and regret nothing, words that I heard all before through my Uncle Muscles was nothing more than a reminder to me.

We finally made it in between my sheets to slow grind the vim away as she gave me some of the most intense sex that I never knew about. Her shit was better than DaVita, Dana, Jackie and Lamaar's all put in one.

As my body rested over Batina like a million bird feathers, our tongues locked like two tangled snakes as I slowly penetrated her warm fudge.

"Pinch my nipples," she said, gripping my lower back for support.

Pinching her nipples and plunging inside of her turned her vaginal canal on to profuse ungodly. The life of exotic dancing must have paid off big time; she was kinky as an indocile animal in the jungle. We traded places and I was inside of her from behind, I guess the feeling of filling one hole wasn't satisfying. So she smeared some of her juices on her rectum and began to stroke the tiny ant hole herself.

"Faster… Faster," she begged, as her tits bounced in rhythm.

The more I stroked and she pleased herself, the more she relinquished unyielding orgasms. She released cum like bathing bubbles while moaning out of pleasure and biting my sheets from the attention I paid inside of her. Just before I came I asked Batina to stare back at me as I palmed her ass with her back fully arched and her finger still maneuvering in her second hole. She gave me a passionate look that could have sat the moon inside the rainbow if her eyes had powers. As I reached my peak and focused on her look, some crazy shit happened. Blood began running from Batina's nose, all over my sheets and I couldn't believe my fucking eyes.

"What the fuck!" I yelled, pushing away from her.

Being mentally alert she must have known exactly what I was referring to because she clinched her nose and ran into the bathroom. I was mad as fuck, not because of her nose bleed but because the hoe messed up my nut, I should of did some pimp shit and kept going but the sight of it turned my stomach.

"Yo' are you alright in there?" I asked, knocking at the door. She was mumbling something to herself in tears as I tuned in with my ear to the door.

"I'm fine," she replied, in weeps as I heard the toilet flush.

"Do you want to talk about it?" I wanted to comfort her.

"Talk about what? There's nothing to talk about Kyle."

By the pitch in her voice I could tell that she was lying or hiding something so I decided to investigate for myself while she got herself together in the bathroom. I snooped through her personal belongings, her jeans, jacket and her pocketbook. I struck gold in her pocketbook which was filled with a bunch of money and heroin. Since the days of working for my Uncle Muscles I always had an eye out for different labels and products of dope. The dope that she has in her purse was called "Kiss," with a stamped print of lips on the bags. The dope was dubious to me and I had to inquire but first I took a few packages of the dope and held on to them until Batina came from the bathroom.

"Let's talk about this," I said, waving the baggy of dope in her face.

"I can't believe that you were snooping through my shit... I'm so out of here," she snapped, putting on her clothes.

Grabbing her arm with force I stopped her in motion and threw her on the bed, it was my first physical encounter with a female. "What the fuck is wrong with you?" she asked, kicking me in my abdominal area. She knocked the wind out of me as I backed into the bureau.

She tried hopping up and get to the bedroom door as I tried regaining my breath but I snatched her leg faster than a bird pecked bread. "Get off of me, let my fuckin' leg go," She said, trying to kick loose. I had to tussle around on the floor until she submitted and gave in.

"Alright... Alright," she said, giving in with a twisted arm, trying not to resist. Batina stood in front of the bureau's mirror and gave me explicit information about the dope and her dealings with it while brushing out her ponytail.

Her clerk job at the towers was another justification and cover up for what she really was doing for a living. She was a runner, except she didn't make deliveries she was sort of like a trustee. She held money and drugs for these two heroin lords by the name of Gary and Pooks, who had two major dope operations on 2nd and Erie Streets and 5th and York Streets.

Batina, who was introduced to Gary and Pooks by her deceased boyfriend Shan, began holding product and counting money for them once Shan was murdered. She seen no harm in doing the procedure for the boys and she was profiting more money than she could ever vision. They were paying her $2,000 a week but her reason for getting a job was to escape the "Operation Sundown" investigation that was taking place in the city. Batina wasn't precise but she had a feeling that Gary and Pooks were being surveillance and on the verge of getting indicted and she wanted to be extra prudent.

As she continued braiding her hair, Batina stressed that she began dibbling and dabbling with dope to alleviate stress and agony. It was something just to get by on but times could have been much worse she explained teary eyed, putting the finishing touches on her hair.

"You'll be alright," I said, grabbing Tina from behind, wiping her tears. "Everyone goes through depression sometimes." As I continued to foster her pain Batina cheered up a little and continued to enlighten me on Gary and Pooks' operation.

Gary and Pooks labeled their dope "Kiss," because it was affectionate to the mind and body in more ways than one. Sort of what a kiss would do in a passionate relationship, giving off a warm attachment. Batina expressed that snorting a good bag of dope was similar to getting a massage in a hot tub. That's why Batina's sexual stamina was so invigorating; Janice was that way as well as the tavern owner Dana. The dope didn't just relax them, it made them horny also.

I had to get an estimate of the figures that Gary and Pooks may have been putting up on the two strips they were trafficking prior to our conversation coming to a close. I stayed with various tricks up my sleeve and no one had any idea of what I was capable of doing. I just liked to stay two steps ahead of everyone else.

"2nd and Erie and 5th and York both bring in about two-hundred and fifty grand a week," Batina said, as she nibbled on my ear and rubbed my chest. "I can't tell you how much Gary and Pooks are actually worth but I can tell that there were more then seven digits between them."

My mind's light bulb lit up immediately when I heard those digits, a come up off of Gary and Pooks would of definitely put me in a seat on the heroin bus. The $390,000 dollars that I possessed wasn't going to last me forever and was soon to run out. Stinging them two money makers would have been remunerative but I needed Batina's keen mind to get my foot in the door.

I looked my gainful jewel in her eyes, seeing nothing but dollar signs and gently kissed her soft lips just to make her feel comfortable again. But, in all reality she was my meal ticket to Gary and Pooks. The warmth of my kiss got us back in the mix of sexing but my second round with Batina wasn't for enjoyment. It was to get her in the palm of my hands and control her like a puppet.

$ $ $ $ $

Easter Sunday rolled around and I hadn't been out of my apartment since I brought my car and hooked up with Batina. I don't know what came over me, I wasn't sick or depressed. The time must have been met to seclude myself from the rest of the world and relax. A few days before Easter my mother called me up to ask if I could join her and Aniyah for morning church service that Sunday. No disrespect to my mother or the man up stairs but the last time I attended church, pimping was the number one hustle on the streets. I was Lucifer himself, I had did so much sinning since then there was no way that God was letting me in to his gates of heaven. I took my mother up on her offer anyhow because I did need some soul searching and to pay my tithes for all of my unanswered deeds.

Easter Sunday down at St. Johns Baptist church in Cramer Hill was more vigorous than a Guns and Roses concert. The church's band was on key, the choir sang in praise and the reverend's biblical testimony about being "A part time believer in God," was phenomenal. My perception of second guessing the almighty above or any divine supernatural was preposterous. The ideology of self superiority that didn't believe were fools, life didn't just form on earth and say throw air here and put animals there. It was you believed or you didn't, there were no reasonable doubts.

While everyone in attendance focused on the Rev's daily sermon, my attention was focused on the females who worked the aisle around me. I was in the Lord's house trying to get myself right for a change, lusting with my eyes. If that wasn't backsliding I don't know what was but from my observation of the folk that were inside, half of them were thinking just like me. Church is where a lot of folk acquainted to meet their soul mates and done some of their best pimpin'. I'm Standing 6'1", chocolate in a cream double breasted suit with some reptile leathers on my feet and to top it off I was handsome. I knew a couple of them tongue speakers were checking me out.

My lustful thoughts must have put me to sleep after while because my mother woke me up five minutes before church service was about to end. Just as the choir was due to perform their last selection, I stood to clap in praise to the song and my feet fell asleep on me. I was clapping with a million ants running through my toes; it would have been ignorant for me to have sat down because I already had dozed off.

My mother held her anger in the entire service because when I got home she left the most profane statement on my machine like I was her man and I got caught cheating. I knew better than to embarrass her at service but I wouldn't say it was embarrassment to me it was inattentiveness. How was she embarrassed when the majority of folk were nodding off more then me? And that wasn't from any lack of sleep, which came from being liquor sippers and staying up all night. My uncle always made me aware of the church goers who owned liquor stores. The good Lord said drink when thirsty not while praising him, but, in my mother's eyes I was the bad guy.

That same night I got flashy fly and dipped in my entire splendor to attend the biggest skating party of the year. Everyone in the tri-state area was anticipating the Easter Sunday, no school Monday Skating Bash at Skate Land. The new hot rap duo Eric B. and Rakim was the featured artist and was set to perform their smash hit Paid in Full. I was spiced in a yellow and white M.C.M. velour sweat suit and a pair of white and yellow Gucci sneakers.

As I slow rolled pass Skate Land to find a parking spot there were so many cars parked off of Mt. Ephraim Avenue and Vanhook Street you would have thought it was a parade happening on the strip. The entrance door was packed to a capacity with ladies and gentlemen eager to find out what was jumping inside. The boycott line extended from the front door all the way to Kentucky Fried Chicken's parking lot; which was next door. The law was stationed across the street out in front of Jock-A-Moe's bar, observing everything riding up and down the Avenue.

I had to put something in my stomach before I went in the rink, so I went into Kentucky Fried and ordered a four piece chicken meal with potatoes wedges and some macaroni and cheese. Leisurely the waiting line moved with ease, there were about ten people in front of me. As I waited patiently to pay my twenty bucks, I bumped into my sister's boyfriend Jingles and a few of his homeboys.

"Yo' slim you're my girl's little brother right?" he asked, recognizing my face immediately. I shook my head in approval, shaking his hand simultaneously. "Follow me," he said, as he and his stepped to the front of the line to the security men that were taking money and tickets.

I didn't know what kind of relationship Jingles had with the security men but they had some type of mutual understanding between them. Jingles whispered something to the two men, pointed in our direction and handed one of them a few bills. The security guys took the money, looked in our direction and opened the doors for us. Jingles must have had V.I.P. status because we had to jump at least a hundred and fifty people that stood out in front.

The inside extravaganza was enchanting, and the music was bumping and the three-hundred spectators and skaters were enthusiastic. I couldn't tell the difference from the people skating on the floor, the floor was packed and everyone was skating at a rapid pace. All I seen was black, brown and white skates, some having colorful pom-poms.

While I observed the rink like a camera, Jingles came over and introduced me to dudes in his circle. There were more to meet but most of them were taking care of other business, I only got acquainted with the four that were there with him. I shook hands with Sayo and Jam first, they were two flamboyant brothers who looked no older than seventeen and smoked tones of reefer.

Miguel, who looked Hispanic resembled Jingles a little bit but was shorter then Jingles and had more bulk to him. We shook hands next but the entire time we conversed he kept looking around like he was targeting someone. His head turned from right to left so much that it caused me to keep looking over my shoulder.

Last but not least was Bumpsy, he was the tranquil one, and it felt like I was talking to a brick wall. Bumpsy shook my hand and went on about his business and from his impression I assumed he didn't take to me well. Until Jingles made it clear to me that Bumpsy never talked, he was like that since they were kids but he listened more than anything. Jingles called him the diamond in the rough, the one that everyone could count on in there time of need. As I continued to talk with Jingles I noticed that two out of the four guys were wearing the "G.W." rings; Sao and Jam were missing there's. I didn't even bother to ask Jingles about that issue because it didn't concern me none.

I decided to maneuver around the rink after getting acquainted with Jingles' crew. I bumped into a lot of people from the city and Centerville that I had to be concise with, half of them didn't even deserve a single word out of me.

I ran into Ebony at the food counter on my way to get some Twizzlers, the last time we talked or seen each other was a year ago. "How have you been?" I asked, giving her a hug.

"I've been doing fine, working, trying to stay out of trouble. You know."

"Yeah, I can dig it, and the family?"

"My mother is doing splendid but I really haven't talked to my dad's side of the family every since he passed from cancer five months ago."

"Jahee passed?" I said, shocked by the news. "Oh, I'm sorry to have heard that."

"It's okay we all have our day to meet the maker."

"So how's Lamaar? Have you heard anything from her lately?"

"I was just about to ask you the same thing, I haven't heard from her since she skipped town, I'm so worried about her."

"She wrote me a letter but left no return address or number to be reached at."

"That's my sister, she always been secretive."

Ebony and I conversed for about ten minutes before we parted in different directions. I could see in her eyes that she was still discouraged and depressed about her father's passing and Lamaar not being around. She took my number for consolation purposes and she told me she would be in touch.

I ran into Kyron as I made my way back over to Sao and Jam near the arcade games, he had just rolled off the rink from skating. "What's been happening slim?" I asked, partially hugging him with my right side. "I see you haven't lost your step since elementary school."

"Yeah you know the feet work is still nice, I have to stay in shape in order to be ready for my final season as a Panther."

Since basketball was our topic we began talking about his situation with Deedra and the predicament that Wayne and Raman got into. Kyron elucidated that Deedra was five months pregnant and had no intentions of getting rid of the baby. He was stressed for a few months but gradually he regained his mental strength. Kyron's mind was already made up about his college choice; the University of Michigan was his pick. They were willing to accept him, Deedra and there baby if he committed to the school. All he had to do was make the grade, score points and win in order to be an official Wolverine.

"Wayne and Rasaan are fucking finished," I said, moving on to them as the topic.

"And the fucked up thing about that is they both left the burden on me to carry out."

"What'd you mean by that?"

There was a huge article in the USA Today's paper about the two former Panthers and Kyron. The title read: [Will Owen's be next to follow in ex-teammates footsteps]. Going through the adversity with his girlfriend Deedra's pregnancy, Kyron knew that his child-hood friend's predicament with the law was another heavyweight on his shoulders. He was just waiting to prove to the world that the weights weren't that heavy.

"It's fucked up how the media and tabloids can stereotype an inner city kid's dreams of making it because of his peer's mistakes."

"Hey, that's the way of the world just prove them wrong, you know I'm behind you a hundred percent no matter what," I said, giving him some love.

Kyron told me he was going to call me in a few days to enlighten me on this summer tournament he was going to attend. I concurred to his statement before letting him roll back out on the rink. I felt like a damn celebrity, the way I smirked and waved at people I knew inside the rink. I stumbled over a lot more people after I finished with Kyron and he rolled of on me to go back into the roller frenzy.

Two of my cousins - Twiggy and Cree - who were with a gaggle of females, had me in a tight headlock for about a half an hour. I was enjoying myself even more because they both knew the game and as soon as I walked up Cool Cree passed me some Rum and Coke and told me to get right. And, Twiggy reached in her pocketbook and handed me a couple of Lifestyle condoms, allowing me to pick from her crew of flat backers. As bad as I wanted to sex one of her lady friends all crazy, my mind was focused elsewhere.

"Cousin you stay on your sexy shit," Cool said, peeping the lay that I was dipped in. Cree was my grandmother Ann's niece, her mother's mom was my grandma's sister.

"Do he," Minnie said, aroused by my presence. "All that choco-late will give a bitch like me pussy diabetes. Somebody needs to hurry up and lock you down before I arrange a new engagement... Damn!" Minnie was a bricked shit house Amazon; she was fuckable but was too goofy for me.

"Please hoe my cousin ain't even into thick milk shakes," Twiggy added, jokingly. "He want'em working the run way." Now Twiggy's father was my grandfather Khalif's brother on my dad's side of the family.

"Stay single and smooth cuzzo," Cool said, selling someone another bottle of liquor.

Eric B. and Rakim were set to perform at the strike of midnight and it was eleven thirty when I eased away from my cousin's circle and went over to the Pac-man machine. DJ Fade was on the wheels of steel, playing everything from the Sugar Hill Gang to Boogie Down Productions; keeping the floor packed with skaters.

Korey Carr, who administered the skate parties, had the rink's attention along with his two brothers - Keith and Brian - and younger sister Taniesha. They had everyone on the floor moving to the step of the soul train line. I couldn't skate so all my soul was in the line of the pellets that Pac-man was gobbling up.

Surprisingly, Kelli came over by the games completely messing up my concentration and I was on the last stage with no power men left to continue if I lost. "Can't return any of my calls," she said without saying hello.

"What?" I replied, glancing her way but kept my focus on the game. "I returned all your calls but your never home."

"Me working has nothing to do with you leaving a message."

$ $ $ $ $

Kelli came off vulgar, like she was my girl or we slept together or something, her attitude made me want to walk away from her and the game. I didn't care how many quarters I wasted in the machine, she wasn't worth me losing. But, it was her appearance that immobilized my furious thoughts.

She had these short, crimped curls wrapped in a green, satin head scarf, matching from head-to-toe. Wearing a green, white, and yellow blouse, some green, plaid Capri pants and a pair of knee high, yellow Gucci boots. And, if I wasn't mistaken she definitely was out to catch a guppy.

"You look cute," Kelli said, inserting a piece of gum in her mouth.

"So do you and what brings you to an affair like this anyhow? I thought things like this didn't interest you... Looking for a date?" I asked raising my eyebrow.

"No! I'm not thank you, I came to see Eric B. and Rakim, plus I knew you would be here."

"Oh really?"

"Yes."

Kelli's conversation was concise and her demeanor didn't show any kind of appreciation of my presence. Still and all she was looking forward to seeing me after Eric B. and Rakim did there thing in the middle of the rink. And, from the way she was looking in those Capri's, there was no way that I was passing her up on that offer.

I bumped into my sisters and their friends over by the picture stand after leaving Kelli. Wadeelah and Alesha had just walked in about ten minutes before I came over in their area. Big Scott, the promoter of the skate bash was controlling the camera and was giving out special deals on pictures. Buy three for ten and get one free, I couldn't refuse that offer and I took at least fifteen pictures with my sisters and their girls before Eric B. and Rakim got on.

It was ten after twelve when Eric B. and Rakim entered the oval shaped shake fiesta. The pandemonium from the crowd was outrageous; everyone from the food court to the walking aisle crowed the rink's wall to get a glimpse of the famous duo.

"What's the deal Camden," Rakim said, yelling thought the microphone, pepping the crowd up before his partner Eric B. dropped the beat. "Make some fuckin' noise."

From all of the yelling and screaming it felt like I was at a concert in the Spectrum over in Philly. "Yo' Bee drop that beat," Rakim said to his vicious DJ, who scratched the 12" vinyl on the turntables.

When the beat dropped to the body moving smash hit "Paid and Full," the pandemonium increased to a peak that was uncontrollable. With about ten security guards securing the rink floor, Rakim pranced around spitting venom in all his truck jewelry.

By the time Rakim performed his second song "I ain't no joke," my attention was diverted to this brown sugar that I had a crush on in junior high school named Tala. I glanced back and forth from the rap star to her with every blink I took. Tala Waters was her name and being gregarious was her game, she was best friends with one of Wayne's old dames, this honey dip by the name of Yolanda.

Full figured from head-to-toe, Tala's physique was eye candy, her complexion was honey, and she stood 5'5", petite with a pair of knockers much bigger than Batina's. Her eyes were the main attraction and they were chink cut like Japanese blood ran some where through her bloodline.

Standing behind her with my hands rubbing on her thighs I whispered seductive things in her ear, like wanting to eat her like a bowl of strawberries. She giggled a little to the humor of my fervent speech while massaging my hands simultaneously. We talked and gently caressed each other through the remainder of the performance. I gave Tala my number without receiving hers in return just to see how deep her interest was since our junior high days.

Eric B. and Rakim ended their three song performance with the invigorating song "Microphone fiend," before going over by Big Scott and the picture stand to sign autographs. The entire time that I was having a two way conversation with Tala and Yolanda, the bitch never told me that she had a nigga or was seeing anyone; my hand was around her waist when her dude approached me with two of his homies.

"Hakeem what's happening cool," I said, extending my hand for a shake in return.

"My girl's what's happening cool," he boasted, pushing my hand away.

My premonition on the ensuing incident didn't allow me to moe an inch, I watched as Tala and Yolanda cringed in fear of what was about to jump off. This was my second altercation over a female with a sucker for love. And as bad as I didn't want any problems, I couldn't see it going any other way. I knew Hakeem from the Polock town and Parkside areas, we swung a few episodes together but, I prayed he didn't show his ass for the two whores standing next to me.

"That's your dude?" I asked Tala, hoping Hakeem wasn't precise. She remained mum, giving me this stupid fucking look. I wanted to smack the bitch myself. "Go ahead some where with that Hakeem," Yolanda, the chocolate, tall bomb shell said, pointing her finger in his face. "You no she's been over you."

"Fuck you floozy," He said, spitting in her face. "You need to mind your fuckin' business that's why you're lonely now."

All eyes turned on us as Yolanda and Hakeem continued to go at each other in a profane manner. I observed Sayo and Jam to my right watch the entire incident go down and as I went to push away from Tala and head into their direction, Hakeem started babbling off at the mouth, just like Kenny's fat ass did in front of Lamaar.

"Fuck you Kyle you jive ass nigga, don't let me catch you around my girl no more." Without verbally bickering back and forth with Hakeem, I turned and snuffed him out. All over his boney ass like orangutans on vines all I could hear was 'Stop, let him up Kyle.' I hit Hakeem with a few hay makers before these enormous gun shots rang out.

I jumped over the rink wall once the tandem, clamorous gunfire kicked off, heading for the nearest exit. The entire place was on the move for cover, there was nothing but clashing bodies and a lot of pushing going on. Pocketbooks, coats and jewelry was flying all over the place in the mist of screams.

I was midway through the rink and about ten feet away when I dropped my fucking keys, instead of them falling in one spot they slid behind me. I was furious because I had to chase the keys like they were my damn kids.

I happened to glance over my shoulder after grabbing my keys and saw Sayo and Jam from a far, standing over near the orange lockers firing massive ammunition from their hand guns. It was like the two young loonies got a kick out of pulling the trigger because the more Jam fired it excited Sao. Bullets had no name though; Sao's laughing pleasure wasn't going to stop me from getting hit.

It seemed like the entire Camden police department was outside Skate Land as I trotted to my car. Half of Mt. Ephraim Avenue was cluttered with police cars, making sure people made it out safely. Standing around being nosey got people killed also but I wanted to wait and see if Sao and Jam made it out the rink without being noticed. But I didn't want to be figured out either, cause the chaos was definitely being front paged in the Courier Post's headlines the next morning.

# Chapter. 17

T he time was a quarter to three in the morning when I strolled in
to the Glamour Towers from Church's Chicken. Church's was the
after hour hang-out spot on Haddon and Kaighns Avenue, directly
across from Donkey's steak place. All of the violent agitation back
at the rink drew hunger pains in my stomach.

Batina was the only one inside the lobby when I entered, sitting
comfortably behind the counter wearing a pair of dark sunglasses
while reading an Ebony Magazine. I spoke respectfully just so she
could recognize me as I checked my mailbox. I got no feedback
in return though and I got peeved by being ignored, especially by
Batina who broke her neck to speak to me any time she saw me.

"Not speaking today I see," I said, moving the magazine from in
front of her face.

"Hi Kyle," she answered, in an aggressive tone. I sensed that she
was bothered by someone or something, her demeanor was shabby
and she had an angered facial structure.

"What's wrong with your eye?" I asked, reaching for her glasses,
Batina was hiding a bruise underneath the shades. But, if she didn't
care neither did I, I grabbed my meal and mail off the counter and
began to step towards my apartment.

"Kyle!" Batina yelled out, I stopped and turned around.

Batina came over to me with her glasses in hand and the biggest
black eye I'd ever seen. Looking like the dog from the little rascals,
I wanted to scream out "What the fuck happened to you," but I just
stared with a pair of wide eyes. I gently touched the bruised area
while she explained the situation. Because of the little addiction she
experiences with dope, Gary and Pooks labeled her a thief and said
she was stealing money and drugs from them to support her habit.

So they brutally pistol whipped her and tossed her from a first floor window.

"I swear Kyle, I never stole anything from them," she cried, resting her head upon my shoulder. "Everything I used or spent was out of my own profit, Gary and Pooks just want to take their emotional loses out on me because they no I'm weak."

$$\$ \$ \$ \$ \$$$

Half of her story was believable, but the other half was kind of shady and I wasn't about to take her side because she in fact got high. I accepted her story for what it was worth to get next to Gary and Pooks. Batina wanted to retaliate by getting even, but the odds were against her because she was in it alone.

"Whenever you want to sit down and plan your revenge you just let me know," I said, kissing her forehead. She was working a double so she needed some time to delve up some edification on the two boys.

I took the back staircase instead of the elevator to Kelli's apartment, just to play it cool in front of Batina. By the time I reached the thirteenth floor from the staircase, I felt like lying on the floor. For five minutes I stood in front of Kelli's apartment knocking and ringing the bell and I hoped she answered because going back down thirteen flights was out of the question.

"It took you long enough to get here," Kelli said, in a raspy voice, allowing me inside. "If you weren't here by three-fifteen I was going to sleep."

Without explaining the shooting that took place at Skate Land or going into detail about me stopping at Church's chicken, or being stopped by Batina in the lobby. I just went with the flow and kept my composure. "I apologize if I kept you waiting."

Kelli must have prayed to Cupid for some love, or had an irritable pussy itch for some dick because no soon as we got settled on her water bed, the art of being salacious took over her. Our tongues locked romantically as I positioned myself in between her thighs while our hands pressed on each other's private area in rough passion. I squeezed her breast hastily, as my erection rubbed against her panties in rash action. Far from being naked, I felt that I had Kelli right where I needed her to be. Under the spell of my thrusting thunderstorm, she moaned seductively, groaned from my sensation and held me close from the aura's moment.

"Stop... Wait Kyle," She said, pushing back.

"Wha-What's wrong? Is it something I did?"

"No... No Kyle there's anything wrong." Without hesitating or sugar coating her issue, Kelli told me that she never engaged in a sexual encounter before, and that she was a mere virgin.

"You never been penetrated or fucked?" I asked, in such vulgar astonishment.

"No... Never!" A twenty-five year old virgin, I was shockingly flattered because if I shot my dice the right way, there was no way that I could crap out.

My game face was on and in her fire place as I hit nothing but lucky numbers. The sensation of my tongue gyrating around her sultry kumquat slowly made Kelli's eyes roll like dollar signs. As I heard the casino man scream nothing but 'Winner,' in my ear, Kelli's feet locked around my neck as my tongue latched on to her sweet nectar even more and her hands pressed down on the back of my head. The number seven couldn't even match the numbers that I put on Kelli's casino table. He was no match for me because I definitely was controlling his dice game.

Kelli's multiple orgasms caused her pussy to erupt like volcano juice, making it much easier for me to dominate her. But instead I just left it oral because if I massaged her walls, she would've been a predator preying on me three or more times a day. And, that wasn't my style, to be stalked; I was in

to woman that gave me as much space that I gave them.

The time was 4:30 a.m. when I came from Kelli's tunnel and got some shut eye, Kelli cuddled behind me securing her warmth. The weirdest shit happened in my dreams; I had children and was doing the picket fence thing with Kelli, all of that I thought from a shot of oral sex that I didn't even receive. I don't know if it was in her plans to have my mind spinning on love's merry-go-round and I felt that only time would tell. But at four in the morning, it felt like time had already spoken.

$$\$ \$ \$ \$ \$$$

I drove to Cooper's rehabilitation center out in Voorhees that Wednesday to visit my Uncle Muscles. I didn't just want to see how he was improving, I also wanted to consult to him about a few things and find out some imperative information.

My uncle was up and rolling around in his wheel chair when I entered the TV room at the facility, he looked like his normal self except his legs were immobilized. The way that he hugged me felt like he regained every bit of strength that he had before he was even hit.

We got into a succinct discussion about our family's matters before I got into the issue I really came for to get some clarity on. He was highly upset with the fact that my two aunts had kids by my pops but, he said that Gracey and Sissy always dabbled in the same water. Out of the triplets he felt that my Aunt Debbie was the innocent one and could be trusted with anyone's life. Every since my uncle has known my pops it was something about him that kept a third eye out on him, feeding him with a long spoon. Out of respect for my mother, Uncle Muscles never really wanted to war with Big Kyle because he knew exactly how Olivia truly felt about him back then.

Discursively, moving on in topics, I consulted with Muscles about having dealings with Jingles Johnson and his Good Wood retinue. I needed his advice because he was the only one that would steer me in the right direction of the street underworld; he was the streets in my eyes. It was my time to come up, I was tired of being just a worker, I needed a boss amongst bosses position and I was really in the game to take over and win.

Muscles thought it wasn't a good idea to have dealings with Jingles and the Good Wood boys because they didn't play fair ball. But, who did play fair in an odd game that every man wanted to control. Muscles elucidated that the Good Wood Boys were treacherous and that he hadn't seen a group of young men like that in his entire street tenure. If they were up against any competition, challenges, or seen other corners and strips putting up numbers like they were - they wanted a piece of it!

The Good Wood Boys were part of Muscles' reason for leaving Centerville, most of the guys he paved the way for and helped make it in the game tried taking advantage of him. Hireling him for their own personal gain, like Big D.S. and Big Kyle who pushed him aside like he wasn't a stern factor. All which took place in 1978 before he went up state for tax invasion but after he touched in '84 he could no longer claim Centerville as his throne. Because there was a new breed of hustlers such as the Good Wood Boys controlling the streets. Not wanting to jeopardize what he had already made in the streets of Camden for a piece of territory that was uncontrollable.

Muscles was great friends with Jingles' father William "Ol 'man Willie" Johnson, also Big Kyle's godfather. Ol' man Willie was the main reason Muscles didn't leave Jingles with the earth worms and maggots. Killing Jingles was like killing himself because there were boundaries and guidelines to follow and once he cross those lines and broke those rules there was a price to pay at the end for that act.

But, Willie Johnson wasn't your average Joe; he was well respected and knew sources that known many sorcerers. That's how Jingles got the power and respect to quell outsiders and mark his territory because of the path Willie paved for him. Muscles said if he was in my shoes, he would have passed on dealing with Jingles and his crew. He told me to start fresh, put together my own team and crawl before I walked. Putting together my own team was going to be a crux because I didn't trust just anyone and the people I did trust were either dead, missing or living an ironic life. Besides, I came in the game standing on my own two feet, so crawling was a past option.

Walking by his side as he rolled with me around the recreational area, I needed to know who this William Holmes guy was. The name began surfacing the air and popping up in all the wrong places. My Uncle's wheel chair came to an abrupt halt when he heard the name.

"William Holmes?" he asked, giving me a leer look.

"Yeah, I came across the name a few times during my inquisition with other inquiring minds. He was to be the owner of the Glamour Towers until they were sold months prior to a guy by the name of Eyeball Jenkins. And, the name has been on numerous pieces of mail at the home of Terry's pad in Pennsauken. Something isn't adding up, there's a huge piece missing from the puzzle."

Billy is William Holmes; my ears went numb when my uncle said his name because Billy was playing possum. "Billy is in on Terry's deceptive motive," I said, making my uncle aware of Billy's unforeseen nature.

"What! Who Billy? No fucking way," Muscles replied, putting his wheel chair back in motion.

"I know its' hard for you to believe because of the history you two share but you have to take my word on this one." Everything Billy explained to me and all the information he enlightened me with about leaving the game alone and what he and my uncle planned to do futuristically, I adduced back to muscles.

It was evident that Billy and Terry were working together and against my uncle for reasons they only knew about. Every since Billy's last message he's been missing in action and my uncle didn't even know about it. He and Billy discussed everything, minor things included, like going to the grocery store.

Cousin's Food Market, the vacant building for the Rosa Park's daycare center and the Glamour Towers didn't ring a bell to my uncle. "As long as Billy and I have been partners he's always been a Jew and I was the gentile," Muscles said, wondering when Billy executed all those business plans.

If Billy owned anything, Muscles was the appraiser to all of his assets, which really wasn't much. More than half of Billy's money was managed through Muscles. The last time Billy visited Muscles was a week prior to him leaving me the coded message. Prior to the abrupt situation Muscles and I both received a lot of inscrutable prank calls from Terry, Billy and his disappearing act, Lamaar's letter and, the William Holmes name appearing on legitimate documents.

"What would make Billy turn against me to join forces with the enemy?" Muscles asked, rubbing his mustache. "Who and what went wrong?"

"That's what we're trying to pinpoint and get to the bottom of," I answered, pushing his wheel chair.

I told my uncle to give me a few days to see what I could find out about the demented incident that was spiraling backwards. When and if I received any information, I told him that he would be notified. Sitting around in the yard with him, trying to unscramble pieces that weren't there wasn't doing anyone of us any good. So I had to leave my uncle and attain to my business of scrutinizing the streets.

# Chapter. 18

That night at my townhouse in Centerville, while contemplating on my next move of solving the inescapable drug puzzle. I received a few calls that had relevance to what I tried vigorously to find out. Keith and Derrick called to let me know that they found no match or information on the William Holmes name. This wasn't a hassle because I already struck gold from my reliable source. I felt bad because I didn't spare them the trouble, I didn't need them to my footwork. When I told them who William Holmes really was they almost shit themselves but perplexed at the same time; some how we got disconnected.

Keith and Derrick couldn't believe that the creep Billy was a snake in the grass, dealing with Terry on the level that he was and having disloyal expectations towards Muscles. But the boys did manage delve into their archives and get significant information on the house that Terry use to live in. The deed was titled to William Holmes and the day the home was purchased, a checked was signed and dated for $105,550 by Billy; co-signer True Williams. This was on the date of February 19th 1982. 'True Williams,' I said, tranquilly to myself, wondering what the hell was happening before my own eyes.

True was my uncle's wife, why was she the co-signer for a home that was purchased by Billy and that Terry was living in? Why didn't Terry sign for the home Muscles paid for? Clues just weren't adding up, the closer I got to solve the puzzle the more pieces came out of no where. I told Keith and Derrick to stay on top of the William Holmes name and to dig up as much information as possible. Even if they had to swim in the fucking sea to grab the glass bottle with the note in it, we needed more facts.

Right after I hung up the phone with Keith and Derrick, I received a call from Ebony. She told me that she didn't want to really converse over the phone and that it would be best if we talked in person. What she had to tell me could cost her life and she wanted to keep a low profile.

"Say no more," I said, wanting her not to go into any further details. I told her to meet me in front of the Glamour Towers, on the North side in forty-five minutes. Unintentionally, Ebony hung up in my ear without saying goodbye.

$$\$\ \$\ \$\ \$$$

The information that Ebony wanted to spill had to be relevant to the things that I was trying to figure out. Making it to my condo in ten minutes via Interstate 676 which sat directly behind the Chelton Terrace townhouse complex, I want to straighten up my place before Ebony got there.

I ran into Batina on my way through the lobby, damn, that was just my luck. "Hey Mr. Moore," Batina said, as I tried easing by her like she wasn't even behind the counter.

"Oh, hey Tin' how's everything today love?" I asked, impatiently standing by the first floor entry door.

"Very well I may say, now that I've seen you."

"I'm flattered, listen give me a buzz and we'll talk then because I have to use the bathroom extremely bad," I feigned, shivering at my knees.

"Alright I'm not going to hold you up but one more thing before you go."

"What's that?"

"I arranged a meeting for you to see Gary and Pooks tomorrow night. I told them that you were a relative coming in from out of town and you were looking to buy the house."

"Whoa! I can't meet with them tomorrow."

"Why not?"

"Because I'm unprepared, I don't have any strategy and I need to know how there operation works, what's their likes and dislikes… Get familiar with people in their organization. Besides I don't have anyone that I can trust to come with me."

"Listen, just follow my lead, find somebody by tomorrow night that you can trust and see if you can get a hold of a briefcase that holds money. It doesn't have to be any money in it, just bring it with you."

"What! That's idiotic, why no money?"

"Trust me love I've been around these kinds of plots for years and wear a suit so you can look presentable or show your toughness or whatever ya'll call it and I'll handle the rest."

Batina's plan and details made me nervous; I never trusted a bitch while in the line of doing something malicious. When the pressures on, the whores tend to bust pipes and that causes for a ruin of the entire operation. Things had turned out for the worst when we brought Summer along to do the mission at the Rotti shop. Even though we made out in the end, it could have been extremely catastrophic and I still haven't caught up to Big D.S. yet.

"Tomorrow night I'll see you then," I said, pulling the door open. "Oh, oh can you do me a big favor before I forget," I added.

"Anything daddy," Tina replied, caressing my chest seductively.

"I'm expecting some company, when she arrives can you buzz her in for me?"

"She?!" Tina exclaimed, shoving me lightly.

I knew where the situation was getting ready to escalate too so I tried nipping it expeditiously. "Yeah, she... Her name is Ebony and she's my cousin."

"Yeah, I heard that all too many times before."

"Trust me, it's not what you think."

I had no clue as to why I was standing there like a jack ass, explaining myself like she was my significant other or wife. "Just do me that favor please," I said, kissing her cheek.

This particular night wasn't my night at all; I should have met Ebony at a remote rendezvous outside of the city. Just as I backed off of Batina, Kelly was exiting the elevator. She glanced in our direction, stopped, sneered at me and headed out the door. I felt like shooting myself in the head at that point. Caught red handed, it was evident that Kelli's eyes wasn't deceiving her. That wasn't important though, in the mean time I had to rearrange my thoughts to justify what she observed because I knew that she was going to confront me about it.

With only ten minutes on my hands before Ebony was due to arrive I managed to ditch Batina so I could straighten my domain a little. I hoped what Ebony had in store for me would bring some sunshine to my inclement day because I was definitely sitting in a pile of dog shit.

$$\$ \$ \$ \$ \$$$

Batina buzzed for me to let Ebony in around ten minutes to twelve at night, if that was a late night creep to Batina, she couldn't bear the differences. After midnight, insecurity was a woman's strength like power pellets were to Ms. Pac-man. They knew once the sun went down anything beyond that point was a secret society.

Ebony showed up to my place in some of her best attire, dressed very exquisite and smelt extremely good. It was as if she was invited to a candle light dinner but, for her to be a plus sized female she was overly attractive. She didn't quite fit my eye because I never thought of her to be a sex object.

"This is a nice place you have here Kyle," she said, taking a seat on the leather sofa.

"Thanks."

"Illegal money does come in handy huh?"

"It helps," I replied walking towards the kitchen. "Would you like something to drink?"

"Yeah water... Thank you."

Sort of a clairvoyant moment while in the refrigerator, I noticed something peculiar about her aura and demeanor while in her presence. I hoped it wasn't what I thought it was but from the look of things it was like Ebony was vulnerable.

"Here's your water," I said, taking a seat next to her.

"Thank you."

"So what was so important that you had to tell me in person?" I asked, placing my right leg over my left.

"Well since my sisters not around to tell you and was basically hiding thing from you in the same sense, I feel that It is my duty to make you aware of some things."

"Make me aware on things such as--"

"Wait but before I do," she said, taking a sip of the ice water. "You have to do something for me in return."

Immediately, our eyes locked like a dog preying on a cat, I was trying to visualize what favor lied between her muddy brown eyes. It was either one or two things, the second thing wasn't a problem, and it was the first thing that had me a little shook up.

"Oh yeah and what's that?"

"I need you to fuck me like this would be your first and last time ever getting some nappy dugout."

I knew it, I fucking knew it! I sensed the scene before it even happened; not wanting to talk over the phone, meeting at my place after hours, and dressed to catch with an appealing fragrance it was very obvious.

"We both have something that is beneficial to our needs, well at least you do anyway," she said, in laughter. "Even though you and my sister--"

"Ebony," I called, intervening. "Your sister's not here and really ain't my concern anymore. My concern is the information you have for me, so let's get to the issue at hand shall we?"

Before Ebony and I got into what was important she gave me a few rules and guidelines that would be useful to my needs. I had to take a piece of my clothing off and by the time I got to my draws she would have explained to me everything I needed to know.

Prior to my dealings with Lamaar while in a relationship with Kenny Morales, she was dealing with Joe Riley and Billy.

"Billy!" I asked, in an astonished tone. "My uncle's Billy? How'd that happen?"

After Lamaar found out about Kenny and Terry's furtive affair and how they were trying to kill her, she went to Riley, not only for help but to plead her innocents for the foul play on Terry and Kenny's behalf. While in motion of doing all of the above, Lamaar noticed Billy was being around Riley and Domino more than she could every suspect.

In promptness, I removed both my tank top and T-shirt, because the information was getting interesting and I needed to know more.

Billy became questionable to Lamaar but she was uncertain about what was going on between him and Riley. When Lamaar started fraternizing with Riley to get back at Kenny, Riley made it clear to her that Billy was a close friend on a business level and nothing more. After being enlightened, Lamaar thought otherwise and went on about her business. Since Lamont Muscles - a close friend of Lamaar's family - was incarcerated at the time, she assumed Muscles knew about Billy doing business with Riley and Domino; but Lamaar was wrong and things became drastic.

Before the last words could roll off of Ebony's tongue I came out of my pants and took of my boxer shorts. Standing in front of her bare ass with a limp muffler, I yearned for more of the story on top of what was already revealed.

The entire time that Lamaar was sneaking around with Riley - from the beginning of 1981 to the end of '82 - he treated her more than a lady, she was his queen to be. Everything was going smooth until Domino got involved between them.

"What happened there?" I asked, trying to perceive why Domino added his two scents in his brother's street romance.

Riley, who had the world in the palm of his hand by both seas, from money, power to respect. And, who gave out orders and never had to answer to no one, to his brother Domino, Lamaar was his kryptonite. Riley bowed down to the feet of his young, voluptuous dame like a homeless dog in need of food. Thirty years Lamaar's senior, Domino couldn't foresee what his brother seen in Lamaar but was destined to find out.

One day Riley and Domino had a fight because Domino smacked Lamaar in front of him. Reason being, Domino said that he was putting Lamaar before what was necessary and needed (Business and money). Their plan was to use Lamaar to get back at Terry, their oldest sister, for using Kenny to deceive them. Riley on the contrary fell in love, instead of using and abusing Lamaar. Riley sensed jealousy and envy from his younger brother.

Riley did the unthinkable he took his gun, put it to Lamaar's head and made her disrobe herself until she was naked in front of Domino. They both took her into a bedroom, tide her up and shot multiple modicums of dope into her blood stream until she was unconscious. By the time Lamaar regained her conscience, she awoke to see Kenny tide to a chair in front of her. In similar form, bloody, drugged and unconscious, Lamaar went into shock and begged for them not to kill Kenny.

Ebony elucidated that Riley and Domino gang banged Lamaar in front of Kenny for hours, to show Kenny how much of a floozy she was. Lamaar told Ebony that Kenny was so drugged all he could do was stare in a daze at the matter of misfortune. He could barely breathe let alone comprehend the sexual act that took place in front of him. Lamaar was drugged once more after being treated like a tamed porn star.

After days of being brutally injected with heroin and sexually sabotaged, Lamaar managed to check into a near by hospital for treatment about her illness. During her weekly stay in the hospital, she called the only person she could trust and talk too - Ebony.

Ebony stated that when she arrived to see her sister lying helpless in the hospital bed, malfunctioning in a disabled position. Ebony had a malignant way of thinking to whomever it was that hurt her sister and she was far from violent.

Lamaar explained to Ebony what had happened, piece by piece, she told Ebony not to tell anyone.

"Wait, wait… What happened to Kenny after all of this took place?" I asked, trying to keep the order of events tandem.

"I'll get to that, let me finish first," she replied, caressing my chest.

Since Billy, was well associated with Riley and Domino, Lamaar came up with a way to get even with them. She made Ebony get in contact with Billy the best way she knew how, even if she had to search the city with a magnifying glass. Within days Billy was reached and in Lamaar's presence.

Lamaar's plan was to make it seem like Billy was the cause of her abuse, after Lamaar explained the entire situation that took place. She put a little salt in the game and twisted the story around. Telling

Billy that she over heard Riley talking to Domino about how they were going to kill him. For the simple fact that he wasn't trying to be a third partner to their operation and because he was partners with their little sister who was their nemesis. It was sort of a chain reaction, Riley and Domino used Kenny to get close to Terry so they could shut her operation down. And, Terry used Billy to get close to her brothers while she manipulated Kenny into deceiving her brothers so they could falter. Billy was caught in crossfire between Terry and her brothers.

$$\$\ \$\ \$\ \$\ \$$$

Lamaar also added that Domino told Riley that Billy was having a furtive affair with her to seek information so that he and Terry could for the big score and complete their mission. That's why they abused her the way they did, to set and example. Billy was infuriated with the information he received. He came up with his own stratagem, by going on a search with for Kenny hoping Riley and Domino didn't separate the soul form his flesh. Billy wanted Kenny to be a part of what was going to take place. It took Billy one phone call to Poohshaun to find Kenny, he was alive and stable just playing low key.

At the round table with Poohshaun, Kenny, and Lamaar, Billy brought upon a mission and plans about getting Riley, Domino and their affluence was discussed. The mission was to kill Riley and Domino and get every penny, dollar, and business establishment that they ever possessed. But the big thing was to keep their names alive by distinguishing their street legacy by planning and maneuvering the way that Riley and Domino maneuvered.

Billy played his cards right, with a straight game face and by Riley and Domino's hands. As if he knew nothing and nothing was ever mentioned to him. A vacation was booked for Billy and the two brothers to the Bahamas for two weeks. The three of them left together but when the two weeks were up Billy was the only one who returned. Due to Lamaar's relationship with Riley, she knew where all Riley and Domino's important paper work and money was kept.

She had Kenny and Poohshaun wipe the safe out.

Billy and Terry took control of Riley and Domino's entire operation and drug franchise. This was once in the palm of the Dominican brother's hands and, in an out of the hands of Shake and Bake. Billy and Terry became the overseers while Kenny and Poohshaun handled the streets.

"So Riley and Domino been deceased?" I asked, trying to conjoin as many clues as possible. Ebony nodded her head concurring to my question.

"Billy and Terry play ghost to Riley and Domino's appearance for what reason though?" Ebony shrugged her shoulders.

"That's what where trying to figure out."

"Billy and Terry have been deceiving my Uncle Muscles the whole time but for what reason?" I asked, thinking to myself. "What does Muscles have that they want from him or what did he do for them to go for his juggler? This entire underworld mystery is an outrage."

Skeptically, I looked at Ebony in confusion she could tell that the situation was wrecking my nerves. I could see that the issue was jumbling her also, because I had to stop her leg from shaking a million bounces per minute.

"Thanks for the information," I said, holding her thigh, kissing her on the cheek simultaneously.

The kiss on the cheek set the mood for Ebony, I had her right where I wanted her and the passion from the kiss mellowed her disposition. It was my first time being with a big boned sistah, so my obligation was to treat Ebony like a model on the cover of an Ebony Magazine. I was hoping while undressing her slowly that she wasn't insecure about her body because that's how most big females were. But she was confident and broad minded about her physique, as she helped me remove her attire.

$ $ $ $

I gave off astonishing facial expression once I seen her naked, to be a 44DDD and a size 12 below the waist, Ebony's body was delectable. She had a few rolls but it was more cushion for the pushing' in my eyes. No stretch marks and her skin was smoother than flaxen fabric.

With a firm grip Ebony pulled me towards her as I lied in between her thighs, missionary style. She caressed the back of my head and back gently while I sucked on her neck simultaneously. With one blink and one deep breath Ebony guided me inside of her lava tunnel. The sensation immobilized my body into relaxation, and I closed my eyes to enjoy the warm feeling. Ironically, Ebony was so good that my eyes didn't open until the following morning.

I awoke to an empty bed, no Ebony in sight and a note that dangled from the center of my bureau's mirror that read:

Kyle, Good morning!

*I hope last night was affectionate for you as it was for me, sorry that I couldn't wake up in your arms but I had some matters to take care of. I left some breakfast on the stove for you to fill your tummy and regain your strength. I'll be in touch and remember always think big.*

*Love, Ebony*

Throughout my entire sexual tenure, I must admit that Ebony was the best I ever had. She put the rock-a-by-baby technique on me and had a cunning way of doing it. Lamaar had the look but Ebony had the feel and I was glad that Ebony waited to show me her other side because she would have sparked confusion between Lamar and I. Plus, I would have been doing vacuous things like being blatant with the both of them. Even though females were the slop in a pigs bowl, they definitely were the key to success.

# Chapter. 19

The following day I was scheduled to meet with these two treacherous mongers, Gary and Pooks, through Batina. Something was telling me not to follow through with the procedure due to my own feared assumption. Batina's insight on what Gary and Pooks possessed excited my mind to the point of me having a "Fuck it," kind of attitude. The golden rule was to think first before moving and I was just moving. All I scene was dollar signs and now I felt my moves haunting me and my thoughts were skeptical. I was driving into a dead end with no breaks, dealing with complete strangers, and two muthafuckas that I never seen in my life and a whore who sniffed dope.

$ $ $ $

The meeting wasn't scheduled until after hours when all the good civilians were a sleep and evil lurked the streets. I wanted to rain check Batina's offer and get back to her because the Cowboys and the Steelers game was coming on at nine o'clock and I didn't want to miss that for the life of me. Plus I had some big money on the Steelers that I couldn't afford to lose.

During the day, I made my way over to South Camden, on Mechanic Street to pay my man Kylee a visit. I needed to know more about his brothers, Jingles and how the entire Good Wood cadre was organized. The time was a little pass eleven o'clock in the morning when I arrived at Kylie's front door; I knocked like I was the police.

"Their in there," This Brown shinned elderly man said, sitting on the porch next door, smoking a cigar. "Those damn junkies kept me and my wife up all night long with all that damn racket, fuckin' addicts. They got one more time to carry on the way that they do and I'm going to send them muthafuckas up in smoke. Go on keep banging' its enough of them in there, eventually somebody will open the door."

As I continued knocking on Kylie's door, the old gangsta and I continued on in our conversation. "So if you don't mind me asking, how long has this disturbance been affecting you and your wife?"

"About a year and a half now, we done been to the highest authorities, police, and landlords... They ain't worth a damn."

"Sometimes you have to take the law into your own hands," I replied, constantly banging on the door.

"Bing!" he said, pointing at me with his pointer finger.

"Sir let me see if I can give you and your wife a helping hand by giving my eccentric family a word of mouth."

The O.G. who happened to be in his late sixties shook his head in approval of my suggestion. When addicts get that adrenaline rush after using a narcotic drug. Or when their habit goes untreated, physically they go into a psychosomatic process. Which affects the mind from the disturbance of bodily symptoms that comes from not getting their daily treatment. Something that Kylee, Nanoo, and Limboo are affected by all to well.

After about fifteen minutes of banging, I finally got an answer at the door. Some filthy looking floozy having a nappy wig came to the door, scratching and smelling like two day old milk. Unmannerly, the whore didn't even ask who I was or what I wanted. She just opened the door like she was expecting me or some shit, she turned around and headed back into the living quarters. The house had a fetid smell of dirty clothes and dried up piss, it definitely was a junkie festival. Fiends, beer cans, rolled up dollar bills, belts and empty bags of heroin was all over the living room as I made my way through.

With the top part of my shirt covering my nose, I headed straight up the stairs to Kylie's bedroom. It was the same routine on the upper level of the house. Overtly, a Boogie Nights rendezvous, in an addict atmosphere.

Kylie was dreaming of how good things were in retrospect for him as a kid, when I entered his bedroom; sleeping like a baby. Reaching over about five bodies, I hit Kylie with a George Forman body shot, sending his stomach to his throat.

"Man, what the fuck!" he exclaimed, hopping out of his bed like a human grass hopper. "Damn-it man, what the fuck that's about slim/'"

"Good morning to you too, what was all what about? Oh the punch, I'll explain that to you later. But, right now there's something more important that you and I have to discuss. Get yourself together first and meet me sown stairs in the kitchen."

I sat at Kylie's junk yard brand kitchen table listening to the wonderful aura and sounds of junkie nature. The cacophonous sounds made me believe that I was in a human zoo. The only thing that was missing was pedestrians, cages, and animal trainees.

After Kylie entered the kitchen, we went out into the back yard to sit down and converse. His face was livid and tight for unknown reasons; it gave me the indication that he needed his early morning wake up medicine.

"Are you alright my man, you look like a corpse?"

"Yeah, yeah I'm cool," He replied, rubbing his nose, snorting in unison. "Cool as a fan and happy like cousin Flappy." From the riddle phrase I could tell that he needed a hit.

Cutting to the chase, I got right to the point of what I needed to know. "Remember a few months back when I made my way up out of the shootout in front of Donkey's place and used your spot for my escape path?"

"Yeah how can I ever forget that episode?" Kylie, replied, leaning back on the fence, crossing his arms and legs simultaneously.

"Well that day before my ride came you were telling me about your brothers Chucky and Bud and their dealings with the Good Wood boys. I need you to finish explaining the story to me from the top, blow by blow."

"Listen slim," he responded, calmly, massaging his goatee. "The shit I know about my brothers and them Good Wood muthafuckas could get me put in a box. How I know that what I'm going to reveal won't go to next lame and somehow get back to the original source?"

Kylie had me convinced about the issue and what could have happened but, the information was needed expeditiously. "If that was the case which in deed it isn't, wouldn't you have already heard something from the little information you did give me the last time?" I asked, with my pointer finger on my temple then I pointed it at him. Kylie paused in thought for a second then eventually came to his senses.

"You were telling me something about how your brothers introduced most of the Good Wood cadre into the came of narcotics."

"Right, Right."

From the end of 1969 to the beginning of '77 Chucky and Bud made ends meet off of this strip known to the streets of Camden as the "Driveway," off of 7th Street and Chelton Avenue. I used to always wonder why my mom wouldn't allow me to go to the Stanley Park playground by myself, or even walk to the far end of the drive way. Where groups of hoodlums maneuvered around on a daily, in neatly pressed attire, jewelry and fancy rides.

The Driveway was an open 24 hour operation which sold powder, cocaine and dope. A guy by the name of Pee-Wee Franklin was the founder and chancellor of the Driveway's organization. The tall, dark skinned, sleepy eyed gambler made enormous amounts of money off of the Driveway. For five years straight Pee-Wee Franklin labored and grinded through cold winter nights and hot summer days to form the Driveway's foundation. Without a lick of education, and no guardian around to guide him, Pee-Wee was competent enough to learn how to make a dollar out of fifteen cents.

Pee-Wee unlike Lamont Muscles, Shake and Bake and their retinues, had done everything on his own from purchasing to distributing drugs with no help what-so-ever.

"Kylie... Kylie," I said, intervening. "I didn't ask you to go into detail about a Pee-Wee Franklin and what he established--"

"But, you said you wanted me to start from the beginning, blow by blow--"

"Yeah I didn't, on your brothers and how the Good Wood boys

branched from their operation and established their own foundation."

The information on Pee-Wee Franklin was impassive to my knowledge; I was tired of getting more superfluous information than was needed. It seemed like everyone that knew something about something had an eternal story to tell.

Kylie's brothers was groomed and educated under Pee-Wee Franklin's street tutelage, in his tyranny since they were teenagers. Instead of replicating the same illegal drug that was an enormous factor in America's thoroughfares, Pee-Wee brought a different product to the streets of Camden, Cocaine. While every nexus, monger, buyer and supplier was at each other's throat and warring over turf for dope. Pee-Wee and his protégés tranquilly raised their stock in the drug market by selling $10 dollars of uncut cocaine.

In the Driveway's eight year run to fame, a portion of that area belonged to Chucky and Bud. Pee-Wee became the nexus and godfather to the Driveway's stardom, as being the only connect to the operation. While the cocaine popularity began to disseminate the inner city to the suburban areas, customers began to mix the two drugs of heroin and cocaine for a faster and more pleasurable high. Known to addicts as speed balling, as the product dissolved through the streets and the money accumulated for Chucky and Bud. A third partner came to share the affluence of the Driveway; a childhood friend by the name of Keithy Kool.

Keithy Kool was a brown skinned, medium height similar build dude who grew up with Chucky and Bud in the Centerville projects. Prior to going up state for numerous crimes that he committed at seventeen in 1971. Subsequently, four years later, Kool for short, became the impetus of the Driveway's prophecy. Fresh home with nothing to lose, everything to gain and the world put into the palm of his hands due to the dedication and loyalty of Chucky and Bud. Circumstances were less innocuous for him and his future for what the Driveway possessed.

Business was an enchanting pleasure for the three childhood partners within a year's time, grossing an astonishing six digit profit by monthly. Stack, flip and, progress was the trio's preparations for hustling. On the contrary, success breeds envy and problems follow money. A local war broke out with Kool and Muscles, and word was that a few of Muscles men that were apart of the Orange Bag squad was furious because they felt like the Driveway was taking their cash flow. In addition to that, Kool came up with a propaganda that would cease all the aggravation and agitation.

Overtly, opening up the heroin and cocaine market throughout Centerville, and flooding the entire neighborhood with both drugs. The Orange Bag crew seen no harm in the matter and was willing to take the chance of getting money all around the board. But, it wasn't the Orange Bag crew's decision on how the tables turned, Muscles was the overseer of the situation.

Reluctantly, Muscles didn't approve of Kool's plan, he said combining the two drugs to sell would do nothing but cause more feuds between factions. Plus, from 10th and Van hook Streets to 8th Street and Ferry Avenue, Muscles wanted that section of Centerville all to himself. Keithy Kool and a couple of Muscles' young mongers weren't feeling the Mr. Grinch attitude of being self autocratic. So in turn, a few of Muscles' men followed Kool and turned the other cheek on the Orange Bag Heroin Gang.

Fly Victor, A-Lucky Lou, Little Fella, Monkey, and Big Tone was just a few of many who crossed over to the Driveway's cocaine operation. Fly Victor, the oldest and most flamboyant out of the bunch had the same interpretations about sharing the street wealth in Centerville like Keithy Kool and, Chucky and Bud. So he took it upon himself at times to be an assailant on Muscles turf any chance he got. Every opportunity that Victor had to become a harmful provocation to Muscles, he used it to his advantage.

After a couple of years of warring with Lamont Muscles for the purpose of trying to amalgamate Centerville into one whole, Victor, Kool and the Driveway boys unanimously got what they needed to get money at all angles. Lamont Muscles went for a long haul on the blue bird to the penitentiary for reasons unknown and automatically Centerville became free land for mongers in the neighborhood. Keithy Kool and the rest of the Driveway boys went throughout Centerville, to all of Muscles' workers and were willing to negotiate and compromise; about flooding Centerville with both narcotic drugs and how it would benefit everyone to get rich. Everyone seemed willing but contrarily there was still one problem that needed to be handled. William "Billy Bad Ass" Holmes, Lamont Muscles right hand renegade wasn't willing to allow his partners turf to diminish and run uncaringly with no sort of order.

The plot of the matter went as follows, the Driveway Boys, Orange Bag Crew, and any other monger who dealt with Muscles, Chucky, Bud, and Keithy Kool had to consult and purchase from Billy. Since there were two main drugs and Billy had control over any movement, he killed two birds with one stone. Making the Driveway boys nexus - Pee-Wee - give him a percentage of what he made from the cocaine operation and cleaned up on the dope. That way he got money all around and kept his partners turf organized.

By the fall of 1978 Centerville was the Las Vegas atmosphere of money, only with no casinos. Everyone from the connections to the addicts was touching a piece of the pie. In addition to the entire street's remunerative affluence, Keithy Kool and Fly Victor decide to merge everyone who was selling both drugs throughout into one section. Roosevelt Manor Projects, on the strip of 8th Street due to too many unnecessary issues happening and stratagem maneuvers as well. It was too much movement and not enough eyes to watch everyone. Plus, Speedy-Speed one of the Driveway's great hustlers and area men had been gunned down and killed on the curb of the Stanley Park's playground. Leaving the neighborhood motiveless and full of assumptions about the death of Speedy that had a misconceiving finger pointed to all of his hustling buddies. By nosey witnesses, prosecutors and homicide detectives that had gut feelings that it was an inside job. Chucky, Bud as well as Kool and Victor decided to shut the Driveway down and move elsewhere.

From 8th Street and Ferry Avenue to 8th and Central Avenue the top brand dope and cocaine was slung. The dame negotiated procedures applied for Pee-Wee Franklin and Billy. With well over fifty mongers in Centerville, 8th Street held a three shift schedule, Chucky and Bud had a shift, and Keithy Kool and Fly Victor had their own shift. Out of the bevy dealers, whoever worked the particular shift, half sold dope and the other half sold cocaine.

The name Good Wood came about from this young jokester by the name of Abby-Ab who lived in the Manor Projects. On a daily while in the mix of the hustle Abby-Ab use to yell out, "Now that I'm getting a little paper everyone wants to jump on the Good Wood. When I was broke and times weren't good you were in the woods nowhere to be found. So for now get off the Good Wood." Abby-Ab became the slang trend setter in Centerville and the founder of a hood orientated - drug organization slogan that changed the community.

At a time, from 1974 to 1978 the Good Wood boys became the good will to their community and began running a philanthropy when Camden's economical system was at an all time low. Capitalism was the heavy hitter; going for self was the main target and the cities amalgamation began to disperse. In a four year span a lot of robberies, breaking and entries, and riots began to emerge on local businesses and throughout Camden's poverty.

The Good Wood boys, even with their engagements of illicit acts, started giving from what they took from the community. Donating lump sums of money to habitat companies for better environmental living, toy drives for children, local charity funds and putting enormous amounts of money into the only two high school's scholarship fund for future graduates. They gave block parties for different occasions and orchestrated Christmas drives for kids who were less fortunate.

Christmas of 1979, the Good Wood boys had two immense tractor trailer trucks from the Kiddies City Toy Company deliver two truckloads of toys, games and bikes for the tenants in Centerville. A true sight to vision and if there was a problem or any kind of disturbance in the neighborhood, neighbors didn't bother calling the police, they took it to the Good Wood members and men from their organization handle the matter. The Good Wood Boys went from inner city slang to a household name in a few years time. Their faces as well as their names appeared on every news paper stand and local news station throughout the Tri-state. That's how the Good Wood franchise was born.

But one knows with much unity and power brings controversy

and opposing views on good living. The mayor's office and the Camden City police department began framing more than half of the Good Wood cadre with any illegal crime that would fit the criteria of the street hoodlum. Only to break up the unification and loyalty that the Good Wood boys possessed, just to make a statement and allow the Camden Community to vision that the law was superior over the unjust.

By 1981, money had slowed up in the Manor Projects, due to connect difficulties and product failure. Pee-Wee Franklin, Chucky and Bud all got sentenced to ten years for racketeering and organized crime throughout Centerville. Other severe charges were file, such as distribution of more than five pounds of cocaine and weapons charges. Billy was a part of the boys' dispute too and took in for questioning about the Centerville organization. His dealing with the three men and the position he with held amongst the crew. After denying any dealings with Pee-Wee Franklin and the Centerville organization, Billy was turned loose; because the allegations and charges had no concrete evidence to hold him. Billy then, secluded himself from Centerville, the Good Wood boys and the dope game after being released from the law's custody.

$$\$ \; \$ \; \$ \; \$$$

A persistent and consistent nexus is what kept an organization together and money rolling in the right way. If a customer or buyer had no straight connect, agitation came into play and reckless things were enacted upon. Reason being is because the more products they received there was more profit. There was no connection, no product, no profit, and those terms weren't good for a hustler.

These happenings brought a lot of unwanted infuriation and feuds inside the Good Wood fellowship. Crossing each other like Broad and Market Streets was the new fad in the Good Wood cipher. Apparently, the relationship between Keithy Kool and Fly Victor became inclement in the family, and sparked unmorally between many others. Kool began doing business outside of the G.W. family after the lost of Billy, Pee-Wee, Chucky and Bud. Without informing

Victor or any other member in the clique, Kool moved his business a block over to 9th and Van hook Street with the help of yet another childhood friend, Johnny "Midget" Money.

Now John Money was this brown skinned, oval head five footer, that's how he got the name Midget. He knew a source, who knew sources, that known sorcerers. After doing most of his childhood in jail he met a few distinguish criminals who were eminent in the streets. Upon release him and Kool - who had dealings prior to his incarceration - maintained contact through letters and phone conversations. Assumingly, Kool must have informed Midget about his dealings with Pee-Wee, Chucky and Bud, Billy and the G.W.B's. And, how things were being operated throughout Centerville, Midget took the depletion of his resources to full advantage with the help of Keithy Kool. They both went out of town to meet with Midget's source from the penitentiary to discuss certain propositions of bringing a new branch to Centerville.

Purportedly, prices and product followed through for the connect, Keithy Kool and Johnny. They brought a few rebels from out of town and opened up the market on 9th and Van hook Streets. Fly Victor and the entire G.W.B crew wasn't too satisfied with the ordeal that was being executed.

The cross began to imbue the faded picture at this turning point; Keithy Kool had an affinity with Victor's big sister "Sweets," before their friendship went sour. Now Sweets despite her curvaceous appearance, strenuous height and mere beauty, was blindly conniving and deceitful under the façade for a smile. She used her tools tandem, behind her wit and charm to build her luxurious castle. This consisted of money, cars, diamonds and real estate. Sweets had been the prize winner to Kool's gold mind and Victor used her to obtain his wealth. But, it took a lot of planning and education for the process to go right. Victor wanted to hit four birds with two stones without having to take four shots. He cleaned out Kool and Midget's wealth, plundering their nexus and taking out the outsiders in one conglomerate strike.

Victor informed his sister about the plot, got her to elucidate the move to their cousin Fatima - Sweet's partner in crime - who was always around when it was time to get grimy. Fame was Fatima's nickname - short for Famous - was put up to the challenge to deceive Johnny. Sweets and Famous together were a sweetly famous tag team, primarily similar to the late Shake and Bake but weren't that knee deep in the game. Fame was a bit shorter than Sweets with the same physical attraction and womanly aura. They were ghetto glamour girls; even their own gender gave them an ogle eye.

Sweets and Fame's mission was to observe Kool and Midgets moves, and take in as much information that would lead them to their money spots. While Victor and some of the G.W.B. members manipulated the outsiders so he could get close to Midget's product resource.

Within weeks Kool and Johnny had been robbed for more than $300,000 dollars and the out of town crew that he brought along somehow vanished. The boys were left mystified having no hard evidence and a lot of finger pointing. In three months time before Kool and Johnny could get 9th and Van hook flowing at a moderate pace, their operation was destroyed completely.

Subsequently, Keithy Kool has smeared his face in more shit as he tried to replace what he go taken for. He got knocked out of town for trying to purchase a pound of cocaine from a pair of undercover agents. His bail was set at a mere $750,000 dollars and he only had half of that to be exact. He called home to Sweets and explained the matter clearly and told her to wait until he got a bail reduction before she posted his bail. But, things didn't go as expected for Kool; he sat in the county jail for three months waiting on a bail reduction. And, when he finally received it, he called home once more to get some disappointing news. Sweets had been robbed for the bail money but, Kool didn't believe her and thought she told a lie to keep it for herself. Kool threatened his onetime love's life with the words of being a "Dead Bitch," when he touched down.

A year passed, and in the spring of '82 Kool went up state to complete a five year prison term. Broke with Sweets out of his life for good and no friends to turn too, Kool got word from some young gossip nigga who was fresh in from the streets. That his man Midget had supreme clientele in the dope game on Phillip Street and

Central Avenue, of off 8th Street in the Manor Projects. Inevitably, that wasn't the only supreme thing Midget had conquered in the game, he even won Sweets over. She didn't have time to waste on a nigga who was doing hard time, Sweets was a top notch sister, and she needed to be where the money was.

Sweets dealings with Johnny sparked conflict between her and Fatima, who didn't appreciate her cousin's mendacious ways. And couldn't believe that Johnny had the audacity to do such a thing but, fame covered her madness and got even.

Fatima wrote Keithy a letter and told everything, how Midget plundered him out of his three-hundred and seventy- five grand, how he always flirted with Sweets behind his back, and the entire time he was away Midget's main objective was to take him under when he came home the first time. Kool's response was succinct and endearing to Famous:

*Fatima,*

*Thanks for the concern and the information but Johnny and his issues are extraneous to my needs at this point and time. It always takes some sort of unnecessary stuff to occur for the truth to be divulged. Just make sure you can vision it before it happens to you and, always walk alone because in the end friends become strangers.*

Kool's brief missive touched Famous' emotional side and she began to take Keithy and his words of encouragement seriously. She put Johnny behind her, alienating herself from Sweets and taking careful steps up life's ladder. After a few back and forth notations Famous started visiting Keithy regularly.

In addition to the matter, Midget and his partner Spirit, some vixen woman who's cupidity for doe was so outrageous that her skin complexion should have been green. They tried to compromise with Fly Victor and a few of the G.W.B.'s, offering them ten keys of cocaine for the administration over Phillip Street and Central Avenue. But, Vick didn't concur, he wasn't expecting the fact that two outsiders

- Spirit from upstate New York and Johnny who'd only been home a year - could monopolize their territory. If Lamont Muscles was home no one would have been thinking about any compromises, let alone try to be in his presence.

Vick rain checked their offer; he needed more time to think things through and, called a meeting with a few stern members of the Good Wood faction. Jingles and Vick were partners in crime, Stereo, A-Lucky Lou, Miguel, Deucey, Little Fella and Bumpsy and Snail. All came to a head to offer substantial view points about the matter at hand.

Everyone but Jingles didn't agree on the move which Johnny and Spirit pushed with persistence. Phillip and Central was Centerville's gold mind, unlike 8th and 9th Streets which were one dimensional. Phillip and Central attracted more traffic then the Lincoln Tunnel at rush hour. Off of Phillip and Central was the Sand Park, which sat on the edge of the Manor Projects and ran from 9th and Central to 9th and Ferry Avenue. This is where all the neighborhood kids came to play, not to mention the Church that sat alone directly across the street from the Sand Park on the Phillip Street side. The G.W.B.'s thought it wasn't a good idea to start something new and allow two outsiders to put product in an area that's been off limits since the Church was built and the park had been reconstructed. Most of them knew that they weren't following the laws of the land but putting crime on silent ground where children played and elders prayed just wasn't their style.

Contrarily, Jingles has a different perspective about the matter, as if he gave two fucks about the kids, the senior citizens or the community. All he saw was dollar signs and he never prayed to god, he prayed over dead presidents. He had a plan that was extraneous to the neighborhood but was relevant enough to get his team rich.

Take Johnny and Spirit's offer of the ten birds, allow them to open the market up on Phillip and Central and get a percentage of what they grossed a week. If Johnny and Spirit moved ten keys a week through the Manor Projects and was buying them for $15,000 dollars a bird. That was an estimate of $150,000 dollars just off of purchase not including the enormous profit that would come out of it all. And the G.W.B's percentage was a fourth of that. So they would have been getting $60,000 dollars plus more to split at the round table. Monthly it was $240,000 dollars just to rent out the land; it was an intelligent business ideal coming from Jingles, all for the price of nothing. They had a ghetto entity not only from which they could capitalize from put monopolize as well. Literally the turf was owned by the city but in street ideology it was controlled by the Good Wood family.

The community, kids, or senior citizens weren't factors to the G.W.B's once Jingles' arithmetical percentages were calculated. They too could only vision dollar signs from being brain washed and decided not to follow through with their decision and go through with Jingles' instead.

With in days Vick not only gave Johnny and Spirit the gang's decision but he also demanded a payment of one-fourth of their earnings by weekly. Unhesitant, Johnny and Spirit took Vaughn's proposal into consideration and, in return told him, "That his team should stay out of their way and everything would run smooth." Johnny and Spirit had big dreams and plans of getting rich then relocate.

Things got off to a slow start on Phillip and Central for Johnny and Spirit in the beginning. But, after about five months of grinding and determination money began to prosper for them both. Things ran smooth for both parties, their liabilities were paid weekly, on time and they had no interruptions from any police or law enforcement. The second quarter of 1981 started out impressive for everyone. That's until word got back to Shaheem "Stereo" Morgan - a general inside of the Good Wood family - that the bitch Spirit was working for the D.E.A.

Stereo got word from these two drug junkies by the name of Rico and Moonie who use to sell for Spirit. Moonie not only worked for Spirit, she was her hair stylist from time to time. Spirit became suspicious to Moonie one night they were out having a good time. The venue that Moonie and Spirit appeared at must have been the D.E.A's cliché for seeking furtive information. Moonie was around people that didn't fit the common life that she or Spirit lived. The atmosphere, language, appearances, and attire were nothing similar to what Moonie was use to seeing in local joints such as Sophia's Café, or Jock-A-Moe's bar.

Moonie was introduced to a few of Spirit's associates, some Black others were Caucasian, something you wouldn't observe even if you were a pedestrian in the ghetto of Centerville. Donny Turner and his family were the only Caucasians who resided in the neighborhood. But, Moonie was recognized and labeled as Spirit's partner and everyone Spirit introduced her to, their response was, "You must be Shonda's partner?"

SHONDA! Who and the hell was Shonda? As long as Moonie had known Spirit her name had always been Sherry or Spirit, not fucking Shonda. That's when Spirit became skeptic to Moonie.

As the night got older and the intoxication surfaced the atmosphere, Moonie was approached by one of Spirit's associates. A white man by the name of Jimmy who wore a mustache similar to Yosemite Sam from the cartoon Bugs Bunny and wore a tooth pick out the side of his mouth. Moonie felt strange from being approached by a white guy because it was unusual to her, something that rarely took place where she was from. Overtly, being the open minded woman that she was, she gave off a regular vibe to Jimmy and began to fraternize in return.

Before the night ended, Jimmy attracted the attention of Moonie so much; they danced, had a few drinks and exchanged numbers. Consequently, in the exchange of numbers Moonie gave Jimmy the wrong number, due to white guys not being her cup of tea.

To prove to herself that her girlfriend wasn't all that she feigned to be, she disguised her voice as Spirit or Shonda and gave Jimmy a call. Jimmy's conversation with Shonda (Moonie), was concise, he said nothing out of the ordinary but, "We need more time," whatever the hell that meant. So to keep all situations parallel, Moonie used Rico to disguise his voice, somewhat similar to Jimmy's and give Spirit a call; making him use the same dialogue which Jimmy said to her. Jimmy (Rico), called Spirit and relayed the dame original message that Jimmy gave. In response, while Moonie listened on the other end of the phone, Spirit had a loquacious tongue. Talking uncaringly over the phone as if her spot wasn't bugged, in response saying, "Need more time for what? I gave you everybody that I know for a fact is a part of the Good Wood organization. And you--"

"The team needs more time," Jimmy (Rico) replied, with the towel over the phone.

"Well you muthafuckas better hurry up because I'm running out of time, patience, product and money to give to them pussies. I can't wait until this entire operation is complete so I can relax."

"It'll all be over before you know it, just have a little more patience with us, I'll call you later."

All three lines hung up, one in a state of depression and the other two fully astounded and amazed about what had just transpired over the phone.

Rico didn't want Moonie to get herself involved in Spirit's bullshit, so he told her the best thing to do was keep her mouth shut. But, it was too late she was already involved being as though she was dealing with Spirit and Johnny, Moonie was her confidant, and had a fling with Stereo. It would have been extremely hard for her to keep her mouth shut, without informing anyone. And, if the G.W.B's got busted an indicted, eventually the situation would have back fired on Moonie once Spirit's name was mentioned of the trial court. Of her being the set up woman or witness, then Moonie's life would have been in danger.

Stereo was immediately informed about Spirit, Jimmy, the operation and what was about to transpire. Stereo found it hard to believe at first, how was he going to take a users word. She was good enough to sleep with then again why not? That's when Rico stepped in and adduced proof on the matter, telling Stereo that he heard it all to clear and witness it all. Being a part of Moonie's scheme to get some information out of Spirit which he was a part of.

Stereo got in contact with every G.W.B immediately and set up a meeting down at Sophia' Café no soon as he got the information from Rico and Moonie. Everyone showed up without interruption, the entire street coalition was at the meeting. From the foot soldiers to the look outs, Sophia's was filled. And, after explaining the situation to everyone in attendance, Stereo thought it was best if everyone went low key until the heat waned and there was no pressure upon anyone to bust a pipe. He also felt that since the issue was brought to his attention first, he wanted to take care of Spirit and Johnny Midget himself.

Jingles on the contrary, had a different outlook on the matter, he felt since everyone was a target that they all should participate to dry out the spell that was erupting. That way no one in the D.E.A. regime could devise a plan to finish off the G.W.B's because time was up for them. So to avoid the penitentiary and indictments Jingles thought it was best to go on a hunt, kill the enemy before the D.E.A. had the chance to clean up. Plus, they wanted to get rid of Moonie and Rico before the cop Jimmy had the chance to have a real conversation with Spirit and find the scheme that was ran. Because eventually jimmy was going to want to know why Monique - the alias Moonie gave Jimmy - gave him the wrong number to begin with. That was another suspicious matter to the investigation table.

The G.W.B.'s all went on the hunt and cleaned house, in a week tops, Stereo knocked off Spirit, Johnny Midget and, Rico after he made Moonie manipulate the three of them and got them to come on Phillip and Central for the purpose of shutting down the operation. When they arrived there was no discussion brewing, just a shut down on their human operation, eternally. Subsequently, Stereo killed Moonie too, because of her tides with the other three victims. Plus, the heat was on her and he didn't want her boiling point to spill and scold the rest of his team.

The killing spree didn't just stop at the four, Fly Victor, Jingles, Stereo, Bumpsy, Snail, Miguel, Deucey, A-Lucky Lou, Little Fella, Bizzy B and Big Tony Vasquez who were all the original members of the G.W.B came to an agreement to murder every look out and dealer who interacted with Spirit and Midget. Out of seven people the guys managed to get three of them and the other four was incognito.

Buddy, Juju, Hakim and, Faheem who were all lookouts for Spirit and Midget, went to the police and explained to them the tragically events that took place. Since the case was federal the D.E.A. interjected and took the four of them into their custody. Jimmy Dartaine, who was the head of the case at the time wanted statements, mug-shots and, names of everyone who was involved with the murders of Rico, Midget, Moonie, the three lookouts and, their essential undercover informant Sherry (Spirit - Shonda) Land. Buddy and Juju gave up statements and the two twin brothers Faheem and Hakim pin pointed the mug shots of every person in the Good Wood Posse, who they accused as being murder victims.

Victor "Fly Vick" Levy, Terrell "Snail" Walton, Marvin "Bizzy" Butler, Author "Deucey" Jamison, Jamal "Ezar" Morgan - Stereo's oldest brother, and Miguel "Nephew" Smith were all captured, charged with murder and conspiracy to sell narcotics to the law enforcement agents. They were all processed and admitted in the Camden County Jail to await a bail arraignment.

Law enforcers had warrants for the bounty of Shaheem "Stereo" Morgan and Darrell "Bumpsy" Walton. Who had fled Centerville and absconded themselves from the City of Camden until the law caught up to them. Jamiere "Jingles" Johnson, Sutton "Little Fella" Hughes, Arran "A-Lucky Lou" Levy and, Anthony "Big Tone" Vasquez were the only names unmentioned in the case of investigation.

Months breezed by before the six suspects had the opportunity to receive a bail hearing, which was invertible and denied by the courts because of their prior criminal history. Once the boys received their discoveries for the indictments, that's when they found out who the informants and rats were in the case. They quickly sent word on the street so the situation could get handled and cleared before the trial started.

The four testifying witness that were all remotely placed in different locations by the D.E.A. and the District Attorney's office, figured that no one was going to find out their testimony until they were scheduled to take the stand. Faheem and Hakim came back into the city as if the word on the wire didn't have them labeled as the rat pack. They were now looked upon as prey to the vicious reptile of the Good Wood gang, what and idiotic decision to make.

Hakim and Faheem were in the hood flaunting themselves like two flamboyant pigeons as if nothing ever happened. Before Jimmy Dartaine or any other agent could get a hold of them and relocate them, the G.W.B's got a hold of them first.

Bumpsy and Stereo who remotely were hiding themselves down in Florida at the home of one of Jingles' relative, came back to handle Faheem and Hakim themselves. It wasn't a wise decision for the two most wanted suspects but when your life's on the line, who could do a better job?

On two separate occasions the twin brothers were murdered and found with multiple gunshot wounds to the head and body. Stereo and Jingles, both, killed Hakim when they caught him coming out of Young's grocery store on the night of November 22, 1981. And, Bumpsy caught Faheem three days later getting out of a car in front of his home and opened him up from chest to navel.

Not to long after the deaths of the twins, Bumpsy was captured at the airport trying to make a furtive get away back to Florida. Stereo still remained on the top of America's fugitive list but managed to diverged himself away from Bumps' troubles.

With Hakim and Faheem out the way the captive Good Wood boys thought the cases that the D.E.A. penned on them were fragile because they had no star witnesses. There was no substantial evidence, no finger prints, gun, not even a relevant motive. Apparently, the D.E.A. grabbed a hold of a sufficient witness for the case, someone who knew everything about the G.W.B.'s, everyone from the ring leaders to the cheerleaders. The law kept close watch on him and covered his appearance even in their presence until the trial date came along.

This material witness was one of the originators and, was a part of the Orange Bag crew that transformed into the Good Wood organization. He knew who originated the name of the kingpins, the middle men, the dealers also the gun clappers. He also knew who planned the murders on Spirit, Midget, Moonie, and Rico but, had no accuracy to who the gunmen were. But was precise about who killed Wadoo and Snapper, two of the three men that were lookout for Spirit and Midget. That was enough for Jimmy Dartaine, the D.E.A., and the D.A. to prosecute the Good Wood Boys and send them up the river for good.

In December of '81 a few of the guys from Good Wood were released on enormous cash/bond bails awaiting their February 1982 trial date. Fly Vick, Bizzy B, Ezar, and Miguel were all out on bail; Snail's bail was revoked due to him having a probation violation. He wasn't charged for the murders but was charged with distribution of a few kilos of cocaine to two female undercover cops. Bumpsy wasn't charged with the two bodies either, but also had no bail as he waited for a preliminary hearing on the deaths of Faheem and Hakim. The D.E.A. barely had any substantial evidence that linked Bumpsy to the murders, but would try to prove beyond a reasonable doubt that he was indeed a suspect. He was a liable suspect on the run when Faheem and Hakim came back to Centerville. Then, he was captured trying to flee the state after the murders and to the law it was something awkward about the way that scenario played out.

Author "Deucey" Jamison remained in protective custody in the county jail, awaiting his day to take the stand and tell tales in his peers trial; Buddy and JuJu sat patiently to add the icing also. Deucey who was eighteen, couldn't handle the pressure of being confined to a cell for the rest of his young life, or maybe he could have but the fact that no one in his crew wanted to dish out bail money for him. Caused him to flip his lip and get the last laugh on friends that he presumed to be loyal. As one of the toughest members out the crew, it was always the ones that became dreadful to many and snitched when the heat arose. The bad thing was Deucey wasn't even there when Wadoo and Snapper were murdered. His testimony was going to be based on the hearsay he received from the guy who really made it happen and that's how the fish got hooked by opening its fucking mouth.

The trial was set for February 19th until the 24th of 1982, the prosecutors has no physical or direct evidence, only the testimony of the three blind mice. Which sent Victor, Ezar, and Bizzy B up the dry river for a twenty year sentence but Bizzy B got lesser time because he wasn't the actual trigger man. He was the get-a-way driver and a juvenile when the tragedies happened; he only got seven years.

Buddy and Juju's testimony didn't even convince the jury to prove beyond a reasonable doubt that the G.W.B. members were guilty for the deaths of Spirit, Johnny, Moonie, and Rico. There were two

unorthodox statements that didn't even align with what was record-
ed by the prosecutors. On the stand Juju stated that he was at the
scene of the crime when Spirit, Johnny, and Moonie were gunned
down. He seen Fly Vick pulled the trigger but when the defense
team played the tape, he said he arrived when the mask men were
fleeing the scene. He gave chase to the mask men but couldn't catch
any of them and never got a good description of any of them.

Buddy and Juju were both at the scene of the crime when a green
family van pulled to the corner of Phillip and Central Avenue and
four men jumped out with hoods over their heads. He identified the
four men as Victor, Miguel, Ezar and Stereo but Stereo wasn't even
at the trial and was never mentioned in Juju's testimony. The four
men started shooting in the direction of a gray, four door Mercedes
Benz where Spirit, Rico, and Midget were waiting for Stereo to
show up. The luxurious car was ambushed and so were the three
bodies inside and they hopped back inside the van and pulled away.
Who was lying and who was telling the truth? Juju and Buddy didn't
know for damn sure, they were just frightened by the G.W.B.'s and
because they were low leveled lookouts for Spirit and Johnny. Not
wanting to be the next two to be amongst the missing, so they made
up a phony testimony to try and put the Good Wood boys behind the
metal cradle before they were put six feet deep.

The trial court and jury allowed the testimony of Author Deucey
to convict the four boys with the murders of Walter "Wadoo" Lewis
and his nephew Samuel "Snapper" Lewis. Both of Deucey's statements from the tape to the stand were accurate enough to convince
the jury of twelve. Deucey admitted to being at the scene the night
the two men were killed and he played the part as a lookout the night
Ezar and Victor ran up in Wadoo's home. Ezar and Victor were undoubtedly the trigger men and, Bizzy B was the driver.

Once the deliberation was finalized, the verdict's reading was
guilty on all counts and the three boys were charged with the murders of Spirit, Midget, Moonie and Rico. Ezar and Victor were guilty
on two counts of 2nd degree murder, Bizzy-B was found guilty of
conspiracy and Miguel walked after being found not guilty for is
alleged actions; Miguel's name wasn't mentioned once in the five

day trial.

Terrell "Snail" Walton took a plea bargain which held a fifteen year sentence in Federal prison. The sufficient evidence that law enforcers had was to severe to get a fair trial or be acquitted on.

Bumpsy was released from the county jail after being acquitted on the two homicides of Hakim and. There were no witnesses and no direct evidence to draw a conviction. Bumpsy even passed a polygraph test that he suggested upon, he said in jail for two and a half years prior to being released.

Author Jamison got fucked all across the board, after giving up a testimony to put his crew away forever, he ended up getting a four year prison term for being a participant in the murder plots. The weird thing was, Deucey wasn't even at the crime scene before or after the action was executed. But, that's how the dice rolled when you stepped a foot in someone else's shit.

Juju and Buddy also got two year jail sentences for falsifying testimony to a jury, not quite what the two fools were looking to receive. Even more bad predicaments that accumulated into the issues that had no meaning in their livelihoods. Conclusively, for Juju, Buddy, and Deucey, after their hard time in the slammer they still had to face the reality of being labeled gray, furry mammals also, classed as prey to the cats that remained a part of the Good Wood Gangs tides.

Four months after the trial ended, Stereo turned himself into the Feds after they were giving an order to kill him on sight, not because he was wanted but for a primary homicide that was committed. A female acquaintance of Stereo's was slain to death in her home where he was hiding out at until his crew's trial ended.

Mindy Mendez, a mother of two who was half Hispanic and Black was shot in the head at close range as she slept peacefully in her bedroom. That was the analysis depicted on the front page of the Courier-Post Newspaper. Shaheem was being held without bail in the Camden County Jail.

The day Author Jamison took the stand and showed his dishonor in the court room at the Hall of Justice. To the four men who gave blood, sweat and tears for him to be amongst their organization and would have given their lives for such a warrior. It cast away a burden of love that would change Centerville forever. The Good Wood circle has never been the same since and everyone strayed and branched off into their own factions. Simultaneously, they kept their eyes on any new or suspicious things that may incriminate them in the future.

After Victor was sentenced to do his twenty year sentence, his built in floor model safe which was in Suton's house was stolen and wiped out for $280,000 dollars. And the night it happened Little Fella was attending a party that took place at Sophia's Café. Two years later, Victor got word from his sister Sweets on a visit, that Jingles was the head honcho at the G.W.B.'s round table. He was supplying the entire hood and call the shots that Vick use to make. She also told him that Jingles was running with these heavyweights from across town in the Cramer Hill section of the city. These renegades, who called themselves Enterprise 33, were the modern day drug cartel since the Dominican Brothers to capitalize and monopolize on money throughout the entire city.

"Kylie," I said, in a furious tone, glancing at my watch. He looked at me dubiously. "It took you almost an hour to tell me that the nigga Jingles is the heir of Centerville?"

"You asked me to give you the history on the Good Wood Boys blow by blow," he replied, taking a seat at the wooden picnic table.

"Yeah well you could have edited it a little." I joined him at the table. "So that brand of dope called Smiley is Jingles' product huh?"

"That's the word on the street."

"What about a stamp called Kiss that's being sold up in North Camden?"

"Never heard of it," Kylie replied, scratching the back of his knotty head. "Kyle, man its so many different brands of dope and cocaine running through these streets, nobody tries to pay attention to names or labels, long as the product is good. And right now that Smiley got users and abusers selling their souls."

"What about these Enterprise 33 lames? You got any significant scoop on them?" I started sounding like a detective, asking question after question.

"Kyle! What the fuck are you the fuzz or something slim goodie? Damn!" Kylie asked, very annoyed from all my questioning.

"I'm curious my man, I need to know as much as I can about this Jingles muthafucka before I get involved with him."

"What?!" Kylie was aggravated by my response.

"What? Did I say something wrong?"

"Hell yeah you did, listen Kyle fuckin' with Jingles, Centerville and them Good Wood muthafuckas is only gone have your mother pulling out that black dress or sending you food packages once a month in the slammer. Them muthafuckas will kill their own kids to escape the pressure of the law or if they sense a bit of weakness in a nigga."

"They're that serious huh?" Kylie's fierce feedback was emasculating my thoughts by the word.

"Serious!" he said, slamming his hand on the table, giving me direct eye contact. No one outside of Centerville enters Centerville. If you don't live there don't go there because they will put you where the worms are. They even got Lamont Muscles and his squad scared to comeback and control the turf that he administered before Jingles and the Good Wood boys were even conceived."

Now that was respect I thought, putting fear in my Uncle Muscles heart was slim to none in the streets. "Besides the Feds and D.E.A still have them under investigation from those prior murders and unsolved drug bust since the beginning of 1980. Now they got them new narcotic teams running down on everything in the city, some new investigation. It's um... Damn!" He said, trying to figure the name out.

"Operation Sundown," I replied, giving him some help. "Yeah, those muthafuckas are trying to shut Camden down for good. Jimmy Dartaine is the captain of the entire operation and he wants everyone that lives under the Good Wood name, including Jingles. He's been after them with a vengeance every since Spirit was murdered."

"How do you know all of this shit?"

"I might get high but I stay alert, I do read and I read in between lines even better. That Operation Sundown shit is the primary attraction 'round here. Day in and day out, on every news station and in every newspaper throughout the Tri-state area."

Kylie convinced me to eradicate my intentions of dealing with Jingles, he and my Uncle's suggestion gave me a haste change of mind. But, I still wanted to dig deeper and derive the information about Jingles and them Enterprise 33 dudes. There was only one person that I could think of that was close enough to Jingles that might give me some insight. My sister Alesha, she and Jingles been together for about ten years, since junior high school' she was my next inquiry.

As I made my way back through Kylie's living room, I noticed the house wasn't as crowded as before. Majority of the junkies and smokers that were lying around smelling like spoiled food had vanished. But, out of my periphery I spotted this man who resembled my dead beat ass dad. With my gun in palm, I made my way over to him and tapped him on the side of his arm with the nose of the hammer.

True indeed it was the bastard; he jumped from the sofa extremely frightened, like a thousand spiders were crawling on his skin.

"Oh shit Marcus!" he exclaimed, backing up with his hands raised. "What are you doing here with that gun?" He swallowed trying to retrieve his conscience. "I mean what's the gun for?"

"Muthafucka you know what it's for, where you have been hiding... I've been looking for you," I replied, thrusting towards him. "I've come to the realization that you take for a joke."

"No, no, no son not at all--"

"I'm not your fuckin' son--"

"Kyle come on jack, not in here... Not your dad man," Kylie said, pushing my arm down.

"Why you ain't tell me this bastard was in here?"

"I forgot that he was even in here." Kylie gave me eye contact but I could hear the fear in his voice. "Limboo and Nanoo invited all those fuckin' leeches any way."

I averted a sharp eye back in Big Kyle's direction, as he stood in front of me looking like a rotten banana. Those drugs were really eating him alive. With sharp flexibility I pivoted in Kylie's direction and hit him wit a fierce body shot with my left hand. Kylie dropped to his knees, holing his stomach, simultaneously I spun off my back foot and turned back towards Big Kyle and aimed the gun at his melon.

"What was that for?" Kylie asked, in a painful baritone.

"For having all these junkies up in here all hours of the night disturbing all of your neighbors."

My day started out on the right foot, I was in luck and as I waited patiently by the door for Big Kyle to put on his shoes and socks. I couldn't believe my fuckin' eyes for a second time as I seen the main I was looking for, head towards me as he trotted down the steps to join the surprise party. I had to rub my eyes just to make sure I wasn't hallucinating, although I was breathing drug fumes and junkie perfume.

"Hey D.S. my man what a pleasant surprise," I said, raising the gun at him. "You're just in time for the meeting."

Terror was written all over D.S. face as he slowly moved down the stairs on at a time. He had a shockingly facial expression as if my physical appearance was an immortal apparition.

"Kyle," he replied, looking over at Big Kyle and Kylie as if they had answers to give him. "This was much unexpected."

"I no," I said, smiling.

"What meeting are you talking 'bout though?"

"The eternal one that the devil has for you, if you don't come up with an excuse of why you robbed Ted, and had me kill him and Jane. And, who the fucks been disguising themselves under Riley, Domino and the Dominican Brothers to get back at Muscles."

Big D.S. was already in disguise, wearing a big, nappy Santa clause beard with an afro bigger than some bushes. He stood in front of me speechless, having no answers to all of the problems that got me shot twice, my uncle confined to an iron horse, and a lot of people killed over the past two decades.

My temperature began to boil as I became infuriated due to them giving me any feedback. So, I took the butt of the .45 caliber ACP, having one in the chamber, on safety and smacked both, Big Kyle and D.S. in the back of the head. Kylie and I tied them up from wrist to ankle with some of his filthy ass sheets and put them in the trunk of Lamaar's black Saab.

I took and dropped Kylie off at my Aunt Debbie's garage that sat in the rear of her home out in Polock town. She had two garages, one that was made into a TV room and the other one was for her car. Kylie and I took Big Kyle and D.S. into the furnished garage.

$ $ $ $

I gave Kylie the gun and told him to watch the both of them until I got back; I had to run a few errands. And, if they even gasped the wrong way he was to knock there ass back out again. And, if my aunt came back there and questioned him, tell her that he was waiting on me to return. And, whatever he did, don't touch nothing in the garage room, just sit and wait for me.

# Chapter. 20

That same night before I journeyed around the corner to meet with the anonymous gangstas, Gary and Pooks. I went and loaded two leather, black brief cases with $380,000 dollars, leaving my last ten g's in the safe just incase I lost the bet on the Steelers to Liquor Luby; the Steelers were having a phenomenal year. I wanted to make a great impression in front of the two men and let them know I wasn't about any games. I wanted it all not some of the shit, like Scarface wanted the world Chico because the empty suit case nonsense was for a muthafucka looking for an early grave. And, funeral homes didn't make a casket to fit my kind of style yet.

My dapper appearance could have melted Pam Grier's insides if she could have got a glance at the sexy shit I was draped in. I was dipped in a double breasted, Italian cream tailor made suit, a black silk tie, some black leather lizard shoes and, a cream top hat with my brim slanted over my right eye; a true, young O.G. at heart.

My white boys were similarly dressed, but instead of the black reptiles on their feet they wore cowboy boots. Only Keith wore a brim hat, Derrick had his hair slicked back in a ponytail. I had enlightened them both about the meeting with Gary and Pooks that following morning after Batina informed me about the mission.

Speaking of the devil, when the three of us arrived at Batina's home which was left to her by her late boyfriend Shan, out in East Camden. Her beauty spoke wonders, truly unexplainable; her golden brown hair was curled down to her shoulders. Laced in a pearl, knee length blouse that lied smoothly over her shimmered brown skin, a pair of cream leather Liz Claiborne heels to match, a pearl necklace and a hand purse to match. Batina and my two hippies acquainted commonly, getting to know a little about each other as we made our way to North Camden.

I parked a block away on 3rd and Front Streets, in front of these stylish row homes that looked like they didn't even belong on the street. Batina thought it was a good idea because Gary and Pooks didn't like anybody or anything that looked suspicious to sit out in front of their building. They dealt with caution and were prepared for anything strange or skeptical that was an impetus to their territory.

"Alright, you two know the plan," I said, turning towards the back seat. "If Tina and I are not out in thirty minutes, make your presence known with your guns sounding like the fourth of July."

"Thirty minutes, why so long dude?" Derrick asked, curiously.

"Because dude, I need some time to get in these muthafucka's head, I want to feel them out a little and make sure your watches are active boys," I replied, opening the driver side door. "Tina you packing that twenty-five?"

"Got it tucked in my panties, massaging the goods," she implied, tapping her loins with a smile.

"Okay then lets go negotiate... Don't forget my boys, thirty minutes."

Eleven-forty-five was the time on my watch when Batina and I arrived in front of this old fire house on 2nd and Front Streets. Gary and Pooks brought the building after the fire department relocated their station on 27th and Federal Streets in East Camden. Gary and Pooks renovated and remodeled the entire building into a grocery store which was on the lower level and an office department which sat above the store.

Two guys dressed in all black and leather Pee coats, searched me from head to toe for weapons and checked the brief cases. They never touched Batina and treated her like she was the queen of England.

"Harvey... Gerard," she called, greasing her succulent lips with Vaseline. "He's clean, ya'll don't have to do all of that. What?! I can't be trusted any more?"

"Where just following the rules," Gerard, the medium height, dark skinned dude said, closing the brief cases back.

"And yes big titis, Oops!" She gave him a reluctant stare. "I mean Batina. Harvey and I trust you a whole lot. Ain't that right Harv'?"

"Umm Hmm a whooooole lot," Harvey signified, giving her an indirect hint.

"Shut up Harvey," she said, smiling, tapping him on the shoulder.

"He's clean boss," Harvey, the tall, brown skin guy said, talking into his walkie-talkie. "Gary said to send you up, Tina you know the way, direct this man to the bosses."

"Not a problem, follow me," She insisted, as we walked through this dark corridor on the side of the building, to the rear of the fire house.

"Let me do all the talking," I said, before taking the back stairs up to the second floor. "You just follow my lead, play your roll with them and stay calm."

"No problem daddy," she said, slapping a big French kiss on me. "I'm always calm."

We were in and instantaneously I was approached, greeted and warm welcomed by these two beautiful ingénues at the back door. Without me offering, the two ladies took my brief cases, suit jacket and brim hat, simultaneously directing me into the spruced comfort zone of Gary and Pooks.

"The bosses will be with you shortly," The tall, trim, well fit valet said, laying my belongings on the plush leather sofa. "Would you like something to drink sir?" She continued.

"No thanks," I replied, wanting to drink her and her side kick.

As I patiently awaited the presence of the two men, I scrutinized their entire office, just in case something fishy jumped off. I knew where to duck, jump and fire my way out the spot.

Their office was more of a luxuriant, modish living room then a cubicle with desk, chairs, book shelves and file cabinets. It was garnished with Persian rugs, a few black leather sofas, elegant wall paintings, a huge chandelier, a built in wall wide screen television, with a stone structured statue having the initials PG13 stationized in the middle of the office. And it had a little fountain pond orbited around it. I was amazed by such swank materials but the statue fountain thing threw me off a tad-bit, in a marveling way. The only time I seen on of them was in the movie Scarface, the seven figure assumption that Batina suspected the boys to have, was visual proof to me. And, definitely in the boys wealth also.

"Are you comfortable?" The tall, poppy-eyed man asked, shaking my hand, as I stood in his presence. "Yes sir, very much indeed," I retorted, with a smile.

"I'm Pooks and you are?"

"Kangaroo... Kangaroo Moore," I replied, not having a clue in the world where I got that weird ass name from.

"That's funny, never heard a name like that before," he said, linking his arms on to his waist. "Tina told me that your name was Kyle."

"She never told you any lies but I prefer Kangaroo its more appealing to me. Like I'm fully aware that Pooks isn't your government name." I returned his answer, in a rasp tone; simultaneously I gave Batina a reluctant stare, as she sat across from me.

Pooks looked to be in his late thirties, brown skin, smooth face having no blemishes, and stood about 6'5" in height. "I take it that you already have met my two beautiful ladies, Francis and Taliyah?" They both bowed their heads assenting too Pook's question.

"Yes, yes I have and beautiful they are," I replied, ogling their appearance.

Francis was the tall, model dame who took all of my belongings when I first entered, and Taliyah was her equal but about four inches shorter. They had the same light complexion and nice petite frames.

"My brother will be joining us shortly, he's taking an important business call," Pooks said handing me a daiquiri that he made at the mini bar which sat adjacent to the wall screen TV.

"Big tits... I mean Batina can you go and see what is taking Gary so long, please... Thank you." Pooks turned on the wide screen and we began watching what was left of the 49ers and the Steelers' game. It was the beginning of the fourth quarter and the Steelers were down by a touchdown (28-21). "Are you a fan of this sport?"

"Oh, very much so." I replied, sipping the daiquiri. "I'm a Steelers fan all the way."

"You too? I've been a Steelers fan for quite sometime now, Steel curtain for sure." I smirked wryly at his zealous response as he nudged me with his elbow. "Com'mon got damn it score, I got a lot of gravey on this game." What a coincidence I thought, I was gambling with ten G's I couldn't afford to lose.

While Pooks and I were being entertained by the game, Gary came out from the other room buckling his green dress pants. About twenty minutes after Batina went in to get him, it wasn't hard to figure out that he was handling his business with Batina while taking his business call.

"Batina will be joining us shortly," Gary said, making his way over to the mini bar. "Yo' slim," he said, looking in my direction. "I'm Gary Ganew, Pooks' older brother. I welcome you to our PG13 establishment." He raised his pinky ring finger in the air, holding his drink up, greeting me as I returned the toast. "Where money talks, product walks and irrelevance runs the marathon. Now if we may, get down to the get down."

The three of us went into the side room where their main office was stationed, leaving Taliyah and Francis behind. Gary shut the doors behind us and headed for another room door that was in the back of the office. He repeatedly called Batina's name before entering, I assumed it was the bathroom or something. Pooks began shooting a game of pool while I watched and we both waited for Gary to return with Batina.

$ $ $ $ $

Gary and Pooks were different in taste and personality, I could tell by Gary's actions that he was the aggressor and Pooks was more sullen and laid back. Pooks' demeanor was open with a calm vibration and Gary on the flip side was talkative, very vigilant and loud. Gary was medium height about 5'10" with a big head, a shade lighter than his brother, bare face with a burn mark on the side of his right cheek.

"Yo slim," Gary said, to Pooks coming from out of the back room. "The whore isn't in the bed room."

"Maybe she took the stairs and went out front to smoke a cigarette or something," Pooks replied calmly, hitting the Q-ball. "Call Harvey and Gerard to see where she may have went."

Gary started pacing the office in a panicky thrust with his gun in hand and walkie-talkie in the other. "Harv', Gerard is Batina anywhere near you two?" he asked talking into the dispatcher. We all heard Harvey's response over the dispatcher; Batina was indeed outside with them. She walked to the car for a minute, to retrieve something out of the trunk.

"Harvey when she comes back tell her to get her ass up here so she can finish sucking my dick." Harvey and Gerard were laughing through the dispatcher, prior to Gary slamming the walkie-talkie on the desk.

I was the only one that knew Batina's real reason for going to the car; she went to get my funky white boys. They were ten minutes behind schedule when I glanced at my watch but I remained cool.

"So Mr. Ahhhh," Gary said trying to figure out my name.

"Kangaroo."

"Right Kangaroo," He retorted, snapping his fingers, leaning back in his red recliner chair behind his desk.

"Tina told Pooksey and me enough about you that convinced us to make this social gathering possible."

"Yeah she said you were a stand up brother," Pooks added, thrusting the eight ball in one of the corner pockets, clearing the pool table. "Contrarily, we've heard that song from a lot of guys who've sat down to aim."

"Basically Mr. Ahhh, Kangaroo what me and my brother are trying to say--"

"I know where you two are going with this and believe me as long as the product is straight, the money is straight, the only cross I got in me is where my neck and shoulders connect. Now am I here to talk about loyalty or are we here to do business because as of right now my streets are being unattained and I'm not making any money," I replied, downing the last of my daiquiri. "Mmm, tasty."

"Okay Kangaroo what you talkin'?" Gary asked, placing his foot above the pool table.

"What you offering?"

"Hmm, you're a funny guy."

"I'm not laughing and you damn sure don't see any clowns in front of you."

"K-Roo where going to cut the bullshit," Pooks said, gently placing the pool stick on the table. "Our offer is twenty at a reasonable price."

"Twenty!" I exclaimed. "You mean to tell me that I came all the way here for twenty ounces?"

"Nah slim you are misunderstanding us, I didn't say you could buy twenty O's, what I meant was that I could supply you with twenty kilos. And if you do buy them, the next time you come to us heroin kings," Pooks said, pointing at himself and Gary. "We'll reduce the original price which happens to be seventy-thousand right now... Down twenty-five percent."

"Eight hundred and forty thousand, not a bad number the second time around but, I might not live to experience the second time around. I live day by day without any futuristic planning. So let's see some baby powder shall we?"

"Oh, oh, oh," Gary said, pushing himself out of his chair. "Bread makes the sandwich complete, so I need to see the doe first."

"Not a problem."

"Fannie, Tee-Tee," Pooks called the ladies at the door. Taliyah was at his side faster than a shark sensing blood.

"You called sir," Taliyah asked, in a weary voice.

"Yeah, where's Francis?"

"She's using the bathroom."

"Oh okay then, go and bring me the goods."

While Francis was handling her business in the bathroom and Taliyah went to get the goods, I went into the living quarters to grab the money. When I returned Pooks was sitting on top of the pool table enjoying a cigar and Gary was screaming over the walkie-talkie for Harvey and Gerard.

"Harvey... Gerard! Where the fuck is those two coo-coo birds?"

he asked, peeping out the window.

"Maybe something suspicious came through and they are check-ing the perimeter," Pooks said, blowing a cloud of smoke in the air.

"Yeah or maybe they went chasing after that whore Batina, where the fuck is she by the way?" Gary looked at me dubiously, assuming that I knew where she could be, like we had a trick up our sleeve.

Francis was still using the lady's room when Taliyah pushed in a cart full of dope; it had to be at least fifty keys on the cart. And, my money wasn't even long enough to buy half of that but I was going to try their chins though.

"Alright Mr. Kangaroo show us some pesos," Gary said, tossing his brother a brick.

I unlatched both briefcases and lifted the tops on them; the two ghetto fabulous bastards couldn't have been happier after visioning both brief cases full of dead presidents.

"Kangaroo going into business with us is the best decision you've made in your fucking life," Pooks said, impinging his pocket knife into the brick of dope.

"Is that right?" I asked, averting my eyes around the room, from Taliyah to Pooks, hoping they weren't up to any sneaky business. I was shitting bricks, all alone with no heat and I was out numbered four to one. Where the fuck was Batina, Keith and Derrick at? I began to get the feeling of funny vibes in my veins.

"That's right brudda, fucking with me and Ganew you can buy you a zoo, ya' dig?" Pooks handed me the knife with some dope on the tip of the blade, I took a dab and rubbed it around my gums. I swear to god my dick went numb in the matter of seconds, I couldn't even feel the salvia accumulate in my mouth that's how potent the shit was.

"You can numb dead corpses with this here," I said, having a gri-mace face, they both laughed at my expression.

"So are we fit to do business or what?" Gary asked sitting back behind the desk.

"Yes indeed--"

"No, indeed you're not," Batina said interjecting, slow pacing in the office with a gun to Francis' head as she stood before the entire office ass naked.

"Tina baby," Pooks said trying to sweet talk her but it wasn't working.

"Don't you Tina baby me, I'm not your fuckin' baby." Francis was shaking more than an earthquake in tears, I could tell that she never been under any severe pressure, like she'd been facing now. "Shut up you stuck up bitch," Tina said, waving the chrome .25 around the room. "All of you go over by the pool table and strip."

Everyone - including me - was looking at Batina like she was crazy. "Oh, what uses think I'm playing?" She fired a single shot into Gary's desk area, letting us all know that she was about business. "The next time I won't miss," She said, pushing Francis over by the pool table.

Taliyah disrobed herself like she never had anything on to begin with, I was in a state of perplexity and half numb and Pooks was taking his good ol' time coming out of his clothes.

"Now Tina I'm only going to ask you one time to put the fuckin' gun down," Gary said, walking around the desk, inching his way towards her with one hand behind his back.

"Gary take one more muthafuckin' step--"

"Gary! Back the fuck off the bitch," Pooks exclaimed, with his hands covering his genitalia area.

Gary looked at his younger brother having the eye of the tiger, knowing that Batina was aiming out of fear and with the courage he had he felt in his soul that he could get her before she would ever think of pulling back that trigger.

With sharpness, Gary whipped his hand from behind his back and a brown handled .357 magnum but before he could fire......

"Suck on this dick, pussy," Tina said, blasting off two shots into Gary's cranium.

"Nooooo!" Pooks yelled, as he began to cry, I was still standing in a numbed daze.

Subsequent to Gary's body dropping, two mask men dressed in all black came into the office carrying two Mac-10 machine guns.

"Damn!" Batina yelled, eyeing the room. "What took you two so fuckin' long?" The two mask men began mumbling verbose words under their ski mask but no one could understand a thing that they were saying. "Just shut up and grab the money and the drugs."

I couldn't detect the mask men, I assumed that they were Keith and Derrick but they were wearing suits; the mask men weren't. Then I thought it could have been Gerard and Harvey because they both wee wearing all black and their physical features were similar to the mask men. I was startled, numb and very confused by the entire situation.

"I knew it was something about you, you black muthafucka," Pooks said, berating me.

"What?" I wasn't following him.

"This entire ordeal was a set up."

"Set up? How the fuck you gone say I set you up and their taking my two brief cases of money and got me leaning on this cold ass pool table, naked. Are you out--"

"Shut the fuck up, both of you fuckers," Tina said, as she rummaged through Gary's desk drawers. She walked over to Pooks, gripped his penis fiercely with one hand and put the .25 to his throat with the other.

"You know Pooksey, you always have been a straight forward man," she said sensually, gently embracing his face with the gun. "And a great fuck in bed, damn! Just thinking' about this dick," She yanked on his dick with force. "Makes me want to drop this gun and ride you til' the sun rises. But eventually dick is not what I'm after right now, I'm on a paper chase and what my two guys have over there in their possession isn't satisfying me right now. I want it all not some of the shit."

"Bitch fuck you," Pooks said, with intense vulgarity. "This empire that Gary and I built from the ground up and all the sweat and tears that we shared on those corners outside of this building, will perish with us before I render my wealth to a drug abusing whore like you." Pooks spit in her face like it was the side walk and laughed. "Gangstas die on top."

"Yeah, just like Shan did huh?" she asked giving him the indication, that she knew that he and Gary killed her ex. Pooks was bewildered by her hysteria.

"What?!"

"You know what bastard," hhe said, wiping the spit form her face. "You and Gary monopolized North Camden and capitalized in the game. After stealing Shan's affluence and had him killed three years ago in front of Tony and Ruthy's breakfast spot.

"That's ridiculous, where did you get that crazy notion or information from?" he asked, averting his eyes in different directions. "I loved Shan like I loved my own brother, if not more."

"Yeah right, that's why you paid Gerard ten stacks to kill him because you and Gary knew with Shan out of your hair so ya'll could terrorize this part of town carelessly.

Batina walked around the opposite side of the pool table where the two mask men were fondling on the bodies of Taliyah and Francis. "What the fuck are you two stupid muthafuckas doing?" she asked, smacking them both in the back of their heads. They both began to mumble unclear things once more. "Just shut up and find the safe, it's in here somewhere."

Pooks turned and faced her, "So that's what this is all about, revenge? You think this is going to relinquish your pain or bring Shan back, huh?"

"It's bigger than Shan and my pain, it's about being in charge, on top, reigning over those who were once in control. You, Gary and Shan are my past nigga, I'm the bossette of this here domain now. You know the rules of the streets, anybody can get caught up in this contaminated game. But the ones who survive are the ones who play as if they were sleep, the ones who hide behind the shadows of the distinguished."

Batina walked over Gary's body, reached down and grabbed the .357 fro the floor, then walked over by the pool table and handed Francis the .25. "If you both want to stay alive," she said, penetrating the .357 barrel in and out of Francis' vagina. "One of use is going to have to kill Pooksey over there."

Francis dropped the gun on the pool table and went into another hysterical outrage. Tailyah on the other hand, was calm as a cat as if she wanted to take the gun and do it herself.

"You no what, that's too easy," Tina said, grabbing the gun from the pool table and walked over toward Gary's desk to take a seat. "I need a little excitement in my life before I kill one of you next," She implied waving both guns around the room. "I want to see all of you fuck each other on top of the pool table, give me a ménage a trois."

No one budged around the pool table, we all gave each other dubious looks, thinking Tina couldn't have been serious at all. That until she fired a shot in the ceiling and said, "I'm not playing, it's either that or I'm a kill all of you right now."

We all assumed positioned on top of the pool table, assuaging Batina's furious mind. Who sat behind the desk with a cinematic smile that went from ear to ear, twirling the .25 handgun around her index finger. I was in the middle of the pool table lying on my back with Taliyah mounted over my face and Francis sucking in between my thighs. I was getting double the pleasure while Pooksey was enjoying Francis' succulent kumquat from behind.

Ten minutes into the session, the two mask men came back to alert Batina that they found the safe. Our pool table show stagnated the minds of the mask men for a second or two, the way they were staring it was like they wanted to join in. But, Batina brought them back into reality way before they had time to fantasize. She walked up behind Pooks and put the .357 to the back of his head and gave him some words of advice.

"I hope you came so your offspring can finish where your life ends." And, she pulled the trigger.

That was the last thing I remembered once I regained my consciousness after taking a blow on the left side of my head near my earlobe. Batina had to hit me last after she shot Pooks, who was hunched over the pool table, lying on the rear end of Francis with his brains oozing down the middle of her back. Francis was still in between my legs, face down, motionless. From my observation she looked dead but I wasn't sure and Taliyah wasn't in my foresight.

Francis had a pulse, I tapped her jaw gently until she became conscience and for the third time she became hysterical after feeling and seeing Pooks' blood all over the place. When I went to retrieve my clothes from the opposite side of the pool table, I stumbled over Taliyah's unconscious body. I tapped her like I did Francis to get her awareness back.

After rinsing the blood off of Francis, the three of us got dressed and exited out through the back of the fire house. Leaving the corpses of Gary and Pooks behind to repose in peace. It was three o'clock in the morning when I made it to my car that was parked in the same place where I left Keith and Derrick. My keys were still in the ignition, when I got in to retrieve the extra set I kept under the mat. My tires burned rubber down Front Street as I headed to one of my places to secure the safety of the ladies.

I took Francis and Taliyah to the Glamour Towers to relax and mend their minds; they both were emotional, scared and ill-humored. Inadvertently, I had to leave them for a while because I had some unfinished business to attain to back at my Aunt Debbie's pad.

Someone was going to pay for the dramatic trauma that I survived, and the $380,000 dollar loss I took and the other $10,000 I lost on the Pittsburgh Steelers, who lost in over time to the 49ers. I beat my head on the steering column the entire drive to my aunt's house. It just wasn't my fuckin' night, not listening to Batina and putting my money in those brief cases was the wrong idea. But, I didn't expect the whore to pull a sting off and manipulate my white boys to do it with her. I wasn't even thinking about the ironic theory, maybe Batina used me as the decoy to pull the sting off and was going to contact me once the heat blew over. But, my chances of getting in contact with her of her reaching out to me were slim to none.

# Chapter. 21

Morton Street, in Pollock Town was tranquil as a desert in a heat warning when I pulled up and parked the Saab in my aunt's drive way. At five-fifteen in the morning I could hear a cricket cry out to the roaming pigeons which traveled the dawned sky.

Big Kyle and D.S. were still in the garage tied up when I went to check on them but, Kylie was gone. Aunt Debbie must have kicked him out when she came in from work and saw him there. She was shaky when coming in contact with strangers, Kylie must have frozen when he saw her and forgot to relay the message. Big Kyle and D.S. weren't in a visible spot so the only way she would have found them is if Kylie told her where they were. They were behind my aunt's couch with a couple of blankets thrown over them.

King and Prince my aunt's two vicious pit bulls were roaming the house when I entered through the back door with my key. They barked out of excitement and jumped all over me when they sensed who I was. The dogs trailed me up to my aunt's bedroom so I could find out about what she said to Kylie before she put him out.

The search for Kylie wasn't difficult at all and I didn't have to inquire about him to my aunt either. Because he was being held captive in my aunt's bed, in between her legs missionary style. I could never seek a bit of triumph because adversity was apart of my immune system. They were so into the intercourse, they didn't even hear me push the door open and step in the room.

It was 5:45 a.m., a time when most common people were getting ready for work or still a sleep. Not in Debbie's bed room though, there were two sex starved people trying to out do the crack of dawn. I stood in the threshold of the door way with my .22 caliber firmly gripped. For about five minutes I watched Kylie give my aunt some of the best strokes of his life. The accumulation of every moan, groan, whisper and assorted position griped my mine to the point of me executing some action. I wanted to do Kylie like Batina did Pooks but I wasn't that insane but, I was steaming though. The hissing sound that I made at a low volume triggered the dogs to bark loud and distract my aunt and Kylie.

Kylie damn near jumped out of his skin when he heard the colossal barks from the dogs reverberate throughout the house. Before he could even turn in the direction of the dogs, the barrel of my gun opposed him like tissue to blow his nose.

"Kyle no!" My aunt shouted, pulling me away from him. "Please, Kyle please do not shoot him."

$ $ $ $ $

I was a thrust of a finger away from blowing his brains all over the cream carpet but self-consciously I retained my trigger finger. I felt that he wasn't the culprit in the situation, my aunt was.

"Put your fuckin' clothes on you sniffling ass heckler," I said, mashing him across the room. "And, your pose to be the innocent one in the family." I declaimed furiously to my aunt. "Up in here fuckin' a guy's brains out that you haven't even known twenty-four hours."

Consequently, I was some what in the wrong, and my irate decorum wasn't even necessary. I came to find out that Kylie use to be my aunt's boyfriend, her old high school sweet heart. The information shook nerves in my brains a little, beleaguering my disposition. The vision of linking my aunt and Kylie as a couple impaired my vision, Kylie's appearance and personality wasn't one that would satisfy my aunt. Her taste in men was completely different; then again some women thrived of ironic taste.

Their relationship became brittle and submerged into turmoil after Kylie committed his time and livelihood into the late Shannon "Shake" Smith. Back in 1966-67 when Kylie dealt with my aunt at seventeen, he was considered one of the prolific, ghetto icons to come out of Centerville. While running with his elder brothers (Chucky and Bud), Kylie wasn't only appreciating his narcotic wealth he was having the time of his twenty-two year old life. One of the main reason he had to wash his hands with my aunt also of my Uncle Muscles enforcing threats and death promised to any nigga that was an insubordinate knuckle head.

$ $ $ $ $

Hence, to avoid any frivolous beef with the powerful column, Kylie isolated himself from the cute and young Deborah Williams; because his character replicated the one of the hoodlum. Muscles wasn't trying to let the bullshit in the streets become prone to his sister's sustenance. Contrarily though, he didn't practice what he preached or tried to induct that proper advice into Debbie's intellectual mind. She mastered the irony that was taught better than her educational curriculum.

Kylie and my aunt discretely seen each other form time to time but, after she found out that Shake was pregnant by him, she disengaged form seeing him; prior to Shake's disappearance in the first quarter of 1973.

Around that time, prior to Shake becoming pregnant she was slyly dealing with Big Kyle. Neither person knew about the other, only Debbie has clear insight of what was going on. Shake was only out to satisfy their bodies to capitalize off of their human income (Pee-Wee Franklin and Muscles). Killing two birds with one stone, Shake not only had the beauty to drop a nigga's pants but the wit and hustling intelligence to profit off of wealth without spending a dime. She manipulated Kylie and Big Kyle with her omnipotent vaginal fruit.

Kylie and Big Kyle were left with broken hearts and personal vendettas against each other. That's when Kylie became a statistical monger in the streets and began doing heroin and Big Kyle was back on the stoop, frustrated, broke and in the dog house with Muscles.

That's until my aunt devise a way for Big Kyle to get back at Shake, reconcile his friendship with Muscles and Billy and become the next franchise player to run Camden. Debbie contemplated on the best way to abolish them, by turning their master mind - behind the ghetto stardom - against them. On their rise to the top in 1971 -'72 Shake and Bake turned on everyone in their retinue except Terry. Without Terry, Shake and Bake's operation never elevated, she knew the business like minutes in a year which happened to be 675, 540; more than enough time to invent a fundamental agenda to profit from.

Terry was credulous after my aunt went to her and told her that she overheard Shake and Bake talking about killing her after they got rid of Lamont Muscles and Billy. Terry absorbed the information and was willing to produce action, she was one that didn't have to be warned a second time.

Terry went to the only person she knew that was infuriated with my Shake and Bake and that was Big Kyle. After enlightening him with the agonized data of hear say, Big Kyle inclined to the assistance of Terry, his yearning vendetta was soon to be compelled. Following, Big Kyle reconciled with Muscles and Billy and brought Terry in not only to acquaint with the two Dons but to explain her roiled relationship with Shannon and Sabina Smith.

Prior to Shake being abducted and submerged into the depths of a river, she gave birth to a beautiful baby girl that no one had any information on. The abandoned child had to be in the current age range of 17 to 25 up until this point of existing. Debbie hadn't seen the infant girl since she was born and Kylie was vacuous minded about his only child's origin.

A few years after Shake's pregnancy she and Sabina were plundered out of fifty keys of dope and a half million dollars and, offered death at the same time. After Shake and Bake's mission became nonexistent, Terry joined forces with Muscles and Billy's affluent cartel. Big Kyle was the next to reign over the underworld after keeping the fifty kilos and the half a million dollars for himself.

Big Kyle attraction for Debbie became even more intensifying after she helped him get back on his feet. But, she declined in having any dealings with him due to him sharing lustful affairs with her three sisters. She wasn't trying to be one to fall victim of his lustful suspense, plus her feelings remained prominent for the lost soul of Kylie; who became a product to the streets himself.

$$\$\,\$\,\$\,\$\,\$$

After listening to my aunt and Kylie babble about their past affinity and acquiring the essential information that came with it. The three of us, along with the dogs marched into the furnished garage to see what we could spill out of Big Kyle and D.S. I really was expecting some substantial answers and pointers to solve the inscrutable, mind boggling puzzle of the underworld.

Kylie and I struggled a little of taking the two bodies from the floor and placing them onto the leather sofa. They both went into an abrupt shock when the covers were pulled from over their frames. Causing them to be finicky and moveable from the way their hands were tied and mouths were sealed.

"Did use come up with any answers about what's been going on the past twenty-four hours?" I asked, fiercely pulling the tape from their mouths. Kylie and my aunt sat quietly on the other sofa behind me, watching meticulously with vigilant eyes.

Avoiding Big Kyle as much as I could because he was trying to plead his innocence and sympathize, I directed my inquisition to the face of Big D.S. Who had yet to give me his street rendition of the coded streets?

"What information can you render about your dealings with Big Kyle and every grimy monger that you have counteracted with in your days with the Camden elite?" I inquired, pacing back and forth slowly, tapping my leg gently with my pistol. "I know you know a lot so spill your guts before I literally spill your guts all over this fuckin' garage."

Big D.S. constrained us all with his version of the wicked games that been played as he witnessed and experienced it. It didn't take long for him to divulge what he knew and didn't know. His story was some what similar to the unveiled story that Big Kyle gave but, far different then the one Dontae had told me a year or so ago.

During his run with Muscles, Billy, Big Kyle and the Rigorous

Rush Girls, he was nothing more than a pawn in the circle. He followed protocol, took orders and, handled relevant issues if any there were. Even when he and Big Kyle took over the streets in Camden, he admitted to being the puppet master who reared Big Kyle's master mind.

$ $ $ $ $

Meticulously, as I analyzed the story, I started to cross exam his dialogue. He gave up more imperative data which became very useful as the Q & A process continued on.

"So you're fresh out of the penitentiary, very indigent and unaware of what had been taking place out in the streets? That's telling me that someone or something had apprised you about what was going down inside Ted and Jane's place of business. Because you and I both know after damn near a decade spent in the slammer, you had no intentions of going to see Ted after you were released. So what I... No, what we want to know is," I said, rotating the gun around the room. "Who are the sorcerers who notified the source with the plot and gave you the orders and, the mission to handle?"

Big D.S. stared at me with dreadful eyes with out attempting to budge his lips, his pupils dilated in size giving me the impression that he wanted to give up all that he ever knew. But, the cat had his tongue and Big Kyle stared him down, hoping D.S. stuck to his guns of not saying a word. While everyone including the dogs waited patiently for D.S. to come clean, I couldn't wait any longer. Having a short man's complex, irritated for answers, I aimed the .22 caliber directly at his foot and banged of a single shot. Causing everyone to freeze in the garage and provoking the dog's bark.

"Okay... Okay! D.S. bawled, squirming vigorously on the sofa, trying to get his hands loose. "I'll tell you... I'll tell you, just don't shoot anymore."

"You addict fucker you better come off something or the next strike is going to be with the dogs and the gun. Now you better choose or I'm going to choose for you."

Kylie was leaned back with a wry smirk on his face as if that kind of action excited his mind and so was my aunt who was just sitting their like nothing was taking place.

"It was Terry and Billy who put me up to do Ted in…"

Once D.S. was released from the slammer, his one main focus and no other intentions but to get rich quick and live his imitated "Super Fly" dreams all over again. Currently, D.S. was trapped in what seemed to be a timeless era, having the same decorum that he had in the early 70's. But, what he wasn't aware of was that the streets had changed since he was booked and put into a cold cell.

$$\$ \ \$ \ \$ \ \$$$

Once he was back in Camden's malicious streets he assumed that majority of his needs and wants would be fulfilled through his old entourage. Ironically, the outcome was different, Muscles was confined to a cell, Big Kyle became a customer to the product he sold heavily, and Terry and Billy were trying to keep a low profile from the Feds. Simultaneously, as they warred with Riley and Domino, the burden of money just falling into his lap was an illusion.

He got word from Terry and Billy that the Rotti Shop was under precautious surveillance and being investigated by Jimmy Dartaine and his lethal Operation Sundown militia. And, since they were two of the operation's main targets, D.S. was best fit to diminish some of their heat because he didn't have a red beam on his back.

At no cost, Big D.S. obliged to handle the matter out of respect, his compensation would come form whatever he was willing to possess from the Rotti Shop which was more than enough to put him back on his feet and, bring his diplomatic service to the boss of the bosses.

"So the twelve kilos and hundred thousand dollars that you possessed, what did you do with it all?" I asked, massaging King around the collar.

D.S. cut his eye over in Big Kyle's direction before responding to my question, as if Big Kyle had the answers for him.

"I um… I sold the twelve keys to Billy for a reasonable price and the money I took and laundered half into a few legal small business markets. Real Estate and commercial businesses, Booney my ol' lady helped me manage my small investments."

$ $ $ $ $

There was still aloof curiosity hidden under the discussion we were having. I was still skeptical about who had been the guise and wealthy torch behind the Dominican Brothers and Riley and Domino's notorious notoriety.

"Hol' on... Hol' on," D.S. spouted, shaking his head reluctantly. "I wanna know why you're interrogating me for information that your dad is more sufficient with than I 'am." D.S. gave Big Kyle a leering gaze for being pressured and tormented for the information that he was hiding.

"Tommy you never told him?" D.S. said, to Big Kyle.

"Told me what?" I ranted, walking towards him. "Told me what Kyle, huh? You holding out on me pussy!" I yelled, back handing him across his face with the gun. "What is it D.S.? What has he been keeping from us all this time?"

D.S.'s sad eyes glared up at me then averted back over into Big Kyle direction before he sluggishly answered, "Terry's an ex-cop."

"Jackpot!" I said, placidly. "That's the information I've been waiting for all this time, and the answer to everyone else's problems."

"She's a what?!" Aunt Debbie howled at the top of her lungs. "Oh my fuckin' Lord... Oh Lord I'm going to jail."

"Aunt Debbie calm down, you're not going to jail, Kylie can you calm her down please."

If my aunt's words were true, then Terry just made a name for herself as a law enforcer because we all had dealt with her to some illegal extent. That meant we were all going down. While Kylie composed my aunt's emotional outbreak, I went back over to D.S. for more enlightenment.

"What else is there to tell D.S.?"

"Nothing more and nothing less then what I just told you."

"Stop fuckin' lying to me!" I aimed the gun at his other foot, knowng more pressure would burst another one of his clandestine pipes.

"Little Kyle don't shoot slim, that's all I fucking know I swear to God." I stepped aside, in front of Big Kyle wanting him to explain what once was hidden.

"Fuck you, you little nosey bastard," He said, directing the crude words to me. "You already know more than enough, I'm not tell you shit. I made you, I brought into this muthafucka, I don't even answer to God, and so what makes you think I'm going to answer to you?" I felt much disrespect from the impolite response, so I knocked him back out with the hammer.

Since Big Kyle remained reticent and stuck to the 5th Amendment by not testifying against himself, I went back to Big D.S. who was more than willing to cooperate.

D.S. illustrated that him finding out about Terry being and Ex-cop came from Big Kyle a couple of years before he went up state to do his time. This was after he was dealing with Shake and my mother at the same time and, the controversy with the Rush Girl's was a distinguished situation; which Kyle had sparked so the girl's could all despise each other. It was only to get even in the tick for tat merriment which hurt and discouraged him.

Furtively, Terry was another one of Big Kyle's paramours but no one ever detected anything because they dealt with each other on unfertile premises. Big D.S. admired Big Kyle's suave decorum; he was a pure lady's man, very smooth and knew how to get a woman in bed without money, a pimp game, or a personal conversation. With a wink of his eye whores would go pulling at his coat tail. Plus, at that time vulnerable woman and whores would sell their kids to get next to a clean, fine, light skin brother. The brim hats and cinematic smile that Big Kyle wore with the sided gold tooth, melted woman's hearts.

Accordingly, Terry who was equivalent in style and character and was not only classy and smooth but, she was a premeditated thinker who studied people as well as things before she obliged, indulged or reacted to any particular thing. She contemplated leisurely like a master at chess, then once she found that right strategy she was a devastating Virgo. She and Big Kyle were two and the same, identical twin but with different parents.

As Big Kyle mingled with Terry the only vitals that he knew was her first name and that she commuted back and forth to Florida occasionally. She never talked about family members, goals, hobbies or, anything that pertained to her personal life. The only thing that mattered to her was money - illegally - without being caught.

Being the keen icon with an eye of a tiger, Big Kyle wanted to know more about the vixen dame known to most as Tabby Terry. He began to delve through her latter lifestyle, wittingly without Terry even suspecting anything suspicious. He would follow her as much as he could, disguising himself as bums, woman and using any other camouflaged attire to stay concealed in her presence. So that his aspiration of finding out who Terry really was, could progress and she could be identified.

After a few years of laborious digging, investigating, and inspecting, Big Kyle struck gold. He had a mechanic name Harry - an old neighborhood buddy - who had his own auto mechanic shop called Guy and Son's on Mt. Ephraim Avenue, a few blocks away from Luby's pool hall. Harry towed Terry's pearl white '73 Fleetwood Eldorado from in front of Club Shake's on Market Street. He rigged the latch on her truck with a special device that molded locks to fit any type of key. Once Terry paid the fine and retrieved her car, she had no idea that Big Kyle was lying in the trunk the entire time.

Big Kyle Drove around in the trunk of Terry's car for three days straight, making a mental note of every location and place that she stopped at. Every time the Fleetwood stopped for a long period of time, Big Kyle popped the trunk to get a glimpse of the area she was in. Terri's locomotion in the '73 Fleetwood would put her in areas and remote locations that were unusual to Big Kyle's photographic memory. He looked for vital signs and symbols most of the time, which could help him where she had driven to. But, his observations always inaccurate, one time Big Kyle almost lost Terry and got himself lost.

He hadn't eaten for about a day or so, and when Terry stopped some place to attain to her concerns, Big Kyle spotted a grocery store near by. He ran inside for a quick second and grabbed a bite to eat. On his way out of the store he observed Terry walking to her car from the other side of the street. He was startled for a second, mind racing for a plan to distract her from pulling off. He spotted this man leisurely ambling up the street and minding his own manners, until Big Kyle broke his concentration. He made the man go stall Terry until he was back inside the trunk and paid the man a hundred bucks for his troubles.

On the third day, after being a confined itinerant inside the trunk, Terry's Fleetwood was back in Camden. Big Kyle couldn't have been happier after finding out from the cashier inside the out of town grocery store that he wasn't in Jersey. But a few hours out side the state, in a town called Annapolis, in Maryland. He had no idea as to why she traveled all the way to Maryland?

Most of Terry's stops back in the city were to the House of Chemistry, Club Shake's and Young's Grocery Store. Club Shake's was a major concern because of Terry's lucrative percentage in the establishment. But, the House of Chemistry on Ferry Avenue and Young's Grocery Store were inquisitive matters to him.

Big Kyle finally found out where Terry rested her head after ending her long, seventy-two hour commute to skeptical places. She resided out in White Fairview, a suburban part of Camden that sat on the south end of the city. The same place where my old jade DaVita lived back in 1980.

She lived in a luxurious, five-bedroom, two and a half bathroom house that was aided with a two car garage and, a swimming pool. She definitely had the money and credit to afford it all without having to borrow or sign for any loans.

Big Kyle waited patiently once inside the garage, to grope the house later on that night when he figured Terry would be sleep. He groped through the somber home lighter than a cat burglar with feathered feet, trying his best not to touch or bump into any compact furniture that would alarm the house. Three out of the five bedrooms were occupied and the other two were vacant.

In the middle upstairs' foyer there were two rooms opposing each other, in one room laid a caramel complexioned female who was sleep in bed. Across the hall, was a child's bedroom where a little girl was sleeping comfortably; at the beginning of the hall sat the master bedroom which was Terry's bedroom. The master bedroom was huge, similar to a mansion's living quarters and how the bedroom was arranged it would have been difficult to observe anyone coming in or out of the room.

Fretfully, Big Kyle's body froze from the scene that was happing before his eyes inside the bedroom. Before him laid an anonymous male figure who was giving Terry rough, passionate sex. For a moment Big Kyle's heart was wrecked from Terry's fervid exhibition but that's why he was there, to identify who and what she really was.

Big Kyle manage to crawl form the bedroom's door and beneath Terry's mammoth canopy bed. He lied under the bed listening to the sexual sounds and vigorous thrust of penetration for a time span that caused him to nod off. The coast was clear the following morning and Big Kyle began scrutinizing the house to make sure that he was the only one inside.

The two cars that were parked in the garage were gone, giving him a big thumb's up to maneuver. The immense, luxuriant home was completely empty and he had more than enough time to search, so he thought.

Big Kyle headed straight back for the master bedroom, he figured that whatever he came looking for has to be in Terry's room. There was also two nice size - his and her - walk in closets. Terry's spouse, boyfriend, or whatever he was to her had a closet full of Italian suits, assorted fabrics and expensive shoes.

Terry's closet had a similar feel, enriched with the finest dresses and shoes, thus the closet was also embellished with a vast amount of artillery, vest, binoculars and secret indictment documentation. After skimming through a few of the documents he found the uniqueness and true individuality of who Terry really was from the veritable information. She was a former investigator for a high intensified drug trafficking task force back in Florida in the mid to late 60's. Big Kyle took a few documents and tucked them away inside the rim of his pants and tried to escape his troubles without being noticed.

Consequently, he faced something unexpected; death faced him with prominence and what he came to notice was that the entire time he was in the house slyly performing inspector duties. He wasn't in the house alone and just as he was exiting the closet, he was approached by a .357 Smith and Wesson. The gun was held by a half naked woman dripping wet in a bath robe and, Big Kyle blamed himself for the nonsensical, half ass inspection because he forgot to check the bathrooms.

There was mere mystification in the bedroom as the female faced him with the gun because they both knew each other very well. The female that opposed him was none other then the carnal appearance of Princess Pooh. What the fuck was she doing in Terry's home? The entire time that Big Kyle and D.S. were doing business with Bobby and Ike through Itchie and Magoo, they were using Terry as a decoy to seek information out of Princess Pooh and Missy Amoure. Big Kyle's mind was boggled, having an inquiring mind to find out what she was doing in Terry's home but he had no time for questions and answers.

Click... Click, Pooh tried firing shots into Big Kyle's head but the fucking gun jammed and his death wish wasn't granted. God was definitely on his side that day because he managed to escape yet another eternal dance with Satan. Kyle then hit Pooh with a boxer's combination, knocking her unconscious after observing the bullet in the gun had wedged on the inside. Big Kyle made it out of the house unharmed, confused, blessed but, with evidence of who Terry really was.

Big D.S. was the only person that Big Kyle could confide in and tell all about Terry being an ex-cop. He was the only person on good terms with Big Kyle at the time because everyone else that he encountered was either dead or in a feud with him.

Prior to Big D.S. pocketing the lucrative amount of cash that was promised to Itchie and Magoo for giving Big Kyle and D.S. the blueprint on how to scam Bobby and Ike Ewing out of their money. And, Bobby and Ike Ewing sending fifty keys of cooking flour to the S & S Brothers and, Missy Amoure and Pooh being found slain. Big D.S. had enlightened Itchie and Magoo about Terri being an ex-cop and the incident that took place at her home with Princess Pooh.

So after D.S. tried short changing Itchie and Magoo for the money that they plundered from Bobby and Ike. Itchie and Magoo wanted to clear the entire board, put an end to Big Kyle and D.S. for their disloyalty, off Terry before she sent the law in to take them under and, off Missy and Pooh just because they were caught in the middle of everything.

Two of Itchie and Magoo's plan were a success but one remained unaccomplished. In accordance, Itchie and Magoo enlightened Bob by and Ike about Terry's situation and Bobby's trollop who was having correlative bondage which was oblivious to him; after D.S. tried getting over and the chaos between them descended a little. Itchie and Magoo also gave them word about what Big Kyle was trying to get them to do once he retrieved the fifty bricks of dope that he planned on purchasing for $2 million dollars.

Bobby, Ike, Itchie and Magoo came together and devised a wily method of their own to kill two birds with one stone. That was to follow through with Kyle's plan for the purchase of fifty keys but in exchange for the cash hand over cooking flour. Find Terry before she managed to contact the Feds and they began to interrogate the entire L.S.D organization. And, since Princess Pooh used and abused Bobby's wealth and love and, never informed him about Terry's street façade, have her and her strumpet girlfriend slaughtered. Sprinkle the cooking flour over their corpses to make homicide assume that the murders had been drug related. But, it was deliberately to send a mix signal to Big Kyle and D.S. to assure them that they were next.

Two of the missions went according to plan but Tabby Terry - everyone's primary target - managed to dodge the ambush that was headed in her directions. Her six senses was more then just a peculiar recognition, it was a dynamic premonition that was uncanny.

In the summer of 1974 aggravation took over Big Kyle's character, having personal vendettas for Terry, Bobby and Ike from the previous plans turning into turmoil. He and D.S. went into the soil of Lake Shore Drive with heavy weaponry and brought out fire works. Once the smoke cleared, five were pronounced dead and many were wounded. Another mission that weakened and went into the sewage drains of the hustling books because every one of the main targets that they aimed for was still on the loose.

In between time, while contemplating on yet another strategic plot to annihilate his adversities. Big Kyle went into a state of depression; he started using his own supply to alleviate the pain of taking major losses and, to ease the pang frustration which kept him mentally eccentric because Terry and Bobby were still alive. Since he couldn't get to Terry and bring down members of the L.S.D crew himself, he brought in an organizational impetus to quell the realm of the operation. He got in contact with a mutual friend Benny Smalls - a sergeant then - at the Camden Police Department. Now a latter lieutenant and who was playing apart in the biggest drug demolition on the east coast. Benny Smalls was offered a lucrative amount of money, off the record and under the table to bring about an investigation on the L.S.D crew.

Benny endorsed Big Kyle's offer and legally followed judicial procedures by going to the superior courts requesting search warrants to encroach the premises and homes of certain members. After receiving anonymous information that there was a major drug ring on the lower south-east side of Camden, in Fairview. He had probable cause to probe the vicinity of Lake Shore Drive and its' wealthy turf.

Benny then contacted his long time friend and superior James "Jimmy" Dartaine, a prolific enforcement agent who was well known for bringing the top dogs in certain organizations down. Jimmy was an impartial personality, after being a cop for more then thirty years he learned to play fair ball and be reasonable. He was the type of authoritative subject that would arrest a person and let them go minutes later; depending on the severity of the charge. Jimmy was very considerate to those living an illegal lifestyle but, if you became a familiar face and he had to arrest you more than he patrolled the streets. You were going to be made and example and shown that he was the streets.

Benny killed two birds with one stone after Jimmy and his team apprehended a great portion of the L.S.D. bandits. But, without notice he flipped the script on Kyle "The Great One" Moore by putting his name on all documentations which indicted the organization and named Big Kyle as the head informant; something that would ruin Big Kyle's reputation in the underworld forever.

By the end of 1974, Big Kyle became apart of the night of the living dead and sex, money and, murder was a secondary option to his primary girlfriend, dope. Big Kyle abused the drug to the extent of becoming absent minded to what was going on in his surroundings. He'd forgotten all about the image that Terry portrayed under her street appearance, his childhood, the business he conducted and, the money he had accumulated in his tenure in the game. He had a vast amount of get away money stashed in a secured place that he can't find and D.S. doesn't even know where Big Kyle put it.

Death became apart of Big Kyle's life like the dark shadows which trailed him, after his nonexistent mind frame had him existing in the streets as a lost soul. The triplets were even trying to repose his soul in the dirt, even Terry for knowing about her discreet past. And, for the sake of Missy Pooh's soul, who allegedly told her about the incident with Big Kyle at the house.

Gracey and Sissy wanted him dead because of his irrational actions towards his two daughters (Alesha and Wadeelah), and how unreliable he was for the care and support of them. Since their conception Big Kyle never claimed them, let alone not even wanting them to exist because of what he thought of Olivia. Gracey and Sissy were just lustful infatuations compared to his significant admiration of Olivia.

Other than Big D.S. - his brother and partner in crime - Big Kyle's trust was directed to only one other person, Debbie. After helping him elevate to being the best thing since Tange and Whop and Lamont Muscles to tyrannize Camden's streets, Debbie became the friend that Big Kyle would never replace.

Contrarily, Debbie began to wash her hands with him once he submerged himself into the depths of dope, he wasn't just a user Big Kyle became an abuser to condemn his life into the graveyard. Debbie discarded comforting him and trying to reform him as a person, so her only other alternative was to take him out herself. She tried poisoning him with Visine eye medication, in his drink but he shunned the meeting of the valley of death once more.

Big Kyle got back in with Terry from the help of Debbie who stuck to her oath of being a Rush Girl for life. Big Kyle wanted to reign over the streets and show his valor as a real money maker. But, it was just what Terry needed to finish Big Kyle off due to his abnormal conscience. His trust and last bit of money that he had went directly to her for the fulfillment of being undisputed in the underworld.

With Tim Freeze in a faded picture, Booby and Ike confined to a mental cubicle and, Billy and Muscles somewhere enjoying their riches. Big Kyle was short a nexus but that wasn't a crux to Terry, who had just what he was looking for. While Terry reached out to oldest brothers for a reasonable proposition, Big Kyle was contriving yet another strategy to rob everyone. Unknowingly, he wasn't conscience enough to know that Terry was a million steps ahead of him.

Krystal's Lounge was where the rendezvous was held, and Big Kyle and D.S. already knew the plan. The same kind of plan they put together on Bobby and Ike, only this time it was do or die and, Big Kyle was available to test the product himself. Prior to the meeting at Krystal's, Big D.S. made it his duty to go down to the lounge himself and hide some guns and extra ammunition behind the toilet in the men's lavatory. Precautious, he wanted to be prepared for any trickery or drastic outburst that wasn't expected.

Riley and Domino declined to partake in the meeting; true bosses never jeopardized themselves, so they thought. Their product was secured in the hands of their baby sister Terry. They all faced each other inside Krystal's bar, Terry and her two pawns and, Big Kyle and D.S. The product was sufficient and all of the money was present but one of the consumers wasn't playing fair.

The two decoys began confuting with each other prior to the product being exchanged for the cash; causing a big distraction while everyone else watched everyone closely. Big Kyle gazed over at Terry who had a devilish smirk on her face and, Big D.S. bawled out, "It's a setup!" Acrobatically, he hurdled over the bar counter with the two pistols that he stashed in the bar's bathroom. He aimed to hit Terry with a few shots but failed due to the inaccuracy of his aim. Simultaneously, as D.S. was going over the counter three people in mask were coming form behind the counter with their guns held high.

Big Kyle reached for one of the brief cases to shield his body from being hit, after Terry released a pump shotgun from beneath the arm pit of her jacket and sent the two pawns to the floor. Big Kyle grabbed both of the .45 ACP handguns from the inside of the brief cases and joined in the ambush with Big D.S. who seemed to have a stuck trigger finger. What seemed to be business turned into a blood war of greed and Big Kyle wasn't the star of his drafted plan.

Big Kyle and D.S. hit two of the mask men who were trying to reclaim the hundred keys of heroin and the other brief case of money that went untouched. One of the mask men got hit twice on the same side of the body, once in the arm and shoulder. The other mask man was struck just above the throat near the chin as the pump shot gun ran out of shells but that didn't stop Terry from being apart of the action.

While grabbing one of the mask men Terry fiercely rang off a .40 caliber in the direction of Big Kyle who was trying to dodge the gun battle. The unwounded mask men sent street sweeping shots across the bar in the direction of Big D.S. who was adjacent to Big Kyle, running across the counter top of the bar. Big D.S. leaped for the door but the impact from the Mac-11 sent him flying through one of the side windows. The knob on the door was stuck as Big Kyle struggled to escape out the front and just as he pushed with force and the door opened he was struck twice from behind. After the two crippling shots came enormous shots that hit Big Kyle as much as they were being fired.

Once the mist of gun smoke cleared, there were two slaughtered decoys and, Big Kyle's body slumped over a chair near the exit door. He was breathing in short, panicky breaths trying his hardest to gasp for air. While his ace D.S. managed to flee from the scene unharmed from the protection of his bulletproof vest. All the goods were gone, the money including the product, even the debris from the clouded dope was gone.

The aftermath of it all put Big Kyle in a coma until the following year, with twelve bullet wounds that came from Terry's .40 caliber all over his body; the way that his body was positioned and curved saved him. Dontae "Big D.S." Wardon Sr. retrograded himself back into the life of petty crime which landed him a nine year sentence for robbing a liquor store for a few thousand dollars but forgot to wear a mask..

Terry was trying to kill Big Kyle for years since the incident at Krystal's Lounge at dawn in 1974. But, she could never catch up with the junkie by day, phantom by night, nine live survivor.

"This mystery is like playing connect the dots." I said, after listening to the version of how the S & S Brothers rose and fail to the powers that were unbeatable. "All of you have been in conjunction with one another for a long period of time and crossing each other for the cost and love of what? Money... Power... Respect?"

My questions were directed to everyone in the garage, "I don't get this shit at all but it's a bunch of nonsense in my eyes--"

"That's because you'll never understand the codes of the underworlds," Big Kyle retorted, tugging his words and trying to find strength to recover. "It's only nonsense because you're trying to play from the outside the fence instead of in the ball park. It's not about questions and answers but it's about quest and achievements in this line of work. You have to get dirty in the underworld before you're able to analyze the theory of the illicit game."

As Big Kyle went in the depths of his explanation, tears began to stream down his face. "The game is to be worked, not sold, nor told that's why this generation is running around like chickens with you're heads cut off. Because you want all the right answers and want to place all the retrospection of past happenings in a certain order, all to get ahead from another gangsta's work. In this life no one is to be trusted... Will be trusted... And will hold that integrity as a burden for future prospects to carry on the torch. When money is involved, control is the cost and if you're not in control of what you possess or want to conquer there's somebody who will conquer it for you. We shoot and kill the guys that come up with us because... Because..." He wiped his tears before continuing on. "There's not enough money for us to split in this shit. It's far from the bucks it's more of the excitement of the rush when you're living out your dreams. D.S. and I had our turn but blew it due to carelessness, never wanted to listen, had too many question, received no answers and thought that the money would stick to our palms forever. A wise man once said, if you lose all your money you lose nothing but if you lose your character you lose everything. And, that's what happened to me... To us," He waved his hand around the room. "We put the money before our characters and eventually this is how you'll end up if you let the money manipulate you."

Big Kyle's vital advice had my ears glued to his lips and meticulous words and it was an emotional moment for us all.

"Junior you either follow these codes or don't even think about profiting from narcotics because life will swallow you alive before you even start to elevate. Try another profession, a legal gig or go to church and pray severely because this line of work isn't for you. You should have stuck to playing baseball." He finished, with a sarcastic chuckle that gave me the impression that he really didn't give two fucks about what I set my mind to do.

His loud laughter irritated me to the point of hopping off the sofa and pushing the .22 caliber so far into his mouth I felt the glands in his esophagus. Just as my finger tapped the trigger to splatter his guts all over the garage my Aunt Debbie smacked my arm down. The might from her hand forced the gun to knock a few teeth out of Big Kyle's mouth before the gun triggered' sending a shot through the ceiling of the garage.

"No Kyle not in here," she said, gripping my arm. "Off the son-of-a-bitch some where else."

My aunt only had to warn me once, I hammered Big Kyle and D.S. across the back of their heads for a second time, then Kylie and I covered their bodies back up with the sheets and carried them to the trunk of the Saab. Taking them out how we brought them in, only this time there would be no returning.

# Chapter. 22

There were two bodies already hogged tied and folded like pretzels in the trunk of my car when Kylie and I went to dump Big Kyle and D.S. bodies inside. I felt like I was hallucinating when I got a clear view of the bodies in the trunk. Derrick and Keith were physically exposed and tide like two pigs on rack.

"I see why there's a shortage of interracial relationships in America between white boys and sistahs," Aunt Debbie mentioned, after inspecting Keith and Derrick's groin area. "I'd be better of fucking my King and Prince my two dogs, shit."

Keith and Derrick stood in the drive way very rattled as my aunt headed inside the house. "Bring them inside here," She said, standing in the threshold of the back door. "Before my neighbors think there's a couple of psychotic rapist out here with infant dicks."

Once we were all inside my Aunt Debbie gave Keith and Derrick some attire to get dressed in, that she had from an ex-boyfriend in the back of her closet. As we explained the crucial situations that happened in the past forty-eight hours there was complete exasperating energy inside the living room.

"Hol' on... Hol' on! You all can't speak at once, one at a time please," Aunt Debbie said, silencing the commotion.

Keith stood first to give us his summary of what took place outside of Gary and Pooks' establishment the prior day. "Dude it's is some weird shit going on and it's beginning to emasculate my brain."

"Who you telling?" I replied.

"Minutes after you and your friend Batina left the car, the ceiling light car blew out and sparks from inside the ashtray began to flare up." Keith and Derrick found a few wire taps inside the light after thoroughly inspecting the car's fuses. "Whomever planted the bugs was experienced because they ran the frequent device from the car light to the lighter inside the astray."

"That was some magnificent work dude," Derrick said, sparking up a cigarette. "Man my father has been electronics and technological studies my entire life and he couldn't even put no shit like that together. If they can bug Kyle's car it's a wonder what else of his... Of ours is bugged?"

"Great fucking question dork," Keith quipped.

"Your sister's a fucking dork shaggy," Derrick retorted.

"Hey, hey com'on this shit is serious my boys," I ranted. "What if I told you that Terry's an ex-cop would you believe me?"

"No fucking way dude," Derrick said, in an astonished tone.

"I believe you without even hesitating for a thought," Keith replied. "The bitch's ingenious abilities got me fuckin' convinced and I mean the cunt can't be traced... She leaves no evidence behind. How do you know that she is anyway?"

I enlightened them with the same indispensable information that Big D.S. unveiled to me. After I finished both of their mouths were walking on the floor.

"Well that explains it all them," Keith stated. "She's the solution to this entire irregular problem."

"I bet you a hundred to one that Terry had something to do with her phones having technical difficulties. Let alone vacating the premises of her home out in Pennsauken once those cameras were inserted," Derrick responded.

"She's a mere fucking genius dude I'm telling you."

While we continued elaborating on Terry and the entire underworld issues my aunt aided us with some lunch to take our minds off the boggling situations. I was still vacuous to the action that took place the night before, I was trying to figure out what and who went wrong?

"I'm telling you man Batina's apart of Terry's coalition," Keith said, biting into his healthy turkey and cheese sandwich.

My two white boys explained to Kylie and me that once Batina and I were inside of Gary and Pooks' place they waited patiently outside the Saab after finding the bugs in the car; which happened about ten minutes after Batina and I left them. While we were inside the GP13 construction Keith and Derrick were scrutinizing Harvey and Gerard like two vigilant owls from a far. The two human shields were out front the entire time pacing back and forth, conversing with each other.

$ $ $ $ $

Two minutes before Keith and Derrick were making their way to the PG13 premises they went to retrieve the ammunition from the trunk. As the trunk ascended in the air, Batina appeared before them with her guns held high telling them to back away from the trunk. As Keith went to question her violent obligation they both were struck form behind and that's all they remembered prior to being stuffed in the congested trunk.

"So you never got a glimpse at any other suspects that could have possibly attacked you in Tina's presence?" I asked.

"Hell no dude," Derrick answered. "It happened like that." He snapped his finger giving a quick demonstration. "With a blink of an eye... Bam! It was lights out."

"Maybe it was them two flunky look outs," Kylie implied, having meticulous ears. "They were the only two outside at the time."

"It couldn't of been them because they were still up the block when we got to the rear of the car," Keith said, quite sure that it wasn't. "Someone had to have followed us it's obvious... The bug in the car--"

"Batina robbing Gary and Pooks for their product, money out of their safe and my two brief cases of cash," I interposed. "Then killing them both but why not murder us all? Why keep us alive?"

"Damn good question Kyle damn good question," Derrick roared. The living room was serene as we all sat in contemplation trying to find answers.

"It's not that complicated if we think about it," Kylie assumed. "You mentioned that everyone who has had any dealings with the broad Terry has been popping up missing or either dead right?"

"Right!" I answered.

"So put two and two together... An ex-cop with her hands tied up in one of the biggest drug mergers in America. Place yourself in her shoes--"

"What are you insinuating Kylie?" I asked, trying to fully apprehend his view point. "We are short on logical motives here."

"Not quite Kyle not quite," Derrick argued. "I'm following what Kylie is trying to imply, if an ex-cop is participating in an illegitimate drug circuit they either have a vengeance against someone, out for revenge or their trying to manipulate the law by destroying legal assets and evidence. Prior to the agents and investigators seizing any significant documents and arresting a Kingpin or average street monger who might fold."

"Right! So they can accumulate as much money as they can from those in the underworld and get rid of those ring leaders and mongers who are major targets in the investigation. Demolishing cases... Indictments and legal operations before they have a chance to execute," Keith said, filling in Derrick's other blanks. "Killing two birds with one stone."

"How many suspects has the Sundown Operation captured thus far?" I asked, assuming they were still at an impasse with only Tarantula and Dre as there top two.

"Only a couple," Kylie answered, having more insight on the follow-up of the operation then any of us. "Reason being is because like you were all assuming, they can't make an arrest when there are no leads, evidence or dead people to arrest. Their arresting the imprudent people that's thoughtless and careless to whom they sell product to. But the meticulous mongers are discreet and low key. The others have already been captured decades ago or they're dead but, there's still a few left out there.

"So what's next where do we go from here?" Derrick asked, sparking another cigarette.

"No where, we render our hands with this shit and go home," I replied, no longer wanting to figure out who was who, what was what, or solve the mysteries that came before me.

"Go Home?!" Keith was aggravated. "We've come to far to retreat and back away, all we have to do is find what we've come to know--"

"That's exactly my point, it's over, Terry and Billy are gone. We have no leads or clues of where they are or could be. All we keep ending up with are presumptions and quizzical information that gives us nothing but one big fuckin' headache. And I'm really tired of thinking right now."

"So it's over?" Derrick said, nonchalantly. "Fuck it Keith Let's head back to Asbury Park, get the van, grab some freaks and go fishing."

The reluctance was all over Keith's face as he stared at Derrick with pain in his eyes as if the underworld matter was his main project. Like he ate, slept and shitted the illicit operation, I could vision through his pupils that he wanted Terry more then any of us in the room. But, we couldn't just wish upon a star or make a wish to an illusionary genie to go get her for us.

"Here's the plan for right now," I said, trying to keep everyone on the same page. "We get rid of everything that might be bugged... Cars and clothes. We even have to relocate for a while because we don't know if Terry or anybody that she dealt with has bugged our resting places. Where not dealing with an amateur that doesn't no the difference between salt and sugar, these muthafuckas are very hi-tech and intelligent. If something comes up or if any of us get some lethal information that will lead us to her or Billy. Then we resume the matter but, as of right now where at an investigational impasse. "

Prior to going our separate ways the four of us consented with each other to keep in contact as often as much and to notify each other if something essential came up. Keith and Derrick were going to borrow a boat from Keith's father and head down to the shore. They gave me a number and an address to a place in a remote location that they only knew about. In return I gave them my mother's information because that's where I planned on staying until the heat died down.

Kylie mentioned that he would be staying with my aunt for the time being, she agreed to be his significant devotee under the circumstanced of rehabilitating his health and organizing his priorities.

He was striving to turn over a new leaf and the life of doing drugs that he once was accustom to, was insignificant at this point and time. We had one more mission to handle before we all branched off and our separate ways.

$$\$ \$ \$ \$ \$$$

We drove in two cars as I pulled my aunt's Buick Park Avenue along side these railroad tracks down by the chemical plant off of Morgan Blvd; adjacent to the Delaware River on the southeast side of town. The day began to fade as the sun set in the mist of it's' twilight which made the silhouette sky look noteworthy.

Together me and my dudes took part in dragging the two bodies into these eerie bushes far behind the chemical plant. The mystery of what lied behind the bushes spooked me and had me not wanting to enter. I peeped over my shoulder often as I could to make sure nothing jumped out and grabbed me while I was dragging D.S.'s body.

Amid the lofty trees and conglomerate bushes with insect sounds of nature's music, lied Big Kyle and D.S. who looked like two glum puppies; knees in the dirt, mouths concealed and hands tied to the rear of their hind ends.

"Com'on Kyle... Man," Keith said, feeling remorseful as he clinched my wrist with his hand, holding g me back from pushing their minds in the dirt. "That's your father Kyle he gave you life." Keith persuaded me as hard as he could not to follow through with my evil intentions.

"Fuck Him!" I ranted. "He's nothing to me, he was never responsible enough to be a father because money was his primary nourishment and I was secondary. He knew exactly what he wanted when he fucked my mother... A nut but literary he got a mental nut."

My former pain reactivated itself again causing me to have a relentless emotional outburst. The agony and stress that I had to live with as a boy that transcended into my manhood deteriorated me internally as if I had a bad case of diabetes. Not only that but, my two sister-cousins had to grow up the same way, without him and that's kind of hard for a woman too endure. The more I thought back and reminisced the more vexed I became.

"I wanted to walk just like you... Talk just like you... often mommy would say I looked just like you and I thought just like you," I said, weeping with tears streaming down my angered face. "How could you let me grow with out you and wear my boo-boo's close to the sole without you and grind in this drug shit to get rich and o broke without you?" I was furious, truly blank minded and I could vision was blood in my eyes.

On the contrary Big D.S. and Big Kyle dreaded my perspective, not because of the gun but because of how I was reacting. It was time for them to spend and eternal vacation with Satan because they both were worthless to the mortals here on earth; they were taking up to much space. Big D.S. had it, blew it, did nine years in the state pen, got hold of it again and now he's one of America's most wanted. I was itching to send his son Dontae a roommate.

Big Kyle was in the same boat as he lied next to his disloyal partner who wasted his time. Living out his false pretense Iceberg Slim fantasies with nothing to show for it; broke, with no woman and using drugs to stimulate his mind from the depression. But on top of everything he was the most prominent target in the underworld, Terry was head hunting for him. And, I was being targeted for his irrational actions which undoubtedly was before my time. I had to slug him for the sake of my mother who tolerated his ridiculous behavior and illusionary manhood. For Gracey and Sissy, my two deceitful aunts who I loved more than life itself, because of the trouble he put them through with my two sister-cousins.

I had to slug them, for my Uncle Muscles who embraced them, showed them the key to life, how to get the doe that niggas owed them, and they still showed my uncle mere dishonesty. This bullet was for the L.S.D. members and Lamaar's father who got indicted and sentenced to numerous years in prison because Big Kyle was a tattletale.

"Does any of use have any last words before I put you in the dirt from which you came?" I asked, checking to see how many bullets were left in the clip.

"Yeah, I got one thing to ask you before you capture my soul," D.S. said, staring up at me. "Why'd you kill my son? He was all I had left in this world."

Sarcastically, I answered him like I could have given to fucks about what he had in this world. "I don't know ask him when you run into him on the other side, he can explain it to you better than I can." Without hesitating I pulled the trigger twice seeping two hot tamales between D.S.'s eyes. "What about you, you worthless maggot?" I said to Big Kyle.

"Yeah I got some last words for all of uses," he said, gazing around to every one of us. "Made men die on top muthafuckas, fuck all you lames and son I'll be waiting on you so I can fuck you up eternally. Pull the trigger you cold hearted bastard so I can go get some pussy with Lucifer the great, its better down there anyway."

At first, prior to Big Kyle talking out of his asshole I absorbed Keith's advice and took it into consideration; having second thoughts about slumping him. But his vulgar dialect burned on my conscience causing my ego to rattle the demon inside of me.

"On the other side tell Lucifer as soon as I get to hell I'm fucking him up first and as for you my man, its self explanatory..." Bang... Bang... Bang!

Three accurate shots put an end to my sperm donor's legacy and, there wasn't any emotions lingering through my body after I killed Big Kyle. Shooting him was like shooting in the air, there was no justification behind him what so ever.

"Now," I said, passing Kylie the .22 caliber. "Everybody has to put a bullet in either one of them for insurance. Just in case one of us decides to fret and have reasonable doubts to turn someone in. That way before you think about snitching you will know that you were an accessory to the crime just as I was."

There were four bullets left in the gun, that's until Kylie used two of them on Big Kyle and D.S. His indication was strong, letting me know that he had never felt guilty for anything he ever done. Unhesitant, my white boys finished the procedure willingly and how ironic was it for Keith to see him penetrate a single shot in Big Kyle's temple; after he tried to sooth my mentality. Derrick emptied the clip by putting the last bullet into Big D.S.'s torso and there were two down and two more to go.

I gave the physical evidence to Keith and Derrick to dispose including the Saab once we vacated the premises but the Saab was their only transportation of getting back home. I told them to ditch the vehicle and burn it once they arrived at their final destination. We gave each other tough love and last regards before parting from each other. A significant street probe that we had in the palm of our hands turned sour; we purchased a puzzle without all of the pieces.

$$\$ \ \$ \ \$ \ \$ \ \$$$

The Glamour Towers became my final stop and resting point after the remorseless action that fell upon Big Kyle and D.S. That evening when I arrived at the towers my cluttered mind was telling me to go and get some rest but my impulsive persuaded me to approach the thirteenth floor of Kelli's apartment. I hadn't seen Kelli or been in contact with her in weeks, my last time speaking with her was at the Skate Land jam featuring Eric B. and Rakim.

Kelli was a restless soul, very mobile, and far from stationary, I sensed this unusual presence of how she maneuvered in my circumference. She was rarely home, mailbox stayed empty and for a beauty of her stature she was too damn antisocial with a concealed identity. I noticed the fickle attitude and odd changes in Kelli weeks ago in the resort's lobby when I was conversing with Batina. Skepticism kicked in and there was something definitely peculiar about Kelli's decorum which had me convinced and convenient for me to probe.

The foyer on the thirteenth floor was tranquil when I tried picking the lock on Kelli's door but wasn't successful. With no other way of picking the lock, I reacted off of my first instinct and that was to trigger the fire alarm and fire a single shot at the lock. One shot from the .38 snub nose pistol I retrieved from my Aunt Debbie handled the job.

As I shut the door behind me the clamorous nose form the fire alarm ceased and the inside of the condo was a mere resemblance of how Kelli expected to be, empty. My old furniture was the only thing that remained was my old furniture that I had left to her. There was no reason for me to depart form the apartment because I came to scrutinize anyhow for any little ting that I could find that could subside my suspicions about Kelli. My gut kept telling me to search, search because there was something in the spot worth looking for. There wasn't much to rummage through but the things I did manage to ransack were to no avail to me. The only objects that were left were the couches and if there was anything significant it would have been in her bed room. 'What the hell,' I thought to myself as I flipped both the sofa and love seats inside out to grab the lose change if there was any.

Bingo! My gut never let me down even when I was starving or had a ache in it, I found some type of identification card that had Kelli's real credentials printed all over it. Ms. Kelli Right was her government name and she resided at 2838 Rosedale Avenue in East Camden; off of Westfield Avenue and across the street from Dudley Grange Park.

Back to the assumption board I went, questioning a question, I just knew that Kelli had ties with Billy and Terry. Why else would she go alias on me and give up fictitious personal information? Once again I was there was my furious side that triggered only because I had a thing for Kelli and was so charmed by her polished sexual persona.

Trying not to be obvious and keeping my cool, I exited through the rear stair case and headed down to the lobby. "Ericka," I called, approaching the front counter. She glanced at me, with the phone in her ear telling gesturing for me to hold on.

"Yes, Mr. Moore," she said, hanging up the receiver. "How may I help you?"

"I was just wondering have you seen Ms. Browning lately, the fine fox that resides on the thirteenth floor."

"Your old place?" she asked, dubiously.

"That's the one, she left numerous messages on my machine and every time I try reaching her through her extension I get no answer."

"I haven't seen Ms. Browning in a few weeks, something strange is going on around here, everyone has been incognito lately."

"Tell me about it," I said, wanting to enlighten her on what's been going on.

"If I run across her do you want me to tell --?"

"No!" I barked, frantically cutting her words short. She looked at me with a queered face. "I mean no you don't have to say anything to her but thanks anyway," I answered, turning to walk away and that's when she said...

"Well if I hear from her or see her I will be sure to let you know okay?"

"Solid," I replied, in stride to my apartment.

My body was worn down from the ripping and running over the pass 72 hours, my stomach growled louder than echoes in Mt. Rushmore and my eyes felt like I needed eternal sleep. But, there was no way I was doing any of that inside the suspicious building. I was very paranoid and uncomfortable but that wasn't going to stop me from getting my things together in the apartment.

As I groped through my place in the dark there were so many irrelevant things burning my brain that I had forgotten all about the two cover girls that I left in the place earlier that morning. They never dawned on me until I got in my bedroom and saw particles of their clothing scattered all over the floor. Now, my place was pitch black as if I never invited Taliyah and Francis to stay but being so weary minded I assumed they might have stepped out for a moment. I didn't even try to second guess my own questioning about the two jades.

When I finished gathering my belongings around 10 p.m. and headed out to put them into my Celebrity Sedan. I remembered that I left my ten grand stashed inside the bathroom in my bedroom. I had to get that so I could pay my bet off to Luby.

When I stepped foot in the bathroom a cloud of steam punched me in my face, it was obvious that someone was in my tub taking a shower because the entire bathroom was moist. With my gun in palm, I pushed the shower curtain back to get a clear view of the suspect but it was only Francis and Taliyah whom I didn't expect it to be. I thought it may have been Batina, DaVita, Ebony, or Terry.

Francis and Taliyah stood before me drenched in steaming hot water caressing each other passionately. 'What a dream come true,' I thought as my fantasy gave me eye to eye contact. Without being asked to join in I took it upon myself to oblige in the erotic episode which steamed my insides more than the shower. I was all over them like bees on a honeycomb as I closed my eyes and allow the two freaks of nature take control of me. Their tongues glided on the surface of my abdominal area like two water snakes, as Taliyah kneeled before me and engulfed my shaft; while Francis kissed on my neck and back from behind.

The shower scene continued in the bedroom and got even more invigorating as we indulged in every sexual position there was for a trio. While I had Taliyah missionary style Francis was mounted over Taliyah's face, French kissing me. Then I switched to penetrating Francis from behind while she had her face in between Taliyah's sweet kumquat. Vigorously we ended our intense sex-capade with a triple threatening orgasm, as I was invading Taliyah's sultriness from behind, Francis was lying over top of her with her legs mounted back as I finger loved her to an exhilarating sensation.

After the bed wrestling was finished, I had no time to play Dolomite with the two fine things. I was on the clock and my time and Livelihood had worn its welcome out at the Glamour towers. Before explaining to the girls my reason of departure from the luxurious edifice, they explained to me that without me they had nowhere to go. Gary and Pooks patronized them financially, with a stable roof over their heads and, cloth and fed them both. Financially, I was hamstrung also that's why I was going back home to mom's place until I could get back on my feet.

The only thing I could do for the floozies was leave them my deluxe apartment, it was fully furnished and a number where I could be reached in case of emergency. Other than that, as far as money went there was a corner store a few blocks from the resort that had tons of Courier-Post newspapers. This held the Classified and subtitled Help Wanted section in it so they could look for a few job positions. I told the two ladies once I settled a few scores and was financially sturdy again I would come back for them.

After leaving the Glamour towers, detoured across town to Luby's Pool hall to pay my remaining debt but from a far as I pulled to the corner of Kaighns Avenue and Louis Street, I had seen that the pool hall was closed down. And, the pool hall's action didn't occur until after hours no way but, it was after one in the morning. There were no cars on either side of the street and no crowds out in front. I pulled in front of the place just to make sure it was shut down and indeed it was.

The only thing I could do was keep my word and hold on to the 10 G's for Liquor Luby until I crossed his path again. My final stop was to 625 Walnut Street, downtown to my mother's place which I had no intentions on leaving until my bank roll was right. I was absconding myself from the streets of the Sugar city until further notice.

# Chapter. 23

The following month in May, was the first time I had inhaled any fresh air from the city's streets and that's only because I took out the trash and walked to the corner store on 6th and Chestnut Streets to get me some penny candy and some oatmeal cookies. It felt like old times again living back home with my mother who had a lot of wisdom for my ears. The only things that changed from 7th Street was my mother, her entire attitude made a complete 360 degree shift, going from a active work-o-holic to a sloth couch potato. She even gained a few pounds since the last time I seen her which was about eight months prior. When I would question her about having work phobia and being around the house all the time, her response would be, 'When you put time in like I have and get it like I have it then you can do as you please and enjoy life.'

Besides Big Kyle my mother never had a sturdy male column in her life except Donald but he came and went for playing his card all wrong. I guess the pain and adversity with Big Kyle over the years kept her distant from the opposite sex; she was self-reliant on another niggas responsibilities and cash. I never knew Olivia to be without work or found herself at an impasse of unemployment. When hard times fell upon us she would formulate a better way to make a buck without having to jeopardize her household or family.

When I use to heckle my aunts and uncles for pocket change or a few bucks when I was a kid my mother would always tell me, 'Now Jr. let your money accumulate quietly and once you're satisfied have fun but keep your composure.' I really didn't understand the concept back then but now I see what she meant by it. She was definitely enjoying her luxurious three-story, five bedroom home with the brand new Cadillac Seville Elegante parked out in front of the house. My mother had the type of comfort zone that it would take a teacher years to accomplish.

Aniyah thought she was the guardian of the house though, very demanding to be a naïve six year old. She was in and out of the house more than my mother was, Aniyah was over everybody's house except her own if she wasn't in school; Alesha spoiled her rotten but she never had time for big bro' and I did all of her dirty work as a infant.

Speaking of my precious, sophisticated sister Alesha through mere coincidence we crossed each other's path when she came to pick Aniyah up one Saturday morning so they could head out to Sesame Place in Pennsylvania. Since the family gathering at my Aunt Carole's home about Big Kyle being her and Wadeelah's father also, Alesha and I didn't see each other that much as we needed to. She had enough time on her hands though for a succinct conversation before she headed off to Sesame Place.

I didn't come straight out and jump into the memoirs about Jingles, his affiliation with the G.W.B's or who the persons inside the cartel of Enterprise 33. I took his where about into consideration and vital livelihood first, then as the conversation extended I drifted into other topics. Alesha's ambition was still dedicated to her nurse's assistant position at Our Lady of Lordes hospital and that she was putting in double the time of laborious hours due to the bad terms her and Jingles had been sharing lately. They weren't meshing like normal and that was her excuse from staying away from him.

"So how did you and Jingles begin courting anyhow?" I inquired, wanting a full elucidation of their history together.

"It all started in 1977 back in Morgan Village for me and Jingles...." She said, reminiscing back down memory lane when things were sweet like the grapes that she grabbed from the refrigerator to eat while she went into detail.

Alesha was living on 9th and Ferry Avenue back then in Branch Village Apartments with my Aunt Sissy; directly across the street from the Sand Park. At twelve going on thirteen Alesha's relationship with Sissy began to shatter due to her strict rules and her consistent drug use. Alesha moved out, and in with Sissy's older sister Blanche - from her father's side - up the street in the Manor projects.

Blanche wasn't as strict and demanding as Sissy, she was sort of nonchalant about a lot of things. But, Alesha didn't use Blanche's kindness to he advantage it was just her aunt's comfort zone that made her more liberated. Other then Blanche having two full time occupations of her own to support her only son Rahmeen and her baby daughter Keisha. Her time was also being occupied by Pee Wee Franklin who Blanche made out of town pick ups for as often as she could for extra money.

Alesha's needs and wants were well taken care of all Blanche wanted was for her to finish school and not to come home pregnant, everything else was irrelevant. As a seventh grade honor roll student and a pure virgin becoming pregnant wasn't even an option. She was too into being fashionable and having the newest-latest materials. Being one of the most attractive redbones in Morgan Village Alesha's popularity started to ascend into high measures when she became apart of the G.G.C. (Gucci Girl Crew). It was an all girl crew that Sweets and Famous came up with to run parallel to the Orange Bag Crew which later altered into the Good Wood Boys.

Sweets and Famous' G.G.C. wasn't into the street life in the beginning, they were a bunch of young girls who liked to dress, look good all the time and tease all the horny boys who tried to shoot game with dripping tongues trying to get a taste of coochie. The G.G.C. became popular throughout the city for the fifty-cent pajama parties they use to arrange weekly down at the Isabel Miller Center.

Fairly new to the G.G.C. and the youngest of them all, Alesha ironically was the most out spoken and spontaneous girl. She never hesitated, always instinctive and if there was something that was beneficial for the entire click she addressed it amongst everyone. If she has something to get off her chest she never bit her tongue and with so much advice to offer and motivational incentive Alesha became the social amender inside the G.G.C.

The description of her persona made me realize that we shared identical genes and characteristics. Having similar ways and actions and there wasn't a doubt in my body that told me she wasn't the late Kyle Tommy Moore's daughter.

As time moved on Alesha became best friends with a former crew member named Takeisha "Taffy" Smith - Miguel's older sister - and the late Shannon and Sabina Smith's younger sister...

"Hol' up... Wait a minute," I said, mystified.

"What?" '

"Shannon and Sabina had other siblings? I never knew that."

"Yeah there the oldest girls out of five children by their mother Niecey Smith. If you weren't a permanent resident in the P.J.'s or Centerville period no one would of ever knew that Shake and Bake were from Centerville because of their classy dispositions. They were the first females in Camden to tyrannize the drug game--"

"Weren't they apprentices to their Uncle's Timmy Tange and Lance Whop Smith?" I asked, throwing back a few grapes.

"They were the ones who showed them how to make a dollar out of fifteen cents. Shake and Bake were the modern day Tange and Whop."

Tange and Whop had all the illegitimacies running on 10th Street in the Deli organization for any unlawful indulger in various fields. From marijuana to Quaaludes 10th Street was a place of variety to cop from. Tange and Whop also used their street prowess as procurers in the pimping business in the Niemo Courts Complex that was adjacent to the Deli's grocery store. For the right price you could purchase the best trim that Tange and Whop had available.

The brother's profited most of their whore mongering money from this luxuriant fantasy of a woman named "Jay Gold," who was the madam in the Niemo Courts Brothel circuit. Jay Gold profited most of her doe from legal customers - Lawyers, police officers, truck drivers, teachers and brokers. Most of them were married but wanted erotic excitement on the side. The word throughout the city and the Tri-state area was addressed to all men in favor that, "You weren't a man until you past Jay Gold's test." Her lickerish was that succulent and delectable that if you didn't try it you were considered gay. Allegedly, prior to Tange and Whop shutting down the Deli operation, Jay Gold had become pregnant and vanished from the jaunty brothel.

Tange and Whop even had a booze operation that was serviced by night in the rear of the grocery store; where the sober got drunk at a low price. The two brothers were corporation inside of corporate America, business men's business men who walked away from the Deli in 1962 and haven't been heard from since. Almost twenty-five years since the two ghetto legend and their Deli Dynasty were the eminent inception of Centerville and the drug underworld.

Nine years after the Deli Organization faded there was the rebirth of the vanished Tange and Whop through the bloodline of their two gorgeous nieces Shannon and Sabina Smith; who was their younger sister Niecey's children. Learning the business portion - product, prices, quality, quantity, imports, exports, manufacturing, distribution, customers and suppliers. And, the personal part - partnership, loyalty, turf, what to expect and what not to expect from their uncles when they were only fourteen years old.

Shake and Bake ascended in the game form $1dollar joints in high school to million dollar drug deals, accounts, Real Estate and luxurious splendor before the age of thirty. With only a three year run in the game, every since they became missing in the beginning of 1973. The Smith family has deeply mourned and prayed for their return, I didn't want to be the spokes person of bad news and tell my sister that Shake and Bake were well off in the promise land some thirteen years ago. So I remained mum and a loud her to continue on...

Similar in features and curvaceous structure Takeisha "Taffy" Smith was Alesha's A-alike. Although Taffy was a shade darker, a few inches shorter and petite too Alesha's thick frame, no one could tell them apart. Their age bracket differentiated them only by two years and Taffy was the oldest. After the liaison between them continued to grow their experience as childhood friends altered into mere sisterhood. Taffy became the distinctive sister that Alesha never had and vice-versa because Alesha was what Taffy missed in Shake and Bake.

Alesha was highly infatuated with Taffy's little brother Miguel who at the time was in a puppy love relationship with a pretty young thing named Tonya Biggs. Tonya was also a competitive, redbone who was a mere attraction to every male figure walking. Contrarily, Alesha slept, ate and fantasized about young Miguel around the clock; she thought he was the most handsome boy in the world with his light, baby face and cinematic smile. Miguel - just like his other four siblings - was a half breed, with black and Hispanic genes. His father Miguel Lopez was a full blooded Puerto Rican but it wasn't Alesha's looks or diabolic infatuation that made Miguel disinterested. It was his conservative social decorum that made him a bit old fashion. He believed in the old cliché of only having one girlfriend; kind of farfetched for a thirteen year old kid. But, that didn't stop Alesha's desire of having him all to herself.

Valentine's day 1977, Alesha went out of her way to present Miguel with a couple of gifts and wanted to give to him in front of his Good Wood crew. She brought him a black Kango cap and a pair of all black Keds sneakers to match. But, Miguel's impassive intentions rejected Alesha's offer and left her standing in front of his boys sadden with a broke heart. Miguel's crew was astounded not wanting to believe that he would - not only - turn down the cool gifts but turn down that Precious girl.

Months passed by without Alesha having a single thought about Miguel, let alone show some consideration for her best friend Taffy. Alesha blamed Miguel's child lie behavior on not wanting to be around Taffy, it was just Alesha's pride - which crushed Taffy's feelings - that made her act snobbish.

During the course of changing classed one day, Miguel bumped into Alesha at her locker, she tried to avoid him but he reached out and grabbed her arm. As she stopped in motion, with a sense of sincerity Miguel told Alesha how he really felt about her; giving her a huge apology on top of his true feelings. After they made up as friends, he hit her with a body blow surprise of news that turned her stomach sour; Jamiere had a crush on her. She couldn't believe the words that rolled off of Miguel's tongue and as a result she gave him a stark grimace face and walked away from him like she didn't even hear him say that.

For weeks on in everyone from the Gucci Girl Crew - including Taffy - would run back and tell her flattering things that Jamiere would say but she wouldn't pay any of it attention. Not because she wasn't interested but because Jamiere didn't have the balls to stand before her and tell her himself.

Alesha couldn't believe that fat, dirty Jamiere with the hazel, cat eyes could even fantasize about something fine and dandy such as herself. The image comparison was no match in her eyes, she was a ghetto movie star and Jamiere belonged to Bill Cosby's get-a-long-gang. Alesha misjudged Jamiere by his appearance without even to getting to know what type of person he really was.

Prior to the end of the school year a drastic change came and with that so did Alesha's thoughts and feelings for dirty ol' cat eyed Jamiere. He approached her one day after school as students traveled up 9th Street to detour to there street address. Alesha and a few of her Gucci Girl peers were walking ahead of Jamiere, Miguel and the rest of the Good Wood hoodlums. Jamiere made his move in front of the expected and unexpected on lookers as Alesha clearly remembered his elegant words that brightened her face with elation. He said, "Sugar as sweet as you shouldn't grow alone especially when one's artificial flavored life is so distasteful. Make my life hyper and be my girl."

After his brief pimp line Jamiere handed Alesha a single rose, she thought his pick-up line was so flattering, especially for a fourteen year old back in 1977. With the compliment and rose Jamiere hit his number and Alesha was his lady to be.

Jingles, who got the name from Alesha because of his chubby cheeks back then was the only boy of three children on his mother's side and his father Willie Johnson's only boy. While his father was doing time in prison for assault and attempted murder, Jingles was being raided by his Uncle Tommy. Big Kyle promised his godfather Willie that he would be Jingles' guardian while he was away.

"What!' I ranted. "You mean to tell me that Big Kyle took care of Jingles for another man knowing that he had three children of his own to raise? That's fuckin' crazy." Alesha gave me a numb look having no answers herself. "Where was his mother around this time?"

The only thing that Alesha knew about Jingles' mother was that she tried to abort him by flushing him down the toilet after giving birth to him. Willie saved Jingles after catching his mother in the act of doing so. And, if it wasn't for his father he would have been nothing more then an innocent spirit. Other then that one incident Jingles never mentioned a thing about his malevolent mother.

During the summer vacation Alesha came to find out that Jingles lived on his own and was raising himself. Big Kyle's support became of no avail to his livelihood due to his own abusive drug addiction. Jingles only way to support his clothing and eating habit was to go out on the corner and hustle drugs to maintain an average way of living. Alesha felt sorry for her boyfriend who was growing up irrational but she stuck by his side because of his pride less courage to survive.

Willie was released from prison that fall and what was once a hapless way of living for him soon transcended into a streak of fortune. In haste motion and not enough time to adapt back to the wick street life, Willie was back to his usual self, running numbers, shooting craps and talking a lot of shit. One's life was that fortunate when money was long as train smoke and there were major connections that linked together like barbed wire. Willie Johnson was a significant maker in the streets, a few of Jingles' teachers in school made sure he passed the required curriculum classes; from a lucrative amount of money and because of the mutual respect they had for his father. He only managed to attend gym class, even passing up the opportunity to sit next to his first love in Language Arts class during second period. And, Ms. Thornton managed to pass him with straight A's in all four marking periods; now that was respect.

While Jingles managed to escape the tough dedication of becoming an honor roll student in school. Willie was educating him on how to become a professional professor in the - School of hard Knocks - streets. Everything that Jingles acquired in the game of hustling he learned most of it from his father. From loading guns, duct taping people for cash, to wrapping thousand dollar stacks in rubber bands for the love of it. Willie Johnson was Jamiere Johnson's distinctive mentor.

The summer of 1979 was the year of Jingles, he was no longer the fat, little, dirty kid with green eyes living on his own. He became a tall, handsome money maker from the prowess and abilities endowed upon him from his father and silent reptile, Alesha.

Somewhere along them lines an insufficient situation happened between Blanche and Alesha. Blanche felt that Alesha was going against her regulation in the household since her dealings flared with Jingles. So she insisted that Alesha find somewhere else to live, prior too, Blanche and Alesha had a cat fight.

Dealing with more problems then his grinding hands could bear Jingles had no choice but to accept Alesha in to his place of comfort. He moved her in with his father's girlfriend Khaliah Trusty until he found better living arrangements. Alesha still felt disowned by Blanche and wanted her to suffer the consequences of her unfair actions. She enlightened Jingles on her and Blanche's disagreement all because she felt that Jingles was breaking up her happy home. Being dismayed by the news Jingles' feelings turned sour for sweet ol' Aunt Blanche.

Since Jingles already received an anonymous tip about Blanche doing business with Pee-Wee Franklin and holding money for him, from a close source. And, with the help of Alesha's information about what her aunt possessed, it was time to turn Blanche's comfortable life into pure misery.

Alesha knew the entire blueprint to the business that her aunt conducted for Pee-Wee Franklin she picked up buy money a day earlier - every other Tuesday of the month - before going out of town on Wednesday to make certain transactions. Twice out of the month Blanche would export - anywhere from - $150,000 to $250,000 dollars to get the best heroin from an out of town connect. When she returned with the product, Blanche didn't immediately go to Pee Wee Franklin and turn over the goods. She waited until that Sunday to take everything to him. That way Pee-Wee could start fresh on Monday for the anticipating user to get high.

Jingles devised a smooth master plan that would have him rich if everything went as planned. He got Alesha to call her Aunt Blanche an hour before she was scheduled to depart from the apartment. So she could feign a reconciled relationship so that her aunt could feel comfortable once again and there wouldn't be a suspicious eye beamed on Alesha. Blanche accepted Alesha back with open arms and told her that she would bring more closure to their meaningless feud after she returned from out of town. Once the two ends on the phones disconnected the plan went directly into effect, Jingles, Alesha and on e of Jingles' henchman squatted outside of Blanche's apartment until she pulled off.

Jingles trailed Blanche from her home to the Philadelphia International Airport in a stolen car. But, before Blanche got the opportunity to get from her car in the airport's parking garage to inside the building. Jingles distracted Blanche by bumping the back of her car to get her undivided attention. When she got out of the car to approach the reckless situation she was then approached by Jingles' henchman with two guns aimed at her head. As Alesha watched from afar Jingles, the henchman, and Blanche got back into her car and found a spot in the parking garage for her.

After Blanche was tied up and the circulation from her mouth cut off until she cooperated, she told Jingles everything he needed to know about going to the Sunshine state to purchase twelve kilos of dope for the price of twenty-five grand a key. She even gave him the password that the Miami connect used so they knew who they were selling to; Jersey devil was the secret code. Once inside the remote place of business Blanche never meant with none of the drug lord diplomats. She slid the money through a mental slot and it was picked up on the opposite side by a mule to be checked and counted. Once everything was accurate the product was slid back through the slot and Blanche was buzzed out to leave. Blanche's information was beneficial but it wasn't enough for her to get turned loose, she lied tied in the back of her trunk until the plan went through.

Two extra, last flight tickets were purchased for Jingles and his henchman to head of into the Sunshine state for a prosperous come up. Alesha impersonated Blanche's roll as the money exporter and client in Miami and Jingles' wasn't a bit worried about jeopardizing his one and only love for something more beneficial than her. Because if he felt she wasn't built for the mission, she wouldn't have told him the plan to begin with. Everything went as expected they all arrived safely at the destination, Alesha used the password, money was exchanged for product, and back to Camden they came; so Alesha thought but Jingles had another trick up his sleeve.

After retrieving the twenty keys of heroin, Jingles squatted patiently inside some side bushes until the mules came out with the buy money that was took to make the transaction complete. Jingles knew that whoever ran the operation wasn't dumb enough to keep the cash where they conducted business; that was like hustling for nothing. His conscience didn't stare him in the wrong direction because him and the henchman observed four guys walk to a car - that was parked out front - carrying two army duffle bags. As Alesha peeked from the bushes with the twenty bricks Jingles and the henchman burst from the bushes with four guns up, one in each palm. Two shots in the air immobilized the men from taking anymore steps. One of the four men tried reaching for a hammer on his waist line but before he could grab it he was grazed across his forehead by a bullet. The man's body dropping ceased all action and the other three men's reactions. The henchman grabbed the two green duffle bags of cash as Jingles held the other three Hispanics face down on the pavement until they were clear to get away.

Back in Philadelphia Airport with two duffle bags filled with $350,000 dollars in cash and twenty kilos of Colombia's finest opium the three of them went back to Blanche's car. Hysterically, Blanche was still inside the trunk thinking her death still awaited her calling. But, it wasn't her time she just took a pounding over the head with Jingles' gun and was left for someone to find her in the parking garage. Jingles and his henchman arrived back into the city as two lucky, wealthy men.

Just as the syndication between the Orange Bag Crew and Pee Wee Franklin's Driveway Boys began to form in unity and accumulate enormous profits together. Blanche came to the table with some aggravating news which made Pee-Wee even more aware of the unusual suspects orbited around him. He didn't fret one bit, his only concern was that Blanche made it back alive and with no serious injuries.

On the other hand, Jingles was a happy hustler who struck oil but managed to remain serene as if nothing ever happened. He split the money and goods with his front line henchman but hid his portion; making it seem to everyone else that he was the same struggling hustler. He became even happier and more serious with his hustle when Lamont Muscles was sent to ride the blue bird up state.

In October 1978 the two street hustling dimensions formed into the Good Wood Boys with Fly Vance Levy as the Capo of the organization. Jingles was nothing more than a go to guy when problems needed to be handled but his character disciplined enough to take orders, his hands called for a leaders roll.

On the rise and cross inside the G.W.B. organization, from donations to charity, sponsoring local events and appearances on the News for their essential contributions. All of it turned into ironic issues, losing Pee Wee Franklin, Chucky and Bud to serve criminal charges of racketeering and enormous drug possessions. With no consistent connect to maintain their lucrative capital in the game, everybody who was somebody in the entourage of the G.W.B. was being targeted by their own comrade.

Fly Vance and Keithy Kool's associating submerged into roiled mud after Kool crossed over and took his business outside the family; Johnny Money became his right hand man. Vance and a few other G.W.B. members' weren't feeling the deception; slaughter was on their minds at that point. But firs, a devised plot from the ingenious, cat eyed mind of Jamiere was more suitable to Vance than the man hunt. And, that was to rob Kool and Midget for their affluence first and then pursue the head hunting. But, Vance hesitated thinking it was impossible because Midget and Kool's street business was difficult to infiltrate; not if you had a big sister and a cousin who shared passionate tides with them.

Sakeema "Sweet" Levy and Fatima "Famous" Levy were needed by Vance and Jamiere to get inside of Midget and Kool's operation. Family came first in Sarema's life so whatever her brother asked of her had to be executed. Sakeema and Fatima didn't even come out of character as they pursued to get furtive information and plunder their charity men's wealth; it was like waling a dog.

In a few weeks time $300,000 plus dollars was confiscated from

Midget and Kool's money spot and the team they had running for them disappeared like rabbits in a hat. Jingles added a hundred plus thousand to his accumulated $125,000 and ten kilos of heroin while also claiming the right hand man position next to Fly Vance; just what he was setting out to do.

The infiltration of cross began to expand so much throughout Centerville that it brought Jimmy Dartaine and the armor of the D.E.A. to stealthily encroach on the G.W.B's turf. After Kool got crossed by his partner Midget who was dealing with his dame Sweets; robbing him for $375,000 dollars in cash. Midget brought in a D.E.A. agent Sherry "Spirit" Land -a mutual friend from up state New York - to conquer and monopolize the streets of Centerville. They brought a proposition to the table trying to compromise with the G.W.B's to hand over a lucrative portion of Centerville; offering them ten keys of cocaine to possess two of their main drug trafficking streets.

A meeting was formulated for the G.W.B's to discuss the matter at hand and the situation was reiterated to the crew verbatim how Fly Vance received it. Everyone had the same conclusive outlook on the solution except Jingles. That it would be bad for the neighborhood for Midget and Spirit to do business on Phillip and Central. Because there was a church and playground amid the plantation which would cause a community up roar.

His neighborhood in Jingles' eyes was already corrupt enough - so he thought - because they all grew up in the dame atmosphere as kids. His morality wasn't for the community it was for his gang and the money that went into their pockets. He wanted the world to be his like Tony Montana. But, the only thing that differentiated him from Scarface was that his balls and word didn't mean shit to himself or anyone else. If Jingles sensed any form of weakness, he was trying to take full advantage of that. And to him Midget and Spirit were weak by trying to offer them out of their own territory; to him that was inexplicable. If a man wanted another man's turf they warred until they conquered.

Jingles suggested that his team accept the ten key proposal but at the same time Midget and Spirit had to page homage to the crew by giving up weekly percentage. Everyone in the crew had a change of mind after summing up the amount they would be taking in weekly for the cost of nothing and all they had to do was sit back and collect. Now they felt like whatever the neighbors despised they just had to deal with it. Because what they wee about to pit into effect with Spirit and Midget was a legal form of grand larceny.

In five months time, after consulting with Fly Vance and the G.W.B.'s, Midget and Spirit brought in so much money to the two connecting streets, she wanted to shut the operation down; because of her mere premonition that something bad was going to happen. And indeed it did, the G.W.B's got some circumstantial evidence that Spirit was working for the D.E.A.; from Monique "Moonie" Mitchell a worker and girlfriend of Spirits. Not to mention that Moonie was a close friend to one of the G.W.B's gun slingers, Shaheem "Stereo" Morgan.

Another urgent meeting was called at the round table and this time no one was leaving until they could pinpoint each and every unusual suspect amid their organization and business. Stereo suggested that everyone lay low while he handled Midget and Spirit but what he couldn't foresee was that it was much bigger then just them two. They were dealing with local authorities and superiors from the Drug Enforcement Agency, two highly advanced forms of government that could infiltrate upon a swamp of snakes and capture the king cobra. The ingenuity of Jingles devised another solution and that was to go on a hunt and murder everyone that had any dealings wit Midget and Spirit, including Rico and Moonie.

In days Midget Money, Spirit, Moonie and Rico were pronounced D.O.A as well as three of seven workers and lookouts in the operation. The other four, Buddy, Juju, Faheem and Hakim went to the police after hearing about their friend's tragedy. They gave up substantial statements and depicted everyone that they knew of inside the Good Wood crew, out of mug shots. Fly Vance, Snail, Bizzy B., Deucey, Ezar and Miguel "Nephew" Smith were all apprehended for the murder and illicit drug trafficking. With Stereo and Bumpsy on the run, Jingles', Little Fella, A-Lucky Lou, and Big Tone were the only ones unmentioned in the investigation; leaving them to vacuum clean the remaining dirt on the streets.

With bail money anticipating the bail hearing for those whom were apprehended, four months later word hit the street about who the inside informant were; to bad that no one who were arrested would have a chance to slaughter the tattletales. Because their bail was revoked after their prior criminal history reports were brought up. Overtly, Hakim and Faheem's lives were revoked subsequent to word hitting the streets about them. Stereo and jingles finished Hakim and Snail left Faheem's body stinking out in front of a near by grocery store. Juju and Buddy were the only two who remained alive to tell their alive to tell their side of the G.W.B's fatality in the streets.

Prior to everyone being released except Snail in the winter of '81, Jingles was hospitalized and labeled in critical condition after being chased in his car by two unidentified men with shotguns. The incident must have been out of retaliation for something that Jingles did in retrospect for the rain to fall heavy on him the way that it did. Miguel was the only person out of the crew that took Jingles' matter into consideration and went to visit him in the hospital; everyone else was seeking their own problem and solutions. Even his soul mender Alesha showed reluctance and inconsistency in visiting him.

During Jingles' time of lying immobilized to hospital bed and the four members from the G.W.B awaited trial. Alesha and Taffy were out enjoying the glamorous life, spending their men's money, shopping sprees and, taking out of town trips in the mid-winter like they lived the lives of millionaire wives; instead of being consolers in their men's lives. Alesha didn't have it like that to spend because Jingles only gave her when needed by taking care of her personal necessities. But, it was Taffy who put Alesha up to having a little fun to walk the red carpet like a true ghetto diva while they spent up Vance's change.

Taffy enlightened Alesha with some shocking news while they relaxed in Jamaica's elegant atmosphere. She elucidated to Alesha that Jingles was furtively sleeping around with Katonya Biggs; Miguel's girlfriend. Prior to Jingles getting shot, she caught the two of them entering the Feather Nest motel on her way out with an anonymous sex figure that she resorted to as B plan excitement. Miguel was never informed about the situation because taffy didn't have the courage to tell her little brother about what Katonya was doing with Jingles; his brother from another mother.

Contrarily, Alesha was reluctant to believe the hear say from Taffy, she thought it was pure envy on her behalf. Alesha felt that taffy was trying to step in and ruin her relationship with Jingles so she could be her replacement. Takeisha always wanted to know what it felt like to have a faithful man Since Vance treated her like nothing more than a whore. Before Taffy tried anything deceiving Alesha felt that she was going to laugh first by beating her to the punch.

Consequently, Taffy and Vance had an unnecessary fight over something irreversible in Vance's eyes, because he felt that Takeisha was cheating on him with another nigga. But, that was just his justification to part from her prior to him going to trial. Needing a shoulder to cry on, how ironic it was for Vance to get consoled from his girl's best friend. Simulating like he was concerned about Jingles condition, Vance really went to Alesha to explain how he truly felt about her. It was just the explanation Alesha needed to follow through with her intriguing desire of being a step ahead of Taffy and satisfied by her best friend's man. What was suppose to turn out as a spontaneous adventure for Alesha soon brought a little feelings along for Vance as well. While Jingles was still stat ionized to the hospital's bed Alesha was putting all her quality time in with Vance and vice-versa for Takeisha's state of loneliness.

Everything was splendid with Vance and Alesha's creep up until the day he was scheduled to appear in court; he was late. Fatima caught him and Alesha cuddling in the bed together. Fatima was so perplexed that she literally got sick and vomited in the bathroom. Alesha and Vance, both, pleaded for Famous not to unveil the secret affair that they both shared. The situation was so severe in Vance's eyes that he gave Famous $3,000 dollars not to mention a word; better yet dissolve it from her memory. In acceptance of the cash she agreed but everyone knows that woman had to squat and piss because they couldn't hold water standing firm.

In the trial courts as the process of the five day examination of witnesses and evidence turned into a twelve hour deliberation. Miguel sat next to his childhood friend - Vance - who had a furtive intercourse with their childhood friend's girlfriend; all because Alesha expected something that was universal in her best friend Takeisha. And, because Taffy explained that Jamiere was having sharing a concealed fling with her younger brother's girlfriend Tonya Biggs; which was in doubt, all dubious to Miguel because everyone kissed but no one told.

After sitting through five days of hear say and testimony from Author "Deucey" Jamison - Miguel and Takiesha's first cousin. Vance and Ezar were found guilty on 2nd degree murder and Bizzy B for being the designated driver. Not to mention that Vance was found guilty of deceiving loyalty by fucking his partner's girl. That was a golden rule that was never suppose to be broken in the life and times of the underworld.

Miguel was cleared of all charges and walked away from a time of confinement in the penitentiary but far from walking away from the lifetime of pain he had to live with for the rest of his life. His blood cousin's testimony on his three friends, the eradication of a loyal underworld family and once he found out about his girlfriend Tonya's fling with his man Jingles; there were a lot of issues for Miguel to grow with and from.

It wasn't long until Fatima's promise was broke and exploited to Jingles whom now was in convalescent stages of being brought back to health. With Vance incarcerated and Taffy and Alesha around in Jingles' livelihood the time couldn't have been better to start some confusion. Jingles didn't act out o character once Fatima broke the news to him about Vance and Alesha bump sessions. On the other end he was a deceiver in his own right of the entire ordeal that took place. But, he got even, even more only this time he upped the ante a bit.

Unmindful of what was going on around her, Taffy accepted Jingles into her sultry kumquat thinking she had another money breaker now that Vance was gone and fulfilling the desire which Alesha placed over her head as a conniving burden that was never in the making from the beginning. As time went on instead of Jingles telling Taffy why he really fell for her, he picked at her brain to absorb enough information about Vance's personal assets. So he could plunder him out of two birds with one stone because Jingles didn't kiss and tell. He was controlling, very manipulative with such a good, young life but enough of Vance's dollar's made sense though while he rode the bench in the big yard's penal system.

Taffy didn't exactly know for sure where Vance's money spots were but she gave Jingles enough insight for him to put two and two together and hit the jackpot. There was only one person - other than Jingles - that was real close to Vance, well that was used for certain missions and agendas. Sutton "Little Fella" Hughes was Vance's personal advisor and proctor in the G.W.B. family. As one of the primary dealers on 8th Street, Little Fella was great with his arithmetic and at the end of the day he was in charge of collecting all the funds that were made. Once he collected the cash he counted the notes out by hand then logged the estimates of how much product was given out and what was brought back.

Valentine's Day 1982, Jingles and the same henchman he took with him to pull off the Florida heist, committed a breaking and entering on Suton Little Fella. Finding a floor modeled safe and taking a mere $280,000 dollars in cash. Adding $140,000 to the $225,000 plus and the ten kilos of dope that he had already accumulated from the prior two stings. Jingles was bubbling quietly in the underworld but not trying to exploit himself as a major figure in the game.

Once a secret to Fatima about Alesha's fling with Fly Vance and Jingles' fling with Taffy; turned into gossip to the neighborhood. Takiesha became to big headed and arrogant about dealing with Jingles, she had to be the only inane mind to display all her luxuriant materials that Jingles garnished her with; also disrespecting her sister and best friend Alesha as well. Takiesha was communicating with Alesha with envy in her heart, saying explicit things to exasperate Alesha's mind by putting unnecessary rumors out in the streets about Alesha and Jingles' relationship. False things like Jingles breaking up with Alesha because she was sleeping with his father. After Jingles denied the assertions of allegedly fraternizing with Takiesha, the outcome became unorthodox.

Takeisha and Alesha battled their friendship and sisterhood into turmoil and violence with each other. And, Jingles stripped Taffy of her intangible goods but he, himself, went into the dog house with Alesha. She separated herself from him because she couldn't handle the dramatic sequence that came her way. After her senior year at Camden High she took her education to the next level at Stockton State University, in Northern Jersey. She eradicated herself from Jingles' for two whole years before returning home and to him before her mother got sick.

"So this has been an on going process for the both of use since the alleged rumors?" I asked, shifting my body at the kitchen table.

"You can say that," she replied, with a gentle but sneered facial expression. "It's on and off... On and off, out break ups to make up be over unnecessary shit. Either because I can't have my way or he can't have his but neither one of us is going anywhere. For the simple fact that I'm one month pregnant and everything Jingles has conquered in the street life from cash to respect is because of me. Plus when you know too much about a person that's played a big part in the drug world, it's hard for them to let you go."

Alesha's conversation about Jingles and the life they shared wasn't to my best interest after she babbled that she was a month pregnant, I was focused on her stomach. "So you're going to be a mommy," I said, gleefully, rubbing my hand over her stomach. "Yup! And you're going to be an uncle."

"Does Jingles know?"

"Yeah but that's the main reason why where not meshing right now--"

"Why not?" I asked, angered by the statement.

"Because he thinks it's not his--"

"What! Why would he assume some shit like that?"

"He thinks I'm still fooling around with some dude name Jayson Walker, some guy I had a fling with a few years ago."

Jingles guess about Alesha's baby being his and who she was dealing with in retrospect was more sufficient then mines. Because that was for them to figure out, my main focus was to probe more into Jingles' underworld ties.

"Not to skip the subject but who are these Enterprise 33 niggas that Jingles' runs with?"

"Some old friends of his that live out in Cramer Hill that is very rich and dangerous, so I've heard. I only know one of them personally and his name is Torri Buggs. Torri is Khaliah Trusty's nephew, Willie's girlfriend. He and Jingles had been calling their selves cousins since they were younger."

"So who and what is this Torri Buggs to Enterprise 33?'

"I don't know about all of that but what I do know us he's the unseen hand out of everyone he deals with... Very hard to find or figure out."

Not if I could help it, nothing was too difficult to search for or detect, all it took was time and patience. Once I got in with Jingles I knew it would be hard for me to get close to the powerful shadows of Torri Buggs.

"So can you arrange for me to meet with Jingles sometime soon?" I asked, taking a piece of her peanut butter and jelly sandwich. "For what Kyle?" she responded, furiously. "You're trying to buy some drugs or something? What are you trying to do?"

"Maybe... I'm trying to get put on."

"I thought you were working with Uncle Muscles, what happened with that?"

I took a few seconds to respond because I didn't want her to know the truth about what was going on with our uncle. "It's a long story... Just know that I'm broke but I'm trying to put a few billion bucks in my pocket," I said, with a wry smirk.

"I'll see what I can do but I'm not making any promises because Jamiere's decorum has been unethical lately," she said, wiping down the kitchen table.

"That answer is good enough just as long as you try, that's all that matters to me." I kissed my big sis' on the forehead and headed out of the kitchen. While she and Aniyah prepared for Sesame Place I went upstairs in the back bedroom to get some sleep. To dream about the excitement of being in the G.W.B's money world of hustling action.

# Chapter. 24

As the summer slowly approached the dull year of 1987, I had high expectations that were being unfulfilled. I needed to solve the inscrutable underworld puzzle, get rich, and then give back to my poor community from which I came. I had no other essential plans on my agenda but to show up for my man Kyron's summer shootout tournament that was going to take place in the next month.

Kyron undoubtedly was controlling all of his successful expectations, having just one full school year left before elevating to the collegiate level of hype. He had not a worry in the world and not another difficult task to pass because he was already a Michigan Wolverine inductee.

While my thoughts continued to stay active and produce plans and strategies, my body became inactive. I became nothing more then a human recluse who refused to venture out into society without a dime in my pocket. I sat around like a grumpy old man waiting for the world to make a move for me. My patience was fading as I waited to hear something from my sister about meeting with Jingles and, a phone call from Ericka about the jade Kelli Right's whereabouts. From flicking the television remote control so much it felt like I had arthritis in my fingers. I watched everything from soap operas, talk shows and local News to pass by the time.

One afternoon after watching an episode of the Three Stooges, I caught an amazing story on the Channel 10 News at 6 p.m. ATF, FBI and Task Force members of the highly fierce Operation Sundown investigation captured a prolific doctor / kingpin by the name of Larry Love out in Reading, Pennsylvania. Love a forty year old Blackman was caught with more than five million dollars worth of cocaine and heroin after informants that were working with the operation directed them to Love. Love had allegedly been supplying all of Philadelphia, most of New Jersey and a few other cities in the Pennsylvania and Delaware region. Selling more than two-hundred kilos of dope and cocaine every four months since 1978. Allegation were being put forth that Love had been importing drugs in from major cities down in Florida, Mexico and New York City.

Also, apprehended in the major drug sting was another wealthy monger named Poohshaun "Uncle Pooh" Miller. Who was captured after Operation Sundown investigators had Andre "Dre" Downes leak some information about his former partner for a reduced prison sentence. Miller 28, was arrested for possession of narcotics after being put under surveillance for more than three years and caught red handed purchasing drugs from Love, himself. If convicted Miller and love could face up to fifty years to life in prison.

Jimmy Dartaine - Captain of the operation - said they were just warming up in the investigation and that was all they needed to get the sweep up and running. My intestines were weak after watching the breaking story as if I was lying in my own excrement. My life as a citizen and a young man in America came to an abrupt halt, in my clairvoyant mind I felt that Poohshaun wasn't built for the duration of time that Operation Sundown was dishing out. Even though I was nothing more than a manipulative peon in the underworld, the boys in them two-thousand dollar shoes were encroaching my presence and I was next to be interrogated.

$ $ $ $ $

The third week in May, the most important response came through for me to meet with the untouchable money man Jingles, himself. I received word from Alesha that Jingles wanted me to attend his father's sixtieth birthday party down at Sophia's Café. The meeting could have been the start of a new beginning for me as a hustler. Being around guys like Jingles and his father, my appearance had to be sleek. I put my triple sole Nike's up and brought out the glossy leather lizard skin shoes. Contrarily, my pockets were full of lint and I had no spare cash to purchase a newspaper from the corner store.

My pride stood between me asking my mother for some money because I was once a six figure nigga and rationalizing with myself, I was suppose to be hitting my mother off with cash. I had no other choice but to spend a few hundred out of the money that I owed Liquor Luby. It had been a month and a half since I lost the bet on the football game; he probably forgot that he made the bet with me.

That night around 9p.m. Alesha accompanied me to Sophia's Café in her brand new Buick Park Avenue. Alesha looked marvelous in all her splendor and my identity was one and the same. She was dressed in a thin, pearl white, satin summer dress with a side split almost to her waist; a pair of high heeled sandals that was designed in colorful rhinestones and colorless artificial gems. I was garnished in a burgundy silk shirt, off white slacks, and a pair of burgundy lizards that would scare a reptile if my shoes were face to face with them.

There were three huge men dressed in fine attire out in front of Sophia's Café when Alesha and I pulled up and parked across the street from Sophia's. 7th Street and Central Avenue were thronged with all sorts of vehicles from one corner to the next.

"Hey Roofie… Tone… Lucky Lou," Alesha said, greeting the men out front as she breezed by them to head in the entrance of Sophia's. In unison they sent there salutations in return.

"Jamiere's inside." The tall dark skinned man with the full beard said, holding the door open for Alesha.

"Thanks Roofie."

"Hol 'on my man," The tall light skin man said to me, stopping me in my tracks. "You have to be searched before you enter the spot."

"But I'm with her," I replied, pointing towards Alesha, using her as my scapegoat to absolve the pat down.

"Lesha Pooh is he with you?" The tall, fat one asked, lighting a well groomed cigar with a book of matches.

She answered them like she had forgotten that I was behind her. "Oh, I'm sorry… Yes he's with me, he's my lil' brother ya'll. Kyle this is Roofie… Big Tone… and Lucky Lou, Good Wood's finest." Big Tone and Roofie, both, greeted me with head gestures, bypassing a handshake. And, Lucky Lou blew a cloud of smoke in my face before shaking my hand.

"Sorry about the smoke in your face youngsta," The corpulent Lucky Lou replied. "But you caught me in the mist of exhaling and we're all sorry for the inconvenience we had no clue that you were Alesha's brother."

"It's cool slim, not a problem."

Roofie and Big tone burst into laughter, I assumed because I called Lucky Lou, slim. I didn't mean it literally it was just a figure of speech. "Fuck ya'll man!" Lucky Lou ranted, tossing his towards the street. "Use can laugh all ya'll want but I bet to ya' girls' my dick is fat muthafuckas."

Sophia's interior house was thronged with people of both sexes and all races, the exterior of the bar and dance floor was so packed that it was hard for people to pass through the aisle. The music reverberated so much throughout the Café, I felt my eardrums pop; I couldn't even hear or understand what people were saying all I could see was their lips moving.

"Make yourself comfortable… have a few drinks," Alesha said, whispering in my ear. "I'll be back I'm going to go find Jingles."

"Take your time I'm going to go and find a seat at the bar."

I went and found a seat in between two gorgeous woman at the colossal, octagon structured bar. I spoke with a head nod and smirk to the lady who sat to the right of me. I figured that would get her to avert her eyes somewhere else because she wasn't my type; to skinny for me. The only thing I could vision to the lady to my left was her rear end because she had her back towards me.

"Hi my name is Dayneil and I will be your barmaid on this end throughout the duration of this gathering, how may I help you?" Dayneil asked, with a beautiful sun tan, caramel complexion, pulling a pen from her ear with a little notepad in hand. I took a minute to respond to her question because her cleavage was whispering for me to come closer.

"Excuse me sir!"

"Ahem… Oh I'm sorry, yes let me have two triple shot s of Seagram's Gin and a Ginger-Ale please, thank you."

No soon as Dayneil turned to walk away the lady to my left turned in my direction. "Hello," she said, very seductive and glassy eyed.

I couldn't believe my fucking eyes; I was smitten by her actual identity that I didn't even return my regards. 'Isn't this a bitch, I can't believe she had the fucking audacity to speak to me. The bitch is so tipsy she don't even remember who the fuck I 'am. I'm going to prolong this conversation and see where it leads me.'

"What's wrong you can't talk or something? I said hello," She said, with a smooth voice.

"Oh! No I'm sorry it was just that your beauty threw me off for a moment. Hi it's nice to meet you though," I replied, thrusting my hand towards her.

"Hel-Lo--"

"And your name is?"

"Excuse me," she said, leaning towards me.

"I said I didn't get your name."

"Ohhh... My name is Myesha but my friends call me Mimi."

'Now your name is MiMi, it figures that a gold digging bitch like yourself would have more than one name. You done so much dirt to people switching up your name and identity is a common ritual for you,' I said to my self as she tried reading my eyes.

"What are you thinking about," she asked, taking a sip of whatever she was drinking.

"How pure your skin complexion is," I replied, making up anything that came to mind. "What are you a mulatto...? Hispanic... Trinidadian --"

"I'm Spanish and Black."

"Is that right?"

"I'm not the type that stares people wrong." Dayneil returned with our drinks.

"How much will that be?" I asked, flickering through the knot of money I retrieved from my pants' pocket.

"Oh no need for that sweetheart, you see drinks around here are on the house tonight."

"Is that right? Well in that case I'll just tip you then," I said, handing her forty dollars.

"Thank you."

"No, thank you," I said in a passionate way. Dayneil turned and walked away once more.

"You definitely have a smooth vibration with females, I must admit," Myesha said, crossing her delectable, high yellow thighs. "I think she likes you."

"Me? Naaaah, sometimes pussy that looks good isn't always good... Catch my drift?" I asked, raising my eyebrow. I threw back the phrase she told me before smacking me over my head, two years ago.

"How can you tell that the pussy you're looking at isn't good without fucking it first? And no I don't catch your drift," She replied, glossing her lips with red lipstick.

"Because good pussy is silent like a predator preying on others. And that to me is a killer because it catches you off guard and its very unexpected. So either way you look at it, it turns out to be some bad pussy."

"So do I look like some bad pussy to you?" she asked, caressing my thigh in a fervid way.

My conscience was telling me to say "Yes," bad as hell but, my dick had an ironic statement. I didn't want to spoil the moment so I said nothing in return; I just allowed my eyes to do all the talking.

"So how did you get that scar over your right eyebrow?" The liquor had her tongue being very discursive.

'Bitch you know how I got the scar, when you smacked me with that gun and robbed me for that brick and a half of dope and sixty G's in cash.'

"I fell off my bike when I was little."

Mimi rubbed it gently before saying, "Excuse me for a moment I have to use the ladies room." Mimi had a strange way about say that to me like she seen a ghost or something. Her eyes widened and she maneuvered haste fully.

Right after Mimi vanished from in front of my eyes; Jingles walked up and positioned himself in her seat. "Kyle what's up dude?" He asked, shaking my hand, sipping on something dark. "Who seat was this?"

"Some whore name Mimi --"

"Watch your mouth Kay, watch your mouth. We here at Sophia's

Café treat our ladies with respect, dig me?"

"I can dig it, it's dug."

"So your sister's telling me that you're having a little financial trouble, what's that about?" he asked seeming concerned.

Cutting no corners, not trying to beat around the bush I got straight to the point, "The money that I made hustling and running for my Uncle Muscles was taken from beneath my feet."

"So you were robbed?"

"If that's what you want to call it but in my eyes I was set up."

"That's a remote circumstance that comes with contaminated game, allow me to tell you something that a wise man told me and never forget this." He pulled his stool close to me and leaned into me, having a serious face. "Cross is the key to success when you're trying to be boss in this profession. Cross will always be boss when you have predators who want to conquer the board."

Jingles reminded me so much of my Uncle Muscles at that very moment I could have sworn it was him sitting in front of me. My Uncle Muscles always had a jewel or two for me to gain a real understanding from.

"So Lamont Muscles is your uncle huh?"

"Yeah," I replied, nonchalantly.

"I use to run for your Uncle at one time too when I was younger."

Jingles took me back to his inception of how things formulated with him and my Uncle Muscles. Their association didn't just happen over night, Lamont Muscles made his way hustling from the support of Willie Johnson; way before he linked up with Timmy Tange and Lance Whop Smith, to accumulate major figures. It was kind of a second passing for Muscles to endow Jingles with the fundamentals of how to ascend in the underworld.

Back in the mid-50's, early 60's Willie Johnson was one of the first street ruffians to come across the powerful drug of heroin and show his other allies and adversaries in Camden how the powdery opium could control the streets. But back then everyone was into numbers, selling booze, brothels, and controlling speak easies. Illicit drugs weren't a primary asset back then. Since nobody was really interested in what Willie had to offer he pushed the drugs to the side and kept doing what he knew best - running numbers. Subsequently, there were some young hungry street thugs whom had nothing to lose and everything to gain and they would try anything once to see the outcome of it all.

Muscles who hung around the older city slickers like Willie, Chucky Mills, and his father Rooster allowed Muscles to tag along with him as a young adolescent. Quickly learned the tricks and trades of how to scheme, scam, and manipulate others out of their possessions. Simply from observing what took place in front of him while being around his father in front of gambling spot and brothels. When his father Rooster was slaughtered in a pool of blood when he was just eleven, Muscles lacked self discipline and made the street life a full time career. Out of respect and loyalty that Old Man Willie had for Rooster and the gratitude that he showed Ann Williams - Muscles mother - he promise to take Muscles into his care and provide for him.

$ $ $ $ $

Muscles started out as a naïve errand boy, cleaning up for Old Man Willie after parties, after hour extravaganzas and making runs for the guys inside the gambling spot. The older Muscles got the more his position increased; he went from errand runner to counting money and logging numbers in books for Old Man Willie which soon altered into running numbers for himself. Muscles showed an enormous disinterest in running numbers after he linked up with a few childhood friends who began slanging marijuana in tiny manila envelope bags called "Coin Bags"; that was a couple of years after he entered into the street lottery business.

Timmy Tange and Lance Whop introduced their ambitious friend Lamont Muscles into the underworld of drugs. William "Billy Bad Ass" Holmes and his younger brothers Stevie, Howie, Spider and Hassan Holmes were apart of the coin bag regime also. After the mutual conjunction with Tange and Whop, Muscles packed his things and left Willie and his family; feeling like all Old Man Willie had done for him didn't matter no more.

On Muscles rise to the top in the underworld, he and his vicious Deli crew were introduced to these two car lot owners through a mutual friend. Richie and Mikey Munez - known as the Dominican Brothers - convinced the Deli Boys that the heroin game was ten times greater then dealing marijuana and once they began accumulating enormous profits they would be attached forever. Ten years or more prior, the Dominican Brothers were the first ones to show Old Man Willie the power behind the powdery drug.

$$\$ \ \$ \ \$ \ \$ \ \$$$

Old Man Willie knew the deceiving intentions Muscles engrossed and how loyalty had no effects for his crew as well as others. That's why prior to Old Man Willie doing time in the penitentiary in 1964, he gave a direct order to Lamont Muscles and his crew, not to deceive or cross his two mutual friends Richie and Mikey Munez. Ironically, the outcome turned out sour for Old Man Willie about seven years later when he read about his two made men in the newspaper. Willie also found out that Muscles...

"Damn! What the fuck am I doing?" Jingles asked himself, cutting his story short. "That's what happens when you drink a bit too much, you begin revealing information that's confidential."

I just stared at him in disgust because he didn't know my intentions of getting to the bottom of this underworld mystery. And, he, his father and his conclusion to the story played a significant part in what I was trying to achieve. I wanted to tell him to finish but I just rolled with the flow.

"Let's go and say happy birthday to my pops," Jingles said, removing himself from the bar.

Through my travels inside the café on my way to acquaint with Old Man Willie, I was scrutinizing as much as my eyes could foresee in the place; searching for Mimi. I couldn't find her if my life deepened on it, it was very peculiar how she just up and left and never returned to her seat. She left her leather purse at the bar and everything I hoped there wasn't anything important in there.

"Happy birthday dad!" Jingles exclaimed, as we walked into what seemed to be the VIP area of the café.

At the present moment it was nothing more than a crap game and everyone's attention went from the dice to Jingles, back to the money on the floor in one quick motion. Of course it was the birthday man who controlled the game as the crowd around him had an intense rush from the excitement in the crap game.

"You heard my son muthafuckas its' my birthday," Willie expressed, shaking the red cubes up and down in his right palm. "I got happy birthday cake muthafuckas... You niggas can't break me--"

"Com'on Old Man roll the dice OG," One bookmaker said, out the crowd, not patient enough to hear Willie's loud vulgarity or the number to come out.

"No more Willie muthafuckas... My game is grown so I prefer you call me William. There goes that stinkin' bitch Ayesha," He replied, slow rolling the dice on to the back wall.

"Snake eyes," Another man called out, from my vision of the old man sitting on a bar stool with a stack of money in his hand. It seemed to me that he was controlling the house.

Old Man Willie's number was eight and that's what he meant when he called for Ayesha to come when he shot the dice. They had their own names for the numbers on the dice, Ayesha or Scorpio stood for the number eight, Snake eyes was the two points on both dice, Bitch for nine, Flowers for ten, Devil for six etc... etc... Willie rolled the dice four times more before hitting his target and scooping up all the money scattered around on the floor near everyone's feet.

"Here Pop Ghost," Willie said, handing him a stack of cash. "I'm a stay on these bones until I break the entire game, let's go." He rolled to seek his point once more.

To be a sixty year old man, Willie sure didn't look or act his age, he was full of invigorating energy too. A couple inches shooter than Jingles, Old Man Willie was brown skin wearing a pair of dark frames covering his eyes and a tooth pick sticking out the corner of his mouth.

"I got tubs of this shit muthafuckas, you muthafuckas just get your rent money out ya' pocket because after I bring this ten back...

Muthafuckas better pay my son whatever is left on the floor."

Old Man Willie was rolling the dice so long that majority of the guys who were bookies too the dice began screaming out, "them muthafuckin' dice are tease... There isn't a seven on those sons of bitches."

Subsequently, no soon as the spectators finished chastising the dice, Old Man Willie hit his number. "I got five grand coming to me from that floor and I don't care how you muthafuckas divide it but give Pop Ghost a thousand and my son the remaining four grand," Willie explained, grabbing his black top hat and suit jacket before heading out of the VIP room.

"Ya'll owe me four thousand?" Jingles said, exuberantly with a smirk on his face. "Ya'll owe me? Let me get that jack 'because I don't have any money on me right now".

After Jingles collected the remaining profit from his pop's slot machines he gave me a grand on general purposes, I guess for just being with him at the time. Then we went back over by the bar to sit with his father.

"A pop this is Lesha's little brother," Jingles said, introducing the two of us.

"No shit! I never knew Sis' had another one of use," He said, eating a hand full of peanuts; I felt kind of strange answering that question.

"Nah, that's my aunt... Big Kyle Moore is my dad, we have the same dad."

"Well ain't that some shit? That damn Tommy always was a crap shooter with his dick. So Alesha's your sister cousin, huh?"

"If that's what you want to call it."

"Did you attend his funeral?"

"No... well I --"

"Let me tell you something son," Willie said, placing his hand upon my shoulder. "No matter the circumstances or whatever you went through with your father. He was still your father and out of all the bad things he may have done to put a scar across your heart for you to despise him. He did one thing right..." Willie paused before continuing on while Jingles and I gave him our intoxicated attention. "He gave you life and brought you into this world."

"Hmm," Jingles gestured, nodding his head. "That's real deep dad... Real deep."

"I would never stare family wrong," Willie said, averting his head back and forth to me and Jingles. "His father was my son before you two were even thought of and the same advice I gave to him at your age, is pertinent to be passed on so uses can pass it down, ya' dig?" He said, shifting his toothpick.

The three of us sat at the bar downing shot after shot after shot. After sharing a few laughs I listened to Old Man Willie explain how he came to terms of raising Big Kyle up.

My grandfather Khalif Moore was what you called a high roller himself back in the fifties and sixties. But the difference between him and Old Man Willie was that my grandfather was illiberal, self-seeking and, a stingy man who looked after himself before he provided for his family; Willie didn't respect my father at all. Grand pop Khalif would go to the local hangout spots dressed in his finest attire and have Big Kyle tagging along with him in filthy, tattered clothing. Willie explained that Grand pop Khalif would leave Big Kyle out side to shine shoes while he was having a good time. Or win about three grand in the gambling house and would never share his winnings with his son, his wife Denise, or his other three children. Willie couldn't stand to see the abuse of Big Kyle suffering any longer so he executed action and intervened.

Old Man Willie gathered up two of his henchmen one night after Pop Ghost's gambling house closed down and caught Grandpa Khalif counting a was of money on his way out. The two henchmen took and pointed two shot guns at Khalif, stripped him of all his materials and money and then told him, "See how it feels to walk in your son's shoes. You run around herein three piece suits with pockets full of money and your son looks like he's living on his own. What kind of muthafuckin' man are you? From this day forward your son is my responsibility."

Khalif had no feed back to give, and then Willie told him, "To get the fuck out of here."

"That's what you told him dad?" Jingles asked, giggling, twirling his organization ring around on his finger.

"Yeah, that's what I told the muthafucka, I hate a greedy mutha-fucka."

I seen nothing but loyalty, dignity, respect and benevolence in Jingles and Old Man Willie as I sat quietly amongst them. That was something I always wanted and always needed to be apart of. There was nothing like a father son relationship and your son was equivalent to you in character like a brother. My understanding became even clearer about why everyone loved Willie Johnson. It wasn't because of his wealth or ghetto stardom he possessed in the streets but because of the respect, care and time he had for others. Big Kyle, Uncle Muscles, nor Jingles were born hustlers but it was due to the knowledge of Willie that birth them men into what they became.

The night was still young but my body felt elderly from the drinks, dancing, and all the fun that came with it. I found myself staggering at times like an alley bum trying to recuperate. Old Man Willie immobilized himself at the bar while Jingles and I roamed the café looking for something or someone else to get into. I had to give it to my sister Alesha; to me she couldn't have found a better dude to call her own. Jingles was the smoothest cat walking on two feet, his character was nonchalant as if he had a worry in the world; he even had cool and calm body language.

His swagger was that of a basketball player like his feet were precious diamonds, the nigga even laughed cool. Every time I turned around or looked up somebody was either screaming his name or shaking his hand. His being was, as if he was conceived from three different sperm cells, having his pops intelligent and heart, Big Kyle's debonair decorum and Muscles aggressiveness. And, almost every time we bypassed a female he knew or a gaggle of ladies who gave him an ogle eye there were two statements that came out of his mouth. "I fucked her," or "those whores wanna fuck me."

I lost Jingles in the mist of our travels through the café, he had two many associates stopping him; every few steps he took. I was trying to get my groove back because my mood was to drunk to be running off at the mouth. Mimi and I bumped into each other once more on my way to the men's room.

"There you go," She said, excitingly, rubbing her hand upon my chest. "I'm sorry that I left you hanging at the bar but not only did I have to use the bathroom, I had to make an important phone call."

"Did you repossess your purse that was left at the bar?" I asked, visioning Mimi and I fucking in the rain. The liquor controlled my train of thought.

"Yeah it's right here." She waved it in my face.

"Listen, I'm on my way home, this party is tiring me out I had enough dancing and drinks for one night and I'm not trying to get caught up with him tonight."

"Who?" I asked, curious.

"Some crazy guy, he's not a factor though but look here's my address… I want you to be at my house in an hour."

I didn't even have to ask why and with a wink of her eye as her hand gently gazed my genitalia area the hint confirmed her desire. 808 State Street was the address which was located in the back of North Camden, the main street that routed into East Camden. She moved because when I use to make my rounds to her house a couple of years back, she lived on Mechanic Street; the same block as Kylie.

Wadeelah and Alesha appeared from out of no where no soon as Mimi took off. "Kyle what are you doing standing in the middle of the bathroom's corridor?" Alesha asked, while Wadeelah stared at me glassy eyed, laughing. I was too drunk to even pay Alesha's question any mind.

"Wha'?"

"I know you weren't just talking to that red bitch Mimi?"

"Mimi who… What?"

"You heard me," Alesha ranted. "I can't stand her fuckin' ass."

"Who Mimi that be with Taffy?" Wadeelah asked, intervening.

"Yeah her… The one always up in Jingles' face every time I turn around."

"Listen I don't know Mimi and Mimi don't know me… An-ee-way Wadeelah what the hell are you doing in here do Aunt Gracey know that your out this time of night sinning?" They both laughed in my face.

"Boy I'm so grown--"

"Not grown enough to get knocked out."

"Pa-ha, whatever," She replied, rolling her eyes, waving me off.

"Stop Kyle," Alesha said, smacking me gently across my shoulder. "She can have fun if she wants too."

"Did you make a college decision yet?" I asked, worrying about her educational status like I was on her level of achievement.

"Man, I have a whole other year to complete before I get into the depths of that." I caught myself talking out of left field, the entire conversation was irrelevant. They truly were blowin' my groove.

"I'm sliding," I said.

"Kyle!" Wadeelah exclaimed, trying to get my attention.

"What?!" I said, without turning around.

"Let me get some money?" I gave her a few hundred from the grand that Jingles had given me; I dropped the shit to the floor as if money wasn't a thing and kept strolling.

Jingles and I reacquainted at the bar where Old Man Willie was still stationed but this time there were more people orbited in his presence. The section of the bar looked like a Mob meeting, everyone sat in silence, drinks in hand with fine, dapper linen on observing everything in the café. I didn't no whether to walk over towards them, take a seat, speak or what.

"Kay." Jingles called, as everyone's head slowly diverted n my direction. He walked over and put his arm around my shoulder. "You look like you're lost or something slim… Having a good time?"

"Fa'sho cool," I replied, with a leering look at all the men at the table that stared me down.

"Solid." He took a few drinks of his drink and said, "I want you to meet some of my cronies." He began introducing me to the men in the Mob section of the bar; we walked by each person individually.

"This is Freddy Fox… Elroy Coles… Gizard Gazoo… Dude Calhoun… Snoopy Pierson… Lord Ticky… And Torri Buggs the great. These are all made men from the notorious Enterprise 33 cadre, I'm a great friend to them all."

Finally, I got to vision with my own eyes who the dangerous faction consisted of; I glared at every individual a few times for photographic purposes. But, my eyes were mainly focused on the "Desperado Don" known as Torri Buggs. He was tall about 6'1", slim, brown skin, wearing a Ko Jack bald head with a lazy right eye. From the tale of his tape, he looked like he did nothing but tell jokes all day long but, looks were deceiving.

While the other men who were at the bar from Enterprise 33 floated and mingled around the café, Torri, Elroy, Fox and Jingles confidentially spoke in codes the entire time I sat at the bar; which was about forty-five minutes to an hour.

"A Jay," I said, getting his attention for a quick second. The time on my watch read twelve-fifteen. "Listen cool, I'm a bout to roll like a doughnut and get out of here--"

"Yeah well let me see you off youngin'."

"It was nice meeting you fellas," I said, paying my respects.

Jingles and I left out of the café's side door as Lucky Lou, Roofie and Big Tone stood out in front of the café attaining to their regular duties when I glanced at the corner.

"Are they apart of the Good Wood family too?" I asked, nodding my head towards them.

"Who the guys on the corner? Yeah they're the gorilla war battle men," Jingles replied, with his eyes in focus on the corner.

Prior to Jingles and I concluding our conversation to go our separate ways an intense, clamorous whistle came from Big Tone on the corner. Keenly, Jingles glanced up the block and returned the whistle.

"Law and Order got eyes on us up the block on Central!" Big Tone yelled, with his hands surfacing his mouth.

Jingles turned in the direction of Central Avenue as we both scanned the area for police activity. Hastily, I comprehended Big Tone's coded message and started looking with sharp eyes of an owl at what was taking place. Jingles spotted two black, unmarked cars before I had the chance to do so. One car was sitting in the middle of Central Avenue and the other car was to our left at the high corner of 7th Street.

"Check the laws style and the way the cops sweat us," he said, staring at the unmarked car sitting on 7th Street. "The number one question is can the Feds get me? I got more vendettas on my hands than I dread to then to worry about these corrupt protectors. Fuck'em though they hate a young, debonair nigga such as myself who's loving his life. They put this illegal shit out here on the market for us to sell and then try to blame me for what they execute and profit from. "The Feds been bugging' my life before my life, dig me?"

I tried to apprehend his slick wisdom but fully didn't understand what he meant by the Feds bugging his life before his life. "Listen slim, I'm not going to hold you up any longer, I need you to get out of here before shit gets thick," He said, leaning up against a parked car with his eyes locked down the block. "You came with Alesha right?"

"Yeah."

"Well look, to keep the heat off you I suggest you take a cab to your comfort zone." Jingles whistled once more up to Big Tone and Roofie. "Get me some yellow wheels out here!" Lucky Lou immediately picked up the receiver on the pay phone that was stationed on the side of the café.

"Here take this," he demanded, handing me five hundred more dollars. "The money I gave you should last you for a few more days."

"Jingles... Man I can't --"

"Don't worry about it Kay, I'll get it back it's nothing, this money is really worthless. I do this street life thing because I'm great at it and I'm pissing these fake so called willies and law enforcers off on purpose," He responded in confidence, slowly walking back to the café's side door. "Call me in a couple of days I want you to take care of something with me... Nothing major, I'll see you later."

"Cool."

When my cab arrived in front of Sophia's I shook hands and said my goodbyes to Roofie, Big Tone and Lucky Lou. Then, I ordered the cabby to take me to my final destination for the night, 808 State Street.

## $ $ $ $ $

When the yellow wheels came to a complete stop in front of

Mimi's domain, the house was pitch black. With literal vision, damn near every home on the block had their lights off, only the illuminaing street lights shined brightly.

"Do you suggest that I pull off or are you staying?" The nappy bearded, brown skin cab man asked, as I patiently sat in the back seat contemplating my next move. "The meter don't stop running you know?"

"Here take this," I said, out of frustration, handing him a fifty dollar bill. "But don't pull off until I get in the house."

North Camden was a dangerous milieu, even in the day time and I didn't even have any protection to defend myself if I wasn't to get in and the cab left me. Before I had the chance to step foot on Mimi's porch and knock on the door, the fuckin' cab driver skirted of down State Street screaming, "Fuck you dick head," with his middle finger raised highly out the window.

The noise from the cab must have triggered the dog on the other side of Mimi's door who was barking loud enough to wake the entire neighborhood up.

"Goldie... Down sexy, go." The voice said behind the door, before opening up to see who I was. "Two hours wasn't what I told you," Mimi said, looking at me for an answer that I didn't have.

"So you're going to breeze by me without giving me an explanation as to why--"

Who needed an explanation when you had a lush tongue and phallus such as mine? Mimi's inquisition ceased when she felt the moistness of my tongue gliding across her tender neck.

In her bedroom, as she stood unclad in front of me, the melodious sounds of Sade played smoothly on her stereo and the fiery lit candles burned like hours around the room; very slow. Mimi favored Sade's elegant features somewhat, except she was taller than Sade and had a wider derriere. Here body was nothing like before, a couple of years ago when she caught me with my feet up. Her chest wasn't as big and skin complexion wasn't as light; preservation was pivotal I guess? Mimi's beauty made me passionately impatient, I wanted to eat her.

"Take your time," she pleaded, massing my hands on her breast.

"I haven't been worked slowly in a very long time."

"Shhhh," I said, placing my finger over her mouth. "Just relax and enjoy."

I licked and sucked Mimi's body clean - from head to toe - before I disrobed myself and rubbed skin with her. From the back of her neck to the quagmire area of her beautiful feet my tongue trail was all over her. She tasted so good; I even sucked under her under arms for my own pleasure.

There was a tight burning sensation when I entered the threshold of Mimi's juices and I wasn't even fully erect or all the way inside her sultry melon and she was dynamically biting my chest and digging her nails into my back. He passionate reaction reminded me much of how DaVita use to act in bed.

"Fuck me until you rip my insides," she whispered, passionately in my ear.

The way Mimi's pussy talked to me was unorthodox as I lied between her soft thighs missionary style. Her vaginal sounds resembled juices being squeezed from fruit, a gushing sound that aroused me. She was the first female to make me moan during sex, the tables had turned and she was the bed aggressor; I was the emotional dictator. Mimi went into an acrobatic position that overwhelmed my loins even more. She put both her legs behind her neck as her coochie thrust with nothing but more flesh to give.

"I al-ways… Uh! I always said I… would try… this with someone who filled all of my sexual desire. Oooh… Umm," she confided, giving me direct eye contact.

Mimi and I had sex in the same position the entire night, orgasm after orgasm was fulfilled without us having to stop once. Mimi climaxed in tandem sensations like it was in her nature to inhale and exhale air.

$ $ $ $ $

The next morning with out trying to wake Myesha from her reposed hibernation, I wanted to furtively leave out her home to keep from having to spend quality time. What I had in mind, to satisfy my conscience was impossible to do right then and there because for one I didn't have a firearm and I had no alibi set up. If I would have killed the whore, homicide would have solved the crime without even second guessing a motive.

I struggled to remove myself from Mimi's bed because when I awoken her dog Goldie was lying beside me. Goldie was a huge ol' bear looking muthafucka, the kind of dog you heard from a block away and detoured to your destination.

The upstairs level of Mimi's home was plush with wall to wall carpet and adorned with glass mirrors across both walls. Everywhere I turned I seen myself about two of three times. The bathroom was garnished with a Jacuzzi, walk in shower, tiled flooring and a matching sink and toilet. Her home was definitely furnished with a hustler's taste. I assumed that her brother Vinnie Parker who had money on top of money gave it to her as a gift.

On my way through the living room I took a quick glance at the living quarters which was also embellished luxuriously. The entire living quarters was decorated white, white leather sofas, carpet, curtains, coffee and end tables, everything I seen had a heaven aura to it. I became very mystified when I observed this huge photograph of Mimi and Jingles positioned on the center wall. Now things began to come together, he was the person she was trying to dodge in the café the night before. And, the reason Alesha was getting worked up when she assumed that I was talking to Mimi.

"So, Jingles got you too huh?" I said, to myself staring into her pictured face.

On my way out the door Mimi was coming in, I did a double take hoping my eyes weren't playing tricks on me, and then I caught myself. "Oh I'm sorry," Mimi said, as we collided with each other.

"And you are?" Her identical identity was very illusionary; she startled my thoughts for a second.

"You look very familiar," She said, retrieving her key from the door knob. "Haven't we met before?"

"Nooo. Not to my recollection," I replied helping her with her grocery bags that were sitting by her feet on the porch. "By the way my name is Kangaroo."

"Kangaroo?" she looked at me distastefully, wondering why my parents would name me such a thing. "Well, I'm Yasming... Mimi's twin sister. But everyone calls me Yum Yum." From Yasming's facial expression it wasn't hard to understand why people called her Yum Yum, she was breath taking.

I was astounded, Yasming's identity amazed and confused me also, because at that very moment I couldn't figure out if it was Mimi who got me set up or Yasming; there was only one way to find out though.

"So Yas... I mean Yum Yum you and Mimi live together?"

"Yeah it's only temporary though until I can find another place because my last home was taken away after it was raided by police. Drugs and guns were found that belonged to my husband and brother, it all happened about a year ago," She explained in an anguished manner.

"Well listen I should be on my journey, I'm on a timed schedule," I said, handing her the bag of groceries. "It was nice to meet you though."

"Yeah you too... Are you sure we never met before because I could have sworn--"

"I'm positive this is our first encounter with each other."

I would have been a nincompoop to reveal an old trick to her, while she was contemplating and assuming I had known for certain that we met before on a few occasions. It wasn't Mimi who set me up it was Yasming the scandalous twin sister who pretended to be Myesha at the time. The same things that make you laugh will make you cry and it became funny to me about all the tears I was getting ready to witness.

"Tell Mimi I'll be in touch."

"I'll be sure to do so," she replied, walking in the house as I made my way onto the side walk.

$ $ $ $ $

I was back at my mother's pad confined to the couch since I left Mimi's home earlier that day. From the verbal chastisement that my mother gave me if I would have known any better I would have stayed at Mimi's place. She was babbling on about the same old issues that obstructed my ears from her irritated advice. Since she left me to carry my own responsibilities on my shoulders as a teenager. Saying that I was a bum like Big Kyle use to be, to lazy not to work or except responsibility the ay she prepared me too. She was putting her faults on me as if I rebelled against her rules and regulations and made it my own obligation to take care of myself. Much as I wanted to give her some explicit feedback, I kept my composure and went downstairs into the den where it was more tranquil.

As I relaxed on the sheep material carpet with my eyes closed the disputer yelled down and told me that someone was on the phone for me.

"Hello," I said, still with my eyes closed.

"Hey Kyle, this is Ericka from Glamour--"

"Yeah what's shakin' cutie, I've been waiting for your call."

"Oh really?" she replied, not to surprised.

'No doubt, what you got for me?'

"The hooker Kelli Browning called here inquiring about some type of identification card that she misplaced and wanted me to go up to her old apartment to look for it. I told her I would and if I found it I would contact her."

"That's it... What else you got?"

"She said if I found it to bring it to her around five tomorrow evening if it wasn't too inconvenient."

"Aaah! That's bad timing." I said, thinking of the meeting with Jingles.

"Is something wrong?"

"Nah, listen... Just... Tomorrow I'm a meet you at your job at four-thirty prompt, not a minute later, okay?"

"Alright but--"

"No buts, I'll be there," I said, hanging up the phone without saying goodbye.

Within a nanosecond of me hanging up the phone with Ericka the phone rang again but when I answered I got no response. Whomever it was hung up in my ear and two seconds later the phone rung a third time but this time there was a voice on the other end.

"This is Francis may I speak to Kangaroo please?"

"This is Kangaroo the great, how may I help you? And, you don't have to sound all proper on the phone either."

"Whaaat? No this is how I 'am all the time."

"Yea right, anyway what's shakin' sweetheart?"

"Nothing much, Taliyah and I were just worried about you and wanted to see how you were making out. "

"I'm still cool as a fan, thanks for the concern though and how 'bout yourself?"

"Everything's going good for Tee and I since leaving us your apartment, we found jobs and everything."

"Yeah?"

"Yup we work here in the buildings laundry department, hourly wages but Eyeball the owner pays us under the table also for out excessive labors."

I definitely was wondering what kind of excessive laboring the two chicks were doing for some side change? It wasn't hard to figure out the kind of activities the whores were indulging in if you was raised with the street sense that was needed to comprehend other people's game.

"Well I just called to see how you were doing, I don't want to hold you up but you would appease our sexual craving if you came by and played a little--"

"Hmm, is that right? I can't play right now… I have some other serious business to take care of before I start playing again. Give me a few days and then we can definitely… definitely have some fun."

"Okay daddy, I'm a hold you to that… we need you in us."

"Later," I replied, in a cool manner hanging up the phone.

I became annoyed after picking up the phone a second time and got no response from the incoming caller. I knew it wasn't anybody that I knew because everybody I gave the number too, I talked to. As I left the den to head back up stairs, I took the phone off the hook on purpose.

# Chapter. 25

I picked Ericka up in my Chevy Celebrity at four-thirty on the nose from outside the Glamour Towers. Our destination was on 5th and Market Streets, where the Hall of Justice, County jail and Bell Atlantic Phone Company sat. Kelli did mention that she was a clerk at City Hall - a block over - on Federal Street.

"There she is," I said, looking out of my rear view mirror, leisurely walking up from a block away. "Take this." Ericka took the identification card. "Spark a conversation with her just to pass a little time, if she asks you to waste a little time, follow along with her--"

"For what? Now you want me to play private I, I'm not trying to get caught in the middle of--"

"Ericka!" I exclaimed, trying to keep her from arguing me down. "It's only for me to get enough time to get out of dodge."

"What, you are going to leave me down here... Downtown at rush hour? Un-Unh, my damn stories are on--"

"Here... Here's a hundred dollars just do what I told you and I'll call you later on."

Ericka stepped out of my car allowing Kelli to see her; she was looking very impatient standing on the far corner waiting for Ericka to show up. Kelli kept glancing at her watch as if she was late coming off her lunch break or some shit, not having enough time to be waiting on an I.D. card. I pulled off once they were face to face I wasn't trying to stick around to see what went on between them. Kelli's location was on hold in my mental disc, I planned on staking out in that area so I could trail Kelli to her new destination; then make my move. But, as I drove through the downtown district my essential option was to get in contact with Jamiere Johnson.

Prior to the rendezvous that I was invited to go to with Jingles, I stopped by Mimi's place to retrieve my gold bracelet that I left on her night stand. Just as before, Mimi's untamed dog Sexy was at the door with clamorous barks that mace me think twice about knocking.

"Which one are you?" I asked, not be able to tell the two beautiful, redbones apart.

"Mimi," she answered, smiling gleefully. "I see you've met my twin sister Yasming?"

"I still don't believe you," I barked, seriously. "If your Mimi then what sexual position did I have you in the past day when I was--"

"Missionary style with my legs behind my head," She battered, with a fast tongue. "Now if you don't come in here and stop playing."

"I just had to make sure I wasn't--" We both entered the living quarters and took a seat on the leather sofa.

"Wasn't what, being tricked?"

"You can say that."

"You came by for the bracelet right?"

"What made you--?"

"Because if you came over for mommy queen," she stated, tapping her chest lightly.

"You would have greeted me with some form of affection, a kiss, hug or something... There's your bracelet on the table."

I averted my head in her direction without reaching for my bracelet and retorted, "My real reason for stopping by was to inquire on the status of your relationship with Jingles."

"If I never mentioned what Jingles and I shared as a couple when I acquainted with you, why is it a big concern now?"

"Because he deals with my sister and I'm feeling uncomfortable that's why."

"Who? Alesha Williams? That's your sister? Pa-ha, that disgraceful tramp--"

"Mimi watch your mouth please, use may have some personal issues with my sister but she's still my sister," I pleaded, sincerely.

"Since you're caught up in the middle of a bad situation, I don't mind sharing my personal life with you."

Mimi was introduced to Jingles through a mutual friend - Yasming's husband Ticky - a year ago. Their familiarity was much unexpected, Ticky happened to come home one day with Jingles and coincidently Mimi was at the house entertaining Yum Yum with girl gossip. Jingles and Mimi were introduced and from there a friendly conversation led to night out on the town and, the date turned into seeing each other regularly.

Jingles told her about Alesha and explained how deep their companionship was for each other. But, his reasons for becoming a fraternizer were because he sensed that Alesha was being unfaithful. Without any substantial evidence on the hearsay about his first love but the hearsay was good enough for him to act out of character. Pivotal adversity had come in between Jingles and Alesha's relationship when Alesha began courting with Camden High's superstar Kyron Ownes

"Whoooa! Not my man Kyron? When did all of this take place sweetheart?" I asked, so curious to the matter.

"I don't know exactly, but Jingles said it was like two years ago."

Alesha only fooled around with Kyron to show Jingles that he wasn't the only live nigga with ghetto stardom that she could have; basically saying that she could have any guy that she focused her attention on. The plot thickened even more and, buzz breezed by his ear about Alesha fucking a friend of his out of the Enterprise 33 team; Elroy Coles.

"He's the joker that resembles Jingles a tad bit only shorter with a little more bulk to him right?"

"Right, that's him."

Clearly, I saw what Syrus - the security guard - meant when he said that he knew a source that knew a source who knew sorcerers, when I was younger. There was always a third eye watching to fill the mouth of masses with a unilateral story that everyone could add their own insight too.

"So... I mean where does your relationship stand with Jingles?"

"I'm just a shoulder to cry on for Jamiere when he's stressed or going through things that can't no one else figure out but me," she answered, nonchalantly. "Physically I satisfy him but it's not mutual, he doesn't gratify me at all."

"Meaning?"

"Meaning his dick isn't the size I prefer!" I could sense the aggravation in her tone of voice. "Plus I'm too spontaneous for him or should I say to fast for him. I may be here one day and in Hawaii the next... With him one night and with you or someone else the next morning. That's just who I' am, I'm an up north gal who's use to the fast life in New York. My motto is to spend and cum--"

"Spend and cum?" I was flabbergasted.

"Yes spend and cum, if I can't buy or have what I want and get pleased sexually the right way then whoever I'm with can't be my item."

'Gold digging bitch,' I thought giving her direct eye contact, Mimi couldn't be trusted and damn sure wasn't the type of woman to settle down with.

"And this is not being directed to you personally, my motto is strictly for them willies and sugar daddies that approach me. It's a different vibration when I seek the unpresuming, like I did when I sparked a conversation with you." The ringing of her phone distracted our conversation.

When Mimi answered she put her finger over her mouth suggesting that I keep quiet. The entire time that I ear hustled in on the phone conversation; I wondered what cat had her tongue? I couldn't hear much of the conversation, only the feed back that she was giving.

"At what time... I'll be there... I'm going to go straight there... No nobody has been following me... I'm going to run it through the machine and take it through the spot... Much as you do for me, would I do something like that? Okay I'll be there in an hour. Bye."

"I can see that your about to handle something important so I'm a head--"

"Not before I taste your head," she said, passionately, licking her pink lips.

"You have Jingles for that," I said, being sarcastic.

"Uh unh see Jingles money maybe long but the brother's dick isn't strong," she retorted, dropping to her knees.

$ $ $ $ $

After the quickie that Myesha and I shared, I jumped in my car and waited for her to leave out. So I could follow her to the destination that she was speaking about on the phone. I trailed Mimi for about twenty minutes on Interstate 676 going south, after we turned off on the Lawnside exit a small town right out side of Camden. Something was telling me to make a U-turn and head back to the city because the police didn't play fair ball in that area; if you looked wrong they were stopping you.

Mimi parked her brown Park Avenue in these complexes called Arbor wood Manor an apartment milieu that was very serene and clean. She got out the car and walked through this walk way that divided two other complexes and disappeared. She was where ever she was for so long that I began to nod off in the front seat of my car. I thought about hopping out of my car for a second to stretch but before could fully exercise the thought Mimi was cutting the corner with two nice size boxes in hand. There had to be something valuable inside the boxes because Mimi was being very cautious, watch unseen eyes that were watching her but there was nothing but diligence in her eye sight.

The boxes were stationed in side the trunk of Mimi's car as I trailed her back to Camden on I-295 North. State Troopers were everywhere on the highway as I drove back with caution; I was an unlicensed driver at nineteen.

I bared off the highway four exits before the North Camden exit, I ran out of patience following Mimi around plus I had bigger fish to fry and her pot of grease wasn't hot enough for me yet. The Morgan Blvd. exit took me right into Centerville because back tracking to North Camden to see Mimi wasn't a necessity; my primary concern was at Sophia's café. For a moment I felt like I owned up to Big Kyle's character but, stalking people wasn't my allure.

There were a few liquor dwellers and old fools out and around the side of Sophia's yapping and drinking when I cruised by searching for a place to park. The time was ten minutes to eight when I entered the café in search of Jingles. The place was no where near as thronged like the day of old Man Willie's party. And, it happened to be one dollar Wednesday, all drinks for a dollar until closing. Over the hump Wednesday wasn't a day that I preferred to drink or a day to drink for some people.

"Yo' nephew," Miguel called, sitting at the far end of the bar. From a distance I thought he was Jingles calling for me but he wasn't. "Have a seat Jingles will be through here shortly. Order what you please nephew I got the tab."

For me to only be in Miguel's presence a few times that was my first time hearing him say a complete sentence out of my mouth. He usually was very tranquil because his eyes did most of the talking.

"So Lesha Pooh is your sister huh nephew?"

"Yeah she's apart of my soul... Not to switch the subject though but I was wondering why do you keep calling me nephew?"

"Instead of me using the words man, boy, nigga, fella, slim, or jack, I say nephew."

To Miguel, nephew was like calling someone brother, the word was part of his unorthodox slang plus it was his nickname. The way he talked to me I sensed that his style was different then the guys he ran with through his body language.

"I'm the reason your sister and Jamiere have been together for as long as long as they have," he said, staring in the opposite direction. "You never really know what you're capable of having until its gone dig me?" Nah! I didn't know but it wasn't long before Miguel began to elucidate what he meant by it all.

At the time of him having Katonya Biggs as a mate and Alesha on the back burner but, wanting to replace Katonya at any given time. It wasn't that Miguel wasn't interested in Alesha, he just didn't vision Alesha doing the things that Katonya was doing for him; pertaining to maneuvering in the streets. Katonya was the type of female that would set a nigga up to get robbed and killed or went out of town to cop for Miguel and if she got caught she stuck to the script. Miguel was that street savvy and he did it to the best of his ability. His ability to be a hustler was handed down from generations of identical identities in his bloodline; from his flamboyant millionaire Uncle's Timothy "Tange" and Lance "Whop" Smith to his gorgeous risk taking sisters, Shannon "Shake" and Sabina "Bake" Smith. His need of a female to be a replica of his older sisters that would elevate him to the top of the drug underworld and being loyal was what he found in Katonya. Miguel didn't foresee Alesha's potential of being one and the same because back then her life style was based on buying materials, not making money.

Coming up in Centerville, growing up with dues like Fly Vance, Bumpsy and Snail, Lucky Lou, and Jingles. Miguel always secluded himself from the in crowd, he stayed to himself more then he did adventurous things with his crew. Miguel learned from his uncles that when you kept to yourself, it was extremely hard for the next person to figure you out, and the burden of other people's troubles wouldn't concern you. He was always there for his team wit it was time to get down, or when they wanted to meet at the round table but more than often he kept to himself.

On trial for this life in 1982 at seventeen and, the youngest member out of the Good Wood cartel all odds were stacked against Miguel Smith Jr., everyone was expecting Miguel to turnout to be the tattle tale that Author Jamison became. So with all of his comrades having the same perception, a few of them had the same intentions of killing him before he had a chance to give the prosecutors any information.

When he was released on bail in the winter of '81, a few months prior to the trial going into effect Miguel walked into a trap without realizing it was meant for him to stick to it. He remembered it as if it just happened to him a few hours ago, on a cold winter night in January '82, Lucky Lou, Jingles and a couple other guys picked Miguel up from his oldest sister Lateeda's house. Blind to the fact that anything was going to happened to him that day, Miguel obliged in taking the ride with his boys. The interior on the inside of the car was covered in white sheets and cloth towels; all the guys in the car were dressed in black with skull caps, gloves and guns.

Half way to Miguel's death point Jingles told the driver to spin the car around and drop Miguel back off. Miguel didn't realize that the plan was for him until after he lost trial and, Ezar explained the situation to him. What saved Miguel was Lateeda, she was the one who answered the door and recognized everyone in the car. So if anything would have happened to Miguel, homicide would have gone to all the known suspects in the car because they all were the last to be seen with him.

While his three childhood friends for losing trial and he was acquitted on all charges Miguel decided to abscond himself from Centerville until the heat blew over in his neighborhood; having extreme intentions of not returning to the environment that he was accustomed too. Because he felt that the love, unity and loyalty were no more inside the Good Wood banner. If Author Jamison could do that to them, how many other dudes inside of their circle had the same intentions? Now the main objective was to seek out who would be the next one to fold but, all the while, cross each other in the mean time.

It was delirious how Miguel found out about Jingles and Tonya's fling, furtively, behind Miguel's back Tonya Jingles went out to enjoy a night on the town. While out enjoying themselves, a female foe of Tonya's happened to be in the same place at the same time as she. Now this is how smooth and mendacious Tonya was simultaneously, she didn't only have Miguel as her main lover boy, and Jingles as her tranquil closet keeper. There was a third party, some guy by the name of Donell but was known to everyone by his nickname "Fat Lip." Donell was some flashy who loved showing off his possessions; he was getting a little paper but spent it on luxuriant materials for attention to procure attractive women. Nothing more than a mere slot machine to Tonya and was the insecure type also.

Allegedly, Tonya's female foe had something going on with the lame Fat Lip and the foe even showed Donell where Jingles lived. Donell, who was furious after receiving the information, squatted outside of Jingles' comfort zone until he got the drop on him and Tonya. The very next morning at dawn, Jingles was on his way out the door to take Tonya home when Donell hopped out of his car and started abusing Tonya. Jingles headed back in the house to retrieve a firearm but when he returned Donell and Katonya had pulled away.

Jingles gave chase until he had the chance to cut Fat Lip off with his car on the block where Katonya lived. With ambition to do Donell in right in front of the whore Tonya, Jingles hopped out of the car with two, twin 9mm handguns and forced them into the driver side of Fat Lip's window, ready to unload. But Tonya jumped in the way and begged Jingles not to shoot Donell so hesitantly Jingles retreated by pulling back his guns and trotting to his car.

Minutes later, Tonya and Donell had a fight inside their home, Donell felt so crushed he pulled out a gun and fired two shots into Katonya's back; leaving her in the house to die. Screaming for her young life not to end she was rescued by two men who just happened to be walking by.

Conclusively, the truth came to light while Katonya was hospitalized from being paralyzed from the waist down, Miguel use to visit her as often as he could. That's when she explained to him what had taken place and, her concealed relationship with Jingles. The entire time that Miguel was offering his love, time and dignity to Tonya she was stabbing him in the back. He left Tonya where she laid as if he never met her and as for Donell "Fat Lip," he went on the run from authorities after they found out the main motive and suspect.

Nothing destroyed Miguel more then when he found out from Katonya who the opposing foe was that enlightened Donell. His own sister Taffy was the one who caught Jingles and Tonya together and forewarned Donell about what she was observing. That's when Miguel realized that he was living and playing in a contaminated game and until this very day Miguel hasn't spoke to his conniving sister.

"So why Jingles?" I asked, astounded by the brief story. "Why continue to put your trust into him and have any dealings with him?" Miguel gave me a dubious look like he had no answer to give back.

"I mean why not deal with a guy who will die for the dame life I live... I mean neither one of us can blame him because money, drugs, whores, unworthy friends, family and cross come with this game here. It's just that you have to read between the lines and seek out those who will and won't get you caught up."

"So which do you think Jingles is capable of doing?" I asked, curious minded. Without a blink of an eye or hesitating at the lip Miguel retorted, "Jingles will never get me or you caught up... He'll kill us both then pull the trigger on himself before he lets some authoritative oppressor that knows nothing about this contaminated game trap us off. And in return I'd do the dame for him, why? Because I was raised in the game to fully understand that cross is boss. But in the end, all the bosses you crossed for gain will come back to haunt and cross you. You ever heard the cliché you reap what you sow in life?"

"Of course."

"Well when you have scattered deception, cross, mischief, and evil within those benevolent hearts of people and turned them into demons just like you. Or your exiling them for the means of a wealthy survival, then when the table turns the reaped shall figure your intentions out and come back for you. I know that the reaped of souls that I have annihilated are coming for me. I'm just patiently awaiting there return because what goes around comes around a hundred times harder.

Damn! Karma was a muthafucka and as I sat with my ears locked to Miguel's vital words of wisdom, I could feel the souls and hear the voices of Dontae, Kenny Morales, Big Kyle, D.S., and Lamaar's sister Pam orbit themselves around me giving me a sudden chill. As they began to whisper, "We're coming for you." The more I learned about the illicit life, it feared me even more then Almighty God in spirit. What was I suppose to do? Stop? Never, it was too late for that procedure to happen even if I could rewind the hands of time back to my adolescent days of living on 7th Street. Danger existed upon me so by all means I had to go all out or die trying.

"I still don't understand what you meant when you said, you never really knew what you're capable of having until it's gone," I said, eating a hand full of pretzels. Right before Miguel had the chance to give me a clear explanation, Jingles and Bumpsy were entering the Café. But, they didn't put a stop to what it was I was trying to get to make me understand.

"Alesha turned out to be a true trooper," he said, eyeing Jingles and Bumpsy as they slowly approached us. "The type of lady you need by your side that will love you when your broke or when your filthy fuckin' rich. There isn't too many niggas that women like Alesha will die for but when it comes to Jingles he's one warrior that she will die for. I had her but I let her slip through my finger tips, and if I could turn back the hands of time I would keep everything the same because it made us all into the people that we were written to be. Jingles don't really know the potential that his diamond possesses. Because if he did he wouldn't treat her like she wasn't apart of him being who he is." He winked his eye and ceased his words in unison as Jingles and Bumpsy walked up.

The three men embraced each other with hand shakes and smiles. "Kay," Jingles said, having an elated face. "What's good in your life time dude?"

"Everything's good," I replied, shaking hands with him and Bumpsy.

"Miguel you ready? Come on let's go handle this situation." Jingles and Bumpsy headed towards the exit door.

"Come on nephew your in on this too," Miguel said, removing himself from the stool.

$ $ $ $ $

The U-haul truck was in motion as I sat blind to my surroundings and tranquil in the back of the truck with Miguel. I didn't have to ask what type of mission we were going on because the mask and gloves that Miguel gave me spoke for themselves. Twenty minutes into the ride the U-haul truck came to an abrupt stop, making me aware that we had arrived at out destination. After Bumpsy unlatched the backdoor and let me and Miguel out, it was difficult to visualize the location because it was very gloomy.

Jingles knocked on this side door that was stationed over this garage; the stairs was adjacent to the garage.

"What's the word?" The thin voice on the other end of the door asked.

"Gorillas... Wolves... and Bears is what I fear," Jingles answered, as the lock on the door clicked and the door opened sesame.

"What took ya'll so long bee?" Sao asked, standing in the thresh old of the door with a joint dangling from his lip. Bumpsy just looked at Sao and walked inside.

"Aiight, let's make things happen," Jingles said, putting on a pair of black, leather gloves. "Everybody strap up... Jam you and Sao bring them muthafuckas out here." Jam who was sitting on the brown cloth sofa, took his time going into the back room to get whatever Jingles was asking for.

As I sat in the room with vigilant eyes trying to figure out what was going on I felt a part of the wall; everyone was attaining to something, paying me no attention. The only furniture that was in the room was a long sofa and a wooden coffee table that had an enormous amount of firearms and ammunition lying on top.

Sao and Jam came back into the front room, slowly pushing two chairs and there was two people sitting in them with sheets covering their bodily structures. The two bodies were alive, aggravated, moaning and gesturing for help fiercely.

"Man shut the fuck up!" Sao exclaimed, smacking the small figured anatomy over the head with the pistol.

"Cool out slim," Jingles replied, with out saying his name, while Bumpsy chuckled under his breath behind him.

"Yo' dude," Jingles said, nodding his head in my direction. "Come over here." I moved like a cadet in training, following all orders. "You gangsta my man?"

"Why wouldn't I be," I responded, shuffling my hands together.

"Aiight then grab two of those guns from the table over there--"

"No offense but I don't need too, I got two of them right here." Jingles averted his eyes around the room, nodding his head as everyone seemed impressed by my approach. I slid both barrels back quietly as I patiently waited for further instructions.

"Pull the covers off those two dead men breathing." Jam went to reach but Jingles stopped him in his tracks. "Nah slim let him do it."

I positioned myself behind the two chairs and pulled the sheets from over the bodies simultaneously, then I walked in front of them to get a clear look at who I was about to snore for all of eternity.

"Oh shit!" I yelled stepping away from the two bodies, all the guys in the room began to laugh at my frightful disposition.

My Uncle Muscles and Liquor Luby were the two men who were hog tide and taped up to the sturdy wooden chairs. After seeing my uncle and Luby in a frantic stage of fear I truly wanted to render my partaking in the mission; there was no way that I was killing my uncle.

"What's all this about?" I inquired, facing Jingles.

"Let him tell you," He replied, pulling the tape from Muscles' mouth.

"I'm not telling my nephew shit... Nephew stay--" Jingles cut his words short by sealing the duct tape back across his lips.

Jingles removed himself from the couch, stood up and took his black T-shirt off, revealing his flaccid upper body. "This is what this is about," He ranted, showing everyone his healed up bullet scars on his back. "The next time you send muthafuckas to kill me it will be in hell... And it better be all of Satan's Disciples."

In 1981, Muscles set word from the penitentiary to have Jingles exiled from Camden's rough streets. Jingles was shot in the back twice from long range with a twelve gauge shotgun, was hospitalized for a few months but managed to escape eternal sleep.

"Since your inception of dealing with my father and hustling in the city's streets... Cross has been your main objective," Jingles explained, circling the chairs. "You've crossed my father... My mother, who I don't give two fucks about but it's just the principles at hand, you've done so much fuckin'--"

"I wasn't' the one who put the hit out on the Dominican muthafuckas... Mikey and Richie," Muscles pleaded, blind folded. "And your mother... She, she was a fuckin' whore--"

Block-a! Jingles fired a single shot into Muscles' thigh and everyone else aimed their pistols in his direction. "You might have been one of the reasons she tried flushing me down the toilet to abort me."

Evidently, your past did come back to haunt you, there was a lot of deceitful things that my uncle committed in his past which crept up on his cordial soul. Deep within I thought that Uncle Muscles had a caring heart but everything that looked good wasn't always good for the all Seeing Eye. I also perceived the fact that my uncle never took any time out to widen my horizons and conscience about the inscrutable underworld. Precisely, I was assuming that it was some information that he was stealthily hiding.

"You think we don't know about you killing Shannon and Sabina thirteen years ago--"

"Them whores deserved whatever came their way--" Block-a! This time Miguel fired a single shot into the upper part of Muscles torso.

"They what pussy?!' Miguel had the face of a raging bull. "They were killed because of their equality and loyalty to you. All they wanted was to share a piece of the streets you solemnly claimed but they were raised up in."

"The drug underworld has no place for conniving women, "Muscles uttered, through a painful tongue.

"I can't tell they were the same two women who made you and your crew bow out of the game back in the day." Muscles sat silently. "Yeah the streets know everything, yo' Jay do this worthless muthafucka."

"Nah Armstrong, if Kyle has love for this game like he says he does then it's his obligation to put an end to Lamont Muscles Williams... The most dangerous man alive." Jingles laughed as he gave me the look of a malicious killer in a room full of vultures who were bred just like him.

Before I even budged there were a lot of dubious things that I needed to know prior to the handling of the two men, like... "What's the reason for Liquor Luby being here?"

"Because he's one of the main reasons why the operation sundown investigation is sweeping through the city. And, also the reason why the prices of heroin and cocaine are at an all time high."

Back when Luby accepted the shipment position from Muscles, Terry, and Billy to export lucrative amounts of money down south in exchange for imported drugs. Luby expanded his business, to a lot of other influential mongers in Camden including Jingles and the G.W.B's. But, what he didn't know was that the nexus " Chocolate Bippy," who Terry acquainted him with, was a law enforcement agent from Florida.

Hence, Liquor Luby was put into a compromising position, give us names of the mongers, buyers and suppliers who you take trips for, the estimate of cash and product exported and imported, and we'll promise you immunity and no jail time; also Luby got to keep the money and drugs.

"The streets are craving for product and it takes a weak link like this nigga to literally starve them," Jingles confide, very relaxed and calm on the sofa. "Anything else you want to know before we proceed?"

"Nah honcho, I'm cool."

"Well show us what you're made of."

I turned and faced my uncle and his intoxicated friend, positioning the gun in front of them, one on each side. I took a few deep breaths as if I was the victim and they were my last, exhaled vigorously, closed my young eyes and squeezed. Pop... Pop... Pop... And twenty-nine more ferocious rounds came behind them, followed by a few more clicks after I ran out of bullets but kept squeezing the trigger. I felt that if I could kill my own father what made me think I couldn't put my uncle to sleep. After I observed my uncle and Luby's soul slowly render their spiritless lives. It was at that exact moment in the room where I stood around a bunch of gun slingers and figured out that I was a natural born killer.

"Miguel and Bumpsy get rid of the bodies and Sao and Jam clean this spot up thoroughly," Jingles demanded, giving orders. They all concurred without any feedback.

"Kyle come with me I have something for you."

When Jingles and I left out of the apartment above the garage we hopped in his black Buick Park Avenue which was amid a bunch of trees and undergrowth and, drove back to the city.

We arrived at the Crestbury apartment complex right of off 8th Streets and Morgan Blvd. The apartments were some low income housing tenements that were being occupied by woman who were on welfare or that had low income paying jobs. Jingles used his apartment for business matters only, to count money, cut blow or a one night stand session with a whore so he wouldn't get caught up by his main honey dip Alesha.

There wasn't too much furniture inside the one bedroom apartment at R-1 Oak Walk. Only two leather sofas, a television and a kitchen set. I was uncertain of what was in the bedroom because my eyes didn't make it that far. But, Jingles did, he returned to the Kitchen with a brown paper bag in hand.

"What'd you know about this?" he asked, dumping two wrapped packages on the glass table.

"I can't answer that because I don't know what it is," I said, grabbing one of them.

"It's two keys of dope price at ninety-thousand a whole one. Since the D.E.A caught one of the Tri-state valley's major distributor... Larry Love a few weeks ago. It's been a mere drought out in the city right now, doe and cocaine is at all time highs like its Wall Street dude. Now I'm paying a half a bird more over the original price which was sixty-thousand a brick. It's cool though dude because you have to spend money to make money in this game."

Ninety-thousand a kilo was too steep for my short pockets, I couldn't even afford a ninety dollar cassette player let alone nine-thousand stacks in rubber bands. My Uncle Muscles was the only diplomat that could put money into my personal safety deposit box like that. But, I killed my obsolete "Come up," for a more lucrative one.

"So how much?" I asked, trying to figure out how much more money did Jingles need to live happy and comfortable.

"How much what?"

"How much more money do you need before you reach your zenith and give up the game?"

"Too much in this game is never enough because you can put a limit on what you're trying to make and once you make it, the money comes so fast. So you're like fuck it if it shows this fast I know my next flip will go just as fast then it becomes and intense rush. The next thing you know you have become addicted to the game and, you will do any and everything to keep that rush coming. It's truly a fucked up way of life--"

"So why not stop?"

"Because I'm into deep, the day I resign from the game is the day I dig my own death certificate. When you've done so much destruction and you know a lot about other desperados who have identical lifestyles, it's extremely difficult to get out. A kingpin's kingpin doesn't just up and leave without having adequate reasoning." The drug underworld was no different from the Mob atmosphere, better yet the beguiling government of America.

"Truthfully dude I'm trying to get it down for that fuckin' corporation money... A thousand key money... Role Royce money... China trip money... Las Vegas casino orange chip money, dig me?"

"Nah I don't pimpin' but I'm definitely imagining it." Jingles smiled wryly. "See I was only known for getting another hustler's money--"

"Well the only way to get you own, keep your own and make sure no one tries to take your own from you, is to cross those who are wealthier than you. Always remember that cross will always... Always be boss in the underworld and for the love of money period. You just have to devise an unorthodox strategy which will stand out from the rest of the people who think just like you."

Jingles' unworthy attitude and demeanor could have been one reason why he wanted my uncle dead. Muscles had old ancient money, money that was damn near thirty years old.

"Here's what I'm going to do for you Kyle," He said, lightly tossing one of the keys over to me. "These two bricks of dope are yours to keep."

"What... I ... I mean--"

"Close ya' mouth kid I'm full of surprises but let me tell you one thing, I'm not like my father."

"What'd you mean by that?"

"I mean I don't forgive and forget, my pops was good at birthing dudes into this game to get crossed in the long run. Holding other people's consequences as a burden over your head is worse then doing life in prison. Because even if you're doing good or bad you will always want revenge on a muthafucka."

Jingles paused, closed his eyes and released a strong amount of air from his lungs as if he was fed up with everything and everybody.

"I'm married to this game but I promised myself over and over again that I would never have a kid with it. For the first time in my life it feels like my conscience is eating me so I'm going back on my word. Why? I can't even answer that my fucking self, I guess it's because I like you Kay for one... For two, I have a mere vision of you being the next one to rule in this here game." Jingles grabbed my hand, placing his over mind. "But I want you to remember to never bite the hand that feeds you--'

"Jay you just have to remember not to choke the mouth that you're feeding," I retorted, as we gave each other direct eye-to-eye contact.

"Hmm, no one I've ever dealt with has ever given me such a sharp response the way that you have."

"I'm something great like William Johnson in his prime."

"Grab that," he said, pointing to the product. "So the city can be yours... Let's get out of here."

As we headed back to Sophia's Café so I could retrieve my car, Jingles explained how his operation in Centerville was run. Dope and cocaine were the only two drugs being distributed in the neighborhood. He had two coke flows, one on 8th Street and Ferry Avenue and the other on 9th and Vanhook Streets. There was only one heroin flow and it was on Central Avenue and Phillip Streets where it always was since the inception of a dope corner in the early 80's.

Jingles' reason for the two and one flow was due to his heroin flow accumulating more money in three nights than his coke flow did in a week's time. There was a three shift hustling schedule on each flow, twenty-four hours, and seven days around the clock. Sao and Jam were the runners who passed out the drugs and collected the cash after every shift was finished. They also watched over the hustlers who were on the corners pitching from the mound, hand to handing.

Everybody that hustled during the day or night in Centerville got paid at the end of every shift. There was a three person per shift hustle, nine shifts and, twenty seven mongers in all. They all got paid $300 dollars a night, if they didn't show they didn't get paid - simple regulations. Eighty-one hundred a night and fifty-six thousand, seven hundred dollars a week came out of the Good Wood Profits. More than the average doctor or lawyer made in a single year. Sao and Jam got paid monthly after calculating all the earnings made in that specific month; then they got there cut sort of a hustler's salary. Everyone else like Miguel and Bumpsy got paid off the flip or after the entire product was sold.

"Get with me Friday so I can break down those two keys and package them for you," Jingles said, as I got out of his car to get into mines. "Then on Sunday you can start making your ends meet--"

"What shift do you want me to go on?" I asked, standing in the threshold of the car door.

He looked at me thinking, trying to calculate some things or figure out a good shift for me to start on. "For you Kay… All three shifts, you can come out there all day, everyday. Okay dude?"

"Aiight cool."

I tooted my horn twice at Jingles while by passing him going down 7th Street, as he went to approach the entrance of Sophia's Café he turned and waved me off. The time was 1:30 a.m., an hourly atmosphere that reposed the souls of many working civilians. But to the young and restless such as myself, it was the start of a new day. North Camden was my next and final stop because my phallus longed for Myesha's sweet nectar.

$ $ $ $

A block away from Mimi's domain as I was positioning my car to parallel park, I observed Mimi departing from her home. She was carrying the same two brown boxes that she had earlier that day out in Lawn side. Mimi was dressed in all black attire, averting her eyes around every which way in a paranoid sense, rushing; she was definitely up to something.

"What the fuck?" I mumbled to myself, carefully watching Mimi maneuver. "Where can she possibly be heading to at…?" I glanced at my watch. "…Ten minutes to two in the got-damn morning."

Mimi placed the boxes in the trunk and pulled away from the house while I allowed her to get up in distance. I followed Mimi to the Pink Elephant - a city park that sat behind the Isabel Miller Center's pool - on the Vanhook Street side. She took the back road in her travel's to the park, the down town route, driving up Broadway to Vanhook's perpendicular street.

My car ran out of gas just as I went to make the left turn on to Vanhook Street. But, that didn't stop my foresight from losing track of Mimi's car. She was still under my visual surveillance until she parked her car two blocks away, grabbed the boxes and began to amble under the under path of the 676 bridge. I lost visual contact with her immediately after that, Mimi made a sharp right on to Master Street after walking quickly from the under path. Around the vicinity of the Pink Elephant's park near Vanhook and Master Streets, the area got extremely gloomy after the sun went down. As I trotted up Vanhook Street to regain observation of Mimi and her direction, I completely lost focus of her whereabouts due to the mist atmosphere.

When I reached the corner of Vanhook and Master Streets, I was a little winded and my legs had tightened up from the three block run.

"Damn!' I ranted, out of frustration, bending over placing my hands on my knees. "Where the fuck did she disappear to that quick?"

Mimi and the two boxes she was carrying just up and vanished into thin air, to the right of the park sat a huge field with flat surface grass that stretched about three-hundred yards. From where I stood, I could visualize Sophia's Café and some of the Manor projects on an angle, from a far.

"This shit is crazy Jack... I never witnessed any shit like this in my life," I babbled meticulously, scanning the area; there was nothing around me but land and street.

After giving up on the search I headed back to my car to see if it would start but I had no luck. I walked across the street to this bar that sat on the corner of Vanhook Street and Broadway to use the pay phone. I called for a yellow cab to come and take me to the nearest gas station to buy some gas. The yellow wheels took about ten minutes to come; the Hispanic cabby took me to this gas station a few blocks away from the bar and brought me back free of charge.

"No money papa," he said, having a heavy Spanish accent, waving my money off. "Me know how it feels to be stranded too. Plus me made enough pesos for tonight." He smiled, revealing his sparkling gold tooth.

"Primo, Como se llama?" I asked, wanting to know his name.

"Me llamo David... Dave same thing papa--"

"Kangaroo," I replied, shaking his hand.

"Kang - aa- roo, what kind of name is that papa? You no animal papa but Kangaroo cool wit you... Kangaroo cool wit me too."

"Oh one more thing primo before you pull off."

"Que?"

"Tell taxi number 524 that his ass is mine." Dave gave me a weird look like he didn't know who I was referring to.

"Me don't deal with these midea goans out here they loco papa."

"Aiight Spanish Dave I hear you primo, thanks for the ride."

Spanish Dave was long gone after I poured the gas into my tank and got in my car to go home.

# Chapter. 26

Friday morning I woke up with nothing but money and business on my mind, it was time to come up once again and hold my own weight; only this time there had to be accurate decisions made. Jingles called me a day earlier elucidating that he had pushed our session back and scheduled it for the morning because he had some essential business to take care of. Which wasn't a problem for me due to some secondary situations that I had to catch up on.

The time was 9 a.m. when I decided to groom myself and head across town to the Crestbury apartments. Subsequently, as I was grabbing a bite to eat from the refrigerator the phone rang. Contemplating on answering it, I hesitated because I was going to let the machine record the call. When I picked up to say hello, simultaneously, my mother picked up and answered before I had the chance to get the H sound out of my mouth. So, being immature and nosey I decided to listen in on the call and with my palms over the receiver I tuned in.

"Hello, who am I speaking with?" my mother asked, having a wearied voice.

"This is Jamiere." Jamiere! Not Jingles what the fuck was he doing calling my house? I assumed he was calling for me, please God let him be calling for me, I prayed out loud.

"Oh hi Jay, I wasn't expecting you to call this early in the morning."

"I'm sorry if I awoke you... I promise to relax your soul when I see you," He said, sensually.

"That sounds nice, so other then that what has you ringing my phone this early because you know you're a busy man to contact."

"I tried calling you a couple of time a few days ago but some guy picked up... Sounded like your son so I just hung up."

"Yeah it probably was him, he's been staying with me for the past month or so."

So it was the anonymous calls form Jingles that made me discern that there was a stalker on the loose.

"But listen, I might need you to handle some work for me--"

"When?"

"I'm not sure of the date and time but I'm trying to put that into effect as we converse over the horn. I'm making you aware now so nothing won't catch you off guard and seem too unexpected. But, I promise to fill you in when I feel you in, catch me?"

"It's caught, just follow through and don't have me waiting forever."

"You know that's not my M.O., I'm much smoother than that."

"I know that's right."

"Later."

"Bye-bye."

After all three lines disconnected, I wanted to run up the stairs and strangle my mother until she turned purple from my infuriation. I tried to obstruct the incident and act like everything was an illusion, Jingles fucking my mother had to be an erroneous matter; it was just too hard to believe. But, it wasn't that hard to find out and believe me I was going to find out even if it cost me my life.

I got to R-1 Oak Walk so fast that it felt like my wheels and gas tank was filled with helium; all my frustration was in my foot as I drove over to the complex.

"Damn Kyle! What the fuck nigga? You knockin' like the fuzz with a warrant," Jingles said, nervously.

"That's because I was just getting chased by them boys in blue," I retorted, lying through my teeth.

"Did you shake'em?" He asked, taking a second look out of the apartment door.

"I think so... They were in my peripheral before I ran the light on Master Street and Morgan Boulevard."

Jingles waited about a half hour before he started to cut the first key of dope and mix it in a coffee blender with a compound drug called "Morphine." Simultaneously, while he was amalgamating the dope with the cut into the blender, Jingles showed me how to measure the portions of dope with a rolled up dollar bill and package them inside the tiny glassine bags.

Curious minded, the relationship, friendship or whatever kind of social attachment that Jingles and my mother were having, bothered me to the point of inquiring into the situation. As we both attained to our labors of perfecting the opium I began questioning his life growing up around Big Kyle.

"So what was it really like having Big Kyle as a guardian growing up in his presence?" Jingles stopped in motion, dropped the playing card and the glassine bag of dope and began to reminisce on the good old days growing up.

"All man growing up with your pops being my overseer was to fast for my own eyes back then."

He elucidated that Big Kyle was on the go and in the streets so much that he use to take Jingles over various amounts of women's houses when he was a kid - around six or seven - and have them baby sit until he returned. Jingles admitted that Big Kyle was a mere ghetto bachelor in his heyday. He had whores by the dozens that loved him so much that they would die for him if they had to. Jingles respected Big Kyle because his word was everything to him, what Big Kyle said - went and, he controlled his realm with discipline and perfection; Kyle Sr. didn't take any shit.

Prior to becoming a full, ripe teenager at the age of ten, Jingles started to visualize the street life that Big Kyle lived by day to day nothing more than a hustle. Big Kyle and D.S. had him hanging around local brothels, whore strips, card games and bars.

"Big D.S. taught me how to shoot craps when I was ten with trick dice and what numbers to shoot from so my point would come much faster," Jingles said, filling the glassine bags up with dope. "And I got my dick sucked too when I was ten--"

"You jiven," I said, very surprised.

"No shit slim." He began to chuckle while explaining. "Ya' pops got it done for me, he made Shake... Shannon... Miguel's oldest sister did it to me. Your pop was a muthafucka slim when it came to them hoes. I wish Shake was still around so I could have gotten some of that trim now."

Jamiere had a despicable way of thinking when it came to dudes out of his crew or people that were close to niggas in his crew. I could never disparage my friend's family no matter what the circumstances was and still look at him or them as brothers.

When my pop's got addicted to heroin and began to lose all his money, valuables, materials, and women; he lost and forgot about Jingles as well. In a short time span, just when he turned eleven Jingles carried the burdens of responsibility and manhood on his back like a pile of lumber. Indirectly, he stated that a few of Big Kyle's jades tried their best to support him but, they had dependents and other responsibilities to attain too. Plus without Uncle Tommy around things just wasn't the same. Reading between his crooked communication, I assumed that the jades he was referring to, my mother had to be one of them. I was tempting to ask him but, I held back my tongue.

"So that's when the streets came into play for you?" I asked, continuing to package the dope myself.

"That's when the illicit life began to overwhelm my positive expectations in life and, I've been walking the crooked life every since."

I was down hearted by how Jingles grew up, I felt his pain because I was one in the same; facing responsibilities at such a young age. In the same breath though, I was proud of how Jingles matured through his struggles and carried himself as a man who was once a waif.

"So do you have nay other siblings around your age?"

"Yeah," He replied, in disgust. "I have two older sisters that live down south, I see them occasionally when I go to family reunions but other than that they're live their lives. And, I had an older brother he's dead now though."

"Sorry to hear that cool--"

"That's how life operates you known? We all have to go some day," he said, nonchalantly.

Jingles and I didn't converse that much during the remainder of time we had left bagging up the dope. My focus was to finish up and go attain to some other unfinished business that needed to be handled. We finished bagging the two birds at something to two in the morning. When I accumulated all of the firm glassine baggies into a black garbage bag, there were three-thousand bricks that I counted out by hand. There were fifty clips of dope in a brick which was retailed at the amount of twenty dollars. All I kept saying to myself was, 'I'll be a millionaire in one flip if everything went as planned and I sold each brick.' Sunday was my big day and I patiently anticipated the day to come, my eye balls rolled with illuminant dollar signs in them.

"Kyle do not get careless with your hustle or money," Jingles said, cleaning up the residue on the kitchen's table. "From a dollar to a million keep your hustling mentality the same."

"Very low key?"

"Always bubble quietly, I don't want to take back my generosity and exclude you from my family. I've seen the best in the game lose everything due to arrogance and cockiness. Second chances don't come often in this way of life... Don't blow yours."

I absorbed Jingles' every word and made sure it found spot on my brain to burn as I kept repeating the phrases, "Don't get careless," and "Bubble quietly," over and over in my head. The first time a wise man told me those words they happened to go into one ear and out the other; I got real careless and it almost cost me my life.

"I'll see you Sunday morning," Jingles said, from the kitchen as I was heading out the door.

"Sure thing."

"Oh, and one more thing."

"What's that cool?"

"Make sure you store that dope in a cool area or else it will go bad."

"Aiight."

"Do you want me to hold on to it for you?"

"Nah I got it." Thinking with a hustle's mind, like he might sell it to himself, keep the cash and forget all about me, I wasn't trying to take that chance. "Sunday morning," I said, leaving out of the apartment, closing the door behind me.

No soon as I left Jingles I went and stored the trash bags of dope at the town house on 7th Street inside the bottom bend of the refrigerator. Then, I changed clothes, threw on my mission gear and, grabbed my gun that I had hidden inside one of my Little sister's teddy bears; Reason being, there was someone that worked on 5th and Market that had some vital information that I needed, and a lot of explaining to do.

The time was around five p.m. when I pulled in and observed that City Hall's parking lot thronged with cars and I swore to myself I was at Big Hustler's car lot for a second time. The whore Kelli finally came out from a hard day of work to get in her car, after I waited patiently with a frustrated mind for two hours for her to exit the building.

I trailed Kelli from City Hall to a residence to Rosedale Avenue over on the east side. Since it wasn't night fall at that particular time, I watched Kelli from the time she got out of her car until she unlocked the door to the addressed home of 6444. Once the home of 6444 became a photographic picture to my cerebral area, I strolled over to this fast food joint called "Mario's," which was stationed a couple blocks away on Westfield Avenue. I just wanted to grab a bite to eat before the sun submerged so I could make my final move on Kelli. As I waited for my Mozzarella sticks and fries to get done I shot a few games of pool to pass time.

I lost a few quick bucks to this gorgeous, caramel dame by the name of Diyah; she was in her mid-20's, a set of chinky eyes and an anatomy like she was a weight trainer or something. After getting in my pocket for about ninety-dollar Diyah offered to treat me to a few drinks over a casual conversation with my money; she was very smooth.

"So where are you from?" she asked, bringing the drinks back from the counter.

"I'm from South Camden--"

"What part?"

"Centerville."

"Centerville? Oh you're from Dodge City, a place where it's hard to get trapped off at if you know the neighborhood but easy to be targeted if you are not from there."

Dodge City was a new name to my ears, I was assuming that the meaning Diyah expressed to me was mainly the reason Centerville had that nickname. "I have a few relatives who reside out there," She expressed, as I admired her beauty.

"So are you from out here?" I countered her question.

"Yeah, I'm from across the street," She implied, pointing out of the side view window which we at near. "Over there in Westfield Acres."

Westfield Acres were located on Westfield Avenue, directly across the street from Mario's steak place. The building was broke down into about fifteen housing project high rises; the biggest high rise tenement in Camden. I'd never been in the gloomy high rise projects but I was informed that they were no different from Centerville. There was a sign that sat out in front of the building that read "If you don't live here we advise you not to move here." The word on the street was that the only drugs being distributed out of the Acres were cocaine and marijuana.

In the rear of the Acres on 32nd Street below the high rises was a spot known to many as "Unknown." I never had a legitimate understanding of why people called it that; just the name alone made someone be on alert of any suspicious activity. Unknown all so had another nickname called the "Deuce," short of 32nd Street of course. Instead of using the three from the street numbers the hustler's out there took the number two and made a street terminology out of it. The name didn't necessarily mean anything to the mongers who were in the vicinity trying to make ends meet; to them a buck was more important.

"So how much money do you think comes through there by the week?" I inquired, being nosey.

"If you want to find out go over to the Deuce and as them cats for yourself. I don't know shit... Yo' can be working for the Feds or some shit," She said, degrading my character.

"What! Bit--" I caught myself, realizing that I was in the wrong environment to start controversy.

"You got the wrong solider cutie... Feds... Ha."

There wasn't a smile on Diyah's face; the expression she gave me was an expression for me to do something to convince her that I wasn't an informant for the law. We both gave each other direct eye contact with out a single blink, trying to read each other's persona though the pupils.

"Come here," I said, grabbing her from the table and pulling her into the restroom in the back of the store; I shut the door behind us.

"Muthatfucka what are you... Get the fuck off--"

"Shh," I said, putting my hand over her soft lips.

I backed away from her, reached for my waist and pulled out a .44 handgun that was already hard with a nut buster in the chamber; waiting to explode.

"What the fuck you gone do with that?" She asked with aggression. "Shoot me because I figured your lame ass out nigga?"

I raided the .44 about five inches so it could stare her directly in the face, only to calm her. "I like your aggressive character Ms. Tough it's kind of cool," I said, caressing her body with the burner. She gestured passionately from the touch of the gun as if pistols turned her on. "I love when someone disgruntles my manhood because it's a thrill in itself to show other wise. And since you have giving me such a thorough impersonation thus far, I'm willing to show you something that the Feds won't do without probable cause or a warrant. Do you accept my offer?"

Staring at me with a fervid attitude, having visions of me penetrating her insides Diyah answered me sincerely. "Yeees, I accept."

By the time I finished explaining what it was I was trying to do at the house on Rosedale Avenue and what it was that I needed from Diyah the day break had turned into night fall. Diyah believed the lie I told her about some lame that lived on Rosedale who owed me an enormous amount of cash that I had eagerly been waiting for; she was entitled to half of the money if everything went accordingly. Once she heard the word cash roll off my tongue she was trying to grab the .44 magnum from my waist and handle the mission herself.

As Diyah and I ambled back around the block to Rosedale Avenue, she was stopping at damn near every car trying to fix her hair and lipstick.

"What's all that for?" I said, throwing my hood over my head. "You're not going to a blind date sweetheart--"

"So what, I still want to look presentable if somebody comes to the door."

Something was telling me that Diyah wasn't the person she proved herself to be, all hard and tough. I wanted to tell her that it was wrong timing but it was too late for an excuse because we were a house away from Kelli's home.

"Here put on this," I said, handing her a black bandana.

"What the fuck is this?"

"Shhh, a scarf to cover your face with now put it on," I snapped, looking around to see if I spotted Kelli's car. I found it; the car was still parked and stationed in the same place as before.

"When you ring the door bell and ask for Mr. Right turn around and let your back face the door. That way if some one peeks out of the window or the peep hole they won't be able to see your covered face."

Kneeled down behind Diyah's thick, firm legs, I was waiting for Kelli to respond to the ringing of the door bell. Diyah pressed the door bell a few more times after she didn't get a haste response. Without anyone answering the ringing of the bell, I heard footsteps approaching from the other side of the door.

"Just a minute," Kelli's voice pleaded as she began to unlock the door.

While Diyah stood holding the metal screen door with her side shoulder, patiently, I moved once I observed the opening come from the front door.

"Oh my god! Please... What's going on?" Kelli yelled at a high pitched voice, backing into a corner on the inside porch.

"Shut up whore before I push pizza out of your head," I replied, in a raspy voice, with my gun aimed to shoot. Diyah followed suit, without hesitating she quickly shut both doors behind her. "Get up," I said, to Kelli who had a look of dread on her face. "Do as I say and you will not be harmed."

Diyah and I took Kelli up stairs and stripped her naked, out of the little bit of attire that she was already wearing. We placed her feet inside some scorching hot water and tied her hands to the sturdy shower rod. Diyah went and found an empty bucket for us and for every question that Kelli didn't answer or lied about when respectably asked, Diyah was to throw a bucket of hot water on to Kelli's light flesh. And, I was going to follow through with lashes form my thick, black, leather belt.

"Whore, who the fuck are you?!" I asked, patiently waiting for her to lie. I received no feed back so I followed through with my unusual punishment.

After one bucket of scolding hot water and two lashes from the belt, Kelli was hollering for God's angels to come and save her but the only thing was, Diyah and I were the only two people that could hear her cry out.

Three times I followed through with my painful procedure trying to make Kelli confess to her true lies but all I got was her wailing gestures and no success. With tears in her eyes, Diyah began to feel sympathetic for Kelli. She grabbed my arm giving me an indication to stop, Diyah dropped the plastic pale and exited the bathroom; I gave chase.

"What's the matter, why'd you leave out?" I asked, standing in the middle of the upstairs foyer.

"I... I can't bear to stand in there," she said, pointing toward the bathroom. "And see you torture the poor, beautiful woman any longer."

I gave Diyah a look of disgust wondering to myself what happened to the tough, courageous imager she showed back at Mario's.

"Just like I thought," I whispered, hugging her while wiping the tears from her eyes.

When we went back to untie Kelli from the shower rod something peculiar happened. Kelli was in the middle of the bathroom floor, on her knees with her gun raised up at us.

"What the--"

"Don't you do it muthafucker," Kelli cried out, as I went to reach for the steel on my hip. "Reveal who you both are before I grab my cuffs and call in for back up."

Diyah and I both gave each other reluctant looks with eyes of refusal, not wanting to show our true identities. It wasn't like I didn't have other options to choose from because I did; I could have easily turned and ran out of the enormous bathroom while taking a shot in the back. Or take one to the front of my torso after I grabbed hold of my piece and tried licking off a few rounds...

"Please do as I say two homicides isn't something that I want on my conscience for you not following simple directions but I do have the authority to do it... Now please do as I ask."

As I went to reveal my identity by pulling sown the bandana, Diyah went with my first imminent option and took off running. I looked and tried to grab her but Diyah was to fast and out of arms reach. Simultaneously, Kelli fired a single shot towards the threshold of the bathroom door. I had no clue where the bullet landed but it didn't penetrate into Diyah's flesh because I heard no clamorous screams and her body didn't hit the floor.

"Fuck! I missed," Kelli said, aggravated, aiming the gun at me. "But I damn sure won't miss the next time... Remove the fuckin' scarf." She ambled slowly towards my person with red bruises tainted on the front of her naked body.

Kelli was egg-eyed after seeing who the man behind the mask. "Kyle," she said, astounded dropping the gun to the floor. I stood in mere silence. "Baby what are you... Why... I mean," she couldn't even come to terms of my malicious actions.

"Call the fuzz and press charges against--"

No!" She exclaimed, grabbing my hand. "I can't... it won't be any of that, come with me into my bedroom," she said, holding her bruised breast.

After trailing Kelli into the bedroom, she gave me three cloth towels and told me to soak them in cold water so she could soothe some of the burning on her body.

"Why'd you lie to me about your name and who you really were?" I asked, lightly tapping her forehead with a cold rag.

"Because," She paused, and averted her eyes into another direction before speaking again. "I didn't want you to get the wrong impression on me."

"Wrong impression, what'd you mean by that?"

"The impression of me being a cop, trying to get close to you so I could get into your Uncle's operation and bring forth some indictments." I went to respond but she intervened. "Don't ever ask how I know about your dealing with Lamont Muscles, just know that I've been on an investigation unit for four years now... Need I say more?" I didn't even responded, I just nodded my head in reluctance.

Kelli elucidated that her name was indeed Kelli Right and she had become a police officer right after graduating high school. Her extraordinary, strategic abilities and aggressive heart to bust a lot of top notch criminals earned her a position on the Fierce investigation known as "Operation Sundown." Known to her colleagues as "Suicide," due to delving up vital information and, evidence on distinctive suspect and other criminals. By the time indictment time came around, the suspects made it easy on themselves and took the easy way out of eternal circumstances by killing themselves.

"I hate that name too," she stated very relaxed. "I don't mean to be so obnoxious or become excessive about how I go about apprehending my suspects because everybody deserves a fair chance but I love getting the job done. Maybe it's because... Nothing, never mind--"

"No, no continue... Whatever is bothering you please feel free o render your true emotions to this hoodlum," I expressed, displaying a wry smirk.

"Well remember my older brother Ernie that I was telling you about that's suppose to be in the army?"

"Yeah I remember you telling me about him."

"Well he's sort of a commander of his own army and it's not being authorized by President Regan either." She pushed my hand away from her forehead and sat up on the bed. "He's a drug dealer that's caught up in the vehement investigation as well." Tears began to profuse behind her words of truth. "I told him years ago prior to me even joining the force to get out the game and find a more productive profession. But, it was like making lucrative amounts of money were a drug to him and his addiction kept increasing to the point of dying to stay rich."

Ernie Right better known in the underworld as E-Tyson was born and raided in East Camden. He began slinging dope in the Acres eleven years ago when his naïve young sister was only in the eighth grade. A hustle that started out just to stay fly with a couple of duckets in his pocket, soon escalated into a full time career. With the money, power, and respect that he earned from inside of the Acres and throughout East Camden, Ernie managed to form his own "Cream Team." He and three childhood friends, Ali Garrett, Ty Brinks, and Mousey Meeks were the three men he took from clocking inside of the arch's hallway's to building a distribution set in the back of the project buildings on 32nd Street; now one of Camden's prolific drug markets. The Deuce alone profited estimates worth $350,000 dollars by weekly, not including the marijuana cascade that's inside almost every arch in the Acres. The name of the marijuana product called "Pine-sol," was being heavily distributed in the area; going for five dollars a bag. Revenue similar to the cocaine profits at an amazing $275,000 dollar week consumption. Both, the Deuce and the Acres' drug market profits are valued at mere $30 million dollar year equity.

"Will you have the courage to bring him down?" I asked, wondering what her true intentions were. Kelli's face turned livid from my questioning as she looked extremely confused; not even wanting to respond.

"I... I have no choice but to do just that, his ass has forced my hand so much that it's to the point that I don't like playing cards no more."

Prior to Kelli joining the investigation team, her duties as patrol officer in East Camden was not a social inner city drive. She and her ex-partner Dyonne Mays were the reason Ernie and a lot of his friends were never arrested or even apprehended for questioning about homicides and robberies that took place inside the arches of the Acres. Kelli would forewarn Ernie on any raids, search warrants, or specific people that the Camden Administration wanted to put forth or capture. Kelli expressed that she never made a single arrest on her brother's turf in the six years that she'd been patrolling the streets. Any dealer that Kelli caught on the Deuce or inside the arches would be cuffed and, all belongings and money confiscated and given a severe ass kicking. But, would never charge them with any crime, basically purging them of any imputations that they were guilty of. Kelli would literally turn the drugs back into Ernie and give the money to local shelters or homeless people she by passed on the street.

Things went sour for Kelli when her ex-partner Dyonne Mays was arrested in 1985 for importing and exporting drugs and money in and out of Camden city. Dyonne was placed under investigation after Jimmy Dartaine got an anonymous tip that Dyonne was doing illegal business within her daily accountabilities of being an honest cop. Her house was raided after the courts presented a legal search warrant to probe. A hundred pounds of marijuana, five kilos of cocaine and a $100,000 dollars in cash was found inside Dyonne's residence. Dyonne's testimony inside her indictment documentation was firm; she took the weight for all the illegal material; without mentioning any names. Ironically, her colleagues weren't incompetent of knowing that there another faction whom had Dyonne storing their goods; they just couldn't pin point the suspects. Dyonne managed all the weight of carrying two heavy burdens, she didn't rat and she got sentenced to twenty years in federal prison.

After the bust on her long time friend and partner, Kelli was placed on convenient supervision while she went under six months of interrogating investigation because of her ex-partner's imprudent behavior.

"When I first joined the force I told Dyonne and my brother to render their sexual relationship but my words were like stone to them," She said, wiping her tears across her face. "She chased his money and he couldn't stop chasing her panties. It hurts like hell to now when I receive vital letters from her and she tells me that everything's going to be okay and no matter how hard things may get she never wanted me to blame Ernie for being a product of his environment."

2005 seemed like forever in Kelli's eye, picturing Dyonne being released from jail when she's forty-seven would be like being acquainted with a stranger all over again.

"What about Ernie do he and Dyonne still keep in contact with each other?"

"Rarely… So imagine what the outcome will be in eighteen more years? It will be like Ernie never existed to her."

Ernie did manage to give Kelli five-hundred thousand dollars to put away for Dyonne's return. But, to Kelli money wasn't the issue, her friend's life and freedom meant much more than all the money in the world.

"It's a must that I make him feel her pain," she replied, with the devil in her eyes. "That's the only way I will be able to ease the rigorous pain inside of my heart."

To calm her nerves Kelli took a warm shower for relaxation, what made the shower even better was when she invited me to join in. She wanted to compensate me for the tongue bath she received a while back; our passionate sex scene was déjà vu all over again. Kelli stood over me with one leg positioned over my back as I kneeled down with my face inside of her sweet licorice my tongue simulated he mind so good that she almost drowned herself under the show head, as she searched for air.

After a fervid struggle of trying to penetrate Kelli's warm tunnel I was satisfied with the fact that I was the first nigga to make a passage way through her vaginal area. She was so tight that it felt like my skin was burning as I stroked in bitter-sweet pain, Kelli moaned out of mere pleasure.

"Oh god… You feel so good," she expressed, impinging her nails into my back.

Kelli held a firm grip on the shower rod as I had her pressed into the corner of the tub, fucking her like I never knew her. Fifteen minutes tops, I was weak on my knees and gasping for my own air; Kelli's trim was that delectable.

"Kyle once you rejuvenate I need you to get dressed, I need you to take this ride with me somewhere," she said, stepping out of the shower. It was like our intercourse had no affect on her decorum what-so-ever. She made me feel like I was the receiver and she was the giver.

Kelli wanted to give me insight on the fierce investigation that's been impatiently anticipating some success for a long time. Kelli figured it was the least she could do since I was already caught up in the drug quest and her brother was too. She told me to follow her lead and directions so everything could run smooth. The time was twelve midnight when we arrived at this remote establishment where the Operation Task Force held their head quarters. I was hand cuffed in the back seat of a gray unmarked Grand Marquis; she had to falsify the apprehension so no one would give her a suspicious eye.

"Look sit right here let me go and check to see if everything is clear so I can bring you in quietly," She said, unbarring the driver side door.

I couldn't help but to get a hard look at the Operation's establishment and the vacant vicinity around me; it was for future references. With the furtive stratagems that lied dormant under my sleeve it was quite possible that I was trying to destroy the head quarters. But, the head quarters sat in a deserted atmosphere like whoever owned the acres of land orbited around the establishment, had knocked down an enormous amounts of Mansions, leveled the soil out and left the homes where the head quarters was for their own personal use. After scrutinizing the vicinity, for the life of me, I had no idea where Kelli brought me too.

"Okay it's clear in there," Kelli rejoiced, grabbing her personals from the front seat of the car. She opened the rear door to let me out and unstuffed me. "I only have an hour to show you bits and pieces of the information and evidence that we have before the one o'clock shift storms in... So pay very close attention."

I was inside but the further Kelli took me to probe, the more I fretted, why? Because the entire situation felt like a set up, there was desk phones, paper, confidential documents black boards and, pictures everywhere on the inside of the main office area. The place was very hollow and gutted out like a huge gymnasium. Through assumptions the place looked like it belonged to a famous entertainer or entrepreneur.

"This is our main objective for the investigation of Operation Sundown," Kelli said, showing the first page of what looked like a ten page document.

Drug importation and exportation from South America into America, southern states into Camden, New Jersey; unknown drug related homicides encountering the massive drug market; and destroyed personal evidence which was sufficient to the operation and cases prior too; that was the entire objective.

"Since the early 60's Camden has been a prominent city for purchasing and distributing tones of narcotics," Kelli stated, walking towards the huge blackboard that had a depicted picture outline from the labeled drug lords to subordinate street scramblers. "And here's who it start's with," Kelli said, pointing to the two men at the top of the board. "Eric Cabrera and his long time partner and relative Jose Colon, known to corporate America as the Sons of Escobar."

It wasn't like Kelli was tell me something that I didn't know but what was essential to my livelihood was, how was so much narcotics being imported into Camden without any law agencies making any bust or captures of the drug lords?

Eric and Jose's facial appearances were no different from vicious Mob bosses. They looked to be in the early stages of the forty-fifty age brackets. Eric had flaxen salt and pepper hair, dark eyes and a ruff skin tone. Jose on the other hand, had faded hair almost bald, smooth spotless skin, a neat goatee and, a black mole under his right eye; they both had emigrational drug lord appearances.

"But why Camden?" I asked, trying to figure out what Camden had that other major cities such as Philly, Baltimore and New York didn't have. "Why would two affluent, bean eaters from a South American city, that's populace holds more than fifteen million people, make a city that only holds over a hundred thousand citizens, its' major drug investment and exchange? Why not California or Texas?"

"Think about it for a minute, when you have a city that's amid three major cities... Two of them being metropolitan areas. Washington D.C... New York and the other one being Philadelphia. Why not find a local city that has three major highways and interstates, no coast guard department to inspect any strange boats or ships moving up and sown the Delaware River. And a police department that's on the outskirts of the urban show case that has been under investigation since the inception of the prolific drug war. There was no firm protection, rules, or guidelines for the residential mongers to live by."

In June of 1966 the Camden police department which use to be stationed downtown adjacent to city hall, was blown up and demolished. After two unidentified men, suspected to have been apart of the city's drug realm, which was ran by Richard and Michael Munez. They walked in the department with C-4 explosives strapped to their bodies, grenades in hand and, took a walk on the wild side so the inflation of Camden's drug market could excel.

Seven hundred people were killed behind the disaster and, there was no one to blame or any logical motives to probe as to why the matter took a horrifying turn. Subsequently, during the reconstruction of the city's downtown area and the pursuit of state troopers and the FBI coming in and out of the city to fulfill their duties of protecting and serving. The Camden drug market became the east coast atomic bomb, exploding narcotics all over the place.

The city of Camden's name quickly was changed and became the "Sugar City," sue to its successful production of qualified narcotics and quantities of federal reserved notes.

"And don't misconstrue the prowess and intelligence of the Sons of Escobar, they are definitely a world wide name and major distributor," Kelli expressed, showing me a few photographs of Eric and Jose meeting with other men whose status favored theirs out in Las Vegas, New York, and Los Angeles.

"It's just that no other geographical city has the architecture or structure as the one built in Camden into other outer towns and cities.

Every name that had been mentioned to me followed with insight was on the aligned drug board. The Sons of Escobar without Kool Kirby and Cuban Pete, the Dominican Brothers, Lamont Muscles, Big Kyle, Billy Bad Ass, Dontae "Big D.S." Wardon, Riley and Domino, the R.S.D. crew, Jimmy Fidell, the Good Wood Boys, Ernie Right, Larry Love, Timothy Freeze and the gorgeous faces of Shannon and Sabina Smith.

There were so many other distinctive faces on the black board; I only had enough time to get a glimpse of the ones that I knew by name. There were hundreds of names and pictures but majority of the photos had big, red X marks on them which implicated death. The only faces that I didn't observe on the board were the ones of Terry, Princess Pooh, Missy Amoure, Chocolate Bippy and, Tange and Whop.

Desks were garnished with old photographs of aforementioned drug lords and low leveled mongers by the boxes. Each box was labeled by the year, time, and rendezvous; wrapped in thick rubber bands. Pictures of on duty cops shaking hands with street thugs and local dealers, cops apprehending suspects and, photos of local tenements and remote establishments that were put under surveillance during certain investigations. I didn't have any more time to view the thousands of photographs that were on display but there were two specific pictures that caught my attention and marveled me.

One picture had Jimmy Dartaine and this other black man standing by an unmarked car dressed in suits with their guns out. "Who are the two guys in the picture with the expensive suits on and the guns?" I asked, pointing to the photo.

"Oh, they were two of Camden's most lethal detectives thirty years ago... James Dartaine who is now Captain and Chief of the Camden Police department and Operation Sundown. And, Keith "Quarters" Inglewood... Captain Jimmy's old friend and partner. He was looked upon as the ancient Shaft before Richard Roundtree's role was even perfected. He was killed in the line of fire in 1961, word was that he was a corrupt cop who got excessive money on the side by keeping dealers out of raids and jail. Also making sure local drug lords got their imported shipments on time--"

"A local conspirator?"

"Without question... Vets on the force believe it was some of the street ruffians who he often compromised with, that killed him."

"And, what about this picture?" I positioned it over top of the other one I held. "Who are the three gorgeous females in the picture with the guy Keith that's shaking hands with Lamont Muscles?"

"I'm not sure... They look as if they can be his daughters, why is there something wrong?"

"No not at all, just curious," I said, knowing exactly who one of the girl's were in the picture.

Terry was the teenage female standing in the middle of the other two females who was standing alongside her in the picture. I'd recognize her face if it was decomposed, the other two young females looked familiar but I couldn't place an accurate description on them. Keith Quarters shaking hands with my Uncle Muscles with Terry and two other girls in the photograph. The question was what did him and my uncle have in common and, what was the real reason he had Terry down with him? Since Quarters and muscles both were dead, Terry was my only leas of finding out the truth.

"It time for us to be going," Kelli suggested, glancing at her wrist watch. "We have ten minutes before the morning shift gets here to set up."

"Let's go," I replied, pocketing the two pictures without her seeing me. "I wouldn't want you to get into any trouble for having an insignificant suspect inside a classified head quarters."

"Turn around Kyle I have to re-cuff you," She answered, placing the cuffs on me.

"I have one question... Why?"

She turned me towards her, giving me direct eye contact only this time with a suspenseful gaze. "Because Kyle unlike most I know, I respect the struggle and strugglers who've dedicated themselves to keep food on tables and roofs over heads. Without illegal funding the corporate world will never function properly. I'm not complaining about my salary that I'm receiving on both ends, understand?" She asked, winking her eye at me alluringly.

Without thought Kelli was definitely understood, only God knew how the world would function if society was only legally cultivated. Then again he might have held back on his vision and testimony because it was the deception of humans who corrupted the world. Only the Devil could clean up the corruption that he started and that was like asking him to befriend God; it would never happen.

From the answers that Kelli gave me she definitely earned my trust with that response. Strugglers, hustlers and even malevolent criminals didn't find too many people like Kelli who looked at her job as a pay check only and not a full time career. But, showed her dignity and gave her gratitude to her own kind who was trapped in poverties all over the Garden State.

After leaving Operation Sundown Headquarters, Kelli and I went back to her place and warmed up her sheets. We sexed until the rise of dawn but my sheet romance wasn't a start or finish of round two of gratifying Kelli's new life into the world of orgasms. But, too keep my enemy even closer so I could weather the storm the way that I wanted to when it was my time to defend my crown. Kelli knew things that she probably didn't even imagine was conscious enough to be deemed classified and that was what I needed to keep her as my main key to the success of the contaminated game.

### THE PLOT THICKENS.............................

# Contaminated Games:

---

## Anybody Can Get Caught Up
### Vol. 2

# Chapter. I

F our-thirty a.m., Sunday morning I stood on the corner of Phillip Street and Central Avenue waiting for Jingles to arrive so he could guide me through my first day on the job. My body was fatigued calling for the bedroom but my mind was fully energized; thinking of nothing but dollar signs. The atmosphere inside the Manor projects was extremely tranquil as if no tenants resided in the area. The streets were clean of any trash, there was no graffiti on any of the walls or the buildings, no sneakers hanging from the telephone lines and, there wasn't a single person ambling on the project's plantation.

A white four-door Cadillac pulled near the curb of Phillip and Central where I stood in frustration. The driver side window slowly descended as I looked up to see who was in the car.

"What up my man... Kyle right?" Sao asked, plainly from the driver side window. I answered with a head nod. "Get in cool."

After I got in and shut the door Sao pulled off at an easy pace. "Jingles told us you would be here," he said, implying to him and his partner Jam who was asleep in the passenger seat. "I'm quite sure he already explained to you how this operation works so I'm not going to repeat it... Really I don't care... All I care about is you making that fuckin' cash. The two cats that will be on the shift with you will show you the ropes--"

"I thought there was three who--"

"One of them was fired so you could fill the position," Sao said, staring at me through the rearview mirror.

Sao turned a few corners and went down a few streets before parking into one of the Project's parking lots. "You hungry slim?" Sao asked, turning the car off. I nodded once more. "Cool let's eat... Jam!... Jam!"

"I'm up slim, damn stop shaking me," He replied, grabbing the gun from his lap, adjusting it under his shirt. Jam looked over his shoulder to see who was sitting behind him and his first words to me were...

"You packin' a burner?" I had a brand new, stainless steel .38 snub nose that never was fired, inside a black book bag that I carried with the dope in it. It was a gift from Kelli who told me that I needed it for the line of work that I was in but, I didn't want anyone to know.

"Nah my man I'm not holdin'," I replied, in a calm manner.

"Here take this," Jam said, handing me a fully loaded 9 millimeter with one in the chamber. "Sao and I got tools like this by the box... plus you need as many as possible when you're a victim inside this contaminated game. Let's eat."

$ $ $ $ $

We went to eat breakfast at a relative's home of Sao and Jam, Aunt Liddy was her name and she was responsible for cooking meals on a daily basis for members inside the G.W.B. crew and others who lived in the neighborhood who wanted a special platter or order. Aunt Liddy's two bedroom tenement was the local fast food joint in the hood, she not only got paid for the meals and the orders that she took but was compensated monthly by members of G.W.B to keep her business opportunities prolific. Liddy was no older than forty, short about 5'2" with a nice physique. Her skin was a dark shiny complexion like mocha, and she wore her hair in thick colorful curlers.

Sao whose real name was Samiere and Jam (Jawuan), were like two naïve angels in Aunt Liddy's circumference. The modification of their decorum didn't confuse me one bit because even though they were hoodlums by circumstance they still were raised with proper morals. I could tell that the two sixteen year old teenagers were very generous young men.

Aunt Liddy treated me like a child of her own; she demanded that I make myself comfortable. Catering to me as if I was a man with a lot of power and she was my special house attendant. She stuffed me with so much of her delectable breakfast to a point that I began to pick over my plate.

"So Kyle where are you from?" Liddy asked, cleaning off the stove and countertops.

"I'm originally from up the street in Chelton Terrace but now I reside across town on Walnut Street."

"You're from out here? Who are your peoples?" She asked, curiously.

"The Moore's... The Williams'--"

"No, I mean who's your mother and father?"

"Oh, my mother name is Olivia and My pops --"

"Olivia? What Olivia... The triplets' sister Olivia?"

"Yeah that's her."

"Boy I should beat your ass," She replied, in a joking manner. "Your mom and aunts are like my sisters, we all grew up together and Kiss is your father?"

"Kiss?" The name confused me, I never heard it before.

"I meant to say Kyle but Kiss was a nickname that he was given back in the day because he greeted all the ladies with a succulent French kiss. Whew! Kiss was something else in his heyday," She expressed, going down memory lane. "I'm sorry about his passing I attended the funeral at Carl Miller."

After local authorities found Big Kyle's remains a couple of weeks prior to his going home service, Big Kyle and D.S.'s corpse had to be thoroughly sanitized because of all the larva and maggots that had eaten away at them. Big D.S. and Kyle had their funerals together; I didn't attend. But, I heard that the place was thronged with friends and family members from all over. It was farewell to the S & S Brothers who came into the life of the streets from the cradle to the grave.

I had to console Liddy who stood holding the dish cloth with watery eyes. "It's time we got a move on," Sao said, putting his plate in the sink. "You don't need anything do you Aunt Liddy?"

"No, I'm fine Samiere."

"Okay we'll see you a little later."

"Alright... Use be careful out there now ya' hear?"

"We hear you Auntie," Jam voiced, kissing Liddy on the cheek.

Phillip and Central looked like a neighborhood rally when Sao made the right turn off of 8th Street. Customers and dope fiends were chasing for that Smiley Face, it was so many people standing in the vicinity that it made me scared to even get out of the car. A tall, slim, dark skin cat road up on a freestyle bike and tapped on the window.

"Sao, what's up we no smiling today?" The guys asked, leaning over the driver side window with his forearms. "The morning rush is bananas out here... It has to be at least twenty gees out this chumpy right now."

"We smiling'," Sao replied, hitting the gadget that opened up the trunk, Jam got out and went to the rear of the car.

"You know Kyle right Mikey B.?"

"Yeah I know Muscles' nephew... Damn Kay you got tall as shit slim." We shook hands.

"Where's your brother?" Sao asked, searching around through the car window.

"He's across the street in the Sand Park." Jam came from around the rear of the trunk with a big, black gym bag and handed it to Mikey.

"Mike-n-Ike here's the key... Open up shop... All the walkie-talkies and scanning equipment is in the bag. Oh and don't forget to show our man Kyle the ropes."

"I'm on the J.O. my nigga... I'll see you dudes at three," Mikey said, shaking Jam's hand.

"Yo' Manny!" Mikey yelled towards the park, motioning his hand for him to come over. "Let's go it's on."

After Sao and Jam pulled away from the strip Mikey and Manny took me to one of the tenements that was stationed a few rows behind the dope set. 827 was the address on the front door of the apartment in the red bricks, this was the spot where all the dope was kept for that particular day, the money was counted and, meticulous listening over the scanners for any suspicious calls that were headed into their territory.

The inside of the apartment, down stairs was garnished with the finest furniture and glass mirrors. The living room had wall to wall carpet which ran to the top of the hallway stairs and the kitchen was laced with marble counter tops, a tile floor and a shinny wooden kitchen table and chairs.

The upstairs was the complete opposite, three metal folding chairs and a long picnic table was the only objects inside of the front bedroom. In the bedroom adjacent to the front sat a 36" inch television stationed on some milk crates with an Atari 2400 video game hooked to the back of it. The bathroom was the only cubicle that had a similar aura to the downstairs part of the place.

"All eyes that are on post in Centerville check in at 827," Manny said, talking into one of the walkie-talkies. Manny's physical appearance was similar to his younger brother Mikey, dark skin, tall, and slim. The only difference was that Mikey was a few inches shorter and had bigger ears.

"827... This is your eyes on tenth and Vanhook checking in," A masculine voice said over the walkie-talkie. "Good Wood.'

"Good Wood," Manny retorted back.

After the first voice checked in to the project head quarters, seven more tandem voices came behind the first voice from all the other post in the perimeter or Centerville. There were lookouts on almost every corner; 10th and Vanhook, 10th and Ferry Avenue, 9th and Vanhook, 9th and Ferry, 8th and Vanhook, 8th and Ferry, 7th and Ferry, and 7th and Central out in front of Sophia's Café.

The G.W.B lookouts weren't your average walking examiners with a walkie-talkie in hand that looked suspicious. They all had ways of disguising themselves by doing constructive activities to fool the police. A few of them vended their own services on the corners by selling merchandise, toiletries, video and cassette tapes, and clothing. The others wee either disguised as bums or local neighbors doing community service.

When the G.W.B's addressed and answered one another using there team slogan it was merely to greet each other with respect.

While Manny stayed behind at the apartment I ventured out in the projects with Mikey B. to sell some of the finest dope that Centerville had to offer. The time was five-thirty in the morning and I was riding on a brand new G.T. Freestyle bike in a black sweat hood and a pair of black shell top Adidas. When Mikey and I got back around to the strip twenty minutes after getting settled into the apartment, the customer count had doubled.

"Aiight peoples this is how we operate," Mikey said, stashing two trash backs full of dope in one of the green street dumpsters which was stationed a nice distance from the selling spot. "We sell on foot but use the bikes for get away purposes... Don't run up on any cars, let the customers get out and come to you... If any customers ask you any questions or ask you what you're selling, walk away from them. Because Smiley's been rockin' every since we switched our stamp over from Black Death three years ago."

'Black Death!' I yelled subconsciously, rattling my own mind for a moment. That was the stamped dope that the perished brothers of Terry were allegedly distributing under the name of the later Dominican Brothers. There were a lot of loopholes in the past information that I had received. What the fuck was going on in the underworld? I had to just keep playing by ear.

"Black Death? I thought that was someone else stamp back then," I said, helping him stash the dope.

"Someone else like who? We got that name from this cologne that Jingles' uncles use to purchase for all the ghetto groupies that were a main attraction to them. There would have been dead men every where if another street corner was selling our product. We only changed our stamp because that dope was putting fiends out of their misery... It was only on the streets for three months."

Mikey filled his pockets and sweat hood with bundles and bundles of Smiley before we went over by the park and moved it. "We take turns while selling and if a customer only wants to specifically cop from either of us we don't listen to them, the order still goes. The product means more to them then the person who's selling it."

Once we got by the park muthafuckas were running up on Mikey B. like he was a famous celebrity signing autographs. People were hopping out of ambulance vans, parked cars and, tractor trailers for the dope.

All I could hear was Mikey yelling out, "Back the fuck up... Wait your turn... How many... Count mines out," in a verbatim order. In fifteen minutes tops Mikey B. sold one trash bag of dope before I could even sell a bundle. I made a single trip back to the apartment to drop off all the money and pick up another trash bag. Mikey B. sold half of the other bag that was in the dumpster prior to me returning on the set.

At eight o'clock we shut down the operation due to school hours going into progress and we weren't scheduled to open back up until nine o'clock. Mikey and I headed back to the apartment to help his brother's count the cash separately by bills.

"Let's separate all of the big bills from the small ones... Kyle turn on the switches to all four money machines," Manny said, pouring a trash bag of money on one of the tables.

I went into the back room and played Atari while Mikey and Manny ran the bills through the accurate machines. The money count took up about a half an hour of our nine o'clock delay. The other half hour was being consumed by conversation.

Born and raised in Centerville in a one parent home, Mikey and Manny Bucks began hustling at the age of twelve and fourteen back in 1972. Only because their mother struggled with the income of the household and literally they were growing up poor. Known to their peers as the "Burn Bucks Brothers," because they made money swiftly and they were the fastest two boys to run on foot in Centerville; Mikey and Manny were the two human inceptions to the G.W.B.'s heroin flow getting started. They are the oldest two runners to slang heroin on any shift of the drug flows in Centerville. Reason being, they helped formulate the structure and they were the only two merely to know every escape route through the Centerville maze of the housing projects; they had never been arrested before.

Manny and Mikey made enough money to move their mother and little brother Mufee out of the projects and into a nice remote location. And, even though they saved enough money to purchase the finer things in life, they still chose to reside in their childhood apartment on 9th and Vanhook Streets. The two brothers stated that they loved being runners with authority because it was a lesser risk than being an overseeing drug lord. Plus they loved when others perceived them as being "Nobodies" in the game.

After the $15,000 dollars was ran through the four money machines and wrapped in G-stacks rubber bands, Mikey and I went back on the grind. From nine a.m. to three o'clock p.m. Mikey ran through so many trash bags of Smiley, it was like hustling was a legal occupation.

On the contrary, I only managed to sell ten bundles out of the enormous amount that I thought was going to be gone on my first day. Five thousand big ones was a good accomplishment for my first day, the fiends and customers didn't recognize my unfamiliar face on Phillip and Central so that gave them a reason not to cop from me; I had no clientele.

At the end of the shift all of the lookouts that had a watch corner in Centerville came by the apartment to collect their daily pay and to do neighborhood clean up. Neighborhood clean up was for the kids who were coming home after school and wanted to play outside. They wouldn't have to play in a lot of trash or paraphernalia that was left behind by the junkies. I assumed that was the reason why the neighborhood was so up to par.

"Kangaroo how'd you do on ya' first day hustla?" Sao asked, ambling towards me as I swept trash off the side walk.

"I made five gees and some change--"

"That's all?" He asked, appalled by the numbers. "Knowing that I should have made much more. Mikey and Manny were hogging up all the sales... I should of--"

"Nah, nah nothing of the sort shorty, I just wasn't that familiar face that the customers were use to seeing that's all."

"I hear you, I hear you... We smiling' the next day though, catch up with you tomorrow." Sao jumped back in his Caddy and slow rolled down Phillip Street.

$ $ $ $

The following six days of hustling in the Ville was the same scenario like my first day out there. Setting up at the apartment, moving trash bags of Smiley with Mikey and Manny, counting doe in the money machines and, cleaning up when the shift was over had become apart of my livelihood.

Fifteen thousand was all I accumulated throughout my first week of pitching. Mikey and Manny sold almost thirty bundles an hour on the productive morning shift. I felt that I was making more money running packages all around town for my uncle; it was like I settled for less dealing with Jingles and his dope flow.

$ $ $ $ $

Word must have got back to Jingles from Sao or Mikey B. about the product sold and the cash I profited for the entire week. Because Jingles called for me over the walkie-talkie to meet with him at a house on 7th and Ferry Avenue, which was a hop, skip and, jump from the dope set.

"So you're not managing to sell what I gave you to sell out by the park?" Jingles asked, as he headed back into the living room area, from opening the door for me. There was no greeting or hand shake intended as I trailed behind him.

"No not really... It's not what I expected but--"

"But things will fall into place youngin', it's truly beneath me to have you on a million dollar flow and your not getting your fair share also. That shit is an insult to the caliber of hustler that I 'am."

Jingles grabbed the butt of the talking device and called for someone to respond at the apartment. Standing in the middle of the empty living quarters, in a white tank top and a crisp pair of black Jordache Jeans with his metallic, cowboy belt buckle dangling, Jingles impatiently waited for a response; he couldn't stop tapping on his leg with the device.

I was in a bewildered mind state, glancing around the house knowing I had been in the establishment before, sometime ago. If my eyes weren't deceiving me, I knew the house I was standing in use to be the House of Chemistry.

"Jay didn't this house belong to my Uncle Muscles at one time?" I asked, having a precise conception that it definitely was.

"I couldn't tell you Kay, my aunt sold me this spot a couple of years ago after it caught on fire," he lamented, finally receiving a response over the walkie-talkie. "Listen, this is the deal," He implied, talking into the hand device. "Starting next week no one is to sell on any shift on Phillip and Central but Kangaroo, copy that? I'll let Sao and Jam know also that everyone will continue to get paid for the time being but no one will work but Kyle, dig it?"

"Like a shovel," the mushy voice replied, over the device.

Jingles gave me total control over his dope flow so that I could get rid of the two keys of heroin that he accommodated me with. He also stated that Mikey and Manny could stick around so they could watch my back and keep the operation in order. But, I had to compensate them out of my own profit which was $3500 a week.

"Are you up for it?" he asked, turning the volume down on the walkie-talkie.

"Hell Yeah."

"Aiight just let me know when you are almost done so you can re-up. Birds are up to an astonishing hundred and thirty grand... Forty thousand more over the original drought price. That right there makes a nigga want to close up shop and go collect some cans or some shit."

Another large shipment was confiscated by the U.S. Coastal Agency a few days ago in the Delaware River. News reporters claim that the Coastal Authorities seized more than fifty pounds of heroin and cocaine; that allegedly was being sent from the Coast of Florida. In my opinion, that wasn't a justification to shut a consistent operation down. I was always told that scared money didn't make money and, if you had it to buy, never hesitate because there was always somebody willing to step in your shoes.

"Are you willing to chance your money?"

"Sure, why not? If I don't produce I'll never gain." Jingles smirked.

"You have a great hustling attitude due, I like that. Hold on," he said, running up the long flight of steps.

I glanced around the house once more, decorating the house with my eyes like Terry and my uncle use to have it a few years ago. The fulfillment of the house was identical to the vacant white walls that orbited around me. If Jingles aunt sold him the house, my uncle had to sell it to her because it was his home, or wasn't it?

"I said I'll take you when I come back!" Jingles exclaimed, thumping down the stairs in haste, tossing a T-shirt over his head.

"Jamiere hurry up back," the redbone standing in the middle of the stairs said, wearing nothing but a purple, silk blouse. "You always say that you're coming right back and leave me in here all night--"

"Taffy where'd you put my keys?" he asked, paying her no attention.

"There up stairs in my Gucci purse."

"Can you... Fuck it I'll get'em," he ranted, slow rolling back up the stairs.

I finally got to see what the gorgeous Takeisha "Taffy" Smith looked like; set aside from all the fabricated stories that I was told about her. She was definitely a lot of competition for my sister Alesha who couldn't stand her guts. For a moment, when I made eye contact with her as she stood seductively on the staircase, I could have sworn that she was Alesha; Jingles definitely had an obsession for high yellow girls. Alesha, Taffy, and Myesha were all in that complexional category.

Twenty minutes after jingles went up stairs his keys were finally found, in an innocuous manner Takeisha brought his keys to me.

"Jamiere said take the car he's on bed rest right now," She expressed, with an erotic giggle. "He'll be stuck in the bachelor pad with me for a few more days."

A Champagne, four-door 750 BMW was parked out in front of the house waiting for me to heat her up and coast away. The entire time I rode comfortably in the expensive car, I managed to stay level headed and didn't over exceed my welcome of the fine life. I just used the car from getting to point A and point B because it was obvious that the Feds had the car on file and currently were taking pictures.

information can be obtained at www.ICGtesting.com
the USA
1130812
00010B/2/P